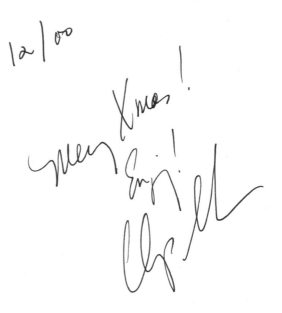

12/00

Mery Xmas!
Enjoy!

The Last Bookmaker

ALSO BY THE AUTHORS

Diner Guys by Chip Silverman
The Block by Bob Litwin and Chip Silverman
Aloha Magnum by Larry Manetti and Chip Silverman

The Last Bookmaker

Bob Litwin
Chip Silverman

BORDERLANDS PRESS
GRANTHAM, NEW HAMPSHIRE ❏ 2000

ISBN: 1-880325-18-7

Library of Congress Control Number: 00-131729

Cover Photograph by Gloria Uhl
Cover and jacket design by T. F. Monteleone
Typesetting, layout, and interior design by Elizabeth Monteleone

Printed in the United States of America

First Edition May, 2000

Borderlands Press, Post Office Box 1529, Grantham, NH 03753

DEDICATION

In memory of
Ted and Julie,
and
Bea and Ben.
O how we loved you;
Though we hardly knew ya.

ACKNOWLEDGMENTS

To Renée Silverman, once again, for transcribing, typing, proofing, editing, and shaping this manuscript into what it has become. She is truly the best!

Special thanks to Andrea Savoye, Doug Ware, and Gloria Uhl.

And finally, thanks to the many others who contributed in so many ways, but prefer to remain anonymous.

"Gambling is as American as the Gold Rush, the boom in Internet stocks and other quests for quick riches. George Washington, who deplored rampant gambling at Valley Forge, supported a lottery to help build the city that bears his name. Lotteries helped build Jamestown, General Washington's army, Harvard, Princeton and Dartmouth.

Time was, Americans probably gambled because life—getting to America; getting across America, through Comanche territory; getting out of the mills and mines in one piece—was a gamble.

Perhaps nowadays gambling appeals because the rest of life is enervatingly predictable."

—George F. Will
Syndicated Columnist
June 27, 1999

Louis Dante, a.k.a. Mr. D, walked out of the Windy Valley Farms Restaurant and Carryout after using the pay phone sandwiched between the men's room and the pinball machine. He looked sophisticated and "country-ish," wearing chocolate-brown slacks, a camel sports coat, and a lightweight white turtleneck shirt. His face was tan, and his long hair bounced against the back of his neck and jacket in the cool breeze of the early spring in Baltimore County, Maryland.

It was 8:45 p.m. and Dante was meeting his fiancée, Shirley, a beautiful, red-haired, statuesque woman. She had parked her car and was already sitting in the passenger's seat of his Mercedes convertible when he came out of Windy Valley. The restaurant was empty, but the ice cream stand in the front of the store was busy dishing out homemade favorites to the customers, as Louis slid into the driver's seat.

Three casually dressed men left the stand carrying different flavored ice cream cones, licking them in various circular motions. As they walked past Dante's car, they stopped, purposely leaning over the Mercedes and letting the ice cream drip onto the tan leather upholstery.

"Outta the car, big shot," ordered one of the men, opening the driver's door. He was heavyset and wore a herringbone tweed sports jacket.

"You can leave now, Miss," encouraged the thin man as he courteously pulled the passenger door ajar.

The third man, medium-sized and muscular, wearing a blue cardigan sweater, slid into the car and began to search it.

Dante was forced to "assume the position," and was humiliatingly searched as a small crowd of onlookers, ice cream cones in hand, gathered around. A search warrant was waved in his face as he was read his rights.

To the right of his car, by the three newspaper dispensers opposite the restaurant, Dante saw the figure of a man in a dark suit. He knew immediately whom the figure represented; the ultimate in trouble—the feds.

When Dante first saw the joint Baltimore City and County Gambling Task Force reps, he was mildly irritated, but now he was worried sick.

"I wanna call my lawyer," Dante insisted as he was shoved into the passenger's seat of his Mercedes.

"Fine," said Byron, the thin man from Baltimore City Vice. "Use your car phone and tell him to meet us at your place 'cause that's where we're headed."

The muscular Vice cop, Feldman, also from the city, confiscated Mr. D's briefcase that contained two cellular telephones, placed it in the back, and drove Dante's car north. Byron, his partner, drove with Copley, the herringbone tweed sports coat, in the Baltimore County Police vehicle.

When they arrived at Mr. D's home, his lawyer, Richard Karson, was waiting at the door. He reviewed the warrant carefully before the police entered Dante's house.

As the three Vice cops hurried in, Karson cautioned them.

"Gentlemen, don't wreck the place for wrecking's sake."

"Actually, I feel lucky tonight," said Copley, who walked directly to the bedroom and into Dante's walk-in closet. He pushed some hangers aside, located a caftan, shook it upside down, and dumped several hundred thousand dollars onto the hardwood floor.

Book One

CHAPTER 1
Fall 1989

Lanny was beginning to lose it.

Shortly after Mr. D was arrested, the wiretaps picked up some very strange calls on Lanny's cellular phone. Between lay-off numbers and sports betting calls, Lanny's obsession with obscenity moved into high gear. He would phone doctors' offices and others.

"Hello," a polite receptionist answered, "Dr. Simpson's office. Can I help you?"

"Yes," Lanny replied. "I'd like to know if I could make an appointment to come into your office. Do you have someone there who can jerk me off?"

"Oh, please," begged the startled receptionist as she hung up the phone.

Other calls to physicians followed, and receptionists would, invariably, slam down the receiver. Undaunted, Lanny spent further hours calling randomly all over town hoping for a female to answer the phone.

"Hi," Lanny purred, "how're ya doing? Listen, I thought I'd come by and take your panties down for ya. Okay?"

"Who's this?" asked the bewildered housewife.

"C'mon, baby," implored Lanny, "just gimme your address."

The phone, as usual, went dead.

Mr. D was totally unaware of his trusted employee's bizarre behavior until his lawyer played the tapes for him.

The lawyer's "paper" detective speculated on the dynamics of the situation.

"It's just that he figured that the operation was over. He's gonna be outta work, and he's got a free phone to use. No one will ever trace it back to him, and he's having a ball!"

He added, "If Lanny ever turns state's evidence, gives up Mr. D, then I'm gonna play all three hours of these obscene tapes on a stereo before the judge, and ask Lanny how long he's suffered from this perversion!"

CHAPTER 2
Fall 1990

So Mr. D would read, watch TV, listen to some music, and things would disappear from his mind—the bad things. But when he'd finish reading, or watching TV, or listening to a tape, reality would flood back into his mind, and he'd start to worry again.

"All right," said Hayden, "lemme ask you this. Describe the room."

Lanny couldn't wait to answer, to please his interrogator.

"Okay. We're in a little room on the second floor. It's got a desk, a couch, a coupla chairs, a window, maybe two windows, with a TV set to watch the early games on Saturday."

"Just one TV set?" asked Hayden. Will Hayden was an assistant state's attorney assigned to Vice Crimes in the Baltimore City State's Attorneys Office.

"One TV set and two black, old-style telephones, I believe," said Lanny, nodding.

"Push-button or ring-dial?"

"Ring-dial telephones. And then two ultra-modern cellular phones that people could even use on airplanes, which they did." Lanny added, "We used a red and blue pencil, reversible."

"Why?" Hayden was somewhat bored. A career civil servant, he'd been through similar examinations before. Many times.

"Red for a plus, blue for a minus column, depending on whichever way things went. One was for the guys who were winning and one was for the losers."

Lanny had been caught easily and couldn't wait to confess, to inform, to "rat-out" Mr. D.

Lanny was a loser. True, he'd been somewhat successful in his twenties when he worked for, and later owned, a few high-style men's clothing shops in local downtown districts. However, Lanny overspent, over-drugged, and overestimated his mostly black clientele's demand for leather and suede apparel. By age thirty-one, he was bankrupt. Lanny drifted from job to job, usually forgetting that he was an employee and not the boss.

Now in his late thirties, he did odd jobs, sold some marijuana, and hung out with the gangster element around Baltimore. Lanny was almost bald on top, but he let what hair he had grow down past his neck. At 5'5", he weighed 175 pounds, and most of his bulk was centered in his belly and backside. He always needed a shave and had a bulbous, bright red nose from too much gin.

"What time do you show up? When does work start?" Hayden was impatient.

"Work starts around ten o'clock in the morning, Saturday morning, for the early calls. Calls from the other guys who are taking smaller action, you know, maybe twenty-five/fifty-dollar bettors, hundred-dollar bettors. And Mr. D may have had like fifty or a hundred of those. So he had a guy who just handled his smaller action. The other smaller bookmakers would lay off into this guy, too, and then call in to Mr. D. Mr. D usually took . . . I don't remember anything less than like $500 a game. And guys would still try and call in and bet the Hawaii game late, trying to fool us on the time zones and stuff like that."

The worry was anxiety. The worry was about what was going to happen. His concern about police surveillance and the government's case against him wove through his mind. He per-

ceived himself to be guilty of what he had done, what he might have done, and what people may even had made up about him. He envisioned conspiracies within conspiracies.

"So this went on from ten in the morning on Saturday until eight at night?" asked Hayden.

Tall, with thinning dirty-blond hair, Hayden had a youthful, muscular build and was proud of it. At forty-five-plus, he still lifted weights five times a week. His face, though, was lined from stress and made him appear older. Over the years, Hayden had turned down several offers from big law firms to stay with the State's Attorneys Office. He preferred the life of a prosecutor.

"Till around two or three," Lanny began, "and then we'd be back from six to eight for the late games. He wasn't hangin' in there all day, and it didn't make sense once all the games started."

"So, what was the routine? You walked in there and the phones would start ringing?"

"We'd walk in there, and, yeah, Mr. D would call a couple people immediately, and others would call him. He'd see that everything was in order, and go over figures with his people; who was minus, who was plus, that kind of stuff. And very polite on the phone. We'd have a little sports book that would tell you all the games and the times that they were beginning. You know what I'm talking about? The football books? Then we'd go over if any times had been changed."

Lanny had been a good student of what Mr. D taught him and of Mr. D. He continued, "He was under the opinion that his clients were the rottenest motherfuckers in the world, and they were out to steal him blind and break him. And it was like a life or death thing with him on each call, that he had to be sharper than them, that these guys were gonna try and beat him silly. And he did not respect any customer who ever gambled with him. He thought they were the worst people in the world."

"Low opinion of them?" asked the prosecutor.

"He thought they were the worst, lyingest people in the world; that they would try and steal from him all the time."

"But weren't his clientele kind of like a blue-blood list or something, professionals, business people . . .?"

"Yeah," said Lanny. "Business people, lots of doctors, lawyers. But he considered them the scum of the earth."

Mr. D sought help. He went to a psychiatrist, and he was told that he suffered from what could be called the "Intolerance of Ambiguity." It affected people who knew they were in trouble, but could do nothing about it. It was the unknown, and they could not tolerate the confusion or the ambiguity of what was going on in the unknown—the realization that one's fate was at the mercy of others, and of time, and of circumstance. It happened to petty crooks waiting to be sentenced, Mafia dons waiting to be indicted by grand juries—to everyone . . .

The two men stood in the corner of the room and quietly watched the interrogation. Occasionally, Lanny would look up and observe the men, but he couldn't distinguish one from the other and took them as police. The two men represented different branches of the federal government. One was an assistant federal prosecutor and the other an IRS agent. They were both wearing dark blue pinstripe suits and different, though similar, rep ties, along with starched white button-down shirts. The IRS agent was about two inches taller than the assistant federal prosecutor, and his hair was a lighter shade of brown. Neither man wore a beard or mustache, and both were extremely clean-shaven for so late in the afternoon.

"So let's go through . . . the phone rings, . . ." Hayden knew Mr. D's process well.

"The phone rings. I would go down the list of games and give out the line. There was a certain way to say it: Penn plus nine, USC plus three, and so forth. All the way down to 18, 20 games, as many games as were being played."

"So, you'd have to do that with everybody, or would guys just call and say 'Here's what I want.'"

"No," said Lanny. He wanted to impress Hayden. But then again, all informants wanted to impress the prosecutor. "I had to give them the line first. Then they might tell me who they wanted, and I would write it all down and repeat it to them exactly. I had to repeat everything to them."

"So you go through the list. Let's take a couple games. Say Maryland was playing Penn State, and Penn State was minus seven and a half, and the caller said he wanted Maryland. So he's got Maryland plus seven and a half. And he says that over the phone. 'I want Maryland.' Then you would repeat that back to him."

Hayden glanced at the recording machine just to make sure everything got on record.

Lanny acted out his response. "Maryland plus seven and a half for one dime."

"One dime was the equivalent of?" led Hayden.

"One thousand dollars."

"And a nickel meant?"

"Five hundred dollars."

"What else? Then there'd be two dimes . . .?"

"Two dimes, ten dimes . . ."

"Okay. That's the lingo that you'd use. There was no other, . . . and these guys understood that if they were betting a thousand, it was really eleven hundred to a thousand. Right? Eleven to ten. That was the vigorish?" Hayden was referring to the "juice," the commission due the bookmaker.

Dante knew what it was, and he was constantly thinking and worrying, and he was constantly anxious. But knowing about the Intolerance of Ambiguity didn't make things easier. It only gave him a title for what was causing the worry. So he tried first to use the strength of his mind, but it wouldn't work because his mind could not blot out his thinking about the terrible consequences that lay ahead.

"So the guy would tell you who he wants," said Hayden, "and then you would tell him back on the phone, 'Here's who you took and for how much.'"

"Right. I would repeat it to everybody who called. That was very important. It was very important that I repeated, 'Okay, Tom,' or whatever the name was, 'you bet . . .'"

"But they didn't call with a name; they called with a number or a letter, right?" asked Hayden.

"They usually called with a number or a letter, right. Like this is number 28 or this is G-10," said Lanny.

"How long would each call last?"

"A call could last a minute or two, not very long."

"Mr. D didn't want the calls long because of tracing and stuff like that?" asked Hayden.

"I don't think that was it," continued Lanny. "He didn't want the calls long 'cause he needed to take in the new calls, so you couldn't tie up the phone. He would hand me the phone, and say 'Give this guy the line. I'll come back and take his . . .' 'cause you had to get the line out to everybody. That was the important thing.

"Now, with certain people," Lanny added, "he knew before they ever called which way they were going to bet. So he would adjust his lines. He would already move it a half a point because he knew that this guy always takes the 'overs' or the favorite or whatever. And if it was a big game on a certain day, he knew how to adjust his line even more in his favor."

"And that's why it was important for him to be there. Not for you?"

"Right," said Lanny enthused. "It would take me five to ten years to maybe learn how he could adjust a line to a specific bettor in a split second."

"That was crucial to him," said Hayden. "That could mean millions of dollars in the future?"

"Yeah. It meant the edge. It meant what he thought was an edge."

The psychiatrist prescribed Valium and then Xanax, but again it didn't matter. Mr. D used alcohol, and in another lifetime, would have used stronger, illicit drugs, but it didn't matter. Once he came out of the booze high, it was just as if he came to the end of a book, or a TV show, or a music album. Reality returned. The Intolerance of Ambiguity was still there.

"Okay. So each phone would ring at different times?" asked Hayden.

"Right. We could have the four phones ringing off the hook at one time, but he would sit calmly handling them . . . Now, the rush would come twenty or thirty minutes before game time.

"You know," Lanny added, "if a phone call didn't come in every ten minutes or something like that, he'd click them on and off. Like maybe the phone's not working or something. Meanwhile, they were always working."

Hayden interrupted. "So what would he keep there to write with? Would he have paper that you could destroy right away?"

"Yeah. He had paper for that. Flash paper."

"Which meant what? You flushed it down the toilet? It was water-soluble?"

"I think he could just throw it in a water can," answered Lanny, "and he kept a little water can nearby."

"Now, did he keep any other kind of papers?" asked Hayden.

"No, not really," said Lanny. "I think everything was done on flash paper. Afterwards he would take it home with him, . . . and once somebody straightened up and paid off, the papers were destroyed, and he started a new week."

He decided to try hypnotism. However, his mind, ever inter-woven in other conspiracies, told him that if hypnotism actually worked, what else would the hypnotist talk him into doing, or not doing, or feeling, or not feeling? Who would go along with Mr. D to protect him, and would that person tell the hypnotist to do some-thing else? And he would never know, so hypnotism was out.

"On Sunday," asked Hayden, "he worked ten 'til about four, right? When the last professional games are?"

"No," corrected Lanny. "Ten to one."

"But what about the late games?"

"To the best of my memory, people bet their late games then. He was playing with guys who were betting serious money. There wasn't no fooling around. They knew who they liked and what they were betting."

Hayden glanced at the two feds, and asked Lanny, "Did Mr. D ever mention that bad incident a few years ago?"

"You mean what happened down at his store with those psychos . . . and his wife?"

"Yeah," said Hayden.

"No."

"Is there a slip of paper for each guy?" Hayden returned to his original line of questioning.

"No. All on one sheet. Mr. D would have a ruler like he was a draftsman. And he had everybody in a column with every game they bet, and either a blue or a red mark next to it."

"A blue or red mark meant . . ." said Hayden.

"Money," said Lanny emphatically. "That's how much money the bettors owed or were due."

"I see. And so he adjusted this after each game?"

"Yeah."

"So Mr. D could know seconds after the games were over where he stood going into the next games," said Hayden.

"And he did," said Lanny. "He writes beautifully, very pointy pencils, very meticulous. You know, it was a lot of money. It looked like figures to me, but it was actually green money to him."

"He kept the pencils sharpened?" asked the prosecutor with a faint smile.

"He had a pencil sharpener," responded the informant.

It was on his mind when he woke up. It was on his mind when he fell asleep.

There was no one to fight, no one to get back at, no one to bribe, no one to convince to drop a charge to cool things out. There were too many inevitable things and too many conspiracies.

"Did he watch you when you went through your years of training so he knew what you were doing?"

"Very little. He just wanted me to listen. He was in no hurry for me to do anything except to totally learn from him. And watch, watch, watch. Because the plan was to eventually let me do what he was doing."

"You would meet him there at this apartment. Did you have to drive like somebody might be following you?" asked Hayden.

"I just drove over there," said Lanny. "Of course, I looked a little bit, but couldn't see anyone following me. But I was aware. I was a little paranoid with it. I felt like we were going to be watched. That that was definitely happening."

"Did you ever sense that with Mr. D? Did you ever sense any paranoia with him?"

"Yeah. He knew they were coming. And thank God he told me."

"It was just a matter of time?"

"Yeah, yeah."

"That he was definitely always gonna get busted . . ." said Hayden.

"And that was kind of why he wanted to teach me everything," said Lanny, "so that, I guess, eventually he could have someone who he knew real well and trusted.

"He didn't want to take the overnight bus because when he got busted, they kept him in jail overnight. As quick as he could get out of jail was as quick as anybody. But the police would work it so that he had to stay in overnight. The cops really knew how to play with his head."

"Especially," said Hayden, "if they popped him on a Saturday night. Then he couldn't do anything Sunday. And if they popped him on a Sunday . . .?"

"He couldn't do anything until Monday, yeah. They always waited 'til the big game weekends . . ." said Lanny.

Oh yes, he could run away. There was nothing stopping that. But, if he ran away, what about the people who counted on him for their survival, for their livelihood, for his companionship; and he for their loyalty? So to run away, to escape would leave them behind, and then he would still worry.

The assistant U.S. prosecutor cleared his throat. It signaled Hayden to digress.

"Lanny, did Mr. D do all of his own banking or did someone else? What about you? Did you ever deposit any money for him?"

"I never touched any money. Maybe one of his other boys from his store, but I'm not sure."

"Was there anything else in the room? Were there certain foods there?" Hayden always looked for a total profile of his adversary. The more he respected his adversary, the more in-depth he wanted the profile.

"Hot dogs, potato chips, a sub," said Lanny. "I might run out and go to the sub shop. One of the other guys who would work on Sundays would bring in big bags of potato chips and pretzels, and we would nosh on that. Mr. D would snack very lightly. Usually he would go eat with his partner or his girlfriend after one o'clock in the afternoon or something like that."

"Was it a furnished apartment?" asked Hayden.

"It was a business, actually, and there was a little office up on the second floor. And the TV was cable. He had to have phones put in there under fake names. Never his. We had a refrigerator downstairs for Coke or Pepsi, and I was always running down for the sodas. I think he liked pretzels, a certain amount of ice, and a little Pepsi. He always had his Pepsi in there because he talked a lot and needed to keep his voice going. Mr. D was always clearing his throat, or he'd make some kind of sound like that."

"Did he ever have any arguments on the phone with anyone?" asked Hayden as he yawned.

"He didn't have any arguments," answered Lanny. "Well, there was this one incident. He had just been turned on to a new guy who was a doctor who had won some money from him, and then turned around and lost and owed Mr. D, I think, $25,000. But the doctor said he wasn't paying him. Mr. D did tell me: 'I will collect from this guy.'"

"Other than that, he was very courteous?"

"Totally," answered Lanny. "I mean the most professional . . ."

"And yet he looked down on all these guys?"

"Yes."

"And he would say to you 'These rotten motherfuckers, they're this and they're that'?" Hayden asked.

"There was a guy Mr. D had won a million dollars from who he hated the most. He said to me: 'You can never be friends with anybody you bet with because they're trying to steal from you and take you broke, and you're trying to take them broke. You can be cordial, and they can be an acquaintance, but they can never be your friend.' And obviously he was right."

And what if he ran away? What would he do? How would he support himself? And would he have to worry about extradition? He'd have to worry about it in the United States. He'd have to worry about it in countries that had treaties with the United States. Where would he go? What would he do? Who would he be?

"Is there anything else you can remember about being in that room? Any comments or . . .?" asked Hayden.

"Well," said Lanny, "the only comment that I remember is that he didn't need a friend there. He didn't need any help with this kind of thing. He wasn't doing this 'cause he needed someone to sit with him. He had a specific plan. He wanted to eventually be able to travel and do certain things and to have someone who he trusted handling what he was doing. But like 'Don't think I'm doing this for any other reason. I don't need any company to do this,' is what he would always say. 'I can do it myself.'

"He wanted it so he could travel with his girlfriend. He was taking a lot of heat from her that she wasn't getting any attention and travel and all."

"Did he ever talk about his ex-wife?"

"Nah, never."

"Lanny, have you any idea where Mr. D kept his money?"

"Nope. But I'll bet it's hidden away real good."

"Did he have more than one business or apartment where he operated from?" asked Hayden.

"Yeah," said Lanny. "He had a few places that he could go to. We only went to this one place because it was comfortable. No one was in there on the weekend. The other business in the building was closed. It was just a Monday to Friday business. He wouldn't leave this place, even though he knew it would be smarter to switch around his places all the time. And he did have some other places to work out of."

"So the worst thing was for Mr. D to get too comfortable in a place. Then he'd get busted. If he moved around, though . . ."

"If he moved around," said Lanny, "he had a better shot . . . yeah. But he was comfortable. He had his cable. And one thing with a gambler, they gotta have the scores. I mean, you would think that after all those years, at four o'clock, you find out the final scores, and you take care of business. But, he was involved to a point where he wanted to know the instant that either team scored. And none of that means anything because it didn't matter until the final results came in

"But he would get comfortable in a spot. Where it was comfortable for him, he would stay a little too long."

When Mr. D was busy, he didn't worry as much, so he tried to stay busy. And this time of year was especially hectic. But, since his business was the cause of his anxiety, the worry was never too far away.

Even in those brief moments when Mr. D didn't think of the criminal and tax charges being brought against him, he worried of other problems—his former marriages, his partner, his family, his girlfriend, his business, his past.

CHAPTER 3
November 10, 1990

"Who are you?" asked Ramone Blande, without turning around from his personal computer.

"I'm Paul."

"You're Mr. D's partner? It's great to meet ya!" said Ramone as he swiveled around.

"Louis and I are associates . . . social friends," corrected Paul.

Ramone eyed the elderly visitor to his office. He was a man

to be respected. Paul was tall and thin. He had aged well over the past sixty-seven years. His pants and sports coat were somewhat oversized, and the muted blue tones blended well with his grayish, receding hairline.

"Hi," said a shorter figure moving from behind Paul. Ramone had failed to hear him enter the room.

"This is my friend, Gordon. He advises me on things," said Paul.

Ramone got up and shook the hands of both men. Gordon was forty-ish, overweight, and had an extremely dark complexion. Ramone restrained himself from asking what kind of advisor Gordon was. He'd seen men like Gordon before and understood his look. Gordon had the facial expression and eyes of a live polygraph machine. He was someone to be wary of.

"Louis told us that you could brief us," said Paul, "get us up to date on his problems. But you don't have to be brief. We've got time and we like details. And, of course, we'll see that you're compensated."

Ramone leaned over and turned off his PC. He offered coffee, but was turned down. The two visitors settled in—Paul on a small sofa and Gordon on a wooden chair by Ramone's desk.

"All right," he said. "Where do you want to begin?"

"Tell us about yourself, Mr. Blande. What do you do for Louis?"

"I'm a paper detective," said Ramone.

CHAPTER 4

The paper detective was a short, stocky, half-Puerto Rican, half-Italian homosexual, forty-one years of age. He had long, tightly curled hair and a thin mustache. Ramone wore tortoiseshell-framed Gucci glasses with a distinct tan tint. His dark, camel-checked sports coat almost matched his glasses.

"In many instances," Ramone began, "lawyers will call me if they need something very simple in a mechanical sort of way; such as a tape transcribed when they can't get it done or their girls are incapable of doing it because it's so tricky . . . the listening, the speed of the tape, and all that garbage. And they will send that over to me and I'll have one of my people do it, or I'll find somebody who can. I play the middleman and pick up some money in between."

"These are like wiretap tapes? Those kinds of things?" asked Gordon.

"Yeah. Or court hearings. Most attorneys wait 'til three days before their case is going to court, and then cry, 'Holy Jesus! We didn't fuckin' do this! And I can't present the tape as evidence, and I need to read what's happening.'"

"So that's one facet of what you do," said Gordon. "What's another one?"

"Find experts for attorneys. I'll give you an example. This one was a drug case. A sheet was seized—an accounting sheet. And the feds were going to produce a witness, an FBI agent or someone who worked for the State's Attorneys Office who could analyze this paper; that this was from the sale of cocaine and that's what the sheet means.

"In this particular case, the client was charged with a cocaine violation. But the client doesn't sell cocaine. I don't know what the client sells. It could be pants for all I know, or T-shirts. But this one piece of paper has no names on it and just these figures . . . The highest figure only comes to $30,000. Well, if you're talking any kind of bulk cocaine, you're talking thirty million dollars. So, the lawyer says to me 'I need to find a civilian who testifies in criminal matters who can refute this paper, but who has a background like he worked for the FBI prior or whatever.' And it takes probably a day for me to find that person."

"Your background? You were with the CIA for 14 years?" asked Paul. He already knew the answer.

"That's right," nodded Ramone.

"So, therefore, you have an expertise where you can find experts that other people can't," said Paul. "Especially when it comes to legal issues, criminal activity, illicit stuff like that?"

"Sure," answered Ramone.

"Do you ever do any real detective stuff?" asked Gordon.

"Well, we're not licensed to be detectives, you understand. Do I do real detective stuff? If an attorney hires me and pays me directly, like I'm on his payroll and I represent him, yes, I do."

"But, basically, you're what is called a 'paper detective'?" asked Gordon. He shifted on the hard chair uncomfortably.

"Yes," answered Ramone. "I analyze papers. I investigate investigations. I find out what they did wrong. I don't think like a lawyer. I think like a person who is a former investigator.

"In Mr. D's case, for instance, when the police went down to Howard County, the lawyers don't think of what car the cops were in, what color it was, how it was assigned to them, what time they took it out, or whether it was full of gas . . . That's what I do. Lawyers think of issues. They think, It's an illegal wiretap because the government did this, and it was signed in Howard County.

"Lawyers rarely go back to the very beginning of a case. That's where my office specializes. If you were arrested at a traffic light, we go back to where you were at nine o'clock that morning and how you got to that traffic light. And somewhere in between, especially in a criminal matter, you're going to find that today's law enforcement agencies cannot follow the dictates of the law to legitimately catch their suspects. They have to cheat. They have to cut corners someplace. Not because they're bad people, but because it's an impossibility to follow the letter of the law to win a conviction. And if you can catch the police on a technicality, on just one little thing, you start the prejudice of the court with motions.

"In Mr. D's case, it was an issue about why all of these police and state's attorneys were in Howard County signing the affidavits and wiretaps. That's a big thing to prejudice a judge's mind with. But, we did something to prejudice the judge, Judge Glass, even further in some early motions.

"How the fuck did the police get assigned this car to take them to Howard County? Who assigned them this car? So we issue a subpoena to the city requesting all of the motor-pool records for the two detectives in the Louis Dante investigation. And, on one specific date, what car were they driving, what license plate number did it have, when was it signed in, when was it signed out, and was the mileage logged in and logged out? And that's important for two reasons, about the mileage in and mileage out, because if we know it's 50 miles from Baltimore City to the Howard County State Police Barracks at Waterloo, and that car did 300 miles that day, we would want to question where else they were with that vehicle when we get them on the witness stand.

"In this particular case, it worked out beautifully. I didn't know that there was a law that existed that said we couldn't have that information. However, the prosecutor for the city tripped on his own tongue and said, 'Well, Your Honor, the mileage information doesn't exist anymore, anyhow.'

"That prejudiced the judge, who said, 'What do you mean they don't exist? I'm allowed to see them. The defense might not be able to see them, but I'm the court. I can see them.'

"Then the prosecutor stood there, turned red, and said, 'Well, Your Honor, you know, the city has a standard policy that after 365 days, documents are shredded.' And Judge Glass jokingly said, 'Oh, what did they use? A Vegematic machine?'

"But this is how the defense skunks up a judge's mind," continued Ramone. "I'm sure that there is a city ordinance that states that all papers that are not relevant to a case after 365 days are shredded. I'm sure that there's a policy like that. But in this case, Judge Glass already felt tainted with so many other things that this is one more that he can't stand. And he looked at the prosecution and said, 'How convenient. How convenient about this vehicle and all the papers being gone, because on the day of this trial, we're only 20 days past the 365. Isn't it convenient that the city is that prompt?'

"But that's what my little firm does," boasted Ramone. "We find things that we don't know where they're going to take us, but we throw it all in. The lawyers would never do what my company did."

"Tell us what you're doing about the cellular phone wiretaps," ordered Gordon.

"We did a chronology of the wiretaps by phone number, and then by date, for each of the cellular phones. We did it all on a computer. We listed when the wiretap was brought up, when it was shut down, and how many notes of conversation were logged as having been taken off that tape.

"According to the 'minimization plan' in this wiretap, Detective Byron was the man sitting with the earphones listening to ten tape recordings. There were ten wiretaps on ten cellular phones."

"At one time?" asked Paul.

"No," corrected Ramone. "That's what we did. We found out how many phones were being listened to at any one time. Like between eleven o'clock in the morning until three in the afternoon, Detective Byron had to have on three sets of earphones to listen to three telephones at once."

"Which is kind of impossible," said Gordon.

"Which is totally impossible. It prejudices the judge. How could you follow the law that says you have to 'minimize,' turn the phones down for a little while if there's a personal conversation? What if on line two, which you don't have the headset on, you know, somebody's talking about getting fucked, and you're supposed to, by law, shut that conversation down? You can't do it if you're not listening. So papers were put in the Motion to Suppress, and we followed it with a transcription of a wiretap of a pregnant woman who had a backache. It's the first time she's ever been pregnant. She's talking to her mother-in-law, saying, 'Well, you know, my knees are sore. Does this mean I'm going to have the baby today?' They're talking about the baby and her husband working nights. The kinds of things the judge doesn't like to hear. 'Well,' she says, 'my breasts are sore because it's getting time to have the baby.' Judges don't like to hear that shit in their courtroom when they're listening to a gambling case."

"So that's supposed to be shut down? The second you're on a wiretap and it's unrelated?" asked Paul.

"A minimization plan means you listen for two minutes, shut it down for twenty seconds, then bring it back up to see if they talk about gambling again. Then you wait another two minutes and you shut it down again. With these conversations, no one's shutting anything down because they couldn't have three sets of earphones on at one time!

"What we now know is that they didn't even have to sit there and listen to any of these wiretaps. We don't even know if they were ever there. They were set up on computer. When the line rang, the computer would bring it up, log the number that came in or went out, and it would record; and all the police would have to do is, at the end of the day, come in when the wiretaps shut down. They tell the computer to shut down at nine or ten o'clock at night, and it shuts down automatically. They come in the next day, take it to their office, listen to the tape, and look at the printout from the computer. It's very simple, and they cheat that way."

"Cheating by, if it's not related to gambling?" asked Paul

"Cheating that you're supposed to promise the court that you'll sit there and listen. You will physically listen. Be there listening while it's occurring. What they did was, we call it, post-logging of conversations. It was after the fact of the tapes. You can't do that, according to law. Now, granted, that isn't the greatest problem in the world to win a case for you, but what you do is set up as many little dirty things that you can that the police did wrong until they make one big dirty thing. And you keep bombarding a judge and a jury with these dirty things that were done; civil rights violations, and just how horrifying it is listening to a pregnant woman."

"Isn't a wiretap the greatest infringement there can be on a person's rights?" asked Gordon.

"That's correct," said Ramone. "And Maryland has the strictest law on wiretapping in the country. It supersedes federal. Maryland State wiretap law supersedes federal because it's much tighter and much stronger."

"Is there a reason for that?" asked Gordon.

"Yes. I think there are more criminals in the Washington and Baltimore metropolitan areas than in most other places. The reason for that, I don't know."

Chapter 5
November 15, 1990

There are four courts of law in Maryland: two appellate courts (court of appeals and court of special appeals) and two trial courts (circuit court, which, generally, hears jury trials, criminal felonies, and civil cases over $20,000; and district court, which is non-jury and hears mostly criminal misdemeanor cases, traffic violations, and civil cases under $10,000).

Judge Barry Glass was in his fifth year as a district court judge. Before his gubernatorial appointment to the district court, he had been a prosecutor in the criminal division of the Baltimore City State's Attorneys Office for 16 years.

"The district court," announced Judge Glass, "tapes the proceedings of all cases coming before it. The microphones are very sensitive, and we appreciate everyone in the courtroom being as quiet as possible."

Glass had been sitting at the Wabash District Court in northwest Baltimore for the past six months. The two-year-old courthouse was fifteen minutes from his home and a stone's throw from the new subway station in suburban Lochearn.

It was 11 o'clock a.m., and from his bench, Judge Glass was observing the participants in a case that had all the markings of a major fiasco. Today was a continuance of the first hearing.

The judge had a boyish look for a man in his late forties. Bifocal glasses supported by a thin gold chain slid from his nose constantly. His straight black hair moved from side to side as he spoke animatedly to the court.

"Now," Judge Glass began, "we had adjourned on August the twenty-first at the point of Mr. Hayden attempting to enter as evidence the actual physical wiretap. At that point, Mr. Karson objected because of chain-of-custody problems. My recollection is that we then took a recess so that Mr. Hayden could contact the clerks of the court in downtown Baltimore to ascertain whether they could drive up to this court with the evidence sign-in book. We finally adjourned after Mr. Hayden came back to court indicating that the clerks' sign-in book had no record of receipt for the evidence against the defendant, Louis Dante."

"Your Honor," shouted Attorney Karson, "this wiretap should be suppressed since my client's rights have been violated. The prosecution cannot account for the whereabouts of the original file with the actual tapes, transcripts, and affidavits for over eight months. It's disappeared! Furthermore, the copies of the transcripts and affidavits are not numbered and . . ."

"Objection," interrupted Hayden. "I think 'disappeared' is somewhat strong. We can't recollect . . ."

"I'm going to overrule the objection," said Judge Glass. "Disappeared seems good to me. I mean, . . . you can't account for where they were . . ."

Seated at a rectangular table in front of the first row of the courtroom's elongated benches were Mr. D and his attorneys—four top-flight male criminal lawyers with over one hundred years of experience between them—and a female tax attorney from an elite Washington D.C. law firm who held two graduate degrees in tax law.

Mr. D was impeccably dressed in a double-breasted blue-black suit from Mr. Guy's in Beverly Hills. His pale blue shirt accentuated a navy-blue and gray paisley tie. Louis Dante was 5'8" tall and weighed 155 pounds. He had long, wavy blondish-brown hair that hung three inches below his suit collar. Clean-shaven and slightly tan from a tanning bed he had purchased two years earlier, Mr. D had bushy, but neatly-trimmed, eyebrows over green eyes.

Judge Glass was not naive. There was more to the misdemeanor charges against Louis Dante than met the eye. Why else would five high-priced attorneys represent Dante? Why else would two newspaper reporters be in the courtroom? Why else would a federal investigator from the U.S. Attorneys Office and an IRS agent be in attendance?

Surely Dante was not concerned about another blot on his criminal record, or the fine for this gambling offense, which was considerably less than the combined hourly rate for two of his attorneys.

The judge had done a little investigating of his own. He knew that Dante was facing federal felony charges that would go into effect if he were convicted of the gambling misdemeanor. When the local police surprised Mr. D and escorted him to his home in northern Baltimore County, they confiscated betting information that indicated a gambling empire grossing over ten million dollars a year. They also found $850,000 in cash. The feds were in the process of implementing a multi-million-dollar tax lien against Dante, and had also instituted a bank-structuring case.

Bank structuring is a violation of the Bank Secrecy Act, which requires banks to report cash transactions of $10,000 or more to the federal government. It was designed to combat money laundering by drug dealers, but was extended to cover other types of crimes.

Dante was facing lots of trouble. He wanted his $850,000 back, and he didn't want to go against the U.S. attorney on tax and structuring charges. He needed to have the state's wiretap case dismissed. Without the wiretaps, no other charges could emanate. At least that's what Mr. D and his posse of lawyers were banking on.

"Let me ask you something," said Attorney Harvey Carter to Detective Van Feldman as the hearing proceeded. "You say you've worked on 34 wiretaps in your career, correct?"

"Yes," answered the detective from Vice. A tenacious bulldog of a cop, Feldman was two years from retirement, and feeling very uncomfortable with the line of questioning.

"This document," continued Carter, holding up copies of the transcript and affidavits, "has over 3,000 pages. How come there are no page numbers? Didn't you have a hard time referring to it . . .? If nobody can find the same thing . . ."

Feldman was clammy. He wanted to loosen his tie, but didn't want the defense to recognize his discomfort. "The document was made up of dozens and dozens of smaller documents . . ."

"But," said Carter, "none of them are numbered. Of the 3,000 pages, not one number appears."

"That's true. That's true," stammered Feldman. "I realize that. It's . . . uh . . . a problem. I'm told by my secretary that . . ."

Judge Glass broke in, "In other wiretaps, have you ever had one that didn't have page numbers on it?"

"I have. Yes," answered Feldman.

"Could you tell me when?" asked the judge. "Because I contacted the federal court that deals with these all the time, and I had a federal judge tell me frankly that he would have thrown the whole thing out just based on the fact that he wouldn't have a way to refer to a single page of the 3,000 pages."

Prosecutor Will Hayden rose from his chair and said, "Okay, Your Honor. If the issue is page numbers, the detectives and I will sit down, make copies, and organize them . . . If we're talking about tampering, if there's been some change, that's a very different story. Numbering is an absolutely secretarial-clerical job. So, it's a clerical issue versus somebody actually tampering with pages . . ."

Defense lawyer Karson jumped in, "I don't think it's that at all. I think it's an authentication problem. I think it goes to the very foundation of the admissibility of the evidence in this wiretap. If Judge Glass threw the pages of the transcript on the floor, and Judge Armstrong, who signed the affidavits, could put them in sequence based on his knowledge of this whole wiretap that he understands, page by page, that he signed, fine. But I bet you he can't do it . . . I mean, play pickup sticks on the floor here with these pages. I don't know if one sentence follows another. I think it's foundational, not ministerial."

Funny, Glass thought, how incestuous this trial is. He had attended junior and senior high school with Mr. D, and, although they were peripheral acquaintances at most, even before Mr. D's brushes with the law and his troubles in 1986, the judge was always aware of Louis Dante's history with illegal gambling. One of Mr. D's lawyers, Harvey Carter, was the city state's attorney who hired him as a prosecutor in the sixties. Mr. D's lead attorney, Richard Karson, served with the judge as a fellow prosecutor for two years. The assistant state's attorney and chief prosecutor against Mr. D, Will Hayden, not only served with the judge, he was also appointed by Harvey Carter as well. And Stewart Nunman, another of Mr. D's attorneys, was one of Prosecutor Hayden's best friends. Both men worked out together religiously, lifting weights at the Downtown Athletic Club. As if that wasn't enough, among the numerous clients of Mr. D's who had been arrested for betting with him, many were prominent and successful business-men and lawyers who were friendly with the defense attorneys, the prosecutor, and the judge.

"I can try this case if there's a reasonable explanation as to where the file was." Judge Glass had joined in the cross-examina-tion with defense lawyer Nunman of the other detective in the Dante case, Sergeant Hal Byron. "I mean, even if it turns out that the file was on a closet shelf for eight months. If I find the file hasn't been tampered with, I can legally come to the conclusion that the trial can continue. But first there has to be, in my under-standing, a reasonable explanation as to where that file has been. And what your comment is, just so we're clear, is that it was not in the interior of your police car."

"I did not have it. It was not in that car, and it was not in the trunk," said Byron. He was tall and angular and casually dressed.

"And you did not file it?" asked Nunman.

"I did not file it. No, sir," answered Byron confidently.

"Okay," said Nunman. "And there were two of them?"

"Yes," said Byron. "One for the clerk and one for the State's Attorneys Office."

"Now, for the record," said Nunman, "I want you to read what that file says, in your own handwriting." Nunman was small, under five-feet-three-inches tall, with a large, round head. He was neatly dressed, without even a speck of lint on his black, pinstripe suit.

Detective Byron read, "In Circuit Court of Baltimore, Crimi-nal Section, State of Maryland: It is ordered on this twenty-eighth day of November 1988, that this sealed envelope be filed with the Clerk of the Courts . . ."

"Stop right there," interrupted Nunman.

"Nice touch, Mr. Nunman," said Judge Glass.

Nunman came closer to the stand where Detective Byron sat. "You wrote that down. You wrote that as a Baltimore police of-ficer with 19 years of wiretap experience, and you're telling this judge here that you weren't even concerned that that file didn't go to the clerk's office?"

"Objection," yelled Hayden. "Your Honor, he never stated that he was not concerned."

Judge Glass was becoming frustrated. "Okay, . . . I could be completely off base, but I don't think I am. In the chain-of-custody situation, . . . it's really technically a sealing and storage violation, that if I find a violation of the sealing and storage requirements of the Maryland statutes, I'm supposed to hold a contempt hearing. And that doesn't necessarily mean that the file itself should be suppressed—the file containing the items—as long as you can give a reasonable explanation as to the presence of the file, which weighed over 25 pounds. Even if you could tell me that the file was in a car trunk for eight months, and people just forgot to put it into the file room, and somebody snuck it in the night before. Okay? And somebody's willing to get on the stand and admit to that. It might be illegal. It might be a violation of the state statute, but it's a reasonable explanation as to where the file was."

"We can't come up with the explanation," Prosecutor Hayden admitted. "I mean, we can't manufacture an explanation. I wish I could have the officers testify 'I remember I kept it. I brought it home, and my kids played with it for a little while, and then I took it and filed it with the courts.' But that's not the way it is. These officers have been working on lots of different cases."

Christ, Glass reflected, I don't need this shit. If I rule in favor of Dante, the feds will be pissed; so will a fellow judge, the prosecutors, the police . . . But this case is all fucked up. Of course, I could always cop out, rule against Dante, and let the court of appeals overturn me, which they most certainly would do. And, with what Dante was involved with in 1986 and his old drug conviction in the early '70s, the media wouldn't get too "bleeding-hearted" over a questionable wiretap case. But that's not why I became a judge.

"Your Honor," interrupted the attractive black woman named Yolanda who worked for the courts monitoring the recording of the trial. "There seems to be a glitch in the tape machine. Could you call Mr. Jensen downstairs to come up and check it out?"

The judge halted the proceedings and announced the reason for the delay, jokingly adding, "Perhaps someone here could tell us how to fix the tape recorder."

As Glass used the phone on his bench to call for assistance, he glanced over at the prosecutor's table and sarcastically added, "I feel strangely uncomfortable using the phone."

After the call, Judge Glass instructed the litigants that he would recess the court for an hour and a half, not only to repair the recorder, he needed to contemplate whether to proceed with the case.

CHAPTER 6

The entourage of defense attorneys and staff left the courthouse with Louis Dante and drove to Miller's Deli, a mile northeast on the other side of the subway line.

The deli sat in the middle of a strip center, and served the best hot dogs and corned beef sandwiches in the Baltimore suburbs. It, too, had a history of gambling and the police.

In the early '80s, several regulars at Miller's—home improvement salesmen and retirees—were "booking" small bets, mostly for amusement and relief from boredom. Somehow the police got wind of the "Over the Hill Gang" (as they came to be called by the media) and conducted an elaborate surveillance and wiretap investigation. Twelve old men, sixty-two years and up, were arrested. It was a major news story, but ended up embarrassing the city's Vice Squad. All dozen of the alleged "gamblers" were acquitted after the wiretap was played in court. The noise in the deli was so loud, with most of the discussions centering around food, that the judge threw the case out.

Ramone stood behind Mr. D in the cafeteria-style line waiting to order lunch. He whispered, "Your friends, Paul and Gordon, visited me. Even though I know you okayed it, I'm a bit worried."

"Why?" asked Mr. D.

"I'm not sure what they're looking for, or if they're really concerned about you."

"Ramone," said Mr. D, "they're working on damage control. Since Paul can't be seen in my company, both he and Gordon are trying to assess the damage to our business in terms of who the snitch or snitches are. Unfortunately, there are lots of suspects, . . . and, also, Paul and Gordon are extremely paranoid."

"I understand," said Ramone as he ordered a lean corned beef on rye with coleslaw and Russian dressing. "What with all the investigations involving you . . ."

Louis Dante and Ramone took a table in the nonsmoking section near the bakery side of Miller's to continue their discussion.

They were briefly interrupted by a small, frail-looking man in his seventies wearing a brownish toupee over very white side-burns.

"Hi, Louis," he said. "Just wanted to wish ya good luck."

It was Lindy, the owner of the poolroom that Mr. D had just about grown up in.

"How ya doin'?" asked Mr. D.

"Not too good. I'm livin' on social security. Lost the pool-room . . ."

"Christ, Lindy, I didn't know. I figured you still had your bar mitzvah money. Here, lemme help ya out a bit," said Dante reaching into his pocket and peeling off six one-hundred-dollar bills.

"Thanks," said Lindy meekly. He was a proud man, but sorely needed the handout. He winked at Mr. D and sauntered away.

"What do your sources tell you about my problems—formally and informally?" asked Mr. D, resuming his dialogue with Ramone.

"Well, lemme see," began Ramone. "Some say it was your trouble in '86 that began a long investigation that has developed into today's charges, . . . but I don't believe that and not many others do, either. Another source says that your problems are mainly the outgrowth of jealous cops. Now, don't take this the wrong way, but some people blame everything on your involvement in the past two years with your girlfriend, Shirley. She's considered too greedy and too controlling. They think you became too visible, too ostentatious . . . You were spending too much money on her . . . and building a million-dollar house . . . The cops see that and they want to fuck with you."

"Do you really believe that, Ramone?"

"To be honest about it, yes. I think it's got some merit. But it's not the reason for the majority of your hassles."

"Ramone," said Mr. D, "between you and me, do you think she may have cooperated with the police?"

"There's no concrete proof," said Ramone, "but others believe she may have 'ratted' you out."

"Who?" asked Dante.

"I think Paul and Gordon are leaning that way, although they see other conspiracies at play."

"Like what?" asked Dante.

"Like the six-state federal loan-sharking grand jury investigation where your name's come up. Rumor has it that an informant, perhaps your old acquaintance, Mel, who owns a poolroom and laid off to you, is singing to the feds . . . Oh, and local police are trying to tie you into the death of Clem Watowski."

"How?" asked Dante. He had known Watowski for 20 years. A big, local bookie, Watowski had been found dead three weeks before in his car, an apparent suicide. Although he had a long friendship with Mr. D, Watowski was upset at his own recent arrest, which he blamed on Mr. D's high living over the past two years.

"It's an interesting case," said Ramone. "How does one shoot himself in the back of the head, twice? Some say it was a jealous husband who found out that Watowski was running around with his wife . . ."

"Shit!" said Dante. "He hadn't had a hard-on in ten years."

"Others," said Ramone, "feel that the cops killed him. Ya know, he cooperated with the police from time to time, and I think he may have had too much on the cops, and . . ."

"Jesus," said Dante, "and they want to blame it on me?"

"Wait," said Ramone. "There's more. Although Paul hasn't been busted in over 20 years, I've got a source who thinks that he may have killed Watowski; and that Paul may be so upset with you that both you and Shirley could be next on the 'hit list.'"

"That's bullshit," said Mr. D. "We're bookmakers. We don't kill people. We don't even hurt people. Everybody wants to tie us to some big Mob, like the Mafia. We're businessmen who provide a service to the public, and if we're arrested, well, it's just an occupational hazard."

CHAPTER 7

At thirty-two, Shirley June McCutcheon was one of the most successful stockbrokers in the prestigious investment house of Shofit and Jordan. Aside from being academically bright and savvy beyond her years, Shirley June was a stunner.

Radiant, long red hair hung down to the middle of her back. At 5'9" and 132 pounds, Shirley June's hourglass figure measured out at 36-23-36. She dressed in either bold red or black dresses and skirts which seemed to highlight her deep green eyes and round ruby lips.

Old-timers at the investment house referred to Shirley June complimentarily as "Blaze" since she reminded them of the former world-famous striptease legend, Blaze Starr. She detested the tag, feeling the nickname was synonymous with the "loose" women associated with today's pornography.

Shirley June's presence was so overpowering that she turned as many women's heads as men. She had been engaged no less than twelve times since her eighteenth birthday, but had never married. Two-thirds of the time, she broke off the engagements. The others came as a result of the former fiancés' frustrations over her totally selfish attitude.

The closest Ms. McCutcheon ever came to the altar was with Louis Dante, Mr. D. Although it was her most tumultuous affair, interspersed with three broken engagements, she was weeks away from a wedding when Mr. D was arrested.

Now, leaning over her desk in the firm's downtown office at Fayette and St. Paul Streets, studying the earnings of what would be her newest stock tip, Universal Securities, Inc., a communications and burglar alarm company, Shirley June felt uneasy. She had the distinct impression that she was being watched. Since her teenage years, she was familiar with the stares and looks from boys and men; but these were different observations. It was as though all of her moves were being followed and analyzed, and that the motives weren't sexual. Paranoia and fear played havoc with her mind.

She saw herself as a tool, but for whom? The FBI, Attorney General's Office, State's Attorneys Office, and the local police had all communicated with her. Even the Securities and Exchange Commission and IRS had paid unannounced visits. Then there was Mr. D's defense team of lawyers and detectives. And there were also Mr. D's pals, Paul and Gordon. Of all of them, she found Gordon the creepiest and Ramone the most annoying. But was there someone else? Weren't there enough already?

The wiretap case had given Shirley June a keen awareness of the eavesdropping devices available to anyone. It made her sick to realize that she had been, or could have been, overheard in her apartment, in Mr. D's home, at work, or on her car phone.

"Who?" she whispered to herself as she unconsciously played with the computer. "Dammit, who is fucking with me?"

CHAPTER 8

"She's such a bitch. I just can't stand her," said Ramone in the more effeminate way that he was used to speaking. He had let his guard down since his first meeting with Paul and Gordon, and was now deeply engrossed in a conversation with Gordon in the bar at the Polo Grill, a fashionable restaurant in the Guilford section of Baltimore, across from the Homewood Campus of the Johns Hopkins University.

Gordon had on a black and red Fila warm-up suit, and Ramone was dressed in a double-breasted gray Armani suit with a light orange shirt and orange handkerchief in his suit pocket. He wore no tie, and the shirt was buttoned at the collar. They sat at a round table with four chairs about six feet from the bar and close by the maître d' stand at the entrance to the restaurant. As both munched from a bowl of pretzels, Gordon drank a Heineken beer, and Paul sipped from a martini glass filled with Stolichnaya vodka and three huge green olives.

"So, how well do you know this McCutcheon broad?" asked Gordon.

"Well," began Ramone, "I met her on a number of occasions while she was still going with Mr. D. Since that time, I have uncovered lots of dirt on her, especially after Mr. D realized that she wasn't as dedicated to him as he had perceived."

"I understand that Louis showered her with all kinds of gifts," said Gordon.

"Showered her ain't the word," said Ramone. "First of all, she was the greediest cunt this side of the Mississippi. Not only that, it didn't matter what he gave her. She didn't appreciate nothin'. He spent over a quarter of a million dollars on her in the first three months that they were dating. He gave her cars, paid for her condo, bought her stocks, paintings . . . You name it, he bought it for her. He even let her have the use of his favorite car, the Mercedes convertible. Then he started building a million-dollar home for the both of 'em. The last fuckin' thing you need is for a guy like him to be showin' off all that money. But, he was thinkin' with his cock, although I know he's a romantic at heart."

"So we had a genuine love affair going on, huh?" asked Gordon.

"No way," said Ramone. "They argued constantly. She was never satisfied. She was always asking him to give her more and more. Once he bought her a mink coat, and she told him, 'I don't like the quality of this coat, Louis. You should have gotten me one that cost twice as much.' I mean, nothin' satisfied this woman. Nothin'."

"So they just fought about gifts all the time, and her not appreciating it . . .?" asked Gordon.

"No," said Ramone. "There was always something. Anything. She was a very strange chick. They had this huge 'beef' one time over privacy. While they were dating, she'd come over his place at night, but then she'd go home after they screwed or whatever. And he'd come over to her apartment, and then go home afterwards. Now, Mr. D, besides the sex, he wanted to sleep with Shirley June, and wake up in the morning beside her. But she was always trying to get him out. Every now and then, she'd fall asleep early and he'd manage to stay overnight in her condo. When she awoke, she'd wake him up immediately and insist that he leave. And he would go bonkers!"

"What do you mean, she'd want to throw him out? What had happened?" asked Gordon.

"Nothing really happened," said Ramone. "The problem was that she didn't want him in the house when she had to go to the bathroom. He couldn't understand that. He figured, What the hell? We're going to be man and wife one day. We're doing everything else together. What's the big deal if I'm in the bedroom when she's in the bathroom; or anywhere in the condo when she's takin' a crap? But she had this big hang-up about it, you know, like not wanting someone to hear her in the bathroom . . . It got so that when he was designing this dream-house, he asked her, 'How many bathrooms do you want me to build, and how far away do you want those bathrooms from wherever I'm allowed to be?' Or he'd say 'Am I going to have to go outside of the house every time you have to take a piss? Or should I drive around the block?' She didn't think it was funny and went crazy over it."

Gordon decided to change the subject. "Do you think that Shirley June may have helped the police?"

"I think so," said Ramone. "She had Mr. D's car and used his car phone. She drove it for a good portion of a month before his arrest. If the police were listening to her phone calls, and let me tell you something, her calls would have been way better than anything we've ever heard. I can guarantee you they must have been pissers. But, somehow there was no tape, or no wiretap, from Mr. D's car. And yet we know he made a lot of phone calls from it, and when she had it, she made a ton. I mean, I saw a bill for over $1,500 for one month of her phone calls from his car."

Gordon motioned for Ramone to be quiet as the waitress approached, and they ordered another round of drinks. When she walked away, Ramone resumed their discussion. "It's more likely that the police, after hearing some of her conversations, decided to have a chat with her. We've never really been able to figure out how Mr. D was arrested in northern Baltimore County."

"Which means there had to be an informant?" asked Gordon.

"Mr. D always thought that maybe it was a guy who owed him money or some bookie who laid off to him who owed him money. That was always his belief. But he could never figure out who that somebody was who was out to get him . . . But no one knew the physical place where he was working. It's one thing to know what the cellular telephone number is, but to know where that telephone physically is, is a very difficult part of an investigation. And I asked Mr. D about it. I asked him, 'Did you ever give Shirley June the phone number of the apartment you were using so she could call you there to see when you might be finished at night?' And Mr. D would say, 'No, no, positively not. I'd never do that. I'd never tell anybody where I was.' But, we know Mr. D well enough. Sometimes he talks."

"I know what you mean," said Gordon. "Especially when it comes to a woman he's infatuated with."

"Yeah," said Ramone, "when he thinks with his dick, he gets in trouble. But, as far as Shirley June's concerned, there's no question that we do know that the police did call her and had left messages for her during that time frame. We got that through our investigation into one of the two detectives at Vice in the city."

Ramone ate the thumb-sized olives from his drink and watched as two young students from Johns Hopkins University came over to sit at the bar. They were young men in their early twenties, either seniors or graduate students at the school, who were very handsome. Ramone caught himself staring and continued. "Gordon, think about it this way. You know, if a judge is signing a court order, a big stink could be made about why the police wouldn't want to tap the car phone of a guy like Mr. D. I mean, that's where you're going to get your best information. Also, for some reason, they didn't tap his house phone. I mean, that's where the guy lives, that's where he works. It's my belief that we don't hear about those tapes, at least the car phone tape, because Shirley June made calls on that car phone. And we might have found that she might have called the police from that car phone after they put some kind of pressure on her. I don't know what kind of pressure, but they obviously could have, and, I think, did.

"Mr. D believed that his car telephone was tapped. What's interesting is that you've got all these court orders, but we can't locate the tenth court order, and we've got a funny feeling that that had to do with the car telephone. And there might have been another one that we don't even know about that was for the house phone."

"So, what are you driving at here, Ramone?" asked Gordon, his interest perked more than normal.

"It's my belief," said Ramone, "that another agency probably has those tapes. I have no proof. It's strictly speculation."

"And that agency could be with the federal government?" asked Gordon.

"That's correct," said Ramone. "We now know everybody who has requested trial transcripts and copies of all evidence from Judge Glass's court. The FBI, the Federal Prosecutor's Office, the State of Maryland Attorney General's Office, and the IRS all requested a set. And the reason for that is because the federal and state governments don't like to lose."

"So," said Gordon, "they don't like it that they've been beaten by Mr. D in the past?"

"For a long time," said Ramone, "they'll never forgive Mr. D. And even though he might not be doing anything right now, it's not going to matter. You see, the government doesn't like losing. They've lost to him in embarrassing ways before, and they want him real bad.

"Oh, and here's another thing, Gordon. You recall when the cops broke into Mr. D's home, they knew right where to go. They didn't have to tear any drawers apart to find lay-off slips and papers because everything was in the same place where he always kept it. They went right to that caftan he had with the hood and just pulled everything out. Why tear up the house? They knew where everything was."

"What do you think this judge is going to do?" asked Gordon.

"I would hope," said Ramone, "that he throws it out. But, he may just want to rule against Mr. D and let the court of appeals overturn him. Make the appeals judges the bad guys. He doesn't want judges like himself on the lower court to be the bad guys 'cause they've got to live with the prosecutors, with other judges, and with the cops . . . And, you know, a lot of judges, they're former prosecutors. They're in this kind of close-knit fraternity."

Gordon leaned closer to Ramone and talked lower. "You've been working very closely with Mr. D and his attorneys, and I would like to know, based on the background work you've done and your close personal observations of Louis Dante, what you think about him."

Ramone, who had been dividing his attention between watching the two young men at the bar and speaking to Gordon, now devoted all of his attention to Gordon. He wasn't sure what he was driving at and remembered what a scary person Gordon was, so he wanted to be cautious with his answer. Also, Ramone was upset with himself since his thought process was foggy, having already had two very stiff drinks.

"I've heard from a lot of those gamblers who were caught how upset they were that Mr. D was so ostentatious. Also, that he aggravated cops, like that guy, Copley, by flaunting shit. Building a million-dollar house, being with flashy women, and driving fancy cars causes a lot of jealousy.

"On the other hand, I see Mr. D as a fly-by-the-seat-of-the-pants man. If it's a good deal, he'll move. He's a mover and a shaker. Dante'll take a bet and play the odds . . . And he usually wins. That's what aggravates people. Louis Dante always comes out on top. This arrest has taken its toll on him, but he's not cheap. He'll spend the money to stay free and do what he has to do in order to win. Now, Gordon, there are some people who are dollar conscious who won't take the risks and play the game. Mr. D will. He doesn't go with the flow. He's not a standstill guy, and he's not a crier. Well, all right, maybe he's a crier, but he keeps moving forward while he cries.

"I don't think it's just the cops who are jealous of him. You can probably add to the list these drop-a-dime guys, squealers, other bookies, lay-off guys, guys who bet with him, and guys who borrow from him. Also, I don't think Mr. D knows how to pick good friends . . ."

Ramone paused. He was hoping that Gordon wouldn't take that statement the wrong way—that Paul and Gordon weren't Dante's good friends.

CHAPTER 9

The Jones Falls Expressway, an eight-lane dual highway, empties out of Baltimore City north towards Baltimore County where it dead-ends into the rural, single-lane Falls Road. Most commuters leave the expressway before it ends to pick up the Baltimore Beltway going east or west. Some will continue along out Falls Road to Greenspring Valley. Right before Falls Road begins, there is an Exxon station, and behind it is the small, all-purpose restaurant called Windy Valley Farms Restaurant and Carryout. It had been there for over 50 years serving hot and cold lunches, dinners, breakfast all day, and homemade ice cream. Groceries could be purchased there, as well as lottery tickets. The restaurant also had three antique pinball machines located towards the left rear of the dining area near the restrooms.

Mr. D was stooped over the last pinball machine playing for just under 20 minutes while waiting for his attorney, Richard Karson, to arrive. He was dressed in jeans, a long-sleeve polo shirt, and a red Windbreaker. He hadn't shaved for three days, and his eyes were bloodshot. He cursed the silver balls in the pinball machine as they bounced the wrong way. He felt frustrated and dejected. At least once a week he met with one or all of his lawyers. All of the meetings cost money. He visualized cash registers ringing in their eyes: a hundred fifty, two hundred, or three hundred an hour. It never stopped. There was always something else that needed clarification. Or there was yet another new issue to be resolved with the state or federal government, or even an old issue. More and more questions, never any answers, and never an end in sight. Today would be no different.

Attorney Karson entered Windy Valley and walked over to the counter to order a tuna sandwich on toast and a cup of coffee.

He never even glanced towards Mr. D. After a few minutes, he grabbed his lunch, paid the bill, and walked over to a booth at the end of the left side of the restaurant. Mr. D finished playing his last game, tilted the machine, walked over, and slid in across from Karson. Silently, he watched Karson devour his sandwich.

After Karson washed down the tuna with his coffee, he wiped his face with a napkin, and said, "Louis, I need to cover some things with you very quickly, and then I have to leave. I have a court case in Carroll County that begins at two o'clock sharp, and I must be on time."

Richard Karson had pale blue eyes, short black hair lightly streaked with gray, and a round, cherub-like face. He possessed a warm smile and a deep voice that was reassuring one-on-one, but grew to a loud resonance in a court of law. At 6'4" tall, Karson towered over Mr. D and most of his other clients.

The attorney removed an envelope and flipped it over. He looked at his notes and said, "Louis, here's what I found out so far about the Watowski killing. Funny, but the newspapers always made him out as the main guy in Baltimore for gambling. He always paid his fines and so forth. Right before your trial comes up, he's found shot to death in his car. Some believe it was suicide. Others say you or Paul may have killed him. Then there's a few who think a jealous lover might have killed him . . . I've got somebody checking with the coroner's office to see if they've determined whether it was murder or suicide.

"Personally, I've got to agree with Ramone. It's very difficult to hold a gun to the back of your head and pull the trigger, twice. You see, usually the first bullet would do it. You'd probably drop the gun. It's the second shot that bothers me with the suicide theory. There are too many coincidences coming up here. You've got some police officers involved here who were always arresting Watowski, and were fairly involved with him over the last few years. Suddenly, they're all transferred out of Vice. So you start adding up piece after piece . . .

"Watowski's reputation was that he fucked people for money, and it leads you to believe that maybe he fucked with the wrong person. But, when the police make a statement that somebody can shoot himself in the head twice, that it's probably suicide, well, that's insanity at its highest level. And they're not saying it because they're stupid. Nobody makes a careless statement like that to the press unless there's a reason. You know, in any death like that, that person has become a liability.

"The way I see it, Louis, if someone's involved in a gambling operation that's worth millions of dollars, and someone owes you a hundred grand, well, if you shut them off, don't do any more business with them, then they're really out of your life and out of your hair. You don't have to commit murder for that. So I don't see how you could be involved in something like this. Not for a hundred grand. There are other ways to get back at him . . ."

"But, what about the black bookies, Creek and Bop?" interrupted Dante. "Surely they . . ."

"No way, I'm told, Louis," said Karson. "Solid-gold alibis. Now, there's a rumor to the effect that Watowski, at one point in his life, was very close with the cops, and that maybe he was paying off the Vice Squad. I don't know. But, if that comes to light . . . It's true, isn't it, that Watowski did federal time for obstruction of justice and refused to give up any information on any cops?"

"Right," said Mr. D.

"Well," Karson continued, "those ties, they don't break that easily. These people who gather information and have friends . . ."

Mr. D stared out of the window towards the Exxon gas station as Karson spoke. He did not look back at Karson's face until after Karson finished with Watowski.

Karson asked, "Louis, did you know there's been a Pen Register at your store for a number of years?"

"No, but it doesn't surprise me," said Mr. D.

A Pen Register is similar to caller ID and attaches to a phone. When a call is made from that phone or a call comes in to that phone, a computer at the phone company spits out the number coming in or going out, the time, and the duration of the call. Nothing is overheard. For four years, an enforcement agency had a Pen Register on five telephone lines at Mr. D's check cashing and package goods store called Charlie's in downtown west Baltimore. It was attached to the three telephone lines going into Charlie's and the two pay phones outside—five telephone lines, twenty-four hours a day, reams and reams of paper. The phone company had to spit out thousands and thousands of telephone calls to and from the outlets. And then the police would ask for a listing of incoming or outgoing calls that showed up frequently to see who the number belonged to. They did this to see if there was a pattern developing among the calls. If they found that calls were to an attorney's office or an accountant, they would discount it. If they found it was a nickel-dime residence, and the person was an alleged gambler, then it was a different story. Yet, at a place like Charlie's, it was somewhat ridiculous to check the incoming calls. Charlie's sold legal state-run lottery tickets, and customers would call every day, all year long, asking for the legal lottery numbers. Since many bought their tickets at Charlie's, they felt compelled to call Charlie's. Therefore, among the hundreds of daily calls, it was conceivable that a telephone number might represent someone who was convicted of a murder or rape years ago. This didn't necessarily mean that this person was into some kind of nefarious dealing at Charlie's. However, it could prejudice a judge into giving enforcement people the right to put a wiretap on more phones.

"I'll tell you a funny story, Richard," said Mr. D. "It's probably one of the few funny things I can think of right now with my head so dizzy from all this bullshit I'm in. A few years back, we had this crazy incident down at Charlie's. The cops were always raiding the place. They never found anything there relating to my bookmaking, but they kept coming in, over and over, because there was always something a little wrong going on. You know, like a guy would come in with a case of tuna fish, and maybe I'd buy it. But, it didn't have the sales stamp, and maybe it was stolen from a store. I don't know where it came from. And so there was always some kind of on-going investigation at Charlie's.

"So here's what happened: A guy named Erwin gets busted by the city police. He's a street fence, not a big operational fence. He tells the police that he hustles things like soap, razor blades, and other 'hot' stuff to me or to my store, and that we buy it for a few bucks. So, the cops decide they're going to set up a sting operation on my place, and they send in Erwin, this lowlife fence. He parades in with ten cartons of cigarettes and one of those video camcorders. You know what they are?"

"Yeah," said Karson.

"Herbie, one of the clerks in the store, gives Erwin a few bucks for the cigarettes and the camcorder. Later that afternoon, the police raid Charlie's. They bust us for illegal possession of cigarettes and this video recorder. Two months later, we go to court, and we find out during cross-examination that the camcorder came from Hecht's department store. It was a gift donated by Hecht's to the police department. Now listen to this, Richard, this is a pisser. Hecht's had donated this camcorder, given it to the Baltimore City Police Department. The police give it to a fence, Erwin, and he sells it to Herbie in my store. Okay, that's one thing. Now, Giant Food store donated ten cartons of cigarettes to the city police. The police also gave the cigarettes to Erwin the fence to sell down at my place. The guy representing me at the time, my former attorney, Stan Lessans, says to the judge, 'Your Honor, none of this material was ever stolen—it was donated by the Hecht Company and Giant Food to the city police. Therefore, the police department, knowingly and willingly, gave the donations to Erwin the fence, who then sold them to Herbie, a clerk at Charlie's. It's no theft. There was no purchase of stolen merchandise. No one stole this merchandise. It was all donated!'"

"So what happened?" asked Karson, amused.

"They threw it out. Not guilty. However, the judge made us return the camcorder and the cigarettes to the police. And we never did get our money back from them."

The client and attorney had a relief of laughter over the story, and then Mr. D became serious, and asked, "Richard, I never understand it. After twenty-some fuckin' years of these people coming after me, . . . I mean, if you're a taxpayer of this state, and you know that the most that's going to happen from a gambling conviction is a fine that won't even exceed a thousand bucks, how in the fuck do you justify spending millions of dollars to bust people like me? It doesn't make any sense."

"Louis," said Karson, "you can't justify it unless you're the federal government. As a result of your misdemeanor conviction, they can use that information to go to the IRS, to seize your property and cash, and to institute this new bank-structuring case against you."

"But, how do they justify it?" asked Louis Dante again.

"In law enforcement agencies' minds, gambling is organized crime. If you're a big bookie doing a large volume of business, and they can get the case to the IRS to put you out of business, they think, Hey, we're going after the Mafia, the Mob. They have tunnel vision. Total organized crime, that's their target, whether they admit it or not. The public might think on the surface, Why is the government wasting our time and money on gambling misdemeanors? The answer from the government is 'Hey, this man's a big fish, and his crime organization could be responsible for all types of heinous crimes. Yeah, maybe every crime ever committed.' And, you get these state's attorneys, attorney generals for the state, attorney generals for the feds, okay . . . How do you think they build their political careers? They need to get somebody big. It's a political job. You don't want to be the government's top lawyer just to sit there. You want to go some place else. And you do it on a body count. You get one good case, or one famous case, or perhaps two, and you prosecute one yourself, or maybe have your underlings do it. And that's what makes political careers, Louis. That's what it's all about."

CHAPTER 10

Baltimore County surrounds three-quarters of Baltimore City, and, over the past three decades, has grown so rapidly that its population now rivals the city itself. Crime has also grown, and that means a growing police force and Vice Squad that mimics that of Baltimore City.

The head of that Vice Squad was Clarence Copley. Copley had come up through the ranks during his tenure in Maryland. He began as a deputy sheriff in the town of Denton on Maryland's Eastern Shore, and later became a foot patrolman in Baltimore City. Following that, he was a state trooper for six years. Then he was placed on special assignment to the Bureau of Narcotics and Dangerous Drugs, the precursor to the federal Drug Enforcement Administration. In the mid-seventies, he was offered a position with the Baltimore County Police Department as their chief of Vice, and he had now been in that position for almost fifteen years.

At sixty years old, Copley was quite a physical specimen. Six feet tall and stocky, he was extremely muscular for someone who had never worked out. His years of growing up on a small farm, where his father worked him from sunup to sundown, had helped develop his physique. Copley's face was always flushed, and he had deep scars on his cheeks as a result of severe acne as a youth. Copley had lost most of his hair by the time he was forty, and he wore a cheap hairpiece. But, he didn't seem to mind the stares when it shifted an inch or so from one ear to the other. He had a long torso and short, very thick legs. A no-nonsense type of individual, Copley was an expert marksman with a rifle or a Colt .45.

He hated Mr. D and everything he stood for. Some of it was

envy. He could admit that to himself. But the law was the law. He had grown up that way, and he truly believed it. If you broke the law, you went to jail or you paid a fine. And if you repeatedly broke the law, you stayed in jail longer. That's the way Copley saw it, and he would stop at nothing to get the lawbreakers, even if it meant that he had to violate the law himself. And if his superiors or the state's attorney didn't agree with Copley's law, then he would personally share information with the feds, the IRS, the FBI, the U.S. Attorney, or the Securities and Exchange Commission. Whatever it took, he would get his target.

Copley sat behind the wheel of his parked, idling Ford Taurus, property of the Baltimore County Police Department, his stomach close to the steering wheel. He unbuttoned the herringbone tweed sports coat that he had been wearing since 1977, and loosened his tie. Seated next to him was Detective Van Feldman of the Baltimore City Police Department Vice Unit. Together they had worked on a number of busts, among them, five arrests of Louis Dante. They were not happy campers. As a result of the latest trial, they were trying to find a way to salvage the case against Mr. D. They had worked too long this time. They had also suffered a number of embarrassing defeats in trying to capture Mr. D in the past.

"Do you think that judge is going to throw the case out?" asked Copley.

"I can't be sure," said Feldman. "Sometimes I think he's ready to do it. Other times it looks like he's grasping at anything just to keep the case going. I'm not sure if Judge Glass just loves hearing the way we all botched this thing, wants to release Mr. D, or if he's looking for a reason to prolong it so we can finally convict the motherfucker."

"So," said Copley, "besides the fact that you assholes don't know what you did with that fucking wiretap evidence, . . . and for the life of me, I don't know why you didn't just make up a story. The judge gave you every fucking chance—but, then, that's you guys. Where else did we fuckin' go wrong? I mean, what else do we have to do? You know, I'm in touch with the feds, and they don't want to look bad in this deal. You know damn well that they'll back off and leave us hanging if we don't give them something."

Feldman munched on a crumb donut that he had bought up the street at Dunkin' Donuts, and said, "If Judge Glass lets the case continue, we've got some other issues they're going to try and beat us on. Minimization is one of them. They realize that we couldn't have listened to all those tapes at one time, or even three tapes at once, and that's going to come out against us."

"How the fuck did that happen?" asked Copley.

"Well, it turns out that by mistake the phone company gave one of the tapped cellular telephones to one of their workmen. He was a young guy who went around using the phone in his truck all day, calling his buddies and telling them about some woman who tried to seduce him. That was one thing. The other one is the worst. They tapped a wrong phone, and it was this pregnant woman speakin' to her mother-in-law. You wouldn't believe what they were talking about. When Judge Glass hears it, he'll go nuts! It'll be obvious because if me or Byron were really listening, it wouldn't be on the tape. So they could catch us on that."

"What else?" asked Copley, disgusted.

"Well, the other one is going to be an embarrassment because it deals with where the judge signed the affidavits. He wasn't in the county that he was supposed to be. You know, like where he had jurisdiction. And one of Mr. D's lawyers was involved in that old trial where . . . You know the story about the Wiretapper Lounge?"

"No," said Copley, impatiently.

"Well," said Feldman, "a judge from Prince George's County was supposed to be signing some wiretaps in his home county. Instead, he goes to meet the state police in the cocktail lounge of the Howard Johnson's in Montgomery County. So, the state's attorneys and the cops meet him there. The judge reads the papers and signs them right in the middle of this cocktail lounge. Of course, it could have been thrown out just for the guys being in a bar. It's not a good place to conduct business, but I don't think that would have mattered. However, the case was later dismissed by the Maryland Court of Appeals, which held that it wasn't the proper jurisdiction. As a result of the publicity, they renamed the cocktail lounge in Howard Johnson's, the Wiretapper Lounge."

It was an amusing story, but Copley had no sense of humor, and Feldman, realizing it, held back his own laughter.

Now it was Feldman's turn to ask Copley a question. "Do you think if the case is suppressed in Baltimore City that the state's attorney in Baltimore County will still try it in your county?"

"I'm not sure," said Copley. "She's not like you and I are with these cases. Gambling's not that big a deal with her, and no matter what I try and tell her about Dante and where this money probably goes, she don't want to listen."

"Yeah, but have you played her the tapes?" asked Feldman.

"Well, no, but she knows the story. I'm just afraid that if she sees that judge suppress it in Baltimore City that she would decide not to try it in the county."

"Listen, I've got a copy of the main tape right here. If you want, we can play it, and then you make a decision," suggested Feldman.

"Okay," said Copley. "Let me here it. I'll tell you what I think."

Detective Feldman slid the cassette into a portable recorder he took out of a manila envelope, and played a copy of the tape of Mr. D and Lanny right after Mr. D was busted.

Mr. D: Yeah. How ya doin'?

Lanny: Good.

Mr. D: You know they got me.

Lanny: Oh no! I called and the phone was . . . They said the phone was down . . .

Mr. D: Who said that?

Lanny: The . . . You know, 'This phone is not in service right now.'?

Mr. D: Did you beep me "99"?

Lanny: No. I didn't beep ya.

Mr. D: Why wouldn't you?

Lanny: Well, I just didn't.

Mr. D: It's important to protect one another, you know? See, that's the important thing—protecting one another. They busted me again. I'm gonna have to quit. I mean I can't work under tension. It's got nothing to do with business. We're gonna have to figure out how much you can handle.

Lanny: Shoo. Christ! Now, so what the fuck's going on here? Somebody's got to have a big mouth.

Mr. D: I can't figure it out. But we can't talk about it right now. I'll talk about it with you later. I'll call you. You got your phone list, right?

Lanny: Yeah.

Mr. D: When you get in there tonight, uh, uh, I'll give you a call at five-thirty. Okay? Will you be there?

Lanny: Yeah.

Mr. D: I want you to go into the other room so you can make some calls. I want you to call 101 and get his ticket reconstructed, you know? And, also do the same for J.B. I'm gonna let you call him and tell him to read you his ticket, and tell him that I have a problem and to restructure his ticket and . . . I'll call you at five-

thirty. I've got to get out of here. Okay? All right?
Lanny: Right.

"Okay, that's it," said Feldman. "What do you think?"

"Well," said Copley, "number one, reconstruct a ticket. His lawyers will say he was talking about a laundry ticket, or he was talking about parking tickets. I mean, what ticket? They talk about coming in at five-thirty, or he'll have to find out how much business Lanny can handle. They'll argue a lot of things.

"When I arrested Mr. D in the county, I found 120 telephone numbers on him, and you guys only found 22 phone numbers on Lanny when he was arrested. Now, it's simple to understand. Some people use more than one bookmaker. Some guy might use one guy to bet baseball and another guy to bet football, but it doesn't mean that they're conspiring to gamble . . . Conspiring to gamble means they tell you what the lines are, how much the lay-off is, and the phone call has nothing to do with it, okay? So, that's what we're dealing with. We've got to get this cocksucker!"

Feldman put the cassette away and started to open the car door.

"Copley," he said, "you really hate Dante, don't ya?"

"He's a fuckin' criminal, Feldman," screamed Copley. "And, yeah, I hate the little prick! . . . But I do respect him some. Every time I've busted him, I roughed him up pretty good, especially this last time. Musta kicked him in the balls and stomach about three times. But, ya know, he never filed a complaint about me. Took it like a man . . . But, he's got to go down this time."

CHAPTER 11

"This is very stupid, Louis," said Shirley June. "Why was it so important to see me? Couldn't you have called?"

Mr. D and Shirley June were standing in the Mammal Pavilion of the National Aquarium. Behind them the newest residents, two bottle-nosed dolphins, deftly swam. The Aquarium was located two piers east of one of the East Coast's top tourist attractions, Harbor Place.

"Jesus Christ, Shirl," said Mr. D, "how could I call? Haven't you gotten it through your head how dangerous the phones are?"

"What do you want?" demanded Shirley June. "I need to get back to work."

"I miss you. I still love you. What's wrong?" he said.

"Louis, your trouble has caused me trouble. My parents are upset. My bosses are upset. I'm embarrassed at work . . ."

"Shirl," said Mr. D. "There's some concern about what you may have told the police, and . . ."

"Fuck you, Louis," she interrupted. "I haven't caused you any trouble. It's your business, your organization . . . Sure, I've had to speak with the authorities, but I've said nothing to incriminate you. Hell, they know much more about you than I do . . . I could lose my job and my license to sell stocks."

"I'm sorry, baby," he said softly. "Can't we get together some night? I need you . . ."

"It's too dangerous for me right now. I'm scared," answered Shirley June.

As they spoke, Mr. D tried to brush against her, to touch her. But the sensuous Ms. McCutcheon wanted no contact with Louis Dante. Even with all of his money, he had become a liability. However, she was somewhat afraid to cut him off; afraid of his associates, his enemies. She needed time.

"Louis," she said as she moved towards the ramp leading down to the escalator. "When it's all over, we'll have time to make up for all of this aggravation. You know how I feel about you. Be patient . . . Gotta run."

Shirley June turned and hurried down the ramp. She moved quickly despite her three-inch-tall black high-heels and tight, knee-length skirt. Her black cashmere sweater strained to hold her large, well-rounded breasts, which jiggled slightly as she moved. Her aura overwhelmed Mr. D. It also overwhelmed the people watching her. Not the Aquarium tourists, but Blume from the U.S. Attorney's Office, Detective Hal Byron from city Vice, Gordon, and "Handsome" John Abrams.

CHAPTER 12

Handsome John Abrams was the last to leave the National Aquarium. Blume and Detective Byron were together. They had not noticed Gordon or Abrams. Gordon had spotted the government men, but not Abrams, who hid more from Gordon than anyone else.

By two p.m., Abrams had driven through the city to Rice's Poolroom, where he met with Mel the Tailor.

Rice's Poolroom was situated next to a Baskin Robbin's Ice Cream Parlor in a strip shopping center on Liberty Road in northwest Baltimore. The name "Rice" was an Americanization of "Ricci." Gino Ricci came to the United States from Naples, Italy in the late 1890s. His son, Gino Ricci, Jr., opened the original Gino's Poolroom on Liberty Heights in the Forest Park section of northwest Baltimore City in 1948. By 1969, his clientele had either grown up and quit playing pool or moved farther north to the county as a result of racial changes in the Forest Park neighborhood. Gino Ricci, Jr. closed the poolroom, and with his son, Gino, III, went into the vending machine business. In 1975, at the age of 65, Gino, Jr. suffered a major heart attack while having lunch in Isaella's in Little Italy, and died in the ambulance on the way to Johns Hopkins Hospital.

Gino Ricci, III sold the vending business a month after his dad died. Two months later, he changed his name to Gene Rice, and, several weeks later, he opened Rice's Poolroom on suburban Liberty Road in northwest Baltimore County. Gene had always loved the poolroom atmosphere and its associated characters. He took on a silent partner, Melvale Dennis, a.k.a. Mel the Tailor, who had owned a small bowling alley in the fifties. The business was licensed in Gene's name only.

Gene worshiped Mel from the old days, and was unaware of how devious and deceitful Mel was. Within two years, he was enlightened. Mel "booked" Gene's bets, steered him to questionable investments, and skimmed the profits from Rice's Poolroom. By late 1977, Mel graciously bailed Gene out of bankruptcy. In return for abating Gene's debts for betting and business losses, Gene signed over Rice's Poolroom to Mel.

The business was a great front for Mel, who was a second-level bookmaker, penny-ante loan shark, and small-time fence. He preferred it that way. "Disheveled" was a great label for Mel the Tailor. Everything he wore looked sloppy. Of medium height and overweight with a receding black hairline, now, at fifty-seven, he had a flabby face with at least three chins. Some thought he dressed badly for effect. Mel was very bright, but his facial features suggested that of a nerd. People who dealt with "the Tailor" found out the hard way that very little could be put over on him. Mel relished relationships with con artists who felt they could sucker or scam him. Very few succeeded.

Mel acquired his nickname in the fifties, after his parents had purchased some very expensive, tailor-made suits and shirts for him. Even clothing precisely measured for his body did not change his unkempt appearance.

Mel the Tailor was a jovial man who was considered a great storyteller. His forte was that of a masterful manipulator of people. Even guys who had been "stung" by Mel couldn't help but like him. He was a man's man.

About the only glitch in Mel's persona was his ego when it came to gambling. He never backed off or folded, and, through the years, it set him back. On at least six occasions over the past four decades, Mel the Tailor had incurred major losses totaling $350,000. Five times he came back from the brink of welfare, assisted the majority of times by loans from loan sharks. It was risky, but Mel was a risk-taker. A scam backed by his borrowed money or a series of fortunate gambling wins enabled him to pay back the loan shark, with the associated huge amount of interest, on time.

Except for the last "loan." The Tailor had taken some heavy hits (losses) at the craps tables on his monthly pilgrimage to Atlantic City, and found himself "behind the eight-ball" to the tune of $94,000. He approached several upper-level bookies who occasionally loan-sharked to other bookmakers—among them, Clem Watowski and Louis Dante. Everyone turned Mel down, and he could accept all but one of the denials. Mr. D not only refused Mel, he demanded the repayment of several small debts from years before which Mel had believed to be forgiven. And worse, Mel had to endure a scolding and a long lecture about slow payments and scams from Mr. D in front of two of Dante's clerks at Charlie's. This irritated the Tailor to no end, and he swore in his heart that he would avenge this berating.

Mel had known Mr. D for over 30 years, and during that time, he had developed a love/hate relationship with him. The hate was a result of losing bets to Mr. D, and the love was for times they had won together and his respect for Mr. D's balls as a bookie and gambler.

To Mel's surprise, and also to Mr. D's, Paul Douglas, the mentor and silent partner of Louis Dante's empire, loaned Mel the $94,000. Mel was elated, not just over being able to visit the craps tables again, but he considered it a slap in Dante's face. That was the good news. The bad news came six months later when Mel could not meet the agreed-upon interest and principal payments to Paul.

Gordon Baines, Paul's henchman, paid an unannounced visit one evening to Rice's Poolroom to collect from the Tailor. In front of Mel's buddies and customers, Gordon verbally and physically abused Mel, slapping him in the face numerous times and threatening dismemberment if he didn't repay the debt within a week.

Terrified, Mel ran to the FBI for protection. The agent-in-charge in Baltimore referred the Tailor to the Attorney General's Office in Washington D.C., where they were conducting a six-state investigation into loan-sharking activities. In return for Mel's clandestine cooperation, the feds would provide funds for him to pay back Paul. They also promised to guard him through audio and visual surveillance—a promise they did not keep.

However, Mel had other ideas. He developed an elaborate scheme that he hoped would not only grant him vengeance against Gordon, Paul, and Mr. D, but would enable him to become the top dog in gambling. Based on his testimony to grand juries in New Orleans and Philadelphia and the current troubles of Mr. D, Mel felt certain that the Dante empire would cease to exist. And as the empire deteriorated, an up-and-coming bookie, Handsome John Abrams, would begin to fill the void each time Mr. D and his associates were shut down.

Mel had schooled Abrams in how to endear himself to Mr. D while laying off bets to him; and how to "be there" for Dante to accept large high-roller bets every time Dante's shop was closed by the cops. Handsome John would let Dante's main clients think that Mr. D was behind him financially. Thus, trust would be established so that when the feds finally destroyed the Louis Dante/Paul Douglas empire, it would be a smooth and easy transition for their customers to go with Abrams.

Normally, when these situations occurred, longtime bettors with one main bookmaker would panic and spread their bets among a number of different local and regional bookies. Everyone would benefit somewhat, and they would all spread their lay-off money among each other for protection—protection usually provided by someone like Mr. D. Mr. D was a rarity, being among only four or five individuals in the U.S. who were the "end of the line," or the men who took all of the lay-off action. They were, in effect, still gambling.

In order to balance the books, it is necessary for a sports bookie or a numbers lottery operator to reinsure himself when he receives a fairly large bet or a series of bets on one number or one team. He will bet a portion of this large bet or series of bets with another sports bookie or numbers lottery operator who, in turn, is able to "balance his books" by taking other excess bets from various sports bookies and numbers lottery operators. This operation is known as "laying off," and this second sports bookie or numbers lottery operator is also known as a "lay-off man." These latter bets, which are actually reinsurance, are known as "lay-offs" or "lay-off bets."

Mr. D took a huge amount of all of the sports and numbers lay-offs from Maryland, Washington D.C., Philadelphia, and south Florida; thereby putting his business in jeopardy over and over again for a large numbers hit or a major sports loss. For example, the Redskins were playing the 49ers in football, and the 49ers were a seven-point favorite. Most of the betting world loved the Redskins with the points, so, at game time, after the major bookies had protected themselves by laying off their overage bets on the Redskins, Mr. D was stuck with $900,000 on the Redskins and only $200,000 on the 49ers. He was basically gambling very high stakes on the 49ers. He stood to either win or lose $700,000. Or, he could have been in the position to pay off on a commonly played number that came up, which everyone loved to bet, such as 123 or 111 or 666. Numbers bets such as those could cost thousands . . . But Mr. D wouldn't have it any other way. He knew the statistics—most gamblers lose. And as long as he could sustain the occasional losses, he knew he would be a winner.

CHAPTER 13

Handsome John Abrams also had a vendetta against Mr. D. It went back years, and included a number of Mr. D's high-rolling customers: lawyers, doctors, businessmen, etc.

Lillian Abrams was John's older sister, and she was married briefly to Louis Dante. She was a beautiful and intelligent woman/ child who was infatuated with Louis Dante's high-profile flamboyant lifestyle in the mid-seventies. Lillian had raven-black, long, wavy hair with high cheekbones and a sensuous smile. Though petite in size, she was very well developed, and had an insatiable sexual appetite.

Mr. D was totally smitten by Lillian, and begged for her hand in marriage after only knowing her for three months. Initially, he overlooked her drug problem, accepting it as part of the landscape of the seventies. Later, however, when Mr. D came under investigation for a series of allegations, including one for drug dealing, he demanded she tone herself down. But Lillian had a serious heroin addiction, and she couldn't or wouldn't stop. The marriage was eventually annulled after less than a month.

Lillian sank deeper into that nefarious pond of slow death, and, within a year, had turned to prostitution to support her habit. At first, she was a "kept woman" to a few rather wealthy men who, like Dante, were captivated by her beauty and sensuality. Most of these men were customers of Dante's. But the drugs also scared them off. High-priced call girl was Lillian's next form of prostitution, but the narcotics lure caused her to be too undependable. Physically, she began to slowly deteriorate, and her next stop was that of a hooker made more dependable by her strict pimp.

Her younger brother watched her descent into heroin hell, and pleaded with Lillian to get help. One night, four years after her failed marriage to Mr. D, she called her brother, John, following a terrible beating she had endured from her latest pimp, and told him she wanted out of her present life. Within three days, John came up with the money to send Lillian to a drug treatment center in northern Virginia called "Silent Cry." She was detoxed and moved into the rehab program where she stayed for two months. When Lillian returned to Baltimore, she moved in with John who, by this time, was a nineteen-year-old sophomore majoring in accounting at the University of Baltimore. He also had his sister's good looks, although he was taller and darker.

Over the next three years, Lillian relapsed five times, becoming an on-again-off-again patient of the Sinai Hospital Methadone Program. Her brother John stood by her, always supportive, and in his heart, always blaming Lillian's "fall" on Louis Dante.

Like Mel the Tailor, John had a love/hate regard for Mr. D. For his sister's misery, John could kill him; but for his gambling prowess, John respected Mr. D. And for Mr. D's balls in a big bet, John loved him. John, too, loved the gambling life and its characters. He became a protégé of Mel the Tailor, and it was Mel who had loaned him, with very high interest, the money to send Lillian to the drug rehab center.

After Lillian's fifth relapse, she began to improve. She detoxed from the methadone, enrolled in a drug-free outpatient counseling program, attended Narcotics Anonymous meetings religiously, and got a job as a receptionist at Westinghouse by the Baltimore/Washington International Airport, 15 miles from home. In 1987, five years into recovery, and recently married to an engineer at Westinghouse, Lillian was diagnosed with AIDS-related complex (ARC). A year later, she was dead.

John was the only mourner at the graveside ceremony at Lillian's funeral in the Petach Tikvah Cemetery in Rosedale in east Baltimore County. She was buried near her parents, who had both died in a 1966 car accident on their way to visit relatives in Chester, Pennsylvania. Lillian was twelve at the time, and, with an old-maidish aunt had raised six-year-old John.

All John could think about was how Mr. D had thrown Lillian out without giving her a chance, and how some of Mr. D's prominent clients had used her as a whore. He swore to himself that he would one day settle the score for his beloved Lillian.

CHAPTER 14

Gordon drove his '89 Chevy Cavalier on the Baltimore Beltway west to Route 70 West. He turned off onto Route 29 towards Washington D.C. After going five miles south, he turned west on Route 175 towards the town of Columbia. Just before the Town Center, Gordon made a right turn at Running Brook, and three blocks later, he pulled up in front of Paul's two-storied brick home.

The town of Columbia, situated between Baltimore and Washington D.C., had been created by avant-garde developer, James Rouse, in the late sixties. Rouse had envisioned a Utopian city where people from diverse races, religions, and socioeconomic backgrounds could live in harmony. Although 20 years later with crime, poverty, and drugs evident, living in Columbia was still better than the older urban areas of Maryland. Also, the town and surrounding region attracted high-tech industries that employed a large population of highly intelligent "yuppies." It became a miniature Silicon Valley and a bedroom community of Washington D.C. The public library was the third busiest library in the entire country.

Paul had moved to Columbia in the early seventies with his wife, Beatrice, daughter, Nancy, and son, Jeffrey. The kids left for college and marriage a few years later, and in 1982, Beatrice was diagnosed with Alzheimer's disease. Paul cared for her for two years, but finally yielded to the doctors' recommendations that he place her in a nursing home.

Carrying the morning paper, Gordon Baines let himself into Paul's home with the key Paul had given him seven years earlier when he was hired as his right-hand man. After grabbing a 7-Up from the refrigerator, Gordon walked down the basement steps to find Paul exercising on his treadmill. The white sweatshirt and navy shorts were drenched with perspiration as Paul walked quickly, keeping up with the machine's four-mile-per-hour speed.

"What's new?" Paul asked Gordon, who was standing beside him.

"I spoke to a couple cops I know real well about the status of the Watowski death, and they said no one's treating it with much interest."

Paul stopped the machine and slid into a chair where he began wiping himself with a large tan towel.

"And what do they think happened?" Paul asked, breathing heavily.

"The usual," said Gordon. "Some animal, some nigger saw him sittin' alone and . . ."

Paul shot Gordon a look of such disgust that he figured he'd be fired on the spot. Actually, Gordon knew the moment he spoke that he had said the wrong thing. Twice before he had made disparaging remarks about blacks, and each time, it had cost him dearly. He couldn't understand it. Paul was so conservative in his ways and most of his philosophical views that it didn't make sense for him to become so offended at a racial slur, and yet . . .

But Gordon, who knew many deep, dark secrets about Paul, was not aware of Paul's hidden past. Paul Douglas was an octoroon—one-eighth black. The only person in the Baltimore metropolitan area who possessed the truth was his wife, Beatrice, who now had no recollection of even her own name. The children, both adopted and white, had no knowledge of their father's family tree. The only relative of Paul's whom they had ever met was his brother, Benson, who was as light as Paul. No one, not even Louis Dante, had ever seen the dark-skinned side of the Douglas clan.

Born in the town of Newport News, Virginia, Paul never knew his father. His mother moved the family to Richmond in the thirties. Young Paul was proud of being black, and was actually embarrassed at his white heritage. He and his brother, Benson, grew up tough, since they were constantly defending their color against Negro and white gangs in response to the incessant taunting.

The boys eventually came under the tutelage of their Uncle, "Little Billie," the Negro boss of the illegal numbers business in Richmond. It was Little Billie who finally convinced the Douglas brothers that their success in life would necessitate crossing the color barrier and never going back. Uncle Billie forced the boys to complete high school in a white community to cover their past, and financed Paul and Benson's room, board, and illicit business ventures in white America in the late forties and early fifties.

Today, at ninety years old, Little Billie was one of the richest blacks in America with real estate holdings in over a dozen cities. Until a few years before, Billie still dabbled in politics and played golf. He grew up chopping cotton in North Carolina before moving to Richmond, Virginia in 1927. Early on, he recognized his gift for the illegal numbers business. Steadily, his enterprise expanded, and he found himself fighting for his turf against out-of-town racketeers. A bar Billie owned was bombed in 1939 after he refused to cooperate with Philadelphia mobsters who demanded ten percent of his numbers take. Over the next several years, there were more bombings, killings, and threats, but Little Billie and his cohorts could also play "hard ball" and came out on top; effectively keeping the northern Mafia out of Richmond.

While still running his gambling interests, Billie shrewdly invested in real estate, bars, restaurants, and small businesses, making the transition to legitimacy easier.

In the early fifties, he was subpoenaed to testify before the U.S. Senate committee probing organized crime, where he freely described his gambling activities. Based on his Senate testimony, Little Billie was convicted of conspiring to operate the illegal lottery, and was sentenced to ten years. But Billie never served a day in jail. The Supreme Court, citing the protection of witnesses before Congressional committees, unanimously overturned the conviction.

Little Billie encouraged Paul to move to Baltimore and became his main reference for entrée into numbers and bookmaking with the gambling establishment there.

Uncle Billie's greatest legacy to Paul was his stories of light-skinned blacks who had crossed the color barrier, became successful, and then helped financially with the Negro, and, later, the civil rights movements. Some of the people Little Billie named boggled Paul's mind, especially Walt Whitman, the great poet of the nineteenth century, who was also an octoroon. There were so many, and, in later life, Paul often wondered if Uncle Billie had been embellishing the stories—but he never challenged them for fear of losing faith in himself and his ideals. Paul had contributed over two million dollars, anonymously, for thirty years to civil rights organizations, as well as financing black-owned businesses and college scholarships.

Paul knew he wasn't a benign philanthropist. He lived outside the law and loved it. He had had people roughed up in his day, and he actually understood the use of terror—both verbal and physical. Paul was the architect of the growth of the black numbers and sports gambling business in Maryland, having forged the first alliance of Negroes with his "white" enterprise in the fifties and sixties. That merger gave credibility and legitimacy to the illegal black gambling business. It also made Paul a great deal of money.

CHAPTER 15

Gordon was fortunate that Paul was in no mood to respond to his racial slur. The look was enough.

Silently, Paul got up and walked upstairs to the kitchen as Gordon followed.

"Is there anything in the paper about yesterday's decision by the judge?" asked Paul curtly as he filled a glass with water from the tap in the sink.

"You ain't gonna like it," said Gordon meekly. "It's the lead story on the front of the Metro section."

"What's it say?" asked Paul. Publicity was bad for business, he knew, especially in this era of media grandstanding.

Gordon began reading from the Baltimore newspaper:

"When the lawyers for the alleged operator of a multi-million-dollar-a-year gambling ring walked into Baltimore district court last week, they came prepared with a long list of arguments why the judge should throw out evidence of the organization's sports betting and illegal lotteries gathered from secretly-taped telephone conversations.

The fact that a 25-pound file containing 3,000 pages of crucial documents had been missing for months was not one of those reasons.

The lawyers planned to challenge the yearlong wiretap on 20 different issues, from the jurisdiction in which the court order had been signed to the technique needed to eavesdrop on conversations over eight portable cellular phones.

But they never had to raise a single one.

Instead, after listening to three days of testimony, the judge tossed out the court order permitting the wiretap because the file containing the order—and reams of sensitive, confidential information supporting the use of a wiretap—had been missing for eight months. And neither the prosecutors handling the case nor the Baltimore police could explain where it had been.

The judge's action means information from the wiretap cannot be used in the case.

If Louis Dante, a.k.a. Mr. D, were a betting man, it's unlikely he would have bet on the latest twist in his criminal case.

Going into district court yesterday, the odds of walking away from a gambling conviction were in Mr. Dante's favor. The well-known, high-priced lawyers battling on his behalf had convinced the judge to throw out a court-ordered wiretap and the evidence gathered from it because of the 'disappearing' file. When prosecutors, citing a recent Supreme Court ruling, argued that they didn't even need a court order to tap the eight cellular phones, Mr. Dante's lawyers again persuaded the judge otherwise.

The case—the first wiretap in the country to involve cellular phones—would be over in the time it would take prosecutors to dismiss charges against Mr. Dante, 47, the alleged ringleader of a 10 million-dollar-a-year gambling operation. Or so it seemed.

Instead, prosecutors told the court they are ready to forge ahead with their case, based on an earlier wiretap—this one on a telephone at the Queensberry Avenue home of Lawrence "Lanny" Oswinkle, a clerk in the ring of the alleged chief bookmaker, Mr. D.

The evidence gleaned from the wiretap—hours of secretly recorded conversations about the alleged sports betting operation and over $800,000 in cash seized in raids last year— appeared doomed.

Judge Glass, yesterday, reaffirmed his decision to throw out the court order.

But prosecutors now say they are going to proceed with their case based on the wiretap on Lanny Oswinkle's phone. Prosecutors had asked a circuit court judge for permission to tap the cellular phones belonging to the gambling ring because of information allegedly heard over Oswinkle's phone earlier that fall.

The attorneys for Mr. Dante will now try to attack the legality of that wiretap.

Mr. Dante may also have other battles ahead.

The federal government has slapped him with a 4.3 million-dollar-a-year income tax lien for taxes allegedly owed since 1986. Moreover, two federal agencies and two state agencies have requested and received recordings of the proceedings in this gambling case, suggesting that other probes may be under way.

Mr. Dante's attorney won't say what his client does for a liv-

ing, but . . ."

"That's enough," said Paul.

"Yeah, but it goes on . . ." said Gordon, "tells about 1986 again . . . Paul, all of Louis's problems . . . and ours . . . yours, they go back to '86; even earlier. If he hadn't . . ."

"Gordon," said Paul, "you and everybody else likes to blame Dante's troubles on 1986, or his girlfriend Shirley, or both. But it's not that simple.

"The persecution of big gamblers like Louis goes back a long time. This losing 'war on drugs' is what's precipitated it. The feds and the local cops can't deal with these drug lords, cartels, and posses who run drugs. And they weren't able to stop the epidemic, the demand for dope. They tried a little in the sixties, harder in the seventies, but they really got beaten badly in the eighties.

"The drug dealers played for keeps. Unlike white-collar criminals and petty thieves, or gamblers, the guys who run the dope business have no regard for life. They kill or maim anyone who gets in their way, including cops, judges, anybody.

"Remember that federal deputy prosecutor in D.C.? He was going after that Jamaican cocaine mob, and he told the press and TV that he'd send 'em all away forever. Well, he got himself shot in the basement parking lot of the federal courthouse! How's that for balls? Drug dealers ain't afraid of anybody.

"So, if I'm a prosecutor, maybe I think twice about goin' after those kinda guys. I'll prosecute guys who don't shoot back. Stockbrokers, developers, cat burglars . . . gamblers.

"The enforcement arena needed scapegoats. And if they could tie a scapegoat who was violatin' some bullshit law with drugs . . . and a criminal element, then they'd get back some prestige, some notoriety, some quotas they could impress the media, the legislators, and the public with. Why else spend millions of dollars in this country to bust some gamblers with a bunch of misdemeanors?

"That's why they go after Louis Dante. Unfortunately, Louis had become an easy target. He shoulda learned from the past. He shoulda been low-key . . . And, yes, what happened in '86 didn't help either . . ."

Book Two
1986

CHAPTER 1
Fall 1986

A little after dusk, the time of day when people hate to drive, there was still some light. It didn't matter to them, though, because they weren't on the road. They had circled the apartment complex carefully and cautiously, and had been there for more than 35 minutes, waiting and watching. Now, they were ready to advance.

The complex, made up mainly of senior citizens, sat quietly, suspended in the early, humid Baltimore evening, its occupants oblivious to the movement surrounding the unit housing apartment 3F.

Feldman let the sophisticated binoculars slip down to hang around his neck. His hands were sweating—not from nerves, but from the heat. True, it was fall, but Indian summer in Baltimore was just as humid as mid-July. The detective from Vice gave the signal.

The door busted in and the target, Louis Dante, better known as Mr. D, immediately began running around trying to dissolve the "water paper" and hide his phone numbers; but he had no chance. The police, who were bigger, stronger, rougher, and much more destructive than Mr. D, quickly subdued him.

Of medium build, the pleasant-faced Mr. D was beginning to put on weight as he approached 44 years. He was breathing heavily, more from the chase than the surprise. This was not his first bust.

"Grab the TVs and calculators. He'll have new ones tomorrow," shouted the taller cop, Sergeant Byron, to his partner.

The partner had a gun pointed right in Mr. D's face as they gathered all of the evidence.

Mr. D yelled, "Put that gun away! All I got is a pencil!"

CHAPTER 2
Spring 1954

As Louis was shinnying his pudgy body down the north fence of the Pimlico Racetrack, having been hoisted up by his buddy Marvin, Mr. Heeps, their ninth-grade Latin teacher, approached. The brand-new Pimlico Junior High School was only two blocks away.

"Can I help you, Mr. Dante?" he sarcastically asked.

"No thanks, Mr. Heeps," replied Louis.

"How about you, Marvin?" Heeps joked. "Need a boost over?"

Propelled by fear, Marvin was up and over the fence within seconds.

In a more serious vein, Heeps advised, "It's twelve o'clock, boys. I do hope this is your lunch hour."

Louis was very antsy, and, as he and Marvin moved away from the fence, he called back, "Mr. Heeps, we'd love to stay here and chat about Caesar's Conquest of Gaul and verb tenses, but it's more important to make the double. So, we'll see you in class tomorrow, if we win!"

Little Louis Dante was short and plump. He had slick black hair and chipped front teeth. From junior high school on, he was the consummate hustler and gambler, cutting classes to sneak into

Pimlico Racetrack on a regular basis. He was gambling serious money from the age of twelve, and would engage in ludicrous pool and bowling matches and card games just for the action.

CHAPTER 3
October 1986

Leaving the city lockup at three a.m., Mr. D was talking to his lawyer, the eminent Paul C. Lyons III, and his bail bondsman, Freddy "The Quick" Lang. Wearing his company logo T-shirt emblazoned with "Nobody Talks, Everybody Walks," Lang interrupted. "That was pretty high bail considering . . ."

"They went to a lot of trouble," said Lyons. "And they need to put on a show for the press."

Mr. D looked haggard. "I never get over being amazed at this shit. It had to cost these guys a couple hundred grand in taxpayers' money; and don't forget I pay taxes, too. And for what? A fuckin' misdemeanor offense. A fine of a few grand tops."

"That's society, Louis," answered the distinguished attorney. "The public is not aware of the maximum penalties versus the cost to arrest bookies."

"They ought to legalize it," said Bondsman Lang. "Although I do like the juice from bailing you and your cohorts out every few years."

Lang was diminutive, but built solidly. At fifty-four, he lived more on his past reputation as a street tough, but he could still handle himself with most hoods; especially those who absconded after he posted bail.

"Think somebody gave me up or what?" asked Mr. D.

"No," said Lyons. "I think the state's attorney is very ambitious. He knows the churches and newspapers love these busts. Probably nothin' you could have done to avoid it, Louis."

"Yeah," said Mr. D, "I know. An occupational hazard."

"At least you wasn't alone in this beef, Mr. D," said Lang.

The three men were standing in the nearly vacant parking lot across from the city lockup.

"Actually," said Lyons, "my source tells me you weren't even a target this time. You were caught as an offshoot of an investigation using some new surveillance equipment; and some unusual cooperation with the feds."

Mr. D was shifting from one foot to the other. His eyes were alive, darting about for passersby. "The feds?" he asked. "When they get into it, I know there's more than a fine involved, and I don't like serving even a few months."

"No," said Lyons. "This is strictly a city bust . . . Interesting, though, about the new equipment."

"What about it?" asked Mr. D. They were now leaning on Lyons' new black Mercedes sedan.

"It's called 'trace and trap' and was, until recently, top secret, and only used in espionage cases. And it was never shared with the locals."

Lyons sounded impressive to his client. Much taller and dressed far classier than Mr. D and Lang, he was the attorney of choice of the criminal element in Maryland—if they could afford him. He had silver hair and aquiline features found only on a blue-blooded descendant of the founding fathers of Maryland.

Bondsman Lang broke into the conversation. "By the way, Mr. D, what's the line on the play-off game between Boston and California?"

"Uh, let's see. In Boston, Boston's eight, and nine runs."

"What's eight?" asked Lyons.

"Boston is seven/eight," said Mr. D.

"I never understood baseball betting," said Lyons. "Can't the line be like football? Why so confusing?"

Now, speaking in his trade parlance, Mr. D tried to impress his attorney. "No. In baseball, what you're betting is a money line. So seven/eight means if you want Boston, for every $100 you bet to win, you're putting up $160, which is basically eight to five. Or, if you're betting on California, for every $100, I have to pay you back $140, which is seven to five."

Lang jumped in. "Ya see, the top number or the highest number, in this case the eight over the seven, is always the favorite team. Seven in this case is the imaginary number. It never usually gets quoted, which is why a bookie says Boston is eight."

"Uh huh," Lyons nodded, still not completely understanding the jargon.

Mr. D continued. "Now, you might say, 'How come I only give $140 to $100 if you're laying $160 to $100?' Well, that's known as the juice, and the juice is the $20, or the difference between the $140 and the $160. That's what I get for brokering the bet."

"And the nine runs?" asked Lyons.

"What the nine runs stands for," said Mr. D, "is the number of runs totaling for the final score. The over and under; like football. You have to 'lay,' that is, bet six to five. That means $120 to $100 regardless of which way you bet; whether you say it's under nine runs or over nine runs as the total runs scored by both teams."

"Very complicated, Louis," said Lyons shaking his head.

"Oh, it gets even more complicated," said Mr. D. "There are other ways to bet baseball; but only for guys who are betting a lot more money and a lot more often than the normal person. There are more sophisticated ways of betting."

Lyons became defensive. "But I'm considered very sophisticated. I'm from the original members of Elkridge Country Club."

Mr. D. smiled. "But that's not what I'm talking about. Socially, you are sophisticated. As a bettor, you're a sap."

CHAPTER 4

The interior of the federal prosecutor's office was shaded from the midday sun. Vince Blume, an investigator for the U.S. Attorney General's Office in Maryland was laying out some material. "It worked out well, Mr. Hopkins. They didn't mind us going through the evidence at all; even borrowing this."

"What is it, Vince?" asked U.S. Attorney General Mitch Hopkins.

Investigator Blume came closer. "Mr. Dante's phone book . . . and . . . this other book, which, in code, has names, amounts, dates . . ."

Mitch Hopkins rose and walked over to a table holding a coffee pot, Styrofoam cups, sugar, Equal, plastic spoons, and a small glass of skim milk. "Code? Does that pose a problem?" he asked.

"No," said Blume. "First, any code can be broken. Second, this one's simple. And third, when we put the screws to our informant, everything will fit in nicely."

Blume knew this business. A former army intelligence officer during the early seventies, he was entering his tenth year with the U.S. Attorney General's Office. Hopkins was the fourth U.S. prosecutor he worked for, and each one was duly impressed with Blume's techniques.

CHAPTER 5

Through the sixties, until the urban riots, Pennsylvania Avenue, or "The Avenue," in Baltimore was the hub of the black economic and entertainment district. But, for the last 20 years, it mirrored the urban decay of all major American cities: rampant crime, drugs, unemployment, empty buildings, methadone programs, storefront churches, shattered residential and commercial establishments, busted pavements and streets, shattered dreams, and vacant eyes.

Many businesses moved, many folded, a few stayed. The only constant of the last two decades were the bars and the check cashing stores, and they were disappearing one by one.

Charlie's, on the corner of Fairmount and Miller Streets, was a block off of The Avenue. It was a combined package goods, check cashing, and vending machine store with a luncheonette. Actually, you could buy anything at Charlie's. And, if they didn't carry it, they'd get it. There was nothing—food, clothing, or shelter—that couldn't be had within 24 hours at this most convenient of stores. Charlie's had provided excellent ancillary business support over the years for its proficient, ambitious, aggressive owner— Louis Dante, better known as Mr. D.

The store was located in a three-storied building with a basement. The first floor was Charlie's. The section to the left served as a food service area. It contained a grill and an icebox for breakfast and lunch items. The rear center section contained lottery outlets and coolers for cold beverages and other grocery items.

Checks were cashed on the right-hand side near a semi-modern cash register. A four-foot-tall counter with recessed Plexiglas protected the clerks who evaluated the checks, photographed the customers, and cashed the checks. Behind the clerks were shelves filled with liquor, cigarettes, and a potpourri of consumer goods, including combs, knives, hair products, etc.

Once a customer entered Charlie's through the very secure steel-reinforced door, they were met on either side by video game machines. Other machines were strategically situated alongside any space that didn't interfere with the field of vision of the clerks or places for the customers to wait for either their lunch, a purchase, or the proceeds of a cashed check in the three-sided store.

No fewer than eight clerks at a time worked in Charlie's, although the staff dwindled to only three by six o'clock in the evening. The basement and top floors were off limits to all but Mr. D, his bookkeeper, Juanita, and his two most trusted aides, Cliff and Moe. Items accumulated on the black market were stored there.

Mr. D worked on and off at Charlie's from five a.m. to five p.m. While there, he spent his time in a small office in the rear of the store or behind the check cashing counter, which he loved almost as much as his bookmaking.

Mr. D was carrying on his normal three conversations at once with a prospective buyer for Charlie's, a customer, and a phone call from a wholesale liquor distributor.

"Hey, boss," interrupted Nick, a weasel-like, balding man of fifty with thick round glasses. "This is the third time around for this shit 'paper.' Think we ought to have her busted? Her name's Sweet Cherry."

"Sweet Cherry?" asked Mr. D. "What are ya talking about? Why you calling Mrs. Washington over there 'Sweet Cherry'? She's an old woman. Show some respect."

"She used to be a cough syrup head," said Nick boldly. "Peddled the cherry flavored cough medicine that gotcha high back then. Got arrested a lotta years ago."

Mr. D was getting irked. "Yeah, so what? I don't give a fuck. What's wrong?"

"It's the third time she's tried to pass a bad check on us in a week. Want me to call the police?"

"Hey, asshole," shouted Mr. D, "give her the fuckin' money, understand? That lady lives on the corner over there. No heat in the house. The landlord jacks up her rent weekly. She's caring for five grandchildren and a couple of street kids whose parents 'rolled' on 'em."

Nick was backing off. "Yeah, but . . ."

Mr. D pulled Nick closer to him and whispered harshly, "Give her the money."

"Okay," said Nick, "but it's not good for business."

"It's my fuckin' business, though!" shouted Mr. D.

Ignoring Nick and hanging up the phone, Mr. D turned to the prospective buyer, a late-sixty-ish, Jewish man named Milton Rubin.

"So, whadaya think? I'm telling ya, this business is unbelievable. It's packed like this all the time. We start five in the morning and go 'til nine at night."

"Yeah," said Mr. Rubin, "but you know, I look at the neighborhood. I don't know if there's going to be any more riots. Security is a big thing for me. I'm too old for that kind of aggravation. My son-in-law is going to work here, and he's a little shaky around blacks. Ya know what I mean?"

"Security? These people are the security!" shouted Mr. D. "This store has never been robbed, and it's been here over 20 years. Never been robbed. Nothing. Not even close."

"I don't know," said Mr. Rubin. "I find that hard to believe."

"I'll tell you something, man," said Mr. D, who was inches from Mr. Rubin's face. "Don't you understand that the riots drove those other businesses out? This is the only place around, for I don't know how many fuckin' miles radius, where somebody can get a check cashed. They've gotta come to me. This place goes under if I leave because I get robbed or somebody gets beaten up or something like that. Then that's the end of it!"

"What do you mean?" retorted the prospective buyer, Rubin. His eyes gazed over the clientele. "You don't know every black person who comes in here. They're the dope fiends, the poor ones. And you've got to worry about their . . ."

"Hold it a second!" yelled Mr. D, who was listening to a clerk and glancing at a check. "You don't know what you're talking about. Lemme tell you something. First of all, we're seldom hit with bad paper. Second, I don't care if a 'spade' became president, he's still coming back here. You know why? Spades don't trust banks, savings and loans, any of those places. They don't wanna walk into a place that's polished and brand-new, and where a whole lot of clean-looking, dressed-up white people are running it—people who tell 'em to come back in three days after their check clears. That's not their thing. They still come down here. The ones that left the neighborhood, the ones that moved out into the valley, the ones that run the city right now, they all come here."

"And they don't mind paying a percentage?" asked Mr. Rubin.

"Paying?" Mr. D gave a chuckle. "They don't give a fuck. Hell, I play with the percentage half the time, anyhow. You get whatever you can from 'em. It doesn't matter who you rob. A lot of white people come in here, too. Don't you understand the situation here? The people, they're your security, pal. They're going to protect you forever."

Quickly ignoring any response from Rubin, Mr. D began to address a customer, an elderly retired postal worker. "Sure, babe, lemme see. You got a Charlie's card? You got to have ID or it's going to cost you eight bucks, and I'll take your picture and give you a card. It's honored everywhere. Let me see your driver's license and two backup IDs, and I'll process that check. Did you see the special on sunglasses? I can't tell you where they came from. Believe me, these things sell for eighty dollars, but for you it's six. Do you want them?"

Mr. D was in his element—the consummate hustler. He went on and on, oblivious to the customer's disinterest in anything but his check, as well as to the fact that Mr. Rubin was laughing hysterically at Mr. D's stream of chatter.

"What about a couple of miniatures? Look here. You see this new kind of wine they've been promotin' lately? Red Foxx drinks it. This is great. Want some pretzels? Want something to eat?"

CHAPTER 6
1956

Like the young Louis Dante, Marvin—bigger and heavier— loved to bet on anything, though he rarely won. There was a ko- sher deli called Mandell's that made great kosher hot dogs, which were very, very greasy, and stayed on the grill for hours. The cooks placed them in greasy rolls and added hot, fried bologna, along with mustard and raw onions. Louis bet Marvin that he couldn't

*eat ten of them at one sitting. Marvin ate the first four, threw up,
ate the second four, threw up again, ate the next one, and passed
out. Louis revived him long enough to get paid off.*

CHAPTER 7
October 1986

Laurel Racetrack is in Howard County near the Prince George's County line, bordered by U.S. Route 1 and Maryland Route 197. It is situated on one of the last wooded parcels of the town of Laurel, twenty minutes from Baltimore or Washington D.C.

Racetracks, or "plants" as they are sometimes referred to, are rated by the caliber of horses running there, and Laurel is considered a typical major track. Rated somewhere just under the tracks in California and New York, Laurel is on par with Florida racing and graded slightly above those in Kentucky and Chicago.

Laurel is designed like most racetracks in a half-pyramid shape beginning at the top story with the dining rooms and box seats, leveling down to the clubhouse section, reserve seats, paddock, and, finally, the grandstands on the lower level. In general, the socioeconomic status of the track customer follows the top to bottom layout of the racetrack, although many patrons will roam throughout the track looking for tips and touts.

Standing at the far end of the grandstand area, at the top of the stretch in front of the seats, near a small beer and hot dog stand, were three casually dressed men. To the unsuspecting eye, they appeared engrossed in a discussion of the upcoming race. However, their conversation was of a more nefarious bend.

"Now remember," said Main Man, the chief lieutenant and confidant of Mr. D, "don't call out his name. Act like you don't know who he is 'cause he can't be seen out here. He's 'eighty-sixed' from the track for life."

"Why? What'd he do?" asked Tongue Deacon.

"Well," said Main Man, "about 12 years ago he got busted; so he's a convicted felon. But that isn't the main thing, though. Ya see, he's a bookie, and they think that he's going to book action at the track. So, naturally, the high rollers would go to him and not to the windows to bet."

"What was he busted for?" asked Baker. Len Baker was Tongue's partner.

"Pharmaceutical coke," answered Main Man. He constantly looked around as he spoke. Main Man wore dark sunglasses most of the time. Although he was not completely bald, he shaved his head à la Kojak from TV. Just a shade over six feet tall, Main Man had a pointed nose, reddish mustache, and a chin that jutted out. He wore his normal uniform of khaki pants, a buttoned tan shirt, and tennis shoes without socks.

"Oh yeah? He dealt dope?" asked Baker, somewhat elated.

"No. Not really," said Main Man. "He was just a user who got caught up in it. He would buy large enough quantities to share with his friends. When he got busted, he was holding enough to call it 'intent to distribute.' Somebody gave him up; some rat. Worse yet, it was the feds. They told him that if he gave up all the big names in gambling nationally, they would let him walk for the mere possession call. But that ain't the way Mr. D is, so he had to do two years."

Tongue watched Main Man closely as he sipped a beer. "That ought to help us, ya know. I mean, what we're financing—what we need him for. To loan us some money for this drug deal. He would be sympathetic. Right?"

"He might not be as sympathetic as you think," said Main Man as he glanced around looking for Mr. D. "He has some pretty hard feelings about dope today."

"He'll go for it," said Baker. "He can turn it over into a pretty profit. Make more interest than he ever does booking action. Believe it, motherfucker!"

Len Baker and Tongue Deacon were close friends. They were both around 5'10" tall and wiry, but their arms were muscular. The light-complected Baker had long, shaggy dirty-blond hair, a broken nose, and heavy bags under his eyes. He wore a small hoop earring in his left ear, and always looked like he needed a shave. Tongue, who was half Italian, was olive-skinned and had medium-length, curly hair. He had a full beard and mustache, rotten teeth, and cold, dark eyes. On his exposed left arm was a tattoo of a cobra with "DEATH" written on its head. Both men had numerous other tattoos covered by their clothing.

Tongue and Baker were scary-looking. Now in their mid-thirties, they had met as teenagers in the state juvenile detention facility at Cub Hill in Harford County. They were perennial bad boys, spending most of their formative years in foster homes and reform schools. By their early twenties, they had become members in good standing of the outlaw Python motorcycle gang.

The Pythons manufactured and sold methamphetamines and PCP in southern Pennsylvania and northern Maryland. Together, state police and the DEA were able to drive the Pythons south to the District of Columbia and northern Virginia where they presently operated.

Tongue and Baker had the dubious distinction of being the only members of the outlaw bikers ever to be thrown out. It had nothing to do with the rapes, robberies, or murders they had committed. They were caught by the late Python treasurer, Max Fox, stealing drugs and money from the gang, and were very lucky they were only expelled and not tortured or killed. Tongue and Baker spent half of their adult lives in state penal institutions.

Main Man finally spotted Mr. D leaning on the fence near the finish line. It was difficult to pick him out of a crowd since he always wore a disguise to get into the track. Nothing elaborate—just an L.A. Raiders' hat, a worn auto mechanic's outfit from Gray's Amoco station, and black-framed eyeglasses.

Mr. D's head was buried in the *Racing Form* analyzing the eighth race, the Feature of the Day, a $24,000 Allowance race for three-year-olds and up. Occasionally he looked up at the tote boards in the track infield with their ever-changing odds on the race and amounts bet on each horse.

The fear of being noticed by track officials and police kept Mr. D from looking at the odds boards for too long; that and the fact that Laurel's infield was dull to the eye. It was difficult for East Coast tracks to have beautiful infield areas. Unlike the ambience of Santa Anita in California or Gulf Stream in Florida, with their majestic scenery and exotic birds, the weather made it impossible to maintain an aesthetic landscape of flowers and shrubbery at plants like Laurel and Pimlico in Maryland, or Aqueduct in New York City.

Louis Dante loved the racetrack. He studiously scanned the *Racing Form* and its maze of data, confident that he could pick the winner better than anyone. The novice or occasional bettor had difficulty comprehending a horse's race history and workout results from the numerous classifications of racing terminology. But not Mr. D.

For example, in the previous race, a Maiden-Claiming race, Mr. D noticed a pattern of a horse named Saucy Sarah being moved up and down in various purse races for no apparent reason. A Claiming race means a price is put on a race, per horse, which is the cost to "claim" or purchase the horse from the race. Claims must be put in before the race. Maiden-Claiming races, which are the lowest types of races, are for horses that have never won a race. After they reach four years old, they are considered unlikely to win.

Although Mr. D gave Saucy Sarah only a slight chance to win, he included her in several "triple" bets with the two favorites of the six-furlong race. In handicapping triple bets, the sophisticated bettor tries to pick the eventual winner, and then boxes five or six horses in the "place" and "show" categories.

His analysis had been correct. Saucy Sarah, a 26 to 1 long shot, ran the race of her life, finishing first ahead of the two favorites, Funny Penny and Mystic Nelle. The triple paid $390 for a one-dollar triple bet. Mr. D had a $20 winning triple bet on the race, which paid him $7,800.

Main Man introduced the two drug dealers to the bookmaker, Louis Dante.

He eyed them casually and did not like what he saw. The bikers were dressed similarly: dirty and faded torn jeans, layers of T-shirts, and cutoff leather vests. They smelled of oil and had filthy fingernails.

"Mr. D," said Tongue, "we've got a deal that we feel can turn us some huge profits."

"What's the deal?" asked Mr. D, his face still submerged in the *Racing Form*.

"Me and Baker got this guy who manufactures bootleg Quaaludes. Highest quality. The dude's a world-class chemist. He's the best. No quality like this been around in years, even before they outlawed real 'ludes."

"Yeah, I'm listening," said Mr. D as he glanced around at the crowd and the odds board.

It was Baker's turn now. "We'll, we need $150,000 up-front money for half a million 'ludes. We'll pay you back at a hundred percent interest in thirty days."

"Ya see, Mr. D," said Tongue, "it used to be 'ludes went anywhere from one to five dollars apiece on the street. Well, now the going rate to the consumer is eight to twelve dollars, depending on the quantity that the people want. We already got our distribution networks set up. Our middlemen pay us two bucks each. I mean, it's a piece of cake, and we're buffered. We ain't got no body else in with us, and we ain't rats. So you ain't got to worry about anybody giving you up, Mr. D."

"If I concern myself with that in any deal I get into, it don't even get to the conversation level," said Mr. D, whose gaze was now fixed on Main Man.

"So that's the deal," said Tongue. "We need the cash by the end of the month. That's when we have to pay the chemist, and that's when we get delivery. It's clean and it's neat. There's no sweat here."

Mr. D circled two horses in the *Form* with his Montblanc pen. He looked up at the two drug dealers and said, "Ya know, boys, it sounds sweet. It looks like a nice deal, but I don't get involved in drugs."

"Hey, Mr. D," said Baker, "what are you talking about? You ain't getting involved? We've just come to you for the money. Nobody'll know who it is, and if by the remotest chance we get popped, nobody's giving you up. I mean, how could they prove it? You ain't giving us a check or nothing like that."

Mr. D spotted a detective for the Thoroughbred Racing Commission (TRC) and turned towards the grandstand seats, his back to Main Man. He spoke quietly but firmly.

"Let me explain something to you guys. I did some time for a drug deal once. I learned a lesson. Over the years, the courts, they don't like drug deals. Now it's even worse. The country's gotten real conservative. I've already gone down one time. I'm a convicted felon, and they don't bother me much with the gambling. Drugs, they bother you with. If they get a hold on me in any way, you understand, even if they suspect it, I'm history. That's one thing. On the other hand, I don't do drugs no more. I don't like 'em. I got a thing about 'em. But personal feelings aside, I can't take the business risk. Sorry fellas. I wish you a lot of luck on the deal, but that's it."

"Mr. Dante," pleaded Baker, "don't you think . . ."

"Fellas," interrupted Main Man, "that's it. Mr. Dante is finished." He stood between Mr. D and the drug dealers.

"Again," said Mr. D, "let me wish you guys luck. I hope you find the financing."

Mr. D was looking down again—not at the *Racing Form*, but

at the dirty, heavy biker boots worn by Tongue and Baker. The boots were not very pointy, but had very big heels.

"How the fuck are we going to get financing, man?" asked Tongue, whose anger was now showing. "I mean, who's got that kind of cash available but you? Can't you take care of it? What the hell is it? We ain't asking for too much!"

"I'm sorry, boys," said Mr. D. "I don't even 'book' to a guy who deals dope. With all the phone taps on these guys, the cops would think I was bankrolling their drugs if they called me for a bet."

"Come on, you guys," said Main Man, more forceful this time, but also wary of the bikers, "you've got to move on. That's enough. I'm sorry. That's it."

The horses for the Feature Race of the Day had left the Paddock and were warming up before approaching the starting gate. The conversation with the drug dealers had caused Mr. D to miss viewing the horses being saddled in the paddock area. He always liked to check them out as they left the area for any hints of soreness in their hind legs. Usually he could notice with his binoculars as the horses paraded around the track if they had any nagging physical problems. But he didn't bring them along. He knew an auto mechanic wouldn't possess the high-quality binoculars he used before he was banned from the Maryland tracks.

There are several types of racing categories at thoroughbred racetracks in America. Stakes races, graded at I, II, or III, depending upon the caliber of the horse and the purse, have the top horses. Then there are Handicap races where weights are assigned to horses to even out the field. If a horse is too good, the weight of the saddle is increased, or, for others, it is decreased. Finally, there are various Feature races with a weekend purse from $50,000 to $100,000 involving the best horses on the grounds for different sexes and at different distances, such as six furlongs, one mile, a mile and a sixteenth, or a mile and an eighth.

This was a Friday Feature race, an Allowance race involving horses with potential against a few of the better distance horses on the grounds.

Mr. D gave Main Man $200 to make an Exacta bet (the top two finishers in order) wheeling Double Bunctions and a long shot named A Top Brandy.

Main Man made the bet at the $50 window, held the tickets in his top shirt pocket, and walked over to speak to a retired jockey named Tony Wallace who was standing with his girlfriend, an outrider named Judy.

"Hey, Main Man, come over here a second," called Mr. D. "Let me tell you something. Don't you ever, ever bring me any guys who wanna deal drugs. Don't ever have them around me. It's heaty enough. I ain't supposed to be at the track. You understand? I've gotta come here looking like a bum, hanging around in the Grandstand with the losers. I can't book no action. I'm trying to have a good time. The track's security people, they know who I am. It ain't that tough for them to find me out if they want to know I'm here. And all they've got to do is say they saw me with those two jerk-offs, right? Then I'll have to worry about the drug cops bothering me. I don't need this shit!"

"Hey, boss, I'm sorry," sighed Main Man. "I really didn't understand the deal when they first came to me. I thought it was strictly a loan, and I knew that you knew Baker's brother. So I figured they was okay."

"You don't have to understand!" Mr. D was pissed off. "You don't get paid to think. That's why I'm the boss. They're bad news. Tell 'em to lose my number!"

The race had gone off. The field of nine, three-year-olds and up, at a mile and a sixteenth, had run almost a mile, and Mr. D's Exacta horses had traded the lead running almost three lengths ahead of the pack. But at the sixteenth pole, 200 yards from the finish line, the 6 to 5 favorite, Little Bold John, had gone to the front having passed Double Bunctions and A Top Brandy to win by a length and a half.

CHAPTER 8
1958

An epic gambling match of nine-ball pool for $1,000 a game between Louis and Drake the Fake, a premier carpet salesman, was taking place. Drake shot with one hand while Louis shot with both. It went on every night for four weeks at Lindy's Poolroom, standing room only, during which time the major draw of this match-up was the sarcastic "knocking" that went on between Drake *and Louis during the course of each game. Drake was quite a hustler, but he could never out-hustle Louis. And Louis was only 16 years old while Drake was pushing 21. Louis won the knocking battle for the most part, although it was closer than the pool bets. Louis salted away about $20,000 before Drake finally quit.*

As they were leaving Lindy's Poolroom, a discussion of masturbation techniques turned into a hotly disputed side bet between Louis and Drake over who could "jerk-off" quicker.

The guys walked over to Drake's home, a few minutes away. They went into his bedroom, stripped off their pants and underwear, and set ground rules. Drake chose his fur mitten, and Louis went with a wad of Vaseline jelly. At the count of three, they began masturbating, and in 20 seconds, Louis ejaculated.

Drake, however, refused to pay Louis the $100 bet. He accused Louis Dante of cheating by playing with himself during the three-block walk over to Drake's.

CHAPTER 9
October 1986

Suspicious of the federal prosecutor's cooperation and interest in Mr. D's codebook, City Assistant State's Attorney Hayden called U.S. Attorney Hopkins.

"When can I get Dante's book back?" asked Hayden.

"As soon as we've decoded it," said Hopkins. "Is there a problem?"

Hayden pictured the arrogant Hopkins and tried to maintain a business-only manner. "No problem. But we like to finish up with these misdemeanor cases quickly and get on with more dangerous criminals," he said.

"Why, Hayden," said Hopkins, "we consider Dante a major cog in organized crime and this state's number one crime czar. He's tied to drugs, loan-sharking, prostitution . . . What kind of civil servant are you?" Hopkins was now openly mocking the city prosecutor.

"Who the fuck are you kiddin', Hopkins?" said Hayden. "I'm a career prosecutor, not an ambitious one looking to be governor, senator, or president . . . Dante's just a bookie . . . The biggest in the East maybe, but just a bookie. He's no more involved in the Mob than you are . . ."

"He runs numbers in three states!" Hopkins shouted back.

"Yeah," said Hayden, "and his competition is the state lottery. So what? He's giving the people a better count than the state does. Don't you have any real criminals to go after, Hopkins? Or are you afraid you'll lose a couple of cases and spoil the feds' quotas?"

There was a brief moment of silence on the line. Then Hopkins said menacingly, "Hayden, you'll regret this conversation. I actually had plans for you down the line, . . . but you'll retire where you are. Wish me luck, Mr. Career Prosecutor, Defender of the City . . ."

Hayden slammed the phone down before Hopkins could finish.

CHAPTER 10

The two federal agents began trailing Mr. Dante as he drove off from Charlie's. It was a clear afternoon at three o'clock, and the traffic was light as Mr. D steered his 1981 beige, two-door 320i BMW up Eutaw Street.

At the corner of McMeckin and Eutaw, he suddenly made a sharp right-hand turn, deliberately heading in the wrong direction on a one-way street.

The agents who had been following Louis Dante in a surveillance format looked at each other in disbelief.

"He couldn't have made us," said Agent Carey. "We're too far behind him, and our car is different from the one we used before."

Since they were not in hot pursuit of Dante, the agents continued north towards the suburbs. They would pick him up again at his home or the deli he frequented.

Mr. D came out on Turner Street and then pulled onto Druid Park Drive, where he picked up the Jones Falls Expressway. Unaware of any pursuit or surveillance, Louis Dante was going through a ritual he had been following for years. He was aware that the bigger he became in gambling, the bigger a target he was to the enforcement agencies. He constantly practiced evasion tactics, just in case someone was following him.

Louis Dante not only drove unpredictably to avoid detection, but he also changed cars on an almost daily basis, especially during football season. He used the three cars he and his wife owned, any one of his eight clerks' cars from Charlie's, or daily car rentals.

CHAPTER 11
1959

Following the pool challenges, Louis and Drake the Fake continued with their next series of gambling matches—bowling. There were a number of older guys who formed two-men teams and bowled a series of games at the three major bowling alleys in northwest Baltimore.

The game was called 69-9-No-Count. In this type of betting on duckpins, the object was to score nine pins or more with only two balls. Anything less than nine meant that you received a zero or "no count" for the frame. You had to receive a score of 69 or more to win the ten-frame game. Teams were usually chosen up and they and the gallery bet on everything imaginable in the contest.

Teenager Louis either booked most of the action in the gallery or wagered on certain contestants. Every now and then, he "fixed" the games.

The classic match occurred one evening at the Hilton Bowling Lanes. Drake was bowling and Louis was betting against him

*and booking action. The guy who owned the bowling alley, Mel
the Tailor, was also gambling serious money. He even closed the
bowling alley from Friday night through Monday morning so that
only the guys in action could play.*

*Louis ended up winning $7,000 from Mel the Tailor. They
went double or nothing with Mel putting up the bowling alley. Mel
lost, and Louis owned the bowling alley.*

*For two days, Louis laid around the bowling alley with the
guys making a mess until Mel, in disgust, finally threw him out.
Louis accused Mel of "welshing" on the bet, and threatened that
nobody would ever come near there again to gamble or to even
use his bowling alley if he didn't settle the wager. So Mel decided to
give Louis a $3,000 "take-it-or-leave-it" payoff, which Louis ac-
cepted.*

CHAPTER 12
October 1986

The government agents, Carey and Solomon, sat in their
maroon Chevy sedan in the Rosedale section of Essex in eastern
Baltimore County spying on Louis Dante. Through sophisticated
listening devices planted in the apartment, they could overhear
Mr. D's conversations with his customers and clerks.

Mr. D had rented the top floor of a three-storied town house,
and in the sparsely furnished converted bedroom, he was answering calls on the baseball play-offs, numbers, and college and
pro football games. His numbers clerk, Lee, interrupted him to
discuss with a caller a big win on the illegal lottery. The numbers
player wanted Mr. D to verify whether his number was "recorded"
today since it "hit" and he had $20 on it.

The illegal numbers game, although paying better odds, taking smaller bets, and not having to sign an IRS form for winning
like the legal state lotteries, had problems from time to time with
bets actually being recorded by numbers runners. Thus, because
of the large amount of the hit, Mr. D or a lay-off numbers boss
could have easily lied that the caller's number never came in from

the "runner" (the person who took the bet). However, the bookmaker's honor and word were his only bond, and that's how Mr. D had survived for 20 years—on his honor.

So Mr. D admitted to the caller that his number was on "the ribbon" (recorded). It cost Louis Dante $14,000 (14 pieces or 14 dimes)—but the word of this big hit and Mr. D's immediate pay-off would spread and buy Mr. D millions in good public relations and new customers, most of whom would lose money to him.

At 8:15 p.m., Mr. D and Lee left the town house by the side stairway and drove off in separate cars to their homes. An hour and a half later, after confirming that no one was presently in the town house, the two agents quietly broke into Mr. D's betting office to photograph the place. A discussion ensued between the two FBI agents on loan to U.S. Attorney Hopkins' office regarding the numbers business.

"I thought we were just dealing with the sports betting end of it. I really don't follow the numbers thing," said Agent Solomon. He was ten years younger than Agent Carey and at least a head taller. Solomon wore a dark raincoat, unbuttoned in the front. He was slim and had short-cropped brown hair.

Agent Carey, a stocky forty-three-year-old and an eighteen-year veteran of the FBI, wore a dark-blue suit with a black shirt open at the collar. "In the forties and fifties," said Carey, "the numbers business was huge. Sports betting didn't get like it is 'til the emergence of pro football and TV. The digit is the number. It can be either the legal or illegal number. In Maryland, the terms are the 'male' and 'female' numbers. The male number is the legal lottery. It gets the term 'male' because the legal lottery comes up as a result of using numbered ping-pong balls on TV. The balls mean that it's a male. Get it? And so the illegal lottery is called the female number. No balls. For years, of course, the number has always been called the 'girl,' anyhow."

Jr. Agent Steve Solomon was photographing a stack of papers spread over the floor. He was fascinated, but naive, at the mechanics of the gambling business. "How's the illegal number determined?" he asked.

"Briefly, it's this," said Carey. "You take the last four races at, say, Pimlico Racetrack. The mutuals are added up. Ya know, the mutuals are how the horses that finish in the top three—win, place, and show—run and pay."

"I'm not sure I follow," said Solomon.

Carey was conducting sound checks on the bugs in the room.

"If the top three horses were the eight, two, and six, you would have a winning price on the eight for, say, twelve-fifty to win, eight-twenty to place, and three dollars to show; on the two for four dollars to place and two-thirty to show; and on the six for six-eighty to show. You add up all of those numbers from the sixth race for the winning bets with the winning mutuals from the seventh race, and that would give you the first number. That number would be the first number to the left of the decimal point. Then you would do the same for the combination of the mutuals from the seventh race and the eighth race, and the eighth and ninth races."

Agent Solomon was grinning. As he changed the film in the camera, he said, "Sounds tough to follow. I never thought the players were that bright."

Agent Carey continued as though he hadn't heard Solomon. "Also, the track location changes from time to time. A track that has racing six days a week needs to be used, and it should have the races finishing before evening. After Laurel and Pimlico Racetracks' meets end, the numbers people may go out of state to use a track for the number. Like Monmoth Park in Jersey."

"Why do they use the tracks . . . and that system?" asked the junior agent as he stood up and looked out the window.

"Because it can't be tampered with and because it's carried by all newspapers and radio stations. In the old days, they used, and in emergencies still do, the U.S. treasury balance."

"Why?" asked Solomon.

"'Cause it's a regularly published number and can't be tampered with," said Carey.

Solomon zipped up the carrying case for the camera and equipment and replaced the papers, phones, and miscellaneous objects as they were before the agents entered the room. "Why do we have to worry about Mr. D's numbers business?" he asked. "I always thought the legalization of the numbers game hurt or destroyed the illegal game."

"No, no, no," said Carey as he and Solomon tiptoed quietly out the door and down the stairway. "As a result of the legal lottery, the illegal numbers business did not decrease, but actually increased due to the fact that it became 'okay' to play since the state government was running it. That encouraged new players to participate, and many of the new customers also turned to the illegal game. It actually invigorated the illegal industry."

CHAPTER 13

Following Mr. D's first divorce in the late sixties, his lifestyle ascended beyond "jet set," propelled by his aggressive gambling acumen, partying escapades, and drug-induced relationships. Men and women flocked to him, seduced by his zest for life, charisma, and outlandish behavior.

Although his sexual activities ran the gamut of a *Playboy* magazine reader's wet dream, at heart, Louis Dante was basically monogamous. He preferred relationships with one woman at a time, and thoroughly enjoyed being married—regardless of how many times he'd walk down the aisle. His current wife, Margaret Prelate, was his latest spouse.

Once, he was chastising Main Man over his infidelity to his wife, and later, to a girlfriend of two years.

"It's not good for you to be involved with more than one woman," Mr. D lectured.

"I can't help it," said Main Man. "I love women. They all turn me on. And, besides, Mr. D, I don't flaunt it. My wife or girlfriend have never found out or even accused me of running around on them."

"That's not the point," said Dante.

"Just what is the point?" asked Main Man. "And why don't you fuck around?"

"It's bad karma," said Mr. D. "It's tough enough to concentrate on our business as it is, let alone having to worry about more than one woman. And lying about it and sneakin' around . . . could seriously affect the way I make a line on a game. Say a customer I know calls for a line on a game and I know who he wants to bet because he's developed a pattern over time. I've got to concentrate on who he'll take, and how high I can adjust the spread. How the hell can I do that if I've also got more than one woman on my mind? . . . It's just real bad karma!"

Mr. D drove on Falls Road toward his home, north to the rural countryside. He had lived in the same home for over ten years. It was a sprawling rancher on an acre and a half of land in Worthington Valley, close to several large horse farms. Mr. D enjoyed the drive, and unconsciously smiled at several landmark turns and stops where he had been forced to pull over by Vice cops over the years. His greatest fears in bygone days were not of being found with gambling paraphernalia, which he had recognized early on as an occupational hazard, but with drugs, another habit of his in the seventies. Louis Dante drank Hycodan, a narcotic-laced cough medicine, and snorted cocaine on a regular basis. He knew this would put him out of business faster than anything. But, because he always expected to be arrested, he was able to act quickly and hide or destroy his drugs before a bust could occur.

Fortunately, Mr. D had been clean of drugs for the past few years, and his paranoia level had dropped considerably. Instead of driving at reckless speeds to get home to the stupor his dope once delivered, he now drove at a casual pace, anticipating a good meal and a peaceful, quiet night with his wife, although such nights occurred less and less frequently lately.

Mr. D steered his car up the steep driveway on Raspberry Lane, a quarter of a mile off of Falls Road. He was met by his big German shepherd, Lilly, who came running out from the trees behind his house. Together, they went into the house through the side door to the kitchen.

"Margaret!" called out Mr. D.

"In here, Louis," came the response. She was in the den setting up the table service for dinner in front of the television. This was the room where Louis Dante spent his nights, perched in front of a 50-inch screen, which took its signals from a satellite dish on the side of the house opposite the driveway.

"What's for dinner?" asked Dante, kissing Margaret on the top of her forehead, patting her backside, and unconsciously flipping on the TV with the remote control.

"Crab cakes," she said. "Got them at the Pimlico Hotel on the way home. I also got you a Coffee salad chopped up the way you like it." The salad was a specialty made by an elderly waitress whose last name was Coffee. The dressing was creamy with ground anchovies, secret seasonings, and Parmesan cheese. It mixed delightfully with various salad greens and chopped eggs.

Mr. D sat down, ate, and watched the television while he made small talk with Margaret about her day. He devoured the two jumbo crab cakes and salad in less then five minutes. Margaret was only about two forkfuls into dinner when her husband had finished.

"I got you some Pimlico cake, too," she said as he stood up and walked into the kitchen. Mr. D loved food and tonight's dinner was among his favorites. Margaret seldom cooked. She either picked up meals at restaurants or had them delivered. The Pimlico cake consisted of layers of moist yellow cake and rich, creamy custard with dark chocolate icing. Louis Dante topped it off with two scoops of Hagen Daaz French vanilla ice cream and brought it back into the den.

As he sat back down, his mind wandered from the TV and dessert to his appetite for Margaret. She was a small bleached-blond woman of thirty-six, eight years younger than Dante. A fitness freak, she was still dressed in her workout clothes: a one-piece black body stocking with white short-shorts. Not an ounce of fat was visible on Margaret, who, though petite, was round and firm in all the right places. Her hair was cropped and straight, and her face was very tan. She fit the profile of the quintessential California girl, although she was born and bred in Maryland.

"I'm gonna go to bed early tonight, Louis," she said. "I've got a bike race in the morning, and I need my rest."

"Okay. But just stay up with me another hour and a half while I watch a couple games, and then I'll go to bed early, too," he said.

Louis loved to have Margaret by his side at night while he watched the different sporting events he was booking; even the reruns. She hated it.

Following dinner, Margaret cleaned up and returned to the loveseat where she snuggled up to Dante. She was now dressed in an oversized T-shirt and lightweight gold sweatpants.

"Louis," she purred. "Have you thought about having a baby again?"

"Yeah, sugar," he said. "Maybe in a year or two we'll have one."

"You always say that," she said. "I'm getting too old. Your daughter will have one before me."

Mr. D had a nineteen-year-old daughter from his first marriage.

"Christ," he said jokingly, "I hope she gets married first . . . Look, Margaret, it's just not the right time. Maybe after I sell Charlie's . . ."

"Jesus," she said. "You always throw Charlie's up to me. Even if you had a legitimate offer, you'd never sell it. Don't bullshit me . . . All right, if it's no baby, what about backing me in a little boutique in Pikesville?"

Louis was getting antsy. He was changing channels more often and shaking his right foot.

"Why is it you need a career?" he asked. "There're a million women who would love your lifestyle. You shop, you work out, you eat great . . . Look at all I've done for you. You always have a few hundred bucks extra every day. Look how you're living . . ."

Margaret removed Dante's arm from around her back and left breast and stood up.

"You turn me off, Louis!" she cried. "I need a fuckin' life of my own . . . Good night!"

She walked out of the room towards the bedroom. Dante watched her walk away, turning his attention back to the television, flipping channel after channel.

CHAPTER 14
1963

Louis and Marvin left Baltimore for Vegas with $8,000. They were sure that they were going to make a major score gambling, and then maybe attend UCLA. They checked into the Stardust Hotel and Casino, where they immediately lost $2,000 the first night playing craps. Although they had dreamt for months about how they were going to take Vegas to the cleaners, things didn't go quite as planned.

The next day, Marvin decided to take a job at the Showboat as a busboy. It appeared to be a pretty good move. He was getting a free jacket, bow tie, and a free dinner before work. However, he found the work too hard, and quit the next day. Louis, who had said that he would wait and see how the job went, was happy that Marvin had quit. For the next two days, they proceeded to lose the rest of their bankroll and were totally broke.

A distress call to Louis's and Marvin's parents yielded train tickets home and an extra $150, which they immediately lost in a desperate attempt to break the bank of the casino.

So the guys boarded a cross-country train, destitute. In the dining car, they waited for people to get up and leave so they could devour any leftovers. They even rummaged through trashcans for half-eaten rolls. At a stopover in Chicago, Louis went through the phone booths looking for change and found 80 cents. He bought a submarine sandwich and cut it in half, and it was all they ate again until Baltimore.

CHAPTER 15
October 1986

Baker and Tongue stood on the corner of High and Fawn Streets in Little Italy awaiting the arrival of Stoney Caskey, who sold hot weapons to the criminal element of Baltimore. They were caddy-cornered to Sabatino's restaurant with their feet resting on the white marble steps of a corner row house.

Parked in front of them were their two Harley-Davidson "Flat-head" motorcycles. Baker had inherited his from his late older brother who had stolen it. Tongue's "hog" came to him in a more traditional way for an outlaw biker. As a rookie Python, Tongue got into a fight with a paunchy fifty-year-old member of a rival biker gang, The Dukes, at a Harley rally, and stabbed him to death. Then he stole the dead guy's "momma" (girlfriend) and his motorcycle, an Indian.

The Indian was the first American-made cycle. Considered the Rolls Royce of motorcycles, production of the Indian stopped 40 years ago. It had a 1,500 cc engine and cruised at 120 miles per hour. Within two days, Cautious Craig, the leader of the Pythons "convinced" Tongue to trade the Indian to him for an old Harley that needed lots of work.

Reluctantly, Tongue made the trade, and, over the next two years, rebuilt it piece by piece. He bought, traded, or stole parts, finally ending up with the Flathead of his dreams—one just like Baker's. Painted black and silver; it had big, beautiful handlebars, a customized seat, a three-inch extended front end with a small wheel and no fender, and custom chrome wiring.

"I tried the nigger downtown," said Baker, "and the Jew coke dealer. 'Cuzz' didn't have the bread, but he used another excuse. And the Jew wanted 40 percent of the deal."

"Forty percent!" screamed Tongue. "The motherfucker! . . . 'Course, we do need the money real soon."

"Fuck him," said Baker. "I gotta way to get the money without even paying interest. We're gonna rip off Mr. D."

Tongue leaned closer to Baker, glancing across the street. "I dunno. It could be trouble."

"Believe me," said Baker. "I know him and his buddies from when my older brother ran numbers for 'em 15 years ago. He'd just write it off as a business loss."

The gun dealer pulled his shiny new green Lincoln Continental in front of a driveway a few cars back from the corner of Fawn Street. He slid out and slung a knapsack over his back as he walked towards the front of Sabatino's.

"They might come after us," said Tongue who began to walk with Baker across the street.

"You don't understand," said Baker. "Mr. D ain't Mob. He ain't even connected. Quit watching TV so much. All Mr. D is . . . is a businessman conducting an illegal service that people want. He don't even beat up anybody who don't pay off. They can't afford that stuff anymore."

Stoney Caskey went into the restaurant without so much as glancing at Baker and Tongue.

"Ya mean they're a bunch of pussies?" asked Tongue.

"Nah. Not really . . . I dunno, maybe to you. But ya can't stay in that kinda business as long as him if you was strong-arming or killing people. They only do that in New York anymore . . . or Boston," said Baker as he and Tongue entered Sabatino's to negotiate an arms deal.

CHAPTER 16

Mr. D was once again discussing selling his package goods and check cashing business to two prospective Korean buyers as he moved around behind the various counters cashing checks, selling legal lottery tickets, and working the grill.

"How much money we make?" asked Mr. Wang as he followed on Louis Dante's heels.

"In what?" said Mr. D. "An hour, a week, a year?"

"Ha, ha, ha," laughed Mr. Wang. "How much we take home every year?"

Mr. D loved to "tummel" with the Korean merchants. He knew they liked to play dumb while sizing him up. "Thousands, Mr. Wang, thousands. By the way, do you have enough cash to buy my place?"

"Ha, ha, ha. Yes, Mr. D, we have much cash," replied Mr. Wang.

"And security?" asked Mr. D.

Mr. Wang smiled. He looked at his brother-in-law and answered, "Yes, yes. We have many buildings. Ha, ha, ha."

CHAPTER 17

Main Man was training a new recruit named Lanny, a small-time hustler. They were sitting in the upstairs room on the top floor of the Rosedale town house in Essex.

"Does Mr. D book to a lot of his friends? I mean, what if they call and only want to talk to him?" asked Lanny.

"Mr. D's philosophy is never book to friends!"

"Why?" asked the trainee, Lanny.

"Listen," said Main Man, who stood up and began pacing around the room. "If a guy looks to separate you from your money, it's like your blood. How can he be Mr. D's friend? . . . An example of what happens is this: Say there's a basketball game between Boston and Seattle and this 'friend' of Mr. D's calls up and he hears that the line on the game is Boston by six. He wants to bet Seattle, but instead he says Boston, not realizing what is said back to him by the person answering the phone, which is you. The next day, when he calls for his figures and finds out he lost instead of won, he gets crazy. Even though when you answered the phone you said, 'I'll read it back to you,' and you read it back to him."

"So what would happen then?" asked Lanny as his eyes followed Main Man over to the refrigerator where he opened it, looked inside, and slammed it shut.

"Mr. D gets involved," said Main Man. "This guy is his buddy, but it's strictly business then. It impairs friendship. Other bookies may tend to disagree with Mr. D. To them, they liken it to having a dry cleaning shop where you want your friends to come to you. And let's say something goes wrong, like a button comes off or something. You'll just pay them for the shirt or the coat. Mr. D sees this as a poor analogy because when you're talking about people betting $1,000 or more, and with a chance of error, you're going to have trouble. Also, the bookie doesn't lure people to bet with him as in other kinds of retail businesses."

Trainee Lanny squirmed in his chair and meekly asked, "What's an analogy?"

"A comparison, genius," mocked Main Man. "Anyhow, as Mr. D says, 'Bookies don't make mistakes on the phone. It's their business.' They are dead bulls-eye experts. It's a case of having faith in the system. Say you taught a parrot to say, 'Play Boston minus six.' The parrot would say it. The bookie's worker, you, my friend, are the parrot working on the phones. You read the line back from the sheet. It's tough to imagine any of Mr. D's people reading something back that is incorrect. In 99.9 percent of the time, the player, the person betting, is wrong. It's rarely, if ever, the error of the person taking the bet."

"Yeah," said Trainee Lanny, eager to please. "I can dig it."

Main Man went back to his chair. "And keep this in mind. The callers are always in between things. They're always in a hurry, or they're calling from work or from play or from a bar. Maybe they're somewhere their wife doesn't know they are. Yet the guy who's answering the phone, doing the business, he's like a tiger sitting in a tree, waiting to pounce on somebody. You're standing there with your hands above the phones waiting to leap upon them. You answer on the first sound of the ring."

Main Man held his hand over one of the phones, demonstrating for Lanny.

CHAPTER 18

Margaret's legs extended well beyond her head, held there by his muscular arms which had pinned her thighs to his shoulders. He thrust in and out of her as she moaned, reaching orgasm for the fourth time.

Suddenly, he pulled out of her and ejaculated over her belly and breasts. Spent, he rolled over on his side, breathing heavily as Margaret squeezed her legs together.

Her heart pounded as she gazed towards the closed drapes of the sliding glass door of her lover's garden apartment, north of the city in Towson, Maryland.

Margaret had met her lover, Johnny, at the Towson Health and Racquet Club, minutes from where he lived. She spent six days a week at the plush club, taking an average of two advanced aerobic classes daily along with three workouts a week from her personal trainer, Rich.

Disenchanted and bored with her life with Mr. D over the past two years, Margaret was primed for an affair. She'd seen Johnny at the club often, playing racquetball, where he reigned as the champ of the "A" ladder, and lifting weights in the workout room. He was young, strong, and courteous. He also had a great personality, and she liked that.

Margaret also liked that Johnny listened to her every word. Plus, he was so, so handsome. She had even heard him referred to by some of his buddies as Handsome John.

To Margaret, he was Johnny, but to his friends, acquaintances, and in bookmaking circles, he was Handsome John Abrams.

Unbeknownst to her, he was the brother of Mr. D's second wife, a small-time, but up-and-coming, bookie, and someone who hated Mr. D for what he had done to his sister.

Margaret believed that Johnny was a medical supplies salesman for the Mid-Atlantic region of the U.S. who was going through a horrible divorce from his boss's daughter.

Handsome John liked Margaret and enjoyed the sex, but his real passion was in knowing that this affair would result in some great hurt to Mr. D. That really turned him on.

Louis Dante not only was totally unaware of his wife's transgression, but also liked Handsome John and truly believed that Handsome John idolized him.

CHAPTER 19

Mr. D and his mentor and silent partner, Paul Douglas, sat in the lobby of the Columbia Inn across the street from the mall in the Town Center of Columbia.

"So, what's up?" asked Paul.

"They got the phone book," said Mr. D, "the sheet, everything. Somebody gave me up . . ."

It was seven a.m., and they appeared to be traveling businessmen having coffee and reading the morning newspaper.

"What's it matter? What else?" Paul's mind was elsewhere.

"The digit hit again," said Mr. D. "That's twice in three months. First it was 123 and then 666 on the President's birthday."

"Damage?" asked Paul as he turned his newspaper.

"Four hundred dimes," said Mr. D sipping on a cup of decaf coffee.

"Ouch!" exclaimed Paul.

"And Dantoni owes us 100 dimes, and says he's tapped," added Mr. D.

"How'd you let him get in that deep?"

"He always paid before," said Mr. D. "And anyhow, we've beat him for close to a million over the years . . . And when his father dies, he'll inherit some serious paper."

Paul stood up and went over to the serving table where he poured himself more coffee. He took two complimentary crois-sants and walked back to his chair by Louis Dante, continuing his conversation as though he'd never left. "What else?"

"Fuckin' Main Man brings over a couple of dope dealers while I'm at the track who wanted me to finance a drug deal," said Mr. D.

"Did ya know 'em?" asked Paul.

"Yeah," said Mr. D. "One of them was young Baker. His brother did some work for us in the digit business. You knew Baker better than me. He was scary, but did his job. The other guy, name of Tongue, I think, wasn't familiar. Anyhow, I nipped the deal and gave Main Man a raft of shit for bringing them around."

"Baker, huh," said Paul. A small smile of amusement crossed his face. "If he's half as crazy as his brother was . . . Jesus, don't you remember how nuts Gil Baker was?"

Gil Baker was the ultimate "baddest" guy. It wasn't that Gil was so physically imposing or rough, he was just crazy and didn't bluff. If he said he would kill you, he would kill you. He was six feet tall, 185 pounds, with big forearms, and had an ape-like walk that made him appear somewhat shorter. His blond hair and pale complexion surrounded a beady-eyed, not-unpleasant face which contorted when Gil was angry, evoking stark terror if you were his prey or in his way.

As a businessman, Gilbert Baker consumed other businesses. If a guy ran numbers, sold drugs, hustled hot clothes, etc., he would advise them to give him half of their earnings. Nobody ever refused since this advice was given while Gil held a gun to their ear. And people knew Gil would use the gun. Over the course of 15 years, it was said that he killed anywhere from 75 to 100 guys, not count-ing the people he beat up and left for dead—guys whose limbs were broken and whose eyes were gouged out. Actually, Gil's job de-scription was that of a freelance assassin and hood who would do anyone and anything.

He was insane. He was very scary. He adapted the cowboy way of life to modern times. Gil's favorite line was "You think you're tough? Go get your guns!" And then Gil would draw his from a shoulder holster. Even other killers were terrified of Gil. They didn't want to die. Gil didn't care.

His main job was strong-arm for the union. It didn't matter which union: Teamsters, Seafarers, Longshoremen. Gil once pulled *his gun and stuck it in Jimmy Hoffa's ear when Hoffa came to Baltimore in the mid-sixties to settle a dispute. He only did it to show Hoffa's bodyguard that he wasn't so tough.*

Gil never took "no" for an answer. He heard there was a guy trying to frame him for something that he actually didn't do. Gil caught up with the guy one night, tied him to a telephone pole, then repeatedly drove his car into and around the pole until the guy confessed. After the confession, Gil untied him, gave him a 20-second head start, and ran him over.

Another time, Gil was being interrogated by a captain of the Narcotics Squad because he had allegedly sold drugs to the captain's daughter. He grabbed the captain and started to dive out the window with him. They put Gil in jail.

Once, while he was in prison (he did serve several short sentences), Gil was trying to be good so that the authorities would let him out on an early parole. He improved his image by helping a blind guy get around. The blind guy walked with Gil and kept his hand on Gil's shoulder. One afternoon, it started raining in the jail yard and Gil was getting soaked because the blind guy was slowing him down. He got pissed off, and said to the blind guy, "Come on! Let's run for it! The gates are wide open!" He then ran the guy straight into a brick wall. No early parole.

Gil was finally sentenced to Patuxent Institute, the old Maryland prison for the criminally insane. He fit right in, killing two black guys who tried to stab him. Surprisingly, he was released 13 months later.

Many a hit man, including the criminally insane black guys at Patuxent, tried to kill Gil, but failed. The Mob finally "hot-wired" Gilbert, forcing Gil's drug connection to sell him pure heroin. He OD'ed.

"Anything else?" asked Paul.

"Margaret wants a baby. More of my time," said Mr. D.

Paul changed the subject. "My grandson's driving me nuts. I can't handle him."

"What now?" asked Mr. D, who rarely heard Paul discuss personal or family matters.

"He's out all night," said Paul. "Misses school in the morning. Thinks he's a big shot. And he tried to fix a junior varsity basketball game."

"I love it!" cried Mr. D.

"Sure," said Paul. "Wait 'til you and Maggie have a kid . . ."

CHAPTER 20

It was Sunday afternoon at a northwest Baltimore City bar called The Curb Shop, a neighborhood pub with TVs at either end of the bar. The NFL preview shows were on the air. The crowd was mostly lively, interested, beer-drinkers, and bettors.

Kenny Williams, a bear of a man in his fifties, was a bar regular and a fanatical football fan. He bet too much with his heart and was on a bad losing streak. Since he lived alone and his only expenses were food and rent, Kenny was a pretty big bettor for a grade-12 employee at the Social Security complex in Woodlawn, Maryland.

"That's it!" he yelled at the TV screen. "We agree. 'The Greek' likes Cincinnati minus three and a half at home against the Vikings. Money's in my pocket." Kenny went over to a pay phone and called a beeper. He punched in the number of the pay phone and waited for a return call from Mr. D.

"Yeah?" said Mr. D.

Kenny immediately recognized his voice. "It's me, Six," said Kenny. "Listen, I want two dollars on the Bengals. Minus three and a half, right?"

"Bengals are minus three and a half," repeated Mr. D. "That's two dollars you got on 'em. Anything else, Number Six?"

Two dollars meant two hundred dollars.

"Maybe," said Kenny. "Over/under still thirty-seven and a half?"

"It climbed to thirty-eight. Want it? I got two calls waiting, Six." Mr. D was impatient.

"Okay," said Kenny. "Over for a dollar. I'm comin' back, man. You'll be paying me from here on in."

Mr. D laughed to himself, and sarcastically said, "I hope so. Good luck, Number Six."

CHAPTER 21

"They love him in the neighborhood. He's helped out people who are down-and-out, paid rents, sent food . . ." Senior Agent Carey was catching his breath as he spoke. He was jogging with the U.S. Attorney General's principal investigator, Vince Blume, around the streets of the Inner Harbor, not far from the Federal Office Building.

"But they must know that he's ripping them off in his store," said Blume. "That he's a bookie, that . . ."

It was nighttime and the air was still muggy from the warm fall Baltimore was experiencing. The investigators had been working late Sunday evening with the U.S. Attorney. They were in the early stages of a sensitive interrogation with their prized informant who was reluctant to tell all about Mr. D. Unable to get much out of the informant, they were still optimistic. Exhilarated with their expectations, Blume and Carey had decided to go for a run.

"They don't give a fuck. Blacks respect hustlers and ballsy guys like Mr. D," said Carey.

The two men ran quietly at an eight-minute-mile clip. They wore sweatshirts and shorts, moving deftly to avoid pedestrian traffic as they headed up Pratt Street.

"Can we infiltrate Charlie's? Put a guy inside?" asked Blume.

"No chance," said Carey. "Dante only hires relatives or guys he's known or who have the right references. Even with all the traffic goin' in and out of Charlie's 15 hours a day, it seems that everybody knows everyone."

"What do you mean?" asked Blume.

Agent Carey wasn't in the shape that Blume was, and since he was speaking more, he ran silently for 30 or 40 seconds before responding.

"Charlie's is busy all fuckin' day. There're usually a dozen people inside and about 15 to 20 people loitering around in front of the place, in the street, or on the adjoining parking lot.

"I had one of our black agents hang out there one day and, within 45 minutes, the loiterers made him as a cop. But he was still able to bring me back most of what I'm tellin' ya."

"Anything else?" asked Blume as he picked up the pace, much to Carey's chagrin.

"Yeah. Ninety percent of the men, and women, who frequent Charlie's are armed with knives or guns, or both."

"Christ," said Blume, "does Mr. D's get robbed a lot? Are those check cashers and customers mugged often?"

"No. Those people protect Charlie's and its clientele. They understand that if Charlie's falls, no one is crazy enough to replace it. Hell, some of those sorrowful, degenerate patrons would die for Mr. D," said Carey. "Actually, the place is safer than most of the Pennsylvania Avenue district.

CHAPTER 22

Louis Dante was still home. It was late for him for a Monday morning. He was still trying to reconcile the weekend's profits and losses. Following that, he would set the schedule for dropping off and picking up payoffs from his local clientele. The pickups were evenly divided between him and Main Man.

Margaret came downstairs in her workout gear: white sleeveless thong leotard with matching white leggings, floppy socks, and high-top white aerobic shoes.

Mr. D stopped his paperwork to gaze admiringly at his wife. Although he knew he had probably married too often, he had to admit to himself that each succeeding wife was prettier than the previous one.

"I'm late, baby," said Margaret. She knew that gaze of Dante's. "See you home tonight." With a peck on his cheek, she was out the door with their dog, Lilly, hot on her heels.

CHAPTER 23
1966

Louis married Judy Canzone, whom he had dated on and off for three years, and opened a "string" of submarine and pizza shops—two of them. A year later, a daughter was born to the Dantes.

One of Louis's major sub shop accounts was the Baltimore Orioles baseball team, since his main store was located near Memorial Stadium. Louis and Marvin were both betting a great deal at this point, and they thought they had discovered a scientific way of winning baseball games. It depended on the number of Polish ham submarine sandwiches that Boog Powell, the Orioles' large, home-run-hitting first baseman, ate. This didn't work and they lost more money.

While Louis was running the sub shops and Marvin was working for a clothing manufacturer, Marvin helped bankroll Louis in a real estate partnership buying residential properties. Within two years, Louis bought 60 homes. He also innovated the real estate business. A speculator would call Louis with a house he had purchased for $4,000 and offer to sell it to Louis for $4,200 in cash. If he liked the house, Louis would pay the guy, and then demand the deed to the house, not a contract. He would then take the deed to a savings and loan firm and ask to borrow $5,300. When they requested the contract, Louis would say that he bought it in a cash deal, and, therefore, all he had was the deed. The exact amount of the cash sale couldn't be confirmed. After the settlement, he would end up with $500 or $600 extra, and also own the house. He would then tell prospective renters that he was renting the house to tenants for $38 a week. Most of the major city landlords at the time were receiving $25 per week, but Louis had a novel approach.

"Mrs. Smith," he would say, "we are a full-service realtor. We give you maintenance, electricity, plumbing, etc. All you have to do is give us a $38 deposit, $38 for the first week's rent, and $38 from that time on and you get full service. Nobody else will give you full service."

Of course, Louis didn't have full service, but what did he care? He then cautioned Mrs. Smith that if she missed one week's payment, the sheriff would put her on the sidewalk the next day.

CHAPTER 24
October 1986

"I hate gettin' up this early, man," said Tongue as he slipped into the seat of the 1983 black Chrysler Le Baron. "Where'd you get this car?"

"Borrowed it from my cousin, Mark," said Baker, swinging the car out of the Holiday Inn parking lot onto Cromwell Bridge Road.

Baker and Tongue were currently residing at the Holiday Inn since their return from California to solidify the "designer" Quaalude deal. Ever since their days with the outlaw Pythons, they had lived in temporary settings: weekly apartments, motels, and rental properties.

The bikers were staying in a street-level room, leading out to the rear of the Holiday Inn, about 100 yards from the Baltimore Beltway. They parked their Harley-Davidsons inside the room beside their beds since true bikers keep their hogs as close to them as possible. Although the hotel manager initially objected to the motorcycles, Baker had explained to him that due to the weight of the bikes, over 700 pounds each, the kickstand would sink into the asphalt outside on the parking lot.

"No sense in driving out to Dante's house. I've already located his first stop," said Baker, proud of his initial surveillance on Mr. D.

They cruised in silence two miles north and exited off the Beltway at Loch Raven Boulevard. Tucked amid numerous commercial establishments was the Bel Loc Diner, the site of Mr. D's first meeting of the day.

Tongue and Baker sat low in the car as they observed Louis Dante and Main Man in a corner booth eating breakfast. It was 7:45 a.m.

The first two days of Mr. D's week were set aside for coordinating rendezvous with lay-off bookies, numbers runners, sports betting customers, and his "staff" of henchmen. Throughout each day, there were pickups or deliveries of cash and paper in the metropolitan area. Contact was made by beepers, car phones, and random pay phones in short, cryptic dialogue.

Louis Dante always varied his meetings, calls, and driving patterns. He cursed at the decisions of certain big customers to meet at the same place and time on his Tuesday night deliveries.

Tongue and Baker were experienced at tracking people. They took their time and would rather lose a prey than risk exposure. And with Mr. D, they knew it would be easier than usual since his patterns could only vary so much in a town like Baltimore.

Before they lost Mr. D around three p.m., Tongue and Baker had watched him exchange money with ten customers, four other bookies, and two numbers men, besides stopping twice at Charlie's, eating lunch in Little Italy with Paul, and stopping at fifteen pay phones—all in eight hours.

For Mr. D, there were still three more hours of rendezvous and two more hours of working the phones before he would return home between 8:15 and 8:30 p.m.

CHAPTER 25

The etymology or history of the words "tout" and "handicapper" goes back over 200 years to England. Originally the name of a thief's scout or watchman, the term "tout" was later extended to horse racing as one who observed or spied upon a horse and/or its trainer, using such information for betting purposes. If the horse won, the tout was rewarded, depending upon the amount bet by the person receiving the information.

"Handicap" evolved from a game of chance called "Hand In The Cap" where people challenged one another for articles they owned. If they lost, their forfeits of money or personal items, which were held in a cap, were awarded to the winner. Later, the term referred to a type of horse race where weights (advantages or penalties) were assigned to equalize the opportunity of winning. A handicapper became a public official who assigned the weights. Still later, handicapper or handicapping evolved into the present day definition of a person or service that predicts winners.

Touts and handicappers were specifically related to horse racing until the second half of the 20th century when sports betting grew in popularity. Although wagering on sports was always around, it was only fashionable among a small segment of the American population. However, the enormous growth of professional sports and television, and the risk-taking behavior of this nation's citizens, created what today has been called a 100-billion-dollar-a-year industry; mostly illicit.

The gambling obsession in the U.S. not only created more and wealthier bookies, but, directly and indirectly, opened up new opportunities in associated fields with only a fine line separating legal from illegal.

Nelson Mattesick walked that fine line. As a youth from the Bronx in New York City, he spent his formative years at the racetrack with his Uncle Leo, who sold a daily "handicap card" to racing patrons. Uncle Leo was only an average handicapper of the ponies, but he was a shrewd marketer. Before the final two races, he would rush to his printing equipment in the rear of his truck and reprint his Daily Pics; this time including the winners of at least half of the day's racing card. Then, as the customers who hadn't bought Uncle Leo's tip sheet passed his stand after the final race, Leo would hand them the reprinted card giving the illusion that, once again, had they spent the two dollars for his predictions, they would have all left as winners.

Nelson learned a lot from his Uncle Leo and also became an excellent handicapper. His insight into horse racing brought him big wins as a teenager and a confidence in himself reserved for board chairmen. An All-City football linebacker at 6'5" tall and 250 pounds, Nelson landed a full scholarship to Notre Dame. He lasted two years at the prestigious university before dropping out to marry his high school sweetheart, a very pregnant Sharon Vellegia.

The newlyweds moved to Baltimore in 1966 to be close to Nelson's new territory for the Bobbie Brooks Dress Company, which specialized in casual women's apparel. He was their number-three salesman nationally, and his future looked solid. A natural at selling himself or a product, Nelson had a well-defined, handsome, square face, piercing blue eyes, and chocolate-brown, wavy hair with long sideburns. But Nelson felt unfulfilled. In the evening, he spent hours pouring over the *Racing Form* and analyzing the major stakes races. On occasion, Nelson gave out his predictions on big races to friends and associates he had accumulated over the years. In return, he asked them to set aside a portion of their bets for him. If Nelson's picks were wrong, he lost. He only received remuneration if his horses won.

In 1967, Nelson purchased the mailing list of 5,000 players from a horse race handicapper who was going out of business. For free, Nelson gave out his prediction for the winner of the Kentucky Derby to his potential new customers. A losing pick would end his dreams; a winner could bring untold success. In a brazen and ballsy move, he selected Proud Clarion, a 30 to 1 long shot. The horse won in a breeze.

Nelson quit his job and expanded his mailing list, working in the basement of his home. Two years later, he cautiously moved into an ancillary service, handicapping college and professional football. Although not as adept in analyzing those sports, his expertise at sales and marketing, and his experience gained from observing Uncle Leo, propelled him to the forefront of this new aspect of gambling: the sports handicapping service.

By 1986, Nelson had gone from a "ma and pa" home basement operation to a ten-story office building in downtown Baltimore, which he now owned. His mailing list totaled five million, he had offices in New York, Chicago, and Los Angeles, and his annual gross income was six million dollars. He operated under the name of Big Nick Mason and had even achieved celebrity status, being a much sought-after guest for sports and talk shows. Yet Nelson was still unfulfilled. A gambler at heart, he yearned for other victories in his field, but feared the criminal justice system.

His business was legal, as numerous court cases against him attested to. His lawyer, a former U.S. Attorney from Ohio who practiced law in Washington D.C., earned a six-figure retainer to assure that it was. The state and federal prosecutors and government agencies, such as the Postal Authorities and the IRS, were always investigating him. Yes, Nelson walked a fine line.

Nelson Mattesick, aka Big Nick Mason, sat in a glass-enclosed office overlooking his employees manning their phones, working his handicapping service. His telecommunication equipment allowed him to listen in on any of his employees' calls, which he was presently doing. The employees each operated a computer that immediately flashed the caller's service history on the screen: first, which service he subscribed to—the service's magazine only, lock of the week, gold card games, Big Nick's special play, etc.; second, what sports he played; third, whether he was paid up; and fourth, what were his horse race selections. He would be asked: "How much are you betting for Big Nick?"

Nelson's secretary buzzed him to the phone, which he answered while still listening to his employees with his other ear.

"Nick, Maggie," said Mr. D's wife. "I'm confirming dinner tonight."

"Great," said Nelson. "Let's make it 8:30. Prime Rib Room. I'm bringing Donna, okay? And tell Louis to be on time."

Donna was Nelson's girlfriend of six months. He had divorced his wife, Sharon, three years earlier.

"Sure," said Margaret sarcastically. "Like I've got a lot of control. See ya tonight."

CHAPTER 26

It was late in the afternoon and Mr. D was already mentally exhausted. He drove over to his old friend Marvin's house. The boyhood chums were sitting outside on the wooden deck surrounding the swimming pool. Marvin was in a wheelchair and Louis Dante was spread out on a cushioned chaise lounge. His former partner in his early business endeavors and initial bookmaking business, Marvin was left crippled by a serious car accident years earlier.

"So how'd they getcha this time, Louis? Pen register, wiretap, informant . . . what?"

"This'll kill ya," said Mr. D. "They got me with 'Trap and Trace.' Real sophisticated. The government used to only use it in spy cases. Can you believe that? And for what? A fucking misdemeanor, a fine. Why can't they leave me alone?"

"How's it work?" asked Marvin as he propelled his wheelchair slowly around the pool picking up litter.

"I'm not real sure of the technicalities, but my attorney said it's a technique that traces the origin of a call."

"Like, if I called you, they could trace it to me?" asked Marvin.

"Yeah," said Mr. D. He was facing the last rays of the day's sun and squirming in the chaise, trying to maximize his comfort. "Supposedly they have a guy at the switching station, and as long as they know the time of the call, they can trace the origin of an incoming call . . . and it's the feds' technique, and now they go and give it to the locals . . . Hell, I pay them taxes. It's my tax dollars supplying this shit."

"C'mon Louis," said Marvin facetiously, "your taxes?"

"Hell yeah, Marv. I paid a hundred grand last year, and every year, under miscellaneous income. IRS has no problem taking it. They know what I do . . . and they don't give it back."

"I once knew a hooker who did the same thing," laughed Marvin. "Maybe they ought to just legalize you and her. Ya know, I . . ."

Marvin stopped talking. He realized Louis had fallen asleep and was beginning to snore loudly.

CHAPTER 27

1968

When Louis and Marvin came home in the evening, they stayed up gambling until very late at night. They would phone out to friends (Baltimore transplants) on the West Coast where they were betting certain "late" basketball or baseball games. They even sent the "callee" money so that he could put his telephone by a radio in order for them to listen to a play-by-play of the game. Not only did their phone bills go through the roof, they lost thousands gambling. This did not endear Louis to his wife, and they soon divorced.

CHAPTER 28
October, 1986

The Dantes, Big Nick, and Donna had finished dessert and were awaiting the check at the swank Prime Rib Room a few blocks north of center city in Baltimore.

The discussions for the evening revolved around small talk and local gossip. However, at the bar before dinner and during the ladies' trips to the bathroom, Louis and Nelson mulled over several new business ideas. Primarily, they discussed a joint venture in Las Vegas, a sports book (a legalized betting service).

Each man respected the other's business talents. Mr. D longed to become legitimate, and Big Nick relished the power and aura of the big-time illegal bookie. He even went so far as to propose merging their empires.

When Margaret and Donna, a statuesque brunette wearing an extremely short, low-cut dress which revealed too much breast and too much leg for the restaurant, returned, Nelson paid the waiter and reminded the ladies that he and Mr. D were flying to Atlantic City the day after tomorrow.

As Mr. D was leaving the restaurant, he spotted a delinquent customer, Ray Dantoni, who owed him lots of money. Mr. D went over to the table and loudly embarrassed and humiliated Dantoni. Before shocked diners, Dantoni sat there, flabbergasted as Mr. D quickly regained his composure and walked away.

To the stunned maître d', Dave, Mr. D said, "Look, you know we can't break people's arms, kill them, hurt them, threaten them, or any of that stuff; but we can embarrass these deadbeats, and that's what I'm going to continue to do. I'm going to seriously humiliate any asshole who owes me a hundred grand!"

CHAPTER 29

"You're gonna have a mini race war on your hands if this shit keeps up!" screamed Clem Watowski to Mr. D.

"Why are you yellin' at me, Clem?" asked Mr. D, totally puzzled.

"Bit by bit, I've been losing my numbers territory to that big gorilla, Shadow Creek. First, he did it on the sneaks, but now he's flauntin' it in my face."

Watowski was livid. It was true that his gambling terrain was shrinking and the cause was Shadow Creek's growing aggressiveness on the east side of the city. He laid off to Mr. D whose bankroll was also growing. Mr. D had assumed it was the result of an increase in betting by Creek's regular customers. He wasn't aware that Clem Watowski was losing clientele that he had had for over three decades.

Years ago, Paul had opened up the opportunity for blacks to control numbers on the west side of town. They would have taken it anyway was the way Paul had put it to his gambling associates in the sixties; so it was a wise move to work in harmony at that time. Jimmy Bop was a black Jamaican who received the west side. But Watowski always felt the east side was his forever.

"What do ya want me to do, Clem?" asked Mr. D. He knew the answer.

"You tell Creek that either I get my turf back or it's war!" screamed Clem.

"Look," said Mr. D. "We don't need a war, especially a racial hassle. Business is too good for everybody . . ."

"Not for me, Dante. Not for me," said Watowski. "And I don't like that nigger datin' those white girls that live in my neighborhood either!" He was red in the face. His blood pressure had gone through the ceiling.

Clem Watowski had run gambling in east Baltimore since the late forties. When he began the numbers business back then, he was 25 years old, but looked older. He had been a strong-arm for the Longshoremen, and, at six feet tall and 220 pounds, he was an imposing specimen. He had reddish-blond hair, a bulbous nose, and very fair skin that turned almost blood-red when he was angry.

Now, almost 40 years and 80 pounds later, he teetered on the scale at 300 pounds. He also suffered from emphysema, but never acknowledged it.

Mr. D was very wary of Watowski. He had heard about and seen him in action for over 20 years and knew how dangerous and violent he could be. Dante also knew that Watowski was connected to the Vice Squad more than anyone. But he respected him and enjoyed his company nonetheless.

Louis knew that he would have to get Paul to intervene in this fracas. As much as he hated to get Paul involved in day-to-day activities, he believed that only Paul could settle this dispute. For Paul had an uncanny way with the blacks, and Dante recognized that the major black players in gambling in Baltimore truly respected and listened to Paul.

CHAPTER 30

Big Nick Mason and Mr. D were at a craps table at The Sands in Atlantic City. They had flown there in a twelve-seat Cessna and were picked up by the casino limousine.

After an excellent dinner at the Gourmet Room, the two gambling czars strolled through the casino kibitzing at blackjack and roulette before getting into some serious action at the craps tables.

In the casino, they ran into Mel the Tailor, the mid-sized bookie who laid off to Mr. D, and who ran a poolroom. Mel was considered a sharp craps player, and Mr. D and Nelson decided to go in partners with him shooting craps. Up about $15,000, the three crapshooters rolled into a losing streak, and, two hours later, found themselves down $35,000. While they were playing, Mel began to relate a story of an elaborate scam he and some other gambling associates had played on an old friend of theirs, Lindy, who also owned a poolroom that Dante had frequented as a young man.

Jeff Hall was a nickel-dime bettor, strictly small-time. He was in Atlantic City at a blackjack table at Resorts playing what is called third base, the far left seat at the blackjack table. A "preferred" customer was playing first base, the right-side seat of the table, and was losing heavily. He was blaming his losses on the way Jeff played third base. He continued to berate and ridicule Jeff about playing poor blackjack until Jeff screamed out, "Hey, I can't help it! That's the way I play!" The guy became more abusive and finally went over and tried to physically remove Jeff from the table. Jeff resisted, and, in the course of the scuffle, punched the guy over the table into the "pit" where the "pit bosses" stood to observe the games. Security personnel rushed over and escorted Jeff and the preferred customer to a holding room to discuss the altercation. The preferred customer broke away from the security officers and punched the seated and restrained Jeff in the face, busting his nose and bruising his eyes. The casino personnel realized immediately that they were liable for what happened to Jeff. They made him an offer of $5,000 to settle the case as he wiped the blood from his face. Not thinking very clearly and dreaming of what he could do with $5,000 while still in Atlantic City, Jeff signed the release. He took the money and proceeded to lose it all by the next morning.

Jeff returned to Baltimore and told the story to his buddies, Mel and Handsome John. They decided to keep the story confidential and worked out an elaborate scam to fool Lindy. Lindy was the owner of Lindy's Poolroom, which had moved from the old Pimlico area into a more exclusive neighborhood farther north. Lindy still had the first dollar he had ever earned. He considered himself as good a hustler as anyone around because he had never gotten suckered into any bizarre deals over the four decades that he had run the poolroom

Mr. D, Nelson, and Mel the Tailor had a chance to recoup the money they had lost. They were behind a hot roll of a guy from Texas who was playing with orange chips worth a thousand dollars apiece. Although not betting as heavily, Mr. D, Mel, and Nelson had about $13,000 in bets on the table. They could go out on top with the next roll. Unfortunately, the guy from Texas threw a seven and they lost.

"Louis," said Nelson, "isn't that the place where you made your reputation, Lindy's Poolroom? Was Lindy that slick?"

"I'll tell ya something. I could never con him out of a dime . . .

Go on with the story, Mel. What happened next?" said Mr. D.

Mel traveled to New York to a prestigious law firm where he asked to meet with the managing partner. Mel knew he would never see the top lawyer without an appointment, so while he was waiting, he asked the receptionist for some travel directions. Mel told her that he had to leave very shortly to return to Baltimore, but he had a major accident case he wanted to discuss and could she loan him some paper so that he could describe the case in a letter for her to deliver to the lawyer. The receptionist gave Mel directions, an envelope, and some law firm stationery. Then she went into another office to brief a secretary on several messages. After a few minutes, Mel left and drove back to Baltimore.

In the poolroom the next day, just within hearing range of Lindy, Mel engaged in conversation with Handsome John and another guy about Jeff's altercation in Atlantic City. There was no mention that Jeff had settled the case, just that the casino initially offered him a quarter of a million dollars. They also said that on the advice of a lawyer friend, Jeff proceeded to New York where he was advised by a major law firm that he could make anywhere from 10 to 15 million dollars if he decided to file a lawsuit against the casino. Mel and Handsome John continued to discuss Jeff's situation every few days near Lindy, and then they would walk away.

Around the second week, Jeff went to Lindy to seek advice as to what he should do. He showed Lindy a letter from the law firm (which Mel had typed). The "attorney" explained in the letter that Jeff should be extremely quiet about what had happened; that there were a number of people involved, including the mayor of Atlantic City and organized crime figures; that he was never to mention that his law firm was representing Jeff; that the minimum the case was worth was five million dollars, if they settled quickly; and that he could earn as much as fifteen million dollars if he waited a year.

Jeff told Lindy that maybe he should just settle for the quarter of a million dollars the casino offered. He was upset because the lawyer called and told him that he needed "up-front" money immediately in order to make some initial payoffs totaling $50,000. The money was needed to bribe the Mob, the mayor of Atlantic City, and some Gambling Commission officials. Jeff was glum because he was broke. Lindy, who felt that this was a once in a life-

time opportunity, told Jeff, "Don't worry. I'll give you the money if you'll sign over half of the final settlement."

Jeff balked at Lindy's offer. He thought 50 percent was too much. As the day passed, Jeff "let" Lindy convince him that he should do it after Lindy agreed to cover all legal fees and payoffs down the line. Lindy hurriedly got a customer who was an attorney to draw up the proper documents, which Jeff "reluctantly" signed. Now Jeff had more money than he had ever had before, and he started going to Atlantic City more often and gambling heavily. He was constantly dining out, treating the guys, leaving tips beyond belief, and having the time of his life. Periodically, he would go back to Lindy for additional funds for different payoffs and fees for the lawyer. Naturally, all requests were specified in letters on the law firms's stationery and typed by Mel. Over time, Jeff took Lindy for $400,000.

"I can't fuckin' believe it, Mel. He took Lindy for 400 grand?" asked Mr. D incredulously.

"It gets even better," said Mel. "Ya know what, guys? I'll tell ya, dinner really didn't fill me. Know how nervous I get after craps. Let's walk over to the White House Sub Shop and get a sub. Maybe bring a couple back."

"You gonna eat again, Mel?" laughed Mr. D. "All right, I don't get up here that often anymore, and I always loved those subs. Hey, Mel, is it true that there are guys that make sub runs every couple of months up to the White House?"

"Yeah," said Mel. "These guys are amazing. They don't even come here to gamble. They just drive up and bring back 30 subs. And they keep them for a week, either heat 'em or eat 'em cold. You can't beat those subs."

The attention of the three gamblers was briefly diverted by the ringing of bells in the casino, designating a big slot machine pay out. They turned and watched the ceremonious payoff from the change girl to an elderly woman in a wheelchair whose slot machine announced a payoff to her of $3,000.

"How far is the walk?" asked Nelson.

"It's over on Arctic and Mississippi. It ain't that bad a stroll," said Mel as the three began to walk out of the front door of the casino onto the boardwalk.

"I can't believe the subs are that good. Ya know, in New York I always ate great subs," boasted Nelson.

"Yeah," shouted Mr. D, "we know everything is better in

New York! But, I'm tellin' ya, Mel is right. When I was a kid, I'd go in there, lines around the block. Then, even after the riots, when Atlantic City went bad, you still couldn't get in the place."

The guys headed south on the boardwalk. The salty air was stimulating, and talk of the subs wet their appetites.

"Ya know what?" said Mel. "Sinatra, Jerry Lewis, and celebrities like that still have subs shipped out to them every few months. They send 'em out on Dry Ice or something. It's fuckin' amazing."

"So go ahead, Mel," said Mr. D, "finish your story."

By coincidence, during this period of time, the mayor of Atlantic City was actually indicted, so Jeff went back to Lindy and said that he needed more money to bribe the interim mayor. Lindy, who had been reading the Atlantic City articles in the newspapers, truly believed that everything Jeff said was going on and, again, dug into his pocket.

On the sly, one afternoon, Lindy phoned Jeff's lawyer in New York only to receive the response that they could not discuss any of their clients, which was standard operating procedure for any legal firm.

In the meantime, Jeff took some of Lindy's money and bought his own poolroom. He also gave Mel and Handsome John a portion of the money because they were part of the scam; but he was spending most of the money himself, living a wild and crazy life. He would even tip the employees who worked in the tollbooths when he drove back and forth to Atlantic City.

One day, Jeff was screwing around in his poolroom with a gun he kept there for security purposes. He was a little "juiced up," and, since he thought the gun was not loaded, he was scaring people by pointing it at them. One guy finally yelled at him, "Cut it out! Don't be crazy! There's going to be an accident!" Jeff answered, "Hey, there's nothing in here!" He turned, pointed the gun at his head, and clicked the trigger. Nothing happened the first time, or the second time. But, the third time, the gun, which must have had a bullet lodged in the chamber, went off. Jeff literally blew his brains out.

Jeff was rushed to Baltimore County General Hospital where he was pronounced dead. The news got to Lindy fairly quickly, and a few hours later, in the early morning, he drove over to the hospital demanding to see Jeff's body. He did not believe that Jeff was dead. Lindy had to lie and say that he was Jeff's father (who was dead) before the hospital authorities would take him to view the body. Heart-

broken, Lindy ran outside crying; not over Jeff's death, but over the fact that he had invested over $400,000 in the lawsuit.

Regaining his composure, Lindy realized that he may still be entitled to the money since he had the signed agreement from Jeff that he was to receive half of the settlement. He decided to drive to New York that morning from the hospital. The four-hour drive took him to the prestigious law firm where he rushed in and demanded to see Jeff's attorney. Naturally, without an appointment, the office staff would not allow it. But Lindy carried on so and was in such a state of despair that they eventually got the managing partner to speak with him. The lawyer repeated the statement about confidentiality. Lindy said that he was aware of that because it was in Jeff's letter. He showed the lawyer the letter on the law firm's stationery. The lawyer denied writing it and told Lindy that it must be a hoax, a fraud. Lindy thought that the law firm was trying to beat him for half of Jeff's money so that they could keep it all. He went berserk and had to be physically removed from the building. Lindy returned to Baltimore still believing Jeff's story.

Mel finished relating the scam as they walked the boardwalk to Mississippi Avenue where they turned right and strolled four more blocks to Arctic Avenue. They each ate half of an Italian cold cut sub at the White House Sub Shop and then took a taxi back to the Sands Casino. On the way to the tables, a pretty woman approached Mel. He rudely dismissed her.

"Why were you so rough on the girl?" asked Nelson. "It looks to me as though she likes you. Is she an old girlfriend?"

"Yeah," said Mel. "You know, she hustles tricks, but she also comps some guys she digs. And, she's very sensual. But I'll tell ya, first of all, I ain't into that much sex if things are going bad up here. And if things are going good, I'd rather stay at the tables . . . And besides, man, with this AIDS shit, it's almost like I oughta become a priest."

"Not quite a priest, Mel," laughed Mr. D.

The threesome was again situated around the same craps table ready to play.

"Hey man, you know these hookers, they spread AIDS. A lot of them shoot dope. Their boyfriends shoot dope. And you know they don't give a fuck here," said Mel.

"Mel's got a point, Louis," said Nelson. "When the herpes thing was going on, they had some chicks with the virus up here. Hookers who hated married men would purposely fuck these guys when they were at their most contagious time. They loved to give herpes to married men. Who can you trust nowadays?"

CHAPTER 31

Originally, Margaret was intent on surprising Handsome John at his apartment. All of her previous liaisons with John had been during the day after briefly and clandestinely making plans at the racquet club.

When the night fell and she knew Louis was in Atlantic City, Margaret had second thoughts. Perhaps John dated other women. Perhaps his estranged wife would be there. She decided not to go to his apartment and, instead, hurriedly called Donna to meet for a drink.

At first Donna was reluctant to go out. Nelson Mattesick was jealous and possessive. If he called and she wasn't home, he would be upset. But Donna was young and didn't relish staying at home; so she changed the message on her answering machine indicating that she was going out with Margaret and would not be late.

The ladies met at Alonzo's, a popular pub not far from where Nelson and Donna resided in the Roland Park area of northern Baltimore City.

The pub was crowded, and Donna and Margaret stood in the front of the circular bar, beyond the sound of the blaring TV. They drank glasses of Coors Light drafts. Although they had known each other for a relatively short period of time, the ladies were comfortable with each other and their discussions were frank.

"So, congratulations," said Margaret. "I understand Nelson's divorce is final . . . Any plans?"

"Yeah," said Donna. She was shaking her head "no" to an offer to buy her a drink from a tall preppy-looking young man in a red Windbreaker, which had Chesapeake Lacrosse Club stitched across the back.

"Nelson told me he wants to get married and have more children, but not for another year. He doesn't want to upset his kids too soon. How about you? Still want to have a baby?"

"Oh, God, yes," said Margaret. She was very confused. She loved Dante and wanted that relationship to work. But she also had fallen for Handsome John. Christ, she thought, What's wrong with me? For a moment she even entertained the idea of screwing the preppy Donna had turned down for a drink.

As the girls chatted away at Alonzo's, three miles southwest, Paul and Jimmy Bop sat on a bench in front of the Esplanade Apartments facing Druid Park Lake.

Even though Jimmy Bop had been in the United States since 1958, he still spoke with a clipped Jamaican accent. "Paul, my friend, I hate to bring you into this, but things are becoming messy. That cocksucker, Watowski, has started something that I may have to finish."

"I understand from Mr. D that he's upset with Shadow Creek infringing upon his territory, but Watowski is mostly talk today. Now, 20 years ago . . ."

"No, Paul. He's more dangerous today. A few hours ago I arranged bail for Shadow as a result of Watowski siccing Vice on him."

"How do you know?" asked Paul.

"Trust me. I know," said Bop. "Now, there will be retaliation unless . . . unless you can talk some sense into that goofy Polack."

CHAPTER 32

Louis Dante was fuming. He had just gotten off of the car phone with his cousin, Estelle, and her son, Dickie. The conversation had taken the entire trip from his home to where he had gone to pick up an offer sheet for Charlie's from the Koreans.

Although watching his rearview mirror while traveling down Falls Road and onto the Jones Falls Expressway, Mr. D was oblivious to the two tails: Tongue and Baker in a stolen silver Toyota Tercel, and the government agents, Carey and Solomon, in a dark blue Chevy van. Neither tail was aware of the other.

Mr. D left the expressway at North Avenue and drove west to

Pennsylvania Avenue. The feds, sensing Dante returning to Charlie's, decided to drop their surveillance and head south to the Federal Office Building. The drug dealers cautiously took an alternate route to Charlie's.

Dickie was a twenty-five-year-old "wise guy." He had performed menial jobs for Mr. D since he was a fifteen-year-old dropout. Everyone referred to him as Mr. D's nephew. He and his mom, Estelle, were very close to Margaret, who always intervened on their behalf when they needed help. Louis Dante had helped support them since Estelle's husband left her 15 years ago.

Dickie eventually got a job as a used car salesman at Dude's Chevrolet in south Baltimore. He also worked as a low-level bookie to Mr. D. Unfortunately, Dickie also loved to bet and he had dug himself quite a hole in a short period of time. Lying about his customers' bets, pocketing payoffs, and gambling heavily, Dickie was in serious debt. And when Mr. D found out about his indiscretions, he was livid. He confronted Dickie at his mom's home, calling him a thief and a cheat, and demanded that he reimburse the $25,000 that he had stolen.

Dickie confessed that he couldn't help himself and cried as Mr. D stormed out of the house. A week had gone by, and now Estelle was calling Dante begging him to get Dickie some help.

Mr. D parked illegally in front of Charlie's and walked through the crowd of customers. He took his place behind the check-cashing counter and called a former gambling client, Benny Kroll, who was now a member of GA (Gamblers Anonymous).

"Benny, Mr. D. How ya doing?"

"Hey, Mr. D," answered Benny. "I still owe you money or something? You come across an IOU or a note? What the hell are you calling me for?"

"Benny, I need a favor," said Mr. D. "I've got to get somebody into one of those treatment programs they have now for compulsive gamblers. You know what I mean? You work with that stuff now, don't ya?"

While conversing with Benny, Mr. D cashed a check for a customer.

"Mr. D, are you kidding me? You serious?" asked Benny.

"Hey, this is somebody very close, a relative. It's family, you hear? I don't book action to family or friends. He was supposed to be bringing me new customers, bringing over action. I find out later that he's been betting. He's ripped me off for some 25 grand. I've got to get him some treatment."

"That's great," said Benny sarcastically. "How about the rest of your clients?"

"What are you talking about, Benny, the rest of my clients? I don't have any compulsive gamblers. They're just guys who like to bet."

"Come on, Mr. D, ya know, spare me."

"Hold on a second, Benny," said Mr. D. He was handing over money for a check to a tall black woman around thirty who worked for the city's Civil Service Commission. With Benny on hold, Mr. D tried to weave his sales magic. "How about some cologne, Miss? They sell 'Charlie' all over Europe for $39.95 an ounce. We got it on special today for five dollars, imported."

The customer declined and Mr. D went back to Benny. "I need to get my cousin into a treatment program. He's causing a lot of hate within the family. I've got to take care of the schmuck . . ."

"I'll tell you what," interrupted Benny. "I'll call you back in a little while. You still at the place?"

Alongside a huge trash bin, a half a block south of Charlie's, Tongue and Baker sat in their car observing the front of the store as they swallowed illicit amphetamines. Neither one spoke.

CHAPTER 33
1969

Louis sold the sub shops and his other investments after his partner, Marvin, was injured in a car accident. Dante became a "beard" for a major bookmaker, Paul. A beard was someone who was a front for the bookmakers. They employed a beard as a third party to bet with other bookies when they had a game that they thought was a lock, or, better yet, a "steamer." Steamers were fixed games. Only a handful of people across the nation knew that in the late sixties and early seventies, the Kansas City Chiefs football team was allegedly fixing games. At the very last minute, Louis, as the beard, would lay a lot of money on a bookie betting on (or against) Kansas City. This worked well for a couple of years until the other bookies realized that something crooked was going on and took Kansas City games off the board.

CHAPTER 34
October, 1986

Paul and Clem Watowski sat at a small table near the bar facing the door leading into Shugs, a lesbian joint on the fringes of Little Italy and two blocks south of the black projects on Caroline Street. The bar had been selected for a meeting over the territorial squabble between Clem and Shadow Creek.

It was three p.m. and Shugs was empty except for Paul, Clem, and the bartender, Sherry, a forty-ish woman wearing a tank top, jeans, and sporting a tattoo on her shoulder that read "Love Sucks." She wore no makeup, had a slim, muscular body, and her hands displayed rings on every finger. Her hair was chestnut colored and cropped, and the look she gave men said "hands off."

At two minutes past three, a large dark-skinned figure walked through the door at a brisk pace. Shadow Creek, the black number's boss of east Baltimore was an imposing man. The three-time All-State high school linebacker and former correctional officer at the state penitentiary in Jessup, Maryland was six feet five inches tall and weighed 235 pounds. Following his dismissal from the prison system for allegedly beating up several incorrigible convicts, Shadow went to work for Jimmy Bop.

After proving his loyalty for ten years, Bop "awarded" him the minuscule east side turf, not under Watowski's control, which Shadow developed over a four-year period. Now, at 42 years old, he had expanded his horizons to rival Watowski for dominance of the area.

Shadow never hesitated as he walked directly to the table where Paul and Clem sat and effortlessly picked up the 300-pound Watowski by his sports coat and slammed him against the bar.

"You got me busted you fat fuck!" screamed Shadow. "I oughta kill you . . ."

Suddenly Shadow felt the cool steel of a Colt .45 revolver pressing against the carotid in his neck.

"Only I do the killing in here, you big chocolate thug," cooed Sherry as she cocked the trigger.

Shadow smiled and released Watowski, who slid to the floor, shaken. "Sorry for the inconvenience," Shadow apologized. "It's stress, ya know?"

Sherry pulled the gun away and Shadow bent down, helping Clem to his feet and seating him back next to Paul, who had remained impassive during the brief altercation. Paul shot a quick glance at Sherry who winked at him and went back to cleaning glasses at the far side of the marble bar. Sherry was a fifty-percent owner of the bar with her mom, Lois Collata, who had opened Shugs 20 years earlier with the financial backing of Paul Douglas.

"I'm fucking leaving!" screamed Watowski as he began to rise.

"Hold on," said Paul calmly. "This is business, gentlemen. There's no room for emotion here. Let's try and resolve your differences."

Both men respected Paul and knew that if there was any way they could work things out without violence or without hurting business, Paul could do it; at least temporarily. Shadow and Clem deeply despised each other and it was inevitable that one of them would go down some day.

"Damn it!" said Shadow. "He didn't have to have me arrested. They came to my mom's home. It was embarrassing!"

"An occupational hazard. A business expense," said Paul.

For the next 45 minutes, Paul let each man vent his anger and present his argument. Listening intently and objectively, Paul tried to arrive at a settlement each man could live with from both a financial and egotistical standpoint. Neither man would accept a partnership, second billing, or a buyout.

"This business has become very complicated since I retired," said Paul. "I recognize the problem you both face today, and it was inevitable. Each of you has commitments and expenses . . . and reputations. You also have the resources to wreak havoc on each other and your customers. But none of this is good for business. The authorities know that managers in our corporations can run but cannot hide. The cops and prosecutors see us as easy targets and quotas and good PR, which they need. They want us to fight, to resort to violence. And, of course, when we do that, we play into their hands. Then they paint us as mobsters and sell this dirty image to the media.

"Do me a favor. Since we cannot come to a compromise, let's have a truce for four months while I think of a fair way to solve your differences."

Shadow Creek and Clem Watowski were frustrated. Paul's argument against friction was persuasive, but their egos were large.

"Why four months?" asked Watowski.

"The football season will be over," said Paul, "and Mr. D will be available to help you all deal with this numbers issue without his mind wavering. I'll need his input since you both lay off to him and he's more aware of the money that is the crux of this battle."

"Two months is all I can wait," said Shadow. "Watowski's too close to his cop buddies, and I don't trust him."

"Two months is fine with me," said Watowski. "Creek, here, has been scaring my numbers runners, and I don't know how long I can hold some of my guys off from retaliation."

"All right," said Paul as he slowly rose from his chair. "Two months. In the meantime, if there are any other disputes, I want to hear about it first before there's any bullshit. Agreed?"

Both men nodded. Watowski got up quickly and hurried out of the bar.

"Patience," Paul said to Shadow. "It'll work out."

CHAPTER 35

Mr. D was frequently looking for safe houses and apartments in which to conduct his bookmaking. Whenever he felt that he or his clerks were experiencing heat from the Vice Squad, Mr. D needed to be able to move his operation swiftly.

Dante was holding a business meeting at the counter of the Double-T Diner on Route 40 and Rolling Road in Catonsville in west Baltimore County. He was speaking with Art Weatherbee, an old high school acquaintance who now sold furniture at a retail outlet across Route 40 in a shopping center.

"Look, Art," said Mr. D, "I'll tell ya what. I'm gonna pay your rent and give you a little bonus money from time to time. You just don't be in the apartment from like around 5:30 'til 8:30 at night. But if you have to be there, I'm going to be in one room, and you will never walk into that fucking room. Is that clear?"

"I don't know, Mr. D. I read about you getting popped in Bob's apartment. Suppose it happened to me. What happens?"

"Ain't nothing going to happen to you," said Mr. D. "But if something happens, it happens to me. You didn't know. I was just your roommate. I was sharing the place with you. Believe me, nothing can happen to you. Ask Bob."

"Well, you know, I've got chicks come to see me and all that. I don't think I want to do it. It's nothing personal, Mr. D, but I don't really need help with the rent."

Mr. D sipped his coffee. He thought a bit and then said, "Let me ask you something. Where's your mother living?"

"My mother?" cried Art. "C'mon, gimme a break!"

"Where is she living?" asked Mr. D.

Art was nervous. He remembered how convincing Louis Dante was, and he didn't need any more aggravation.

"She lives over near Seven Mile Lane," said Art.

"I'll pay her rent," said Mr. D. "I'll take care of all her needs: food, clothing, shelter, the whole bit. I don't even care if she's in the pad when I'm there."

"Mr. D, my mother!" said Art trying to control his voice. "They come bustin' in, they break the door down on my mother?"

Mr. D was aware of Art's uneasiness. He picked up the check for the coffee, pulled out five dollars and handed it to the waitress. "Art, don't worry. It only happens once every five or six years."

"Once every five or six years?" cried Art. "That's great. She has a bad heart. She's had three bypass operations. Jesus!"

"Hey," laughed Mr. D, "it'll add some spice to her life, believe me. There's no such thing as busting her. There's not going to be a problem . . . and I'll cover her health insurance, too."

Mr. D waved to the waitress to keep the change. Art had his face buried in his hands.

"My God," said Art. "It's an old women's apartment house. I can't believe that you could even ask me something like this."

CHAPTER 36

Margaret looked down upon Handsome John as she lunged back and forth over him. His eyes were squeezed shut as he lurched upward trying to rhythmically match her frantic pace as she rode him to orgasm.

The phone rang and John paused his thrusting as he reached for the receiver.

"Yeah," he answered as Margaret continued to ride him.

John spoke cryptically for a few seconds and hung up. He returned to Margaret, rolling her over easily, arching high above her, and thrusting deeply within her belly. Two minutes later, he came.

"I've gotta leave. That was a sales tip I've been waiting for," said John as he pulled out of Margaret and walked towards the bathroom.

"John," said Margaret. "Do you like kids, babies?"

"Hate 'em," said John, acutely cognizant of the meaning of her remark.

CHAPTER 37

Juanita Colter was small for a 16-year-old high school junior in 1976. She also had an unusual look that she had inherited from her parents. Her biological father, whom she never knew, was Puerto Rican, and her mother was half African-American and half Cherokee Indian. A reddish hue dominated her chocolate-brown skin, and her facial features were more Spanish/Cherokee than African. Juanita had excellent posture, bony arms and legs, and beautiful, curly light-brown hair.

She and her mother lived on Poppleton Street, three blocks west of Charlie's and four miles south of Douglass High School. Juanita took the school bus every morning and was greeted while descending the bus almost daily by three very large, rough girls who were part of a gang called "The Debs."

The Debs terrorized female students and sometimes even the weaker males at Douglass. They took lunch money and articles of clothing from Juanita, as well as others, and indiscriminately slapped her around.

After two years of terror and humiliation, Juanita, a proud and defiant young girl, had had enough. One Thursday morning, refusing to give up her new white cardigan sweater, she kicked Big Arlene, the leader of The Debs, and then ran toward the principal's office. She never made it. The Debs caught her quickly and dragged Juanita out to the center of the athletic field where they beat her with heavy branches from a nearby tree for 15 minutes.

Multiple scratches and welts enveloped her body, and her face was caked with blood. Her clothes were in tatters. Dazed and embarrassed beyond belief, Juanita walked the four miles back to her neighborhood.

Mr. D was just leaving Charlie's when he drove past the sadly disheveled Juanita. He hardly recognized her from the quiet youth who came into Charlie's with her mother on occasion. Juanita did not respond to Dante's calls as he pulled his car up to her. He parked, rushed out, and brought her into his car. They drove to the nearby Bon Secours Hospital emergency ward where, for the next two hours, she was cleaned up and bandaged. Dante left and, before Juanita was released, her mother arrived.

"I'm never going back to school," she told her mother matter-of-factly. Ms. Colter tried to console Juanita and convince her to return to school or to go home. But Juanita ran away from the hospital and her mother.

A half-hour later, she walked into Charlie's and asked for Mr. D. Refusing to leave until she saw him, one of his clerks finally interrupted him.

"What do you want, young lady?" Dante asked. "Are you all right?"

"I'll be fine, Mr. D," she said. "I just want to thank you and to ask for a job. I'm never, ever going back to school, and I want to repay you for the hospital bill."

"That's not necessary," said Dante, who was impressed with Juanita's inner strength. "But I do need someone to help clean up the place. I'll pay you three dollars an hour, cash."

"That's fine. I'll start right now," insisted Juanita as she began scooping up empty cups and wrappers from the floor.

That was ten years ago. Juanita developed into a woman slowly during her late teenage years. During that time, she rose from assistant janitor to personal bookkeeper for Mr. D. By the time she was 26, she had grown into a beautiful, exotic-looking female of five feet five inches with slim, sensual features that she tried to keep hidden from the lecherous eyes of most men. Intellectually, through experience and extensive reading of business texts, Juanita was as smart as any C.P.A. in Baltimore. She was also fiercely devoted and loyal to Mr. D.

To Juanita, Mr. D was a father figure and more. She had been physically attracted to him since she turned 19, and had had her first sexual encounter with Mr. D when she was 21. Juanita tried to fight off her feelings of romantic love for Mr. D, and over the past five years, she took on several lovers in brief and extended affairs.

Mr. D was monogamous, and was only involved with Juanita between marriages and long-term relationships. But whenever Dante went through a divorce or a broken affair, he and Juanita experienced many tender moments on the top floor of her mother's home. The two got along famously except for those few times when Mr. D would harangue on Juanita's current and former lovers. Deep down, he was intensely jealous of any man who touched her.

Now, as Mr. D, seated at his desk, perused Juanita's record-keeping of his legitimate set of books, she stood over him massaging his neck and shoulders.

"Louis," she said. "You're so tense. What's wrong?"

"It's nothing," he said. "Just the craziness this time of year and . . ."

"Bullshit," she laughed. Juanita knew him as well as anyone, and he knew it.

"I dunno," Dante began. "Every time I get married, my wife always begins to change. While we date and during the first year of marriage, it's fine. But, then . . ."

Juanita wrapped her arms around Louis Dante from behind and snuggled her face into the side of his head. She loved him the most when he was in this vulnerable stage. Instinctively, she knew his current marriage was waning. It made her a little sad since she liked Margaret the most out of his numerous wives, yet she enjoyed the thought that Mr. D would soon be in her arms once again.

"Why do you think it happens?" she asked.

Mr. D swiveled around in his chair and pulled Juanita onto his lap. Stroking her left arm, he said, "I oughta write a book on marriage, ya know. At first, they always wanna listen to me, praise me, love me. After a while, it changes. They hate my lifestyle and don't wanna listen to me or sit with me and watch the games. They want to travel, start their own business, make new friends. They forget where the money comes from. They forget the risks and stresses of my life. I need them to root for me . . . Aw, what the hell. Thank God I've got you. But you'll probably leave me one day too."

"No," said Juanita. "No, Louis, I'll always be here. Always."

CHAPTER 38

The U.S. Attorney's room was dark. The blinds were drawn against the late afternoon sunlight. Agents Carey and Solomon sat together in a corner as they watched Blume steer the informant into Hopkin's office and seat him in front of the federal attorney's plush ebony desk.

The informant's head was bowed and he spoke in a whisper, answering only in single words the questions tossed at him by Blume and Hopkins.

"Why are they being so careful . . . and almost nice to that crumb?" asked Solomon.

"Look," said Carey. "This guy is not a typical informant. He's in anguish that he's gotta rat out Dante. And right now he's only telling us what we already know, . . . 'cept maybe for some details that won't really hurt anyone. Blume is very aware that if they go too fast, tick this guy off, that regardless of what we've got on him, he may back off and not give us what we want."

"Which is?" asked Solomon, frustrated at the slow pace of the informant's interrogation.

"Mr. D is much more than a bookie to the Attorney General. Mr. D is a Mafia crime lord," whispered Agent Carey.

CHAPTER 39

Shadow Creek and Jimmy Bop sat on two chaise lounges on the porch of Shadow's cousin Lolly's house in east Baltimore. Lolly lived on North Avenue by Harford Road, a rough neighborhood two miles north of the Johns Hopkins Hospital. Most of the row houses across the street were boarded up except for one that had been conspicuously broken into.

The fast and steady traffic in and out of the home across from Lolly assured that it was being used as a shooting gallery for drug addicts.

Shadow and Jimmy Bop had deduced that the gallery was for shooting cocaine as opposed to heroin. A heroin shooting gallery maintained a silent ambience all to itself reflecting the nature of narcotic addicts to "nodding out." But the semi-boarded-up house at 9311 North Avenue was too noisy and too active. The screams from the thin cocoa-brown black girl who had entered 15 minutes ago signaled further the stimulating effects of the cocaine. Unfortunately, any female risking a cocaine purchase or entrée into a coke shooting gallery usually ended up being gang-raped. It would be hours before the young girl of 17 would be able to escape—if she ever did.

"Ya know, I gotta get Lolly to move oughta here," said Shadow. "Too many drug houses. And by mistake, the narcs could break into Lolly's and find some of my shit."

"Is Lolly clean?" asked Jimmy Bop.

"Yeah," said Shadow. "You know, I don't think I can wait on this Watowski. He's too close with the cops. I think he's gonna have an accident."

Jimmy Bop got up and moved to the front ledge of the porch, trying to get a closer look at the action taking place at the boarded-up shooting gallery. He could just make out the girl, half-naked, with clothes in disarray, trying to crawl out of the house. She got about halfway onto the porch before two men pulled her back in. Then she disappeared under a tangled pile of four or five bodies.

Jimmy Bop shook his head from side to side. He reached into his waist, pulled out a small Beretta, and started down the steps.

"Don't," said Shadow. "She's probably already dead . . . And I'm not ready to see you die and me take over your business."

Jimmy Bop laughed. "Yeah," he said replacing his gun and walking back up the steps to the porch.

"By the way, Shadow," he said, "forget Watowski for a while. I gotta call from Richmond. 'The Man' said that Paul'll make you and Watowski an offer that'll make it appear as if that fat fuckin' Polack has won east Baltimore. You're to accept it."

"Fuck that!" shouted Shadow.

"I haven't finished," cautioned Bop. "In return, you'll be richly compensated, keep your turf as of last summer, and . . ."

Jimmy Bop paused, and Shadow knew he had saved the best for last.

"And . . ." Bop repeated, "in five years, all of east Baltimore, including Watowski's territory, will be yours . . . for free!"

"Do ya believe it?" asked Shadow.

Bop nodded.

"Then I tell ya what," said Shadow as he raised his six-foot-five-inch frame and grabbed a baseball bat from the corner of the porch. "I've got all this rage inside me and it can't wait five years. So let's perform a public service and get that little lady oughta that hellhole."

Together the gambling bosses ran across the street to the shooting gallery. Shadow with the bat and Jimmy Bop with his gun drawn.

CHAPTER 40

Assistant State's Attorney Will Hayden stood erect in front of the desk of the State's Attorney for Baltimore City. He was the first black elected to the post and figured to be the first elected black mayor. The clean-shaven State's Attorney with short hair, an ever-smiling face, and radiant eyes stared at Hayden.

"The U.S. Attorney pulled me over at the charity Cancer Ball last night. He's very upset with you over the Dante case. Says you're not very cooperative with his office when it come to issues concerning the Mob."

"Mob!" cried Hayden. "What Mob? Who the fuck is that blue-blood snob trying to snow? Jesus, boss . . ."

"Look, Hayden," said the State's Attorney, "I know he's a snotty prick, but the press loves him. And he says he's got evidence this time that'll bury Dante; and prove, once and for all, that he's fronting for the Mob."

Hayden tried to calm himself down. Over the years, he had worked for three other State's Attorneys and recognized the politics of their position. He liked the present State's Attorney and didn't relish a pissing contest with the U.S. prosecutor.

"Baltimore," said Hayden, "make that Maryland, is not a Mob town or state. And it's also not the most corrupt place in America, either. Maybe, around the country, some people believe it because of what happened in the seventies to Governor Mandel and Vice President Agnew, but it's not true. Number one, what we had here, and still do, are very aggressive and ambitious prosecutors. Number two, there are more rats, squealers, and informants in this area than anywhere in the world. We've got people who can't wait to rat other people out, especially people who are visible and successful. I've got a file with hundreds, maybe thousands, of letters and calls, anonymous naturally, from guys droppin' dimes on everyone and anyone. They make me sick."

"Well, Hayden," said the State's Attorney, stretching his six-foot-two-inch frame up out of his chair, "this may be true. But, don't forget, most of our winning cases come from rats. Our jobs basically depend on rats. So, sometimes it's nice to be thankful to the rats."

Coming around his desk, the State's Attorney put his arm around Hayden and guided him to the door.

"You've been around here since I was in high school, and you'll probably be here when my kid's in high school. I, too, have ambition. I just hope it's not at the expense of some little guy gone wrong. But, Dante has had a presence around here for over 20 years, and maybe it's about time that he went down. Not by us, mind you. Vice crimes are far too petty for me to commit the bulk of my resources to. And my people could care less about me busting bookies.

"But, our friend, Hopkins . . . if he wants Dante and publicizes that he's the Mob, that's his business. You'll cooperate to the degree that Hopkins doesn't vilify us in the press. Okay?"

CHAPTER 41

Dante picked up the phone on the fourth ring. It was ten to four in the morning. Margaret never could get accustomed to the late calls.

"Jesus," she muttered as Mr. D answered the call.

"It's me, Schwartzie," said the caller, who immediately hung up.

Mr. D placed the receiver back gingerly and hurried to the kitchen where he opened the refrigerator and removed a tray of ice cubes. He walked into the bathroom, grabbing his briefcase from the hallway. Quickly, he emptied the ice into the bathroom sink and turned on the cold water. When the washbasin was filled, he stuck his head into the water, face first, three times. Dante needed to be awake and alert before returning the phone call.

The caller, Schwartzie, was Dr. Eugene Poo, a Chinese-American plastic surgeon from Boca Raton, Florida. He was Mr. D's biggest gambler. Wagering anywhere from 10 to 25 thousand dollars a football game, Dr. Poo could bet as many as 26 games a weekend—college and pro.

Removing his cellular phone from the briefcase, Mr. D returned Poo's call.

"All right, Schwartzie," said Dante.

"What's the Michigan-Purdue line?" asked Poo.

"Michigan is thirteen and a half," answered Dante, wiping his face dry.

"I want Purdue for 25 dimes," ordered Poo. "What's the Grambling-Mississippi Valley State game?"

"There's no line on black college football," responded Dante, who knew that it didn't matter to Poo.

"Make one," demanded Poo.

Dante racked his mind trying to remember the previous scores of each team, the Sheridan top-ten black teams' rankings, and anything he may have read recently about each school. He also tried to read Poo's mind on who he wanted to bet.

"C'mon, my friend," said Poo. "I've got to be in surgery in an hour making a 60-year-old Jewish woman look 40 and Christian."

"Grambling is seven and a half," said Dante.

"Gimme Mississippi Valley for 10 dimes," said Poo as he hung up.

Dante, standing nude in the bathroom, relieved himself, packed away the phone, and returned to bed. Margaret had rolled over to his side and he sat on her arm, waking her up.

"Why do you do that?" asked Margaret. "Why do you have to listen to him and bet his games at this hour?"

"The guy is betting 25 grand a game!" said Mr. D loudly. "Are you kidding me? I used to be down a million to him and now I'm up a million and a half. I love it when he calls. He's fuckin' juiced up. He ain't got a prayer of beatin' me. Go back to sleep."

Margaret couldn't understand Dante's behavior. "But didn't you guys used to get high and party together? He's your friend."

Mr. D was incensed at her statement. "How in the fuck can he be my friend if he's bettin' against me? We're both trying to take from each other. What used to be, it's all history. This is now. I'm going to beat him for everything I can beat him for. I hope he calls up every night when he's high!"

CHAPTER 42
1970

Paul Douglas, one of the major numbers bookies in Baltimore, was sent to jail, and Louis, as a favor, took over his business for a year.

The bulk of Paul's business was the numbers game, but he recognized that sports betting would dominate the future. Before Paul was sentenced, he taught Louis Dante all he knew about being a B.M. (bookmaker). Then he took him to Las Vegas where Paul introduced him to the man who made the line and showed him how it was arrived at.

Paul and Louis Dante were standing in a small betting shop in Las Vegas called Churchill Downs.

"What happens," said Paul, "is that there are guys in here who set the line. The day before the line is to officially come out, they arrive at a 'number' or 'spread' on a game. Say, for example, the New York Giants are playing Detroit in New York. These guys decide on a spread of 10. (If one wanted to bet the Giants, one had to 'lay' or give away 10 points. If one wanted to bet Detroit, one had to take 10 points. The Giants would have to score more than 10 points over an opponent for a Giant bettor to win.)

"The guys who set the line go to people who are known as sharp bettors to find out who they'll bet. In this case, you can't ask for their opinions 'cause opinions are like asshole—everybody has one. But when you're putting money up, then it's a different story. You can only test what is really going on when money is on the line; and it has to be a lot of money. So the Vegas guys call up three or four sharp bettors from around the country and tell them they can bet the game immediately before the official line comes out. They have to bet it for five or ten thousand dollars. Let's say you call up two of these sharpies and they both lay the ten points for five thousand each. Then you think maybe you should make the line higher. So you make the line twelve, and now the Giants are favored by twelve points, and you call up two other sharp guys, and they go the other way—instead of laying the points, they take twelve points. And, so, you determine that the line should be eleven. If everyone was taking more points, you might go back and keep increasing it until you found people betting the other way. The same thing is done with 'over and under' bets. You're not just calling up these sharpies for one game. You're putting all the games up at a high enough figure of money to keep it honest."

"Am I going to meet these guys, Paul?" asked Louis Dante.

"Yeah, Louis," said Paul. "But, remember to listen, be quiet, and show respect. You'll need them, and they'll need you."

Paul eventually downsized his numbers business and paid more attention to sports gambling, which exploded in the sixties and seventies. However, when Paul went to jail and Mr. D took over his business, there were five major numbers backers in Maryland. They were laying off their bets to another guy who was sent to jail, and they asked Mr. D if he was interested in backing the business. Although Mr. D could not use the money from Paul's business and had just a few thousand dollars that he and Marvin had saved together over the years, he boasted to the five numbers backers that he could do it and had the bankroll. They agreed, but warned him that he had better be straight with them.

At that time, Mr. D's hair was halfway down his back and he was referred to as "Long Hair."

As luck would have it, no one hit a number big for years. Of course, Mr. D sweat it every day until he had a big enough bankroll, eventually realizing millions of dollars over the course of the next decade. Had Mr. D taken one hit, he would have had to leave the country or the other backers would surely have killed him.

CHAPTER 43
October 1986

Mr. D pulled off of South Fremont Avenue towards McHenry Street in South Baltimore. Vacant homes outnumbered occupied houses up and down the two blocks of inner-city row homes. The marble steps, synonymous with the Baltimore City landscape, differed in color from the original white to gray or black—the effects of years of neglect by slum landlords since the sixties.

Yet there was still a sense of pride by the few city dwellers who owned their homes on McHenry Street. Between the marble steps and curb, at the far end of the pavement, sat car tires painted white with petunias growing out of the center in buckets.

For such an innocuous setting, the foot and car traffic on McHenry Street bustled with activity. To some it would signal an area of illicit drug wheeling and dealing. But in enforcement and gambling circles, this two-block area was known as "Numbers Writers or Runners Street."

Numbers betting begins at a very early hour each day, and each writer reports his bets on selected three-digit numbers. The numbers writer obtains individual bets from his betting customers who make their typical twenty-five-cent to one-dollar wager on any one of a number of three-digit combinations from 000 to 999. His work is usually completed sometime before two o'clock p.m. The writer turns in or telephones his bets to the individual known as a "runner." The runner receives bets from a number of writers, and then turns in all the bets either personally or telephonically to an "office." The phone clerk in the office, upon totaling all of his work, then determines what, if any, numbers bets are to be laid off. This lay-off is done by telephone and is usually completed no later than four o'clock p.m. each day prior to the sixth race, at a designated racetrack, the results of which are the beginning of the compilation of the number for the day. Final paperwork is hand-carried from the office location to a final location known as the "bank" by a runner. Another individual, who represents the financial backer, will periodically contact the writers and make cash collections or payoffs. Lay-off is settled on a weekly basis.

Numbers writers, lay-off men, and backers maintain records of wagers and hits placed, telephone number lists, and other gambling records and paraphernalia secreted on their persons and/or at some location of their residence or place of operation. These records must be maintained in order to compute the total amounts wagered on various numbers, and to correctly determine the lay-off and identify the individuals sustaining hits on specific numbers wagers. These records must reflect the daily and the weekly volume of the various numbers wagers in order to adequately supervise the operations. The lay-off man must maintain records of the numbers laid off, telephone numbers, and/or locations of central numbers offices from which lay-off is accepted, as well as weekly totals of what is owed for the purpose of settling up. In addition, the principal figures in a lay-off operation will maintain tallies for the purpose of determining the amount payable to an individual backer who has laid off a heavily-wagered winning number.

With the inception of the legal lottery in Maryland, two new approaches were developed. First, many illegal organizations use the winning Maryland State lottery numbers as their own along with the racetrack pari-mutuel number. This allows for writers accepting the state number up until seven o'clock p.m. while also doing away with arguments over the old method of determining the pari-mutuel numbers at the track. Second, the illegal numbers operators can lay-off to the state game, thereby keeping them from depending on other illicit organizations while maintaining more secrecy.

A numbers writer may roam the streets, operate from his home, or operate in a bar, restaurant, poolroom or barbershop as a customer or employee. Or the writer may work in a factory or business and collect from other workers.

Some of Mr. D's people who wrote numbers had been busted, and a few complained to Main Man that they wanted to quit because they couldn't take the stress of the job. Once this was relayed to Mr. D, he decided to drive over to meet with the spokesman of the disenchanted clique. Dante considered it essential that his field of players be motivated and mollified.

"I just can't take the pressure anymore, Mr. D," said Runner, a nickname for Caswell Oppenheim. "The stress, it gives me chest pains."

Oppenheim was thirty-five years old, but looked sixty. He had been bald since his early twenties, and his stooped-shouldered, frail appearance could gain him access to any nursing home in Maryland. Yet Runner moved as quickly as any track star, which he was in high school, still holding the state record for the fastest 440-yard dash time.

"What stress? What pressure?" asked Mr. D. "I got ya outta jail quick, didn't I? You worried about your police record? I don't think it'll hurt your chances of joining the CIA."

"It's just gettin' to me, Mr. D," pleaded Runner, who sat nervously on the steps of a vacant home.

Mr. D actually loved these situations. He loved to motivate people. "Look at those two guys mismanaging the World Series. They're pathetic. And you know why? They can't handle the pressure. That's the bottom line—pressure! You know what pressure is? Money! All that money is on the line and they choke. Look at Johnson. Look at McNamara. Look at the blunders they made. I should be managing the game. I've been under pressure all my life. I mean, what I lose in a single night, they don't make in a year!

"I was under pressure like that when I was a teenager. You remember the money I was betting. These guys don't know pressure. If I'm managing the World Series, and I'm managing the Mets, you'd never say we lost because we got out-managed. Here . . ."

Mr. D handed Runner some money. "Buy yourself some clothes. Go to the track. Bet some long shots. It'll help ya deal with the pressure."

Unbeknownst to him, Mr. D was being watched from the corner of McHenry and Freemont by Tongue and Baker, and two blocks west with high-powered binoculars by Agents Carey and Solomon.

CHAPTER 44
1971

When the bookmaker, Paul Douglas, was released from prison, Louis Dante handed him $500,000 in cash. As a result, Louis became a full partner and took over the daily operations for Paul's numbers and sports betting business in Maryland. Later that year, Louis bought Charlie's, a package goods and check cashing store.

Louis also renewed his friendship with Bruce Hawk, an old neighborhood pal, and gave him a job at Charlie's. During the fifties and sixties, Bruce Hawk had established himself as one of the zanier and more risk-taking of the Pimlico neighborhood guys, rivaling Louis and Marvin, and surpassing them in terms of the trouble he got into in such a short period of time. Hawk excelled in some very dangerous practices, mostly involving criminal and drug-taking activity.

Tall, with a ruddy complexion, Hawk was an excellent natural athlete. He spoke in a harsh voice and always seemed to be screaming. Recently released from prison, Hawk needed a legitimate job as part of his parole, and Louis put him to work in the store. After three months, Hawk left town. Although this was in violation of his parole, nothing ever happened to him.

CHAPTER 45
October 1986

Silhouetted in the window of the eleventh floor of II Charles Center Condominiums, three blocks north of the Federal Office Building, was a man at his desk, bent over motionlessly.

U.S. Attorney General for Maryland, Hopkins, was preparing a press release and/or a speech in anticipation of his pending grand jury indictment of Mr. D. Rather than wait until the last minute, days, perhaps weeks, from now, Hopkins wanted this to be the springboard for a run at U.S. Senator or Governor; and then . . .

The right words, phrases, and references were essential. He gathered affidavits, internal reports, case histories, and monographs from federal, state, and local enforcement authorities concerning gambling. Picking out words, sentences, and paragraphs, he highlighted with a yellow marker the watchwords and catchphrases that would gain the public's attention.

Finally, his eyes and mind settled on an affidavit filed by the city's experienced Vice Squad and the State's Attorney's Office. It referred to Dante's gambling empire as a pyramid with the bettor as the base and Dante sitting at the top, isolated and secure. With some subtle changes, Hopkins could change it into an organizational chart similar to those of the Mafia crime families in New York.

Then he noticed another statement that could grab the masses: "Although participated in by some middle- and lower-class bettors who basically wager on numbers and horse racing, sports wagering.caters primarily to the affluent. Betting on football, basketball, baseball, and hockey is the king of bookmaking from a gross dollar volume standpoint."

CHAPTER 46

Mr. D, Main Man, and the trainee, Lanny, were back at the betting apartment in the Rosedale town house. Dante was on the phone while Main Man was going over more procedures with Lanny.

"Be cautious," he said. "Always assume you're being followed. If they want you, though, there's not much you can do. But make it difficult! All right, let's go over a couple of things. You know where to call for the line?"

Lanny nodded and said, "I call this number in Nevada and say 'Good afternoon, this is 67,' and the guy gives me the line."

Mr. D hung up the phone and jumped into Lanny's training. "What about betting limits? Let's say Mr. G calls and wants to bet ten dimes on Buffalo minus two . . ."

"I tell 'em . . ." Lanny began.

"Hold it, I'm not finished," interrupted Mr. D. "So you know his limit is ten dimes per game, but he wants to press the bet for another ten dimes. What do ya do?"

"Tell 'em no," said a confident Lanny.

"Wrong, putz!" yelled Mr. D. "You tell Mr. G he can press the bet if he takes the line up to two and a half points. You see Mr. G is worth about a quarter of a million bucks. And if he's betting twenty dimes for ten games and loses, well, we're gonna have problems with him later. So him giving up more points'll make him more cautious. Understand?"

Lanny was becoming frustrated. "But how am I supposed to know that?"

"You do now," said Mr. D.

CHAPTER 47
1972

Wheelchair bound, Marvin was vacationing at the Fountainbleau in Miami Beach when he ran into Louis Dante.

Over dinner, Louis confessed that he had temporarily shut his business down because things had become heaty. He was considering going into the drug business and had a meeting scheduled the next afternoon with some young kid from Baltimore who had a plane-load of marijuana coming in from Bolivia. Marvin tried to enlighten Louis to the public and enforcement's attitude towards drug dealing as opposed to gambling, but to no avail.

Marvin called Bruce Hawk that evening when he heard that Hawk was working at the Diplomat in Hollywood, Florida parking cars. *"Hawk, I need you to explain to Louis about how much danger is involved in drug trafficking."*

Hawk promised to join Louis and Marvin at the racetrack the next day.

When they couldn't change Louis's mind at the racetrack, Hawk told him that he would go along and test the marijuana to see that Louis wasn't being taken advantage of in the deal. *"No matter how good it is,"* Hawk assured Marvin, *"I'll vilify it."*

Marvin left the track separately in a van driven by his nurse.

The young dealer met Louis Dante and Hawk on the track's parking lot after the races, and they drove back toward Miami Beach while Hawk sampled the grass. Its potency was devastating, but Hawk knocked it.

"You call this good shit?" yelled Hawk. *"I've gotten higher smoking toilet paper! Stop the car! We're throwing this pseudo-dealer out now."*

Louis was pissed off. He didn't know what "pseudo" meant. He slammed on the brakes, stopping the car, and pushed the shocked youth out on the 79th Street Causeway.

"Thanks, Hawk," said Louis apologetically. *"I almost made a big mistake."*

After they pulled up to the Fountainbleau, Hawk told Louis to go ahead inside. *"I need to borrow your car for a few minutes."*

Louis split, and 40 minutes later, Hawk was still in the front seat, catatonic. The marijuana's effects were so strong he couldn't move for two hours.

That night over dinner, before Hawk went back to Hollywood, he pulled out and shuffled what looked like a deck of cards in front of Marvin and Louis. It was actually numerous credit cards that he had "found" in the glove compartments of the cars he parked.

"Can you believe how fucking dumb people are? Hiding these in their glove compartments?" Hawk lectured. *"Let me buy you guys something. A suit, television set, dinner. Take some cards home, please!"*

CHAPTER 48
October 1986

"It ain't gonna be that easy to rip him off. He's always on the move or surrounded by people. But we got no choice, Baker. We gotta hit him soon for the bread," said Tongue.

The Quaalude dealers were riding Baker's Harley-Davidson Flathead motorcycle on Interstate 83 towards York, Pennsylvania. Tongue was sitting directly behind Baker, holding on to the back of his belt.

Although the ride was bumpy since the old Harley frame was rigid, neither biker complained. It was macho, and the alternative was sacrilegious—a more flexible Japanese-made cycle. To the outlaw motorcycle breed, the "rice burners" had no character.

"Yeah. Time's right," shouted Baker over the sounds of the road. "But it's gotta be the right moment. Patience, my man, patience."

"Yeah," said Tongue, "we'll tail 'em a couple more days, and try and get to him when he's carrying either his payouts or collecting from his high rollers."

Tongue and Baker had hoped to discover Dante coming or going from a "stash" where he may have hidden millions over the years. However, after more than a week of close surveillance, they were still unsuccessful.

CHAPTER 49

Recovering compulsive gambler, Benny, Mr. D's former customer, had arranged for "nephew" Dickie to receive outpatient treatment at the Nyman Manor Psychiatric Hospital in Carroll County, 20 miles from Baltimore City.

After two sessions, the counselor for Dickie, Miss Joanna, had arranged to have the staff psychiatrist, Dr. Politzer, meet with her, Dickie, Mr. D, and Dickie's mother, Estelle. Everyone agreed that Dickie was progressing in his treatment. However, an argument had arisen concerning restitution.

"I'm not going to break Dickie's legs," said Mr. D, "and I'm not going to hassle him a great deal. You know, he *is* family. I can deal with the losses. The money ain't the point. But the guy owes me 25 grand. I want $250 a month for ten years, and he can miss a month or two and it ain't gonna kill me. It's the principle with a P-L-E on the end, okay? Not the principal, with a P-A-L! He wants to pay me $50 a month, and that's what this counselor here is telling me. That's all he can afford. I know he's making more, and she says that it violates his confidentiality if I know what his actual salary is. Well, Christ, he's telling her anything, and she can't violate his confidentiality! I know just what he makes. He was pulling games on me. This ain't money he lost to me. He stole this money from me!"

Sheldon Politzer was a 42-year-old, conservatively dressed psychiatrist originally from New York. After medical school, he had worked at the Veteran's Administration in Washington D.C. where most of the early research and recognition of pathological gambling was developed. The doctor completed his residency at the Brooklyn Veteran's Administration outpatient hospital, and, later, spent six months in Breaksville, Ohio at the first inpatient facility for compulsive gambling in the world.

"Aren't you ashamed of being a bookie, a criminal, Mr. D, preying on weak, defenseless, sick people?" asked Dr. Politzer.

"Hey, Doc, cut me a break, will ya?" answered Mr. D. "There are more doctors in jail than bookies."

CHAPTER 50
Acapulco, Mexico
1973

Once again single and amply providing for his ex-wife and daughter, Louis Dante became a creature of the drug culture of the seventies era.

Hawk returned to Baltimore and became Mr. D's chief lieutenant, and they began a lifestyle of mind-boggling proportions. Although Dante liked drugs and marveled at the profits, he was strictly into purchasing and using for himself and his friends. Distribution was much too dangerous. The gambling business provided enough income and stress.

One morning, Dante, Hawk, and two devious characters they had partied with named Half and Brute put on Panama hats, grabbed an ounce of cocaine, got into a limo, and rode to the recently renamed BWI Airport for a flight to Mexico. Paul, in semi-retirement, was left to run the gambling operation. The guys were dressed outlandishly and looked somewhat heaty. They flew into Dallas and continued on to Mexico City where the four of them were the only people on the plane. They danced and sang in the aisles, flirting with the stewardesses, as they journeyed to Acapulco.

Once in Acapulco, they checked into the Hilton in the center of the city where they rented the two top suites. They partied constantly, spending money like water, picking up every beautiful woman available, and soon acquired a huge entourage. Dante was buying dinners for 15 to 30 people every evening. The bar tabs were as much as $1,500 a night.

The third day there, their tour guide told them that he could get them some inexpensive "Acapulco Gold" marijuana.

"Get us $300 worth," said Dante. That proved to be a pound. It was just for the guys, and they used it liberally, taking the guide along to party. The next night, they threw a huge party in their suites.

At about eight in the morning, as the party was ending, Dante took a beautiful sixteen-year-old budding actress out onto the beach to wait for a boat that was going to chauffeur the group to a nearby island. After waiting for the guys on the beach for three hours,

Dante suspected trouble and returned to the hotel just in time to find forty Federales in the room. Hawk, Brute, and Half were being led away in handcuffs.

Dante rushed in and demanded to know what was going on. The Federale chief said that they had been caught with marijuana and were being arrested and taken to the courthouse. Dante led the chief out to the veranda and offered him a bribe of $5,000, but the chief told him it was too late, although he contemplated it for quite a while. When Dante saw that he could get no further, he packed up everything, including cameras and stereos, and strolled to the courthouse with his friends.

At the courthouse, they were all ordered to go directly to jail. Dante tried to bribe some other officials, but failed. He was marvelous, though. Ranting and raving, Mr. D shouted that he was the nephew of Joe Columbo, the Mafia boss. (He wasn't.) "If you faggots don't watch it, a lot of people will die in Acapulco; and all over Mexico!"

He was acting like a wild man, while actually being very calculated. Later, even Dante couldn't believe what he was doing. But he was on such a roll he couldn't stop.

The group was taken to the Carsell Municipale which was the Acapulco jail. It was a prison constructed of brick where 300 of the worst criminals dwelt. There were only four toilets which were located in the center of the yard and emptied into the ground. It was very filthy. For food, they got slop in the morning and slop in the evening.

After entering the warden's office with the guys, Dante continued to carry on in such an intimidating manner at being the nephew of Joseph Columbo that the warden allowed him to keep his camera and personal belongings. Incredulously, Dante supervised the guards who locked away everyone's suitcases. Hawk, Half, and Brute were beside themselves and near tears. They thought they wouldn't get out of prison for years. Dante believed otherwise.

As they entered the prison yard, they shockingly ran into a Baltimorean they knew named Mat. Mat had shot a Federale in the shoulder during an escape attempt after being caught trafficking marijuana. He had been sentenced to eight years in jail. Mat explained to the guys, sadly, that they probably wouldn't even get a hearing for about six months. Dante told Mat he didn't have the time to wait. "I have to take my daughter to Disneyland next week. You watch, we'll be out by then."

While Mat was explaining that it would take at least three or four days to get an audience with the warden, two weeks to actually see a lawyer or public defender, and another six months for a hearing, Hawk and Brute began to cry, and Half hyperventilated and passed out.

Dante walked up to a guard and demanded to see the warden in such a threatening way that he got an audience within two hours. He strolled into the warden's office and told him, "Look, Warden, this is yours, this Franklin, a C-note, a hundred dollar bill! Every time I want to come up here to see you, I want to see you right away; and you get a Franklin every time. I want to use your phone, and I want to use the bathroom now because I'm not going down to use that filthy fucking hole in the ground. And I also want to take a bath!"

Dante added, "If you help get me out of here, I'm going to take care of you. And I want you to see that my boys also have no problems."

Dante was on such a high, as Columbo's nephew, that he was having a ball. The warden laughed at Dante as he pocketed the C-note. Dante phoned Paul in Baltimore. He told him briefly what had happened, and asked Paul to get in touch with a girl named Pam who Dante used to date and who was now residing in Canada. Pam used to live in Mexico City and had connections with the Mexican Mob. Dante finally left the warden's office after telling him that he must return the call the next day.

Mat from Hampden, a working-class area of Baltimore, had usurped control of a lot of the prison population. Since Dante was carrying his money with him, they were able to purchase certain cement slabs to sleep upon—and certain Mexican hoodlums to guard and protect them if they happened to fall asleep.

Dante was probably the only guy in the history of the world who had a camera and was taking pictures inside of a foreign federal prison when no one else was allowed even a notebook. He was even calling guards out from their towers so that he could snap pictures of them posing with all of the guys. Hawk and Brute just continued to weep.

The next day, Dante laid another C-note on the warden. He called Paul who advised him that things were in the works. "Pam is in Mexico City, and we're going to try and get you out. It will cost anywhere from $25,000 to $50,000."

Dante instructed Paul that only he should bring the money down and make the deal. He didn't want anybody pulling a scam on him.

The third day, Dante called Paul and was told that the deal was completed. "Tomorrow morning, somebody will be there to pick you guys up and take you to Mexico City."

Elated, Dante told the warden that they would be leaving soon, but the warden didn't believe him and laughed.

Dante went back down to the guys who were still crying and told them not to worry. He then snapped a picture of Hawk relieving himself on one of the cement slabs in the middle of the prison compound.

The next morning, Dante was called upstairs, and the warden, wide-eyed, said they were being picked up within two hours to be taken to Mexico City. Dante gave the warden extra money to get food for everybody and to bring Mat and some of the guys he had befriended up for a huge going-away party. Dante went into the other room in the warden's office, took out his stereo, and, as the guys walked in, he got on top of the warden's desk and began to sing and dance. The guys couldn't believe their ears when they heard that they were leaving for Mexico City.

Two hours later, a huge limo pulled up, and Dante, Hawk, Half, and Brute were escorted, with their baggage, into the car to be driven to Mexico City. Upon their arrival, they had to spend the night in the Mexico City jail where all four were put in one cell. The following day, they were swiftly ushered out, put on a plane, and told never to return to Mexico.

Before Dante left the Acapulco jail, he told Mat that he would come back for him as soon as possible since Mat was such a stand-up guy. Although Mat knew he had eight years to serve and didn't want to believe it, he appreciated the thought.

CHAPTER 51
October 1986

Agents Carey and Solomon were once again inside Mr. D's betting apartment in Rosedale photographing information and testing the audio bugs.

"It's amazing that from a community of degenerates and lowlifes, how this sports betting is almost always done on credit," said Solomon.

"It's also the reason why so many bookies and numbers backers go out of business," said Carey.

Suddenly they heard someone at the door. Solomon looked out of the window hoping to recognize the car of the bookmaker or one of the clerks before he and Carey took cover behind the sofa.

"Whoever he is," whispered Carey, "he doesn't have a key. Someone's trying to pick the lock."

The door opened slowly and then closed quietly. The shadowy figure crossed the room.

"Carey . . . Solomon?" the figure called out.

"Jesus, you scared us," said Carey, standing up. The intruder was Blume from the Attorney General's Office.

"Clean everything up. Leave no trace that we've ever been here," ordered Blume.

"What's up?" asked Solomon.

"Our informant is ready to play. We squeezed him a little tighter, and he's agreed to go along," boasted Blume as he accidentally kicked over a chair in the dark room.

CHAPTER 52

Mr. D became totally disgusted while watching the World Series with Margaret.

"I can't fucking believe it," he said, his voice rising. "First and second, no outs, and he don't have 'em bunt. And now I'm outta the fuckin' inning!"

"Don't scream so loud, hon," said Margaret.

Mr. D ignored her. "What could he have been thinking of, for Christ's sake? The choke. And he's sitting there chewing on them peanuts?" Dante lost his temper. He threw a glass of Pepsi towards the trashcan, missing and shattering it against the wall.

"My God, Louis, it's just one game. You're scaring me." Margaret stood up from the sofa, glaring at Dante.

"One game?" he said. "It's a half-a-million-dollar swing if I lose, and you say just one game. Sit down and root for me." Dante reached up to pull her down.

Margaret was livid. "I'm going to bed," she said as she rushed out of the room.

"Fine," said Mr. D sarcastically, "great idea. I'll go too. This game don't mean anything, you selfish bitch!"

CHAPTER 53
Acapulco
1973

Dante took his daughter to Disneyland the next week, and then called Paul to tell him he was going back to Acapulco with Hawk to get Mat out of jail.

Dante arrived in Mexico City first, and found out from the local mobsters that they could get Mat out for $50,000. Dante considered the price too high, but, realizing that it could be worked out, returned to Acapulco. He spent two weeks meeting different people until he located the right connection to get it done for "only" $25,000. Dante met a guy whose father was the publisher of a Mexico City newspaper, and they arranged a deal to release Mat Maultsby.

Dante walked into the prison in Acapulco wearing a white suit and a Panama hat and carrying a briefcase. The warden almost passed out upon seeing him.

Dante told him, "I hope you've taken care of everybody. It's a good thing we got out, too, or there would have been a lot of dead people, including you!"

The warden swore that he had been nice to Mat and did all he could to get Dante out, before adding that whatever arrangements Dante wanted to make were fine with him. However, he advised Mr. D that he had no authority to release Mat.

Dante partied like crazy with Hawk for the next week and a half. He returned to Baltimore after that to run his business since Paul was going out of town. By phone, Dante set everything up and saw to it that Hawk assisted in Mat's release from prison.

When Mat returned to Baltimore, he ran over to Dante's house and kissed his ring like he was the Pope or the Don of all Mafia people. Soon after, Mat went to work for Louis Dante.

CHAPTER 54
October, 1986

Mr. D and his partner and mentor, Paul, sat at a small, round table in the outdoor cafe of Jean Claude's Restaurant in the Light Street Pavilion side of Baltimore's Harbor Place. Occasionally glancing up at the strollers on the boardwalk and the original American battleship "Constellation," Mr. D was in an upbeat, chatty mood.

"But, you know what, Paul? God was looking down on me. That's all I can tell ya. God takes care of who he wants to take care of; and he took care of me. It was a swing of a half a million bucks. That's a big loss. A lot of guys don't make that in a lifetime."

"I only saw part of the game," said Paul. "How'd we do Saturday?"

Mr. D was smiling and animated. "We're up about 30 dimes going into the game last night. Notre Dame's winning 33-0 and it's the last quarter. They're a 22-point favorite and everybody's bet on 'em. So Navy gets two TDs in the last quarter. I mean, hey, you can't beat me."

Paul nodded and looked around at the lunchtime crowd as Dante continued.

"Oh, I even took action on the Breeder's Cup. Paul, you know, very rarely do I do that—book horse racing. For two days, I hyped it with the guys, and everybody wanted to bet it, and they lost. I was a little worried, though. The Chink from D.C. puts ten grand on a horse to 'show' that was 2-5, and the horse runs out of the money. Do ya love it? And there was that guy, Wallman. He bets five and five on a horse that pays $73, but it's an early race. What happens after that is he begins to believe that he's a big handicapper and starts betting $1,000 a race, and he ends up losing money. It's tough to beat me, Paul, but I wanna win all the time. That's the problem."

"How you doing with Maggie?" asked Paul, changing the subject.

"What am I gonna do about my wife? She wants to be the best that she can be. What the fuck's that? Now she wants a career if I'm not going to be around to spend time with her, or to have a baby.

"Hey, she needs $300 a day to survive, she tells me. Don't know what she spends it on 'cause she bangs the credit cards for a fortune. What am I supposed to do, huh? When I come home, don't you think I deserve some companionship? If she don't like it, she can always roll. But, if she's going to be there, she better come up with more attention. I respect careers. Careers are a lot of fun, but I'm paying for everything. I want her there."

It was a lovely, fall day and Paul was feeling philosophical. "How many times you been married, Louis? Three, four, five times?"

"I dunno, Paul. Legally, I only been married four, I think."

"You've only been married once, Louis. To the action! That's how it is with guys like us. We're different."

CHAPTER 55
1950s

When Paul moved north to Baltimore, his brother, Benson, moved to Virginia Beach where he became involved in the construction business and earned a good deal of money. Through betting, writing numbers, and doing odd jobs for some of the major numbers backers and gambling interests in Baltimore, Paul eventually began his own numbers business as a backer, although his bankroll was sorely limited. Anytime too much money was bet on a sporting event or a number, Paul called Benson in Virginia Beach to see if he would cover him in case he took a big hit.

One day a guy was referred to Paul from a friend who worked at a downtown bar. The referral was an accountant for a major steel corporation in the shipyards, and Paul's friend had fixed the guy up with women. The accountant told Paul that he had to be extremely discreet because he had a very important job at the shipyard, but that he was also very interested in betting sporting events.

The accountant started to bet small at first, but as with many bettors who bet with emotion instead of smarts, he began to lose a lot of money and subsequently exhausted his personal income. Like many dumb bettors, he doubled up on his bets and continued to lose. Although Paul would have cut any other bettor off, he knew that this guy could tap into the resources of his company since he had hinted as much over drinks several months before. Figuring that because of the accountant's fear of exposure, Paul could eventually get whatever money was owed him, he let the account grow more and more on credit. The accountant began to embezzle money from the business, and, over the course of the next few years, he embezzled over one and a half million dollars betting with Paul. During this period of time, Paul went into a partnership with Al Blair, a club owner from Baltimore's Block, the city's adult entertainment district. The club became the headquarters for Paul's numbers and bookmaking business.

The steel company found out about the accountant and the missing money, and he was subsequently indicted. In a plea for leniency, the accountant informed on Paul and Al, and they, too, were indicted. Although they denied any wrongdoing, Paul and Al were convicted and sent to jail for two years. The money was never recovered. The accountant was given a smaller sentence and was fired from his job.

Almost overnight, Paul achieved the reputation of one of the biggest sports gamblers in Maryland due to the trial's notoriety, which convinced bettors that Paul had the resources to pay off all bets. During Paul's incarceration, his brother moved up from Virginia Beach to run Paul's business. The money Paul had accumulated from the accountant was laundered through his brother's construction firm, and tripled in worth.

CHAPTER 56
October 1986

Tongue and Baker had done their homework well—almost perfectly. They knew that on this specific night, Mr. D would get home later than usual since he had a regular "meet" with a long-time client right after he closed the office in Rosedale.

The dope dealers were counting on surprise, darkness, and dirt bikes, as well as Margaret taking Lilly, the German shepherd, in the house for dinner. What they overlooked was a safety habit that Dante had practiced for years.

After Mr. D had parked his four-month-old Audi with darkly tinted windows, cut off the lights, and grabbed his two briefcases, one full of money and the other containing two cellular telephones, he slid across the front seat to exit from the passenger side of the car. Unaware of Dante's late-night car-exiting practice, Tongue and Baker were surprised. They had both been hiding in the hedges in front of the trees on the passenger side of the driveway wearing ski masks. Once the car had stopped, they scurried to the front passenger side of the car where they kneeled, waiting for Dante.

Figuring to go around to the driver's side when Dante got out to lock the car door, Tongue was set to knock him unconscious from behind as Baker arrived from the other direction and scooped up the briefcase. However, as Mr. D exited the passenger side, the door pushed Tongue forward and tipped Baker's left shoulder, causing him to temporarily lose his balance. As Baker slipped back, his hand, holding a .38-caliber Smith and Wesson revolver, hit the blacktop and the gun discharged. Recognizing an impending ambush, Dante pulled the door shut as the two gunmen struggled quickly to recover.

Hearing the gunshot from inside the house, Lilly ran to the living room window, barking and growling, and Margaret hit the burglar alarm panic button.

"What are ya doin'?" Baker yelled, as Tongue tried to open the car door that Dante had locked.

"Stand back," Baker ordered, as he fired his gun through the car window. The glass shattered, and Dante fell backwards, his head resting between the steering wheel and driver's side door. Tongue reached in and grabbed at the briefcase just as Lilly leaped through the living room window and became entangled in the screen.

"C'mon, it's the fuckin' dog!" screamed Baker. Tongue picked up the closest briefcase, and the two masked men ran to the woods. Within seconds, they reached their dirt bikes which they had left leaning against the trees. They were a quarter of a mile down the road when Lilly ran into the woods.

Margaret cautiously came out of the house. She tried to open the Audi from the driver's side and found it locked. Suddenly, Dante's head appeared and she screamed. He had been grazed in the forehead and blood covered his face. He opened the door.

"Turn off the alarm and tell the police it went off by accident," said Dante, calmly, unable to hear the police sirens in the background.

"Louis, are you okay? I'll call an ambulance," cried Margaret.

"No! Don't call anyone . . . Where's Lilly? . . . I . . ." A wave of nausea came over him and he threw up on the blacktop. As he wiped his mouth with the sleeve of his yellow linen shirt, he noticed the blood cascading from his forehead. Dizziness hit and he blacked out.

CHAPTER 57

Mr. D's feet dangled over the emergency room gurney as the attending physician, Dr. William Deming, spoke to him. "Mr. Dante, you've been very lucky. The bullet grazed your forehead, only penetrating about an eighth of an inch. It caused a lot of bleeding, but no internal damage. With some minor cosmetic surgery, we'll be able to repair the dent in your head."

"Dent?" asked Dante, meekly. He still felt nauseous.

"The wound took 33 stitches, and I gave you a tetanus shot," said the doctor, matter-of-factly. He had worked emergency for two years and was all too familiar with gunshot wounds. "Your wife is outside, and so is a policeman named Copley and another man. Who do you want to see first?"

"Leave me a scalpel and send in Copley," said Mr. D in jest. The doctor looked puzzled.

As soon as Dr. Deming finished adjusting Mr. D's bandages over his left eye and forehead, he left. Copley strolled in with a scaggy-looking undercover DEA narc. Pulling up a chair, Copley produced a notepad and belched loudly.

"You're a class act, Copley," said Mr. D.

"Jeez, I'm sorry you got shot, asshole. You know I'd be sick if somebody other than me killed you," retorted Copley, smiling widely and glancing at the narc.

Copley wore his year-round, wool sports coat over khaki pants. He was sweating profusely, but didn't seem to mind. Copley worked the Vice Squad for Baltimore County. Unlike Baltimore City, which spun off narcotics from Vice in the late sixties, the County still included it along with prostitution and gambling.

The narc, Zach Strimer, was wearing a frayed brown sweater that hung shapelessly over his jeans. He had a short, uneven beard, and unkempt black hair with bangs almost touching his oversized sunglasses.

"Who did it, scumbag?" asked Copley.

"Don't know," replied Dante quietly.

"You're a liar."

"Kiss my ass."

"You're lucky you're in here, fuckface, or I'd fuck you up real bad," threatened Copley.

"You're a real tough guy in a hospital ward, Detective Copley!" screamed Dante.

Margaret came rushing in. "What's wrong?" she cried as she hugged Dante and stared at the two cops.

"It's okay, baby. Go back outside. I'll be finished in a minute," said Dante.

Margaret slowly walked out of the curtain-enclosed emergency room cubicle, and Copley continued.

"We think we know who tried to kill ya, Dante."

"Nobody tried to kill me. It was a botched robbery attempt."

"Sure, big shot," said Copley.

"Anything else, fat boy?" asked Dante. The nausea and pain were gone, replaced by anger and frustration at Copley and the robbers.

The narc stood impassively, listening to the verbal sparring.

"Do ya know two dope dealers named Tongue Deacon and Len Baker?" asked Copley.

Dante shook his head horizontally and mouthed the word "no." Inside, he froze up. They were a scary twosome, and Dante's immediate mental calculation was that it most definitely was them. They wanted his money, and since he wouldn't loan it to them, they were planning on taking it. Fortunately for Dante, Tongue and Baker, in their haste, had taken the briefcase with the cellular phones. Mr. D still had the money.

"They want you dead, my man," said Copley. "Better be real careful."

The narc opened the curtain and left without so much as a mutter. Copley followed him out. The two passed Margaret and walked through the emergency room doors to the street. It was chilly, and the narc hugged himself as Copley lit a cigarette.

"What do ya think?" asked Copley.

"They did it, and Dante knows," said the narc, Strimer, almost in a whisper. "I'll hunt Tongue and Baker down and tell 'em that Dante's put out a contract on them. That way, either the dopers'll kill Dante or he'll kill them."

CHAPTER 58
New York, 1974

Dante and Hawk left Ocean City, Maryland to drive to New York. For Hawk it was strictly a business deal—drugs. For Dante it was fun. He had become enamored with cocaine and had been promised by Hawk that he would be able to score anywhere from a half ounce to an ounce of 80-percent-pure cocaine. Dante was like many "fast-laners" of the seventies, the "connected" or celebrity types who became seduced by cocaine.

Dante had a local connection for pharmaceutical coke. But he was out of the drug and was looking to score for himself and maybe to share with some friends. In no way, however, was he involved in dealing cocaine. Dante also had no knowledge that Hawk had been "turned around"—that is, he was now an informant working with the federal drug enforcement authorities. Hawk wouldn't give up any of his friends, but other than that, everybody was fair game.

They were in New York to meet with a big executive from one of the top fashion houses in the country. Hawk was extremely well connected in the illicit drug field. They went to this gentleman's suite at a posh, west side apartment complex, and tested some outstandingly pure cocaine. Dante bought a half an ounce, and it made his trip. He was just having fun. However, Hawk told the executive that he was looking to purchase a kilo, or 2.2 pounds, of coke, an exceptional purchase, especially in those times. The executive got on the phone and made a call to Tennessee, arranging to score the kilo in four days. He gave all of the logistical information for the deal over the phone in the two visitors' presence and then hung up. He bid Hawk and Dante farewell, and they returned to Maryland.

Four days later, Dante read a Baltimore newspaper that a big fashion executive had been busted in Tennessee, as he was about to leave for New York. He was caught with a kilo of cocaine. Right away it dawned on Dante that Hawk was an agent working for the government.

Although shocked and dismayed, Dante knew that Hawk had not given him up and did not intend to. Yet he recognized that his business and social relationships with Hawk had to end.

When the DEA pulled Hawk in to find out what information he possessed, he would occasionally be left alone in their private offices. Once alone, he would ransack the desks looking for things to steal, or information for his personal use.

One afternoon while Hawk was rifling through some DEA office drawers, he found indictments for Dante. He called Dante on the phone as soon as he could to alert him. Short of leaving the country, there wasn't much Mr. D could do except seek powerful legal help.

Dante was indicted after two young men from a hair salon with whom Dante had shared the pharmaceutical coke tried reselling the same coke to a federal agent. They were also "turned around," and gave up Dante. Of course, Dante could have "walked." All the authorities wanted was for him to give up his connections to the pharmaceutical coke and some big gambling figures. But Dante was not the type of guy to give anyone up, and he refused to testify.

During the indictment and trial, Dante had an affair with a local girl named Lillian whom he married. His first courtship and marriage had lasted a few years. This one was somewhat more abbreviated. Dante's new bride was a nice girl, but a serious junkie. Dante found her heroin paraphernalia in the kitchen one morning spread out for everyone to see. He had the marriage annulled after three weeks. The next day, he began a two-year prison sentence.

CHAPTER 59
October 1986

Mr. D's compulsive gambling cousin, Dickie, walked into Charlie's and spotted Dante behind the counter, a bandage neatly wrapped around his forehead.

"Uncle Louis, how are you? Heard about the robbery. You're lucky to be alive."

"Thanks, Dickie," said Mr. D. "You come to pay me?"

"Look, Uncle Louis, I know you're pissed at me and all that, but it's not my fault. The doc says I'm sick. Ya know, like Art Schlichter. I can't help myself."

Dickie was referring to the Baltimore Colt quarterback who was expelled from the National Football League for gambling on pro football games.

"Save the bullshit for the shrink, Dickie! First, you're my cousin, not my nephew. So stop with the 'uncle.' Second, you owe me 25 thousand! You stole it! Your buddies told me what they were betting with you and it never got to me."

Dante's outburst caused the clerks and shoppers to quiet down and look over at the argument.

"I told ya I'll pay ya back no matter how long it takes. Whaddaya want? Blood?"

"No, Dickie. My money. And not $50 a month!"

Mr. D looked over at the people staring and shook his head.

"That's why I'm here," said Dickie. "I'm gonna make it a hundred a month."

"Forget it!" said Mr. D. "Two hundred fifty dollars a month is the least I'll take or don't ever let me see you around again."

"How can you say that?" said Dickie tearfully. "I don't have that much. Christ, we're blood . . . family."

Paul Douglas, making a rare appearance, walked into Charlie's and caught Mr. D's eye.

"Stow that talk, Dickie. Get outta here," said Mr. D. "I'm too busy for you conning me. And, remember, I'm not your uncle."

Dickie stormed out in a huff, brushing past Paul.

"Family reunion, Louis?" asked Paul sarcastically.

"Yeah! My cousin thinks he should be treated like Art Schlichter."

A discussion ensued concerning Art Schlichter, who made national headlines by admitting his gambling problems and receiving treatment for compulsive gambling. Paul and Mr. D briefly reminisced about what they believed to be the true story behind Schlichter. It turned out that a small-time bookie, who laid off to a guy, who laid off to another guy, who eventually laid off to Mr. D, was the guy whom Schlichter was betting with. These were very small-time bookies, and they never intended to pay Schlichter off if he would have won his bets. They figured that Schlichter had no chance at collecting since he had to fear these guys coming after him or going to the football commissioner. The small-time bookie later confided to Mr. D that Schlichter was betting for over a dozen other Colts and that the NFL suppressed the story.

Paul explained to Mr. D that this was not the first time such a cover-up occurred. In the sixties, when the NFL suspended Green Bay's Paul Hornung and Detroit's Alex Karras for a year, rumor had it they were not betting alone, either. At least a dozen of their teammates on the Lions and the Packers were also betting.

CHAPTER 60

Louis Dante wore a tan suit, white shirt, and green paisley tie as he stood solemnly in front of the judge's bench at the old district court building on Reisterstown Road in northwest Baltimore City. It also housed the Northwest Police District. He was surrounded by 11 other bookies, bettors, and clerks who had been caught up in the gambling raids a few weeks earlier.

Four attorneys represented the dozen plaintiffs. There was no testimony. Guilty pleas and fines had been worked out earlier with Assistant State's Attorney Will Hayden. Clem Watowski, Main Man, and Johnny Bop were among the guilty.

The judge, the Honorable Davey Witt, a former political hack, who had served for over three decades, levied fines ranging from $500 to $6,000. He then dismissed the ensemble cast with no further remarks.

As Dante hurriedly walked out of the courthouse and down the steps to Reisterstown Road, Clem Watowski approached him.

"I need to speak to you about the niggers," he said, loud enough for Johnny Bop to hear. Before Dante could respond, Watowski was off in the direction of the parking lot.

"He's such a prick," said Main Man, catching up to Mr. D.

"Listen," said Dante. "Cover for me today and tomorrow. I'm takin' Margaret to Atlantic City. She's still shook up over the robbery . . . By the way, maybe if you hadn't encouraged them to meet with me, it wouldn't have happened."

"Jesus, boss, I didn't encourage them. And I am sorry."

"Also," said Dante. "Put Lanny on the phones. He needs the experience."

CHAPTER 61

Hammerjack's catered to a clientele ranging from outlaw bikers to yuppies. It was a huge bar and dance club located in a warehouse area near the entrance to Baltimore City from the south. Situated under a span of overpasses for Interstate 95, which snaked through south and east Baltimore, Hammerjack's defied the life span of Baltimore nightspots. A very fickle town, Baltimore nightclubs usually stayed in business less than a year. Now in its eighth year of operation, the crowds were still large despite the increases in prices and the decreases in the economy. Loud bands played a variety of current tunes and heavy metal, and, several times a year, "name" groups and entertainers appeared unannounced to practice before setting off on national concert tours.

A local group, Pedestrian, was playing their opening set, and the dance floor in the center of the club was filled. At a side bar, Tongue and Baker leaned. They were looking out over the throng and nodding in rhythm to the song "Fetish Boy" being sung by the Sciuto brothers, Tony, the lead singer, and Michael, the bass guitarist for the group.

Tongue tried to speak to Baker, but was drowned out by the noise. Baker motioned for him to walk outside.

"I haven't seen that sorry fuck yet. What time's he due?" asked Tongue after walking to a secluded spot at the front end of the parking lot underneath of the neon black and yellow Hammerjack's sign.

"His plane should have landed 45 minutes ago. If it's on time, a cab'll get him here soon . . . oh, cool it," warned Baker as the DEA narc, Strimer, approached them.

"Evenin' gentlemen," he said as he flicked the remnants of a half-smoked cigarillo in the direction of Tongue. "How are my two favorite losers?"

"What's a matter, chief?" asked Baker. "Quota time? We ain't doin' nothin' wrong."

An airport taxi pulled up in front of Hammerjack's. It idled roughly while the fare paid the driver and departed the cab. A thirty-ish man of medium build with thick-lens glasses and a neatly-trimmed beard glanced briefly at Tongue, Baker, and the narc before entering the noise and blinking lights of the nightclub.

Baker and Tongue shifted uncomfortably.

"I'm not here to harass you boys," said the narc. "Just passing on a warning. Maybe you'll appreciate it and help me out one day with some information on your old Python motorcycle buddies."

The guys just stared at the narc.

"I've heard through my channels that you two may have tried to rip off a gambler named Dante," said Strimer, pausing for several seconds to let his comment sink in. The volume from the club shifted as the band finished a fast heavy metal arrangement and went into a slow ballad.

"And word has it that he's put out a hit on the both of you. I'd be looking over my shoulder, boys. You owe me one." The narc didn't wait for a response and walked quickly out into the darkness of the parking lot.

"Well," said Baker, "whatcha think?"

"I think we'd better go inside and find the chemist real quick," suggested Tongue. They both hurried back into Hammerjack's.

The chemist was Michael Thompson. Dressed in a forest green Polo shirt, black jeans, and Docksider shoes with no socks, Thompson was close by the stage watching the female lead singer, Vicki Hare, belt out a song with Tony Sciuto. She was a small woman with reddish hair wearing a one-piece black jumpsuit and prancing around the stage, often hanging onto the other band members.

Michael Thompson was considered an accomplished chemist. Originally from Vista, California, a town near San Diego, he had attended University of California-Polytechnic and graduated with honors in 1972. Recruited by several major pharmaceutical firms, he chose employment with the DuPont Company in Wilmington, Delaware and worked there for ten years. On a vacation in 1982 to the Cayman Islands, he fell in with a group of high-living, high-spending, yuppie-like drug dealers who seduced him with dreams, and some reality, of wealth, women, and escape. Within two months, Thompson became an outlaw chemist and full partner in a "designer drug" gang, and left Dupont to return to California. His new friends had convinced him of the future needs of the American public. Sixty percent of the world's botanically grown illicit drugs were consumed in the United States. If the government ever really decided to close its border to dope, the demand would still be there. And that demand could only be met by the production of synthetic drugs manufactured by world-class chemists like Michael Thompson. The profits on the designer drug trade were light-years higher than the current system of smuggling.

For example, China White, the nickname for synthetic heroin, was an analog of fentanyl, a narcotic/analgesic used in surgery. By slightly altering the molecular structure of the fentanyl formula, a chemist could produce a narcotic 30,000 times stronger than heroin. A shoebox full of China White could feed the heroin-using population of California for six months. Besides China White, Thompson's business manufactured Ecstasy (an analog of a potent stimulant), Ice (crystal methamphetamine), and bootleg Quaaludes (a sedative-hypnotic).

Headquartered just outside of San Francisco, Thompson wore several hats in the business. He designed formulas, supervised other chemists, laundered profits, and occasionally negotiated deals on the East Coast.

Tongue approached Thompson and escorted him to the men's room to meet with Baker, who was relieving himself in the urinal.

"Christ, it smells lousy in here," muttered Thompson. "Let's get on with it. Where's the money?"

"We've got it, but not with us, though," said Baker. "When's delivery?"

"Let's cut the crap, guys," said Thompson. He was leaning against a stall and watching the entrance. "The deal's still the same. The ludes'll be in town in three days if . . . if I get my money. I expected to be paid the agreed-to installment this evening and the rest on delivery. But I get these vibes that you guys may be a little short right now. Since we've done business before, I'll keep the deal open for 50 more hours. After that, I'm history."

"No problem, my man," said Tongue. He sounded confident. "Where will you be staying?"

Thompson moved away from the stall and walked out of the men's room with Tongue and Baker.

"I'll be at the Marriott near the airport under the name of Walter Cohen. See ya," said Thompson who walked over to the bar and ordered a club soda with lime.

Tongue and Baker left Hammerjack's through a side entrance near the men's room. They appeared to be two men looking for their car. Instead, they were looking for one to steal. Noticing two girls slam the doors of a two-door blue 1984 Honda Civic without locking them, Tongue and Baker slowed down and watched the girls run, as best they could in tight short skirts and high heels, towards the nightclub.

Baker slipped into the driver's seat and released the hood. Within 45 seconds, Tongue had the car engine purring, the hood closed, and was seated on the passenger side.

"What's our move?" asked Tongue as Baker pulled the car out of the parking lot, down a ramp, and onto Martin Luther King Boulevard.

"Same as before," said Baker, smiling. "We rip off and waste Dante; and anybody else who gets in the way."

CHAPTER 62

U.S. Attorney Hopkins was speaking to the informant. "So, no more bullshit. It's, how do you say in your business, 'game time'? How did you get yourself in such a mess, Mat?"

The informant, Main Man, was choked up and could barely speak. He was sick to his stomach that his personal relationships had caused him to ruin the man who saved his life.

Baltimore, 1983

Main Man's girlfriend, Conceta, had his baby, a son named Lee. For the first couple of years, their relationship was okay, even though they never married. Main Man loved Conceta and the baby dearly, but over time, he noticed some changes in Conceta, such as mood swings, new friends, and less attention giving to the child. He discovered that she was a junkie and had several boyfriends visiting her at their house while he was at work.

Two years later, Main Man hired an attorney, and, subsequently, a judge awarded him custody of Lee. Conceta was livid and swore revenge. She went to the police and told them that Main Man was a bookie. Through the child, during her visitation periods, Conceta found out the location of the betting apartment. It seemed that against Mr. D's instructions, Main Man brought his son to work. He had lost a trusted babysitter and was reluctant to leave Lee with just anyone. Conceta's constant questioning of her son enabled her to determine the apartment complex location of the operation.

She told the police, who put a Pen Register on the switching box in the basement of the apartment building. A Pen Register was a device that recorded the number of calls and phone numbers being dialed. It did not intercept or record conversations. The police received a listing of calls that could reveal a pattern based on the length of the calls and the time of day. In the instance of this bookmaking operation, a clear pattern emerged during weeknights from six to eight p.m. and weekends from eleven-thirty a.m. to four p.m.

So, on one busy Sunday afternoon, Detective Feldman and the Baltimore City Vice Squad broke into the apartment and arrested Mr. D and Main Man; and later rounded up the smaller bookies all over the metro area who laid off to Mr. D. Not only did it ruin a lucrative day for Mr. D, he had to post bail for many of the other bookies who worked for him. And when he found out it was because of Main Man's carelessness in bringing his child to work, Mr. D was livid.

CHAPTER 63
October 1986

The two-hour-and-forty-five-minute trip from Baltimore to Atlantic City was uneventful for the Dante's. Small talk dominated the ride, with Margaret rarely speaking. Mr. D drove north on I-95 up the JFK Highway through Maryland, then across the Delaware Memorial Bridge onto the New Jersey Turnpike. He took Turnpike Exit 3 through Runnymeade and completed the trek on the Atlantic City Expressway.

They proceeded directly to the Resorts Hotel and Casino on South Carolina Avenue, unpacked their luggage, and walked out onto the boardwalk.

The ocean breeze put a mild chill in the late afternoon air as Mr. D and Margaret walked north past the Resorts facility, formerly the Marlborough-Blenheim Hotel. Long before the riots of the late sixties and the decay of Atlantic City, the Marlborough-Blenheim complex, joined by a footbridge, served as one of the grand hotels. From the thirties through the sixties, it catered mainly to the WASP set, nestled within the other hotels frequented by Jews and Italians.

"Louis, I can't take much more," said Margaret, who had been thinking of how to approach her husband for three hours. "You're up at four a.m. You don't come home 'til nine at night. The only vacation time we have together is during the baseball All-Star break and after the Super Bowl. And now somebody tries to kill you in front of the house."

"Whadaya want me to do?" asked Mr. D. "It's my job . . . and it was just a robbery."

"It's your life. You love it. But, can't you give something up?"

"I'm trying to sell the store . . ." said Mr. D.

"Then what?" asked Margaret as she and Louis turned into an opening in the boardwalk guardrail and walked down several steps onto the beach.

"Then I'll have more time," answered Dante.

"For me or you?" asked Margaret as she plopped down on the stony sand, removed her black flats, and rolled up her jeans.

"C'mon Maggie. You know what I am." Mr. D stood over Margaret. He kept his Nike running shoes and heavy gray sweat socks on.

"Louis, I'm scared and embarrassed. I never thought I would be, but . . ."

"Somebody say something?" asked Mr. D.

"No . . . Can't you give up being a bookie? You've got enough to retire handsomely for a hundred years."

"What, and let someone else have all that action? How can I let it go? It's a never-ending well."

"Paul did," she argued.

Louis and Margaret walked close to the small but pounding ocean waves of the Atlantic. She stayed on the outside and let the water roll over her bare feet. Dante was wary of the water and walked parallel to, but four to five feet away from, Margaret.

"Sure, Paul had me," explained Mr. D emphatically.

"You've got Main Man," countered Margaret.

"It's not the same. Look, after I sell the store, and after the Super Bowl, I'll look into some legitimate investments. But let up on me for awhile . . ."

Margaret stopped and turned to the ocean, her back to Dante.

"Let up? Louis, please. I need some time, some attention. We haven't made love for six weeks . . . On weekends, it's awful."

Mr. D put his arms on her shoulders. He pressed himself to her back, oblivious now to the seawater wetting his shoes. He tried to explain his behavior, for himself as well as for Margaret.

"You don't understand. There's a tremendous emotional high and low—an emotional drain no matter what, whether I win or lose. I need an hour or two to calm down after all of the games are over. It's like I just came out of the game myself. On a Sunday night during the football season, I'm not looking to do anything. I mean I ain't up for company at four p.m. on a Sunday if I'm down $150,000 as a result of the one p.m. games. And I don't need to be soothed or pampered, Maggie. And I've got no time to entertain you or your friends.

"I've got the sheets in front of me where there is a million bucks worth of bets. It's like I'm sittin' there with a loaded cannon. How can sex be on my mind?"

Margaret sighed inwardly and decided to change the subject of their discussion. He'd never change, she thought.

"What used to be here?" she asked, pointing to the pilings stacked up stretching from the boardwalk to the water.

"That, Maggie," Mr. D said proudly, "was one of the wonders of the modern world—the Steel Pier. Crowds came in droves to hang out here." He was relieved to digress from their personal life.

"For what?" she asked.

"Everything you can imagine. There was an arcade, a funhouse, two movies, and the world's saltiest popcorn that they sold in glassine bags."

Margaret and Louis Dante walked back up the beach towards the boardwalk and looked at the busted and dry-rotted ads clinging desperately to the withering wood signs. She barely made out the picture of the Tony Grant's "Stars of Tomorrow Review."

"I saw Johnny Ray here once," reminisced Mr. D. "They had to move the bandstand closer to him 'cause he was deaf."

"Who was Johnny Ray?" asked Margaret.

"Old-time singer. Had some hits right when rock and roll began. My dad worked here one summer for one of his uncles who rented space for a game of chance."

"What kind?" she asked.

"He had these three wooden milk bottles, one perched atop the other two. People paid to throw a baseball at them. If they knocked the bottles over, they won a cupey doll . . . but nobody ever won."

"Why?" asked Margaret. "That couldn't have been that hard."

"Hell," laughed Dante, "during the hurricane of '44, which almost destroyed Atlantic City and whacked out the boardwalk, the only thing left standing were the three milk bottles!"

Margaret smiled, recognizing that her spouse's family tree was filled with hustlers and gamblers. She and Louis reached the boardwalk and turned south toward the hotel. As they walked past the front of the old Steel Pier, she gawked at the decaying poster of the Diving Horse, a beautiful thoroughbred flying in the air, snout-first, into the water.

"Did you ever see that?" asked Margaret

"Yeah," said Dante. "But it wasn't exactly like the picture. The horse usually looked like the kind that pulled wagons in the street. They'd drag it up a ramp to this 50-foot platform. Horse be shakin' like crazy. Did it three times a day. The poor thing would shit on the platform and then someone would push it off. It dropped like a stone with the rider holdin' on for dear life on its back. Made a huge splash onto its belly into the enclosed area of water. People'd be screamin' and laughin'. Crazy, just crazy . . ."

Margaret laughed. This was the Louis Dante she'd loved. In her heart she felt sad and guilty. Sad because she knew he'd never change as long as he was a bookie. Guilty because of her indiscretions with Handsome John with whom she'd thought about running away.

CHAPTER 64
Baltimore, 1983

Instead of moving to a new apartment, Mr. D and Main Man decided to use the same place in which they had gotten busted, figuring the police would never suspect it. They parked a mile away, wore disguises, kept the lights off, and moved their desk, phones, and equipment into a large closet where they worked. It was ingenious, except that the police had not yet removed the Pen Register. The amount of activity was such that Detective Feldman figured that Mr. D had to be back. So, one evening later that week, the police again busted the door down. When they got inside and put on the lights, no one was there. Feldman began cursing and, as an afterthought, told his men to search the apartment anyhow. Lo and behold, they found Mr. D and Main Man in the closet. Both the bookies and the cops were still laughing as they entered the police station.

CHAPTER 65
October 1986

Nothing in the world could have made Main Man turn informant against Mr. D—nothing except the thought of losing his son. The federal prosecutor had guaranteed that Main Man's son would be given back to Conceta and would disappear with her in the Witness Protection Program. Thus, he would never see the child again.

It was the federal prosecutor's aim, with Main Man's tainted testimony, to link Mr. D to the Philadelphia and New Jersey Mafia and ride a wave of publicity into the Governor's mansion.

"You're sure the dope deal never materialized?" asked the

U.S. Attorney. They were walking past the grand jury room in the federal courthouse.

"I told you it wouldn't work," said Main Man. "Plus he really reamed me for bringing the deal and those lowlife guys to meet with him."

"Actually, Mat," he said, "you're all lowlife. However, we've still got photographs of the drug dealers and Dante together at the racetrack. It'll all fit in real nice as a criminal enterprise package . . . tomorrow, before a righteous grand jury."

CHAPTER 66

Something looked strange and sorely out of place to the old woman who was dragging her grocery cart along the street in Rosedale. The two men who had walked quickly past her were certainly well dressed in their dark suits, but something didn't click. She shook her head and then forgot what she was thinking about as a neighbor called out to her.

The two suits were Len Baker and Tongue Deacon. Baker's long, unkempt, shaggy, dirty-blond hair, and beard stubble and earring, didn't fit a new suit. Nor did Tongue's full beard; mustache; and cold, dark, death-like eyes. And the heavy old filthy biker's boots they both wore certainly didn't match their attire. But the boots did prove to be handy when Tongue and Baker simultaneously kicked in the door to the apartment atop the town house enclosing Mr. D's bookmaking operation.

Lanny Oswinkle's head snapped back in surprise as he watched the door fall towards the middle of the floor, followed by two men in suits.

"Who are you? Where's Dante?" asked Tongue as Baker moved around the room searching for anything or anyone.

"I've got nothin' to say," said Lanny acting boldly. He assumed they were cops. "Where's your badges?"

Baker walked over and grabbed Lanny by his shirt collar. "Tell me where Dante is or I'll break your fuckin' neck!"

"What about my rights?" asked Lanny. "You gotta read me my rights."

"Well, Officer," said Tongue to Baker, "give 'em a right."

Baker hit Lanny with his right fist square in the left cheek, and then punched him about the face three more times.

"Is that enough rights?" laughed Tongue. "Or do you want more?"

Shook up, Lanny held his face in his hands. "You guys are in trouble. This is definitely police brutality!" he cried.

"Well," said Baker, "if you're gonna file formal brutality charges, we might as well help you with an ironclad case against us."

Baker and Tongue lifted Lanny up from the floor and began to viciously beat him up. As Lanny slipped to the floor, the bikers kicked him in the head and groin area.

Just then, Main Man walked into the room. He was wide-eyed at the scene of the broken door and melee in the center of the apartment. Recognizing Tongue and Baker, he grabbed the phone to dial 911.

"Dumb move, Mat," shouted Baker. He drew a .38-caliber revolver with a silencer from his trousers and shot Main Man three times.

CHAPTER 67

Shortly after Tongue and Baker left the town house and briskly walked two blocks to their motorcycles, a panicky Lanny ran out of the apartment. He drove his car to a 7-Eleven store in a small strip shopping center three miles away and called the police, anonymously. He reported that two cops had shot a man, gave the address, and hung up.

Terrified, Lanny got into his 1984 Buick Regal and sped along the beltway to the Timonium exit and then to Stierhoff's Pub, a bar he frequented. A small bar and restaurant with four tables dominated by a horseshoe-shaped bar, Stierhoff's was nestled just outside of the Baltimore County line on a side street off of York Road.

The sun had fallen below the horizon outside as Lanny sat at the bar drinking shot glasses of Wild Turkey 101 bourbon.

"Seen a ghost? What happened to you?" asked Harriette Wrapper, the early-shift bartender. She was checking out, getting ready to leave.

"I seen the ghost and them that made the ghost," said Lanny. He was breathing heavily and could feel his heart pounding inside of his denim shirt. His face was beginning to swell, his balls ached, and he could feel two very large knots forming on his head.

"Say, Harriette, got anything to calm me down?" asked Lanny.

Harriette smiled as she wiped the bar, looking around at the sparsely occupied pub. She was in her mid-forties, older than Lanny, and her face was weathered from years of drugs and stress. Twice divorced with four children who grew up in foster homes, she still had an attractive body with long legs, a tight butt, and small breasts. Four days a week she worked out at the Hollywood Health Spa for free. The manager, an unhappily married man who commuted from northern Virginia, 'comped' Harriette in return for a couple of sexual trysts a week.

"Gimme a ride home and I'll get ya somethin'," proposed Harriette. She had gotten to know Lanny over the years and liked him. They were both losers.

Lanny paid the bar tab and waited outside for Harriette. They drove over to her place, an apartment less than two miles north of Stierhoff's Pub. Her place was a mess, and, although she had moved in four years earlier, there were still boxes full of household wares strewn about the place.

Harriette went into the bedroom as Lanny settled on the sofa in front of the TV. Within five minutes, she returned, dressed only in a housecoat loosely tied at the waist, carrying a bottle of Absolute Vodka and a vial of pills.

"What ya got there, baby?" asked Lanny as he stared intently at Harriette.

"Xanax," she said. Xanax was a drug used for anxiety that was growing in popularity with the dope taking set.

Over the next few hours, Lanny and Harriette ingested a dozen pills and finished almost all of the vodka. At around six a.m., Lanny stood groggily urinating in the toilet in the tiny bathroom. Recalling the shooting from the past evening, he went to the phone and called Mr. D at Charlie's. He had returned from Atlantic City.

"Yeah," answered Dante impatiently.

"Trouble last night. Mat got shot," said Lanny.

"What!? Is he dead?" asked Mr. D.

"Yeah . . . I dunno . . . I'm not sure," stammered Lanny.

Mr. D hung up on Lanny and began to make another call. Midway in his dialing he stopped, whispered to Juanita what he had been told, gave her some instructions, and ran outside to his car.

CHAPTER 68

Margaret had slept late after she and Dante returned from Atlantic City. He was gone when she woke up. It was after seven a.m. when Margaret stepped out of the shower. She toweled herself dry and dressed for her advanced aerobic class from 8:30 to 9:30; and a possible rendezvous with Handsome John at 10:30.

The German shepherd, Lilly, laid on her side by the driveway, a huge prime rib bone near her mouth. She appeared to be sunning herself during an early morning snooze. On closer observation, however, Lilly was dead; poisoned by the strychnine sprinkled liberally on the prime rib surprise she had found after Margaret had let her outside to relieve herself.

Margaret, who had no fear with Lilly about, had left the side door by the kitchen open, and Tongue and Baker had quietly let themselves in. Unaware that Dante had left earlier in the morning, they were there to rob and kill him. They needed the money before the evening deadline invoked by the chemist.

Tongue waited in the kitchen while Baker silently and swiftly surveyed the house. Four minutes later, he reported to his buddy.

"Fuckin' Dante ain't here," he swore. "His ole lady is in the bedroom. There's some jewelry, furs . . . didn't see any money or a safe. What do you want to do?"

"He's probably down at Charlie's. What's she look like?" asked Baker.

"Real strong, man. She's just gettin' dressed," said Tongue.

"Let's help her," said Baker as they walked towards the bedroom.

CHAPTER 69

Main Man was in the emergency room at Franklin Square Hospital in Essex in east Baltimore County. The doctors had agreed not to move him to Intensive Care until he was stabilized. A floor-to-ceiling curtain surrounded Mat's cubicle as tubes from machines and intravenous equipment protruded from his strapped-down body. The three bullets had severely damaged his right lung, kidney, and abdomen. Twice during the night, emergency room technicians had restarted his heart. The prognosis for recovery was very poor.

Mr. D rushed over to the emergency room desk asking to see Main Man. Through her contacts, Juanita had located Mat at Franklin Square and had called Mr. D in his car as he drove over to observe the town house in Rosedale. The police with yellow crime-scene ribbon had cordoned off the town house. Anticipating this, Mr. D drove by slowly and proceeded directly to the hospital.

The nurse Mr. D spoke with summoned the on-duty hospital guard. Fortunately, he recognized Mr. D from years before when he worked for the Baltimore City Police Department. After a couple of minutes of social amenities and approval from Dr. Constantine Grafos, the emergency room physician, Mr. D was allowed to see Main Man for a couple of minutes.

"How ya doin', pal?" asked Dante. He realized that Mat's injuries were critical.

Main Man could barely whisper. Mr. D bent over, placing his ear near Mat's mouth.

"Sorry, boss . . . It was Tongue and Baker," Main Man choked, resting a few seconds before continuing. "They're out to kill ya . . . I . . ." He began to cough and the doctor rushed in.

"His signs are very bad. Can you contact his family?" asked Dr. Grafos, motioning for Mr. D to leave.

Tears welled up in Dante's eyes and he swallowed hard.

"I am his family," he said as he turned and walked purpose-fully out of the hospital.

CHAPTER 70

Margaret's naked body was stretched face down over the top of the orange ottoman in the bedroom near the vanity. A shiny, silk black scarf tied her hands tightly, and her wrists were held down by Tongue. Baker loomed over her back, his body driving like a piston pounding away at her backside. His large penis seared into her anus. Margaret's short blond hair was still wet and droplets of water shook over Tongue as her head flung up and down. A six-inch piece of duct tape covered her mouth and spread across her flushed cheeks.

Tongue reached behind him and turned on the clock radio. Music blared as he ripped the duct tape off of Margaret's face.

"I wanna hear her scream," he said to Baker. "And I've got some better use for her mouth."

"She's gonna bite it off," shouted Baker.

"No she won't," said Tongue. "If she don't suck it real good, I'm gonna slice off her ear." He pulled out his switchblade knife with his right hand and placed the tip under her earlobe and along her neck.

"Please," cried Margaret as Tongue let her wrists go with his left hand. Still keeping the knife on the side of her face, Tongue unzipped his jeans and pulled out his prick. Grabbing Margaret's wet hair, he forced the head of his cock into her mouth.

CHAPTER 71

Mr. D drove along the Beltway towards west Baltimore County. He had decided to proceed with Main Man's daily chores. He tried to assess the damage done to his business, and to wrestle with the reality of Main Man out of the operation. Mat had been a loyal friend and diligent worker for years since Mr. D had rescued him in Mexico. However, Mr. D had no idea that Main Man had been coerced into turning informant.

As Dante headed to his first pickup in Pikesville in northwest Baltimore, U.S. Attorney Mitch Hopkins and investigators Blume, Carey, and Solomon were running into Franklin Square Hospital, followed by a dazed court stenographer carrying a tape recorder and steno equipment.

They were met by the hospital administrator, Jeffrey Blumenfeld, who personally escorted them to Main Man in the emergency room.

"This won't work," protested Dr. Grafos, who had been on duty for over 30 hours. "He's very, very weak."

"I'll take the responsibility," overruled the administrator, Blumenfeld, as he ushered in the federal authorities.

The court stenographer quickly set up her equipment and switched on the tape recorder. Hopkins leaned over Mat and gently advised him that they would be brief and to try to speak clearly.

"Soon you'll be with your son, forever. We'll take good care of both of you. You probably won't even have to testify at Dante's trial," said Hopkins soothingly.

Mat's eyes moved about the room. He smiled weakly, sighed, and began to cough. His head fell slightly to the left and the heart monitor began to sound a long, steady beep.

The doctor rushed in, followed by a nurse and two technicians. He ordered everyone out of the room as he began working feverishly to save Main Man. Grafos and his aides attempted every means of resuscitation, but nothing worked. Mat was dead.

CHAPTER 72

In Pikesville, a predominantly Jewish community, Mr. D met Ned Weinstein, a wealthy developer, in Fields Pharmacy. Located a half-mile inside the beltway and a half mile before the city line, Fields had served the northwest Baltimore community for most of the 20th century. Besides being a pharmacy and restaurant, Fields was an all-purpose store selling cosmetics, toiletries, greeting cards, and stationery supplies.

After receiving $14,000 in cash from Weinstein, Mr. D noticed Big Nick and Donna seated at the back counter in the restaurant. Realizing that he was driving the Audi with the recently repaired side window that Tongue and Baker had attacked him in the week before, Dante approached Nick Mattesick.

"How ya all doin'?" he asked.

"Fine, Louis," said Big Nick. "Join us for a bite?"

"Actually, Nick, I need a favor. Could I borrow your car for a few hours? I'll leave mine with you."

"No problem. Anything wrong?" asked Nick, grabbing Dante by the arm and walking away from the food counter.

"Maybe . . . Listen, Nick, don't drive the car around too much until I get back. I'm having a problem with a couple of punks and . . ."

"Don't worry about it," interrupted Nick. "Need any help?"

"Nah," said Mr. D. "I can handle it. Where's it parked?"

Big Nick walked Dante out behind Fields Pharmacy, handed him the keys, and pointed out his '83 customized Porsche Carrera. Dante gave Nick the keys to his Audi, shook his hand, and left.

Dante's next stop was Rice's Poolroom, 20 minutes west of Pikesville. Mel the Tailor was standing by the cash register at the door on the telephone, and Handsome John Abrams was shooting pool, alone.

Mr. D received an envelope from each man after he entered the poolroom. Money, numbers, and football bets were in each packet. Dante went over to a pinball machine and examined the contents of each envelope, counting the money twice. While he was engrossed in his work, Lindy, the elderly former poolroom owner who had been scammed by the late

Jeff Hall, Mel, and Handsome John shuffled in. He began arguing with Mel, who came from behind the cash register counter
and grabbed Lindy.

"Get the fuck outta here!" he shouted.

"You owe me money, you thievin' bastard," cried Lindy as
Mel shoved him out the door.

Mr. D did not like the scene and considered intervening in
the dispute. However, recognizing that he already had enough
problems with the shooting of Mat and associated threats, he gathered up the bets and lay-off action from Mel and John and hurried out of Rice's Poolroom.

Chapter 73

Margaret Dante had been in the shower for over thirty-five
minutes frantically trying to scrub away the past two terrifying
hours with Tongue and Baker. She had been repeatedly sodomized,
forced to hand over jewelry, money, credit cards, and furs, and
even had to cook them a breakfast of bacon and eggs. Before
they left, she stood by the refrigerator listening to the bikers de-
bate over how and whether to kill her. Finally, Baker called her
over to clear the kitchen table. As she gathered the dishes, he
punched her in the jaw, knocking her out. When she came to,
they were gone.

After the shower, she dried herself and stood over the phone.
Already convinced that she would not call the police, Margaret
decided to contact her husband and warn him. Tongue and
Baker had openly discussed their decision to kill Mr. D in front
of her. Neither of his cellular phones was operable, all of the
lines to Charlie's were busy, and the car phone didn't answer.
Frantic, she called Estelle and told her to send Dickie over to
pick her up.

CHAPTER 74

"So, are we gonna pick up Dante?" asked Agent Solomon.

"I don't think so," said Senior Agent Carey. He'd been in similar situations over the years when a key witness, informant, or piece of evidence was no longer available. In this case, the death of Mr. D's chief lieutenant, Main Man, had probably ended the U.S. prosecutor's goal. In return for a life with his son, Mat would have reluctantly testified to Louis Dante's criminal empire, which spread across state lines. His testimony, tainted by the prosecutor's zeal, would have given the media an illusion of a Mob organization that extended to drugs, prostitution, loansharking, and more.

Carey believed that the feds could still put Dante in jail, but only for gambling. Yet he knew that Hopkins could not receive the notoriety for a gambling charge that he could have from a bust of a major criminal enterprise. Actually, he would just as soon not continue the investigation or go to court against Dante for fear of being embarrassed at the extent and cost to the tax-payer to nab one gambler.

"What makes you so sure we're not arresting Dante?" asked a bewildered Solomon.

"Take if from me. The silence in the car on our return from the hospital told me plenty. Without Mat, the case is no longer sexy. Believe it."

CHAPTER 75

The lunchtime crowd had grown, and standing room was at a premium at the fenced-in Mulberry Street Projects' basketball court on the corner of Mulberry and Stricker Streets in west Baltimore.

Each weekday, teams made up of drug dealers, numbers

runners, pimps, school dropouts, and the unemployed engaged in full-court games beginning at eleven-thirty a.m. and continuing through three p.m. There were team sponsors, league standings, and wagers on the games. Competition was fierce, talk was tough, and minor fistfights were frequent; but no gunplay, knife-fights, or vendettas followed. The league's commissioners, Jimmy Bop and Shadow Creek, wouldn't allow it.

Bop and Creek were engrossed in the matter of the placement of a new prospect, a six-foot-eight-inch recently paroled bank robber, being drafted by a team called the Fancy Pants sponsored by a pimp named Marvelous Mitch. Mr. D, who had come to collect their numbers lay-offs, interrupted them.

"Workin' hard, boys?" joked Dante.

"Hey, watch that 'boys' shit, Mr. D. There're some dangerous niggers in this cage," said Jimmy Bop. He reached into his double-breasted gray suit jacket and pulled out several thousand dollars tied tightly in thick rubber bands. A small folded sheet with numbers was wrapped around the top of the money.

From his right front pants pocket, Shadow Creek dug out a similar-sized amount of cash and handed it to Dante.

"You headed back to Charlie's?" asked Shadow.

"Yeah, later," said Dante as he watched the warm-up and jive-talk taking place on the court.

"Well, do me a favor," said Shadow. "Tell that fine young thing, Juanita, who you've been hiding up there for years, that I'd love to make her sweat."

Jimmy Bop laughed as Mr. D shook his head at Shadow Creek.

"Don't go near the help," cautioned Dante who recognized the jocular vein of the comment. Just then, the crowd roared as the parolee dunked the ball hard through the chain-link basket.

"Where ya off to in that pretty machine?" asked Bop as Dante headed towards his loaner car.

"I'm gonna see Shadow's girlfriend," he called back. "Clem!"

CHAPTER 76

"Hello," said Donna. She had answered Mr. D's car phone while moving the car into a parking spot after leaving Big Nick at his uptown Pikesville office.

"Who the fuck is this?" came the answer from a near-hysterical Margaret who had forgotten her problems for a moment suspecting she had caught her husband with another woman.

"This is Donna . . . Maggie, is that you?"

"Donna, what are you doing with Louis?"

"Louis switched cars with Nick. I don't know why . . . and I don't know where he is."

Maggie began to cry. Then she told Donna what had happened to her and that she needed to reach Dante. Suddenly the passenger door swung open and Donna screamed.

"Calm down," said the voice. It was Big Nick.

"I saw you get into the car from upstairs and rushed down here. You can't use this car because Louis is having some trouble with . . ."

"I know," said Donna. "Margaret's on the phone." Quietly, she told Nick that Margaret had been raped and that they needed to contact Dante. Nick grabbed the phone and spoke to Margaret. They both agreed that they couldn't alert the police.

"Maggie, you sit tight. I'll have a doctor pal of mine come over and check you out. I'm going to Charlie's to find Louis. Don't worry."

Nick hung up and walked back to his office with Donna. He took off his sport jacket and put on a silver Windbreaker. Opening a side desk drawer, he pulled out a small Beretta automatic and placed it in the right pocket of the Windbreaker.

"I'll call Doc Bowen from the car. You call Maggie back and giver her some moral support. She's at Louis's cousin, Estelle's, home."

CHAPTER 77

"Whatcha gonna work out with me and that black bastard, Creek?" asked Clem Watowski as he watched Mr. D count his lay-off action.

"Christ, Clem, looks to me like you're doin' way better than him according to my tally. I just came from picking up his . . ."

"Don't bullshit me, Dante," interrupted Clem. He and Mr. D were seated in a small booth in the Broadway Market two blocks from the pier at the foot of Fells Point in the east Baltimore section of the harbor. They had bought French toast and coffee in the Prevas Brothers stall at the north end of the market.

"Say, where's Mat? Doesn't he usually make collections today?" asked Clem.

Dante stopped counting and looked up at Watowski. He felt certain that Clem somehow knew that Main Man had gotten shot. Strange how no one except Watowski had inquired about Mat, he thought.

"Nah," Dante lied. "We usually split up the days. Plus, I just got back from Atlantic City.

"Everything okay?" asked Clem.

He was being too inquisitive for Mr. D. "Everything's just great," said Dante. He munched down the rest of the French toast and took two big swallows of coffee.

"I'm outta here, Clem," he said as he ducked out the side entrance onto Thames Street.

"Don't forget about solvin' my nigger problem!" yelled Watowski, oblivious to the two blacks in the seafood stall next to his booth.

CHAPTER 78

"Hey, Juanita, it's Dickie. Lemme speak to my Uncle Louis, would ya?"

"He's not your uncle and he's not here," said Juanita.

"I've been trying to call Charlie's for hours. Phones have been all tied up. What happened? Popular number hit?" asked Dickie.

"Jesus, you fool!" screamed Juanita as she stood up from her desk chair. "Watch what you say on the phone!"

"Listen, Juanita. Tell Uncle Louis that Margaret was raped and beaten this morning by two thugs who are looking for him."

"My God! Is Maggie okay?" asked Juanita.

"The doctor's on his way over now. She's real shook up. Naturally, we didn't call the police. Don't forget to tell my uncle . . . uh . . . cousin . . . that I'm taking care of everything. Goodbye."

Juanita looked at her watch and wondered where Dante was. She walked out into the crowded store from her office and looked around. Blacks from all walks of life jammed the various counters of Charlie's: pimps, prostitutes, bums, retirees, civil servants, and beer truck drivers. An attorney and a district court judge waved to her as they strolled out after cashing several checks. Coming out from the luncheon side, she peered out the front door and gazed up and down the street.

Out of Juanita's vision was the dirt parking lot, which stretched half a block west. In the far back section was a light blue Chevrolet Chevette station wagon with state government license plates. Two hours earlier, Tongue and Baker had stolen it from F Lot near the State Office Complex, two miles south of Charlie's.

The State Office Complex had seven parking lots for state employees. F Lot was located the farthest from the three-building complex. Tongue and Baker had parked their two motorcycles on the street and waited patiently for a returning employee. Ironically, the chief of the State Drug Abuse Administration Office of Drug Prevention was the next person to pull into a parking space. Before she was two blocks from her office, the car was hot-wired and headed to Charlie's.

"You think he's already in there and we missed him?" asked Tongue.

"Nah," said Baker. "He's collecting our money for the drug deal from the other bookies. Plus, I ain't seen any of his cars."

"Yeah, but he uses a lot of 'em," said Tongue.

"Duck down!" ordered Baker as the two slid low in the front seats of the Chevette. Each screwed a silencer onto their gun barrel.

Pulling up to the only empty space on the street across from the parking lot was the somewhat-new Audi of Mr. D's. The bikers recognized it as the same car he was in when they tried to rob him at his home. The windows were darkly tinted, and they couldn't identify the number of people in the car.

"What do you want to do?" asked Tongue. He noticed that no one had opened the car door. "Whadaya think?"

"He's gotta be countin' the money," said Baker. "Let's go!"

Tongue and Baker hurried out of the state car and over to the rear of the Audi. As they debated over which door Dante would come out of, the driver's side began to open. Drawing their guns, they came around and opened fire on the occupant. It was Big Nick who fell backwards across the front seat, his legs dangling in the street.

"Who the fuck is this big cocksucker?" asked Tongue as he and Baker pushed Nick's body aside and climbed into the car. Baker looked out from the partially closed door and noticed that no one in front of Charlie's had seen the assault.

"He's probably a hired security guard for Dante," answered Baker, seeing the gun hanging from Nick's coat pocket. Tongue searched the dead body and whistled at the jewelry and wad of bills he removed from Big Nick Mattesick.

"Our boy's here," said Baker, who closed the car door. He saw Dante stroll into Charlie's after illegally double-parking Nick's Porsche Carrera by the entrance.

CHAPTER 79

Dante saw Juanita's worried look as she motioned to him. He ducked under the check-cashing counter and walked around to the back of the store.

"Trouble," she whispered as they hustled back to his office. "Maggie was raped and beaten by two thugs who are coming after you. She's at your cousin, Estelle's. Dickie called and said a doctor's on the way and that no cops were notified."

"Jesus," he sighed as he dialed the phone. Dickie answered on the first ring.

"It's me. Lemme talk to Maggie," barked Mr. D.

"Gee, Uncle Louis," said Dickie. "She's back with the doctor now. I've got everything under control and . . ."

"See if she can speak to me for just a second," pleaded Dante.

He heard Dickie drop the phone and walk away. In the distance, he heard Margaret screaming something, and then Dickie came back to the phone.

"She's very hysterical," said Dickie. "She says that if you don't quit your business, she'll never see ya again . . . I'll try and talk some sense into her after the doctor leaves."

Mr. D hung up the phone and shook his head. He figured that Margaret blamed him for the assault and hoped that maybe she would calm down later. He felt nauseous as he thought of her.

Then his mind shifted gears. A loud commotion in Charlie's commanded his attention. He heard yelling, screaming, breaking glass, and gunfire. He began desperately searching his desk for a gun he kept there. He hadn't looked for it in years.

Moments before he hung up the phone, Tongue and Baker had burst into Charlie's with their guns raised, silencers removed. They called out for Mr. D as they perused the store. They opened fire indiscriminately on employees behind the counters as the customers hit the floor for cover or tried to run out.

Two check-cashing clerks and the woman who operated the lunch grill lay dead where they had been working. Two other employees and a Budweiser beer deliveryman stirred on the floor, wounded and bleeding.

Baker and Tongue swiveled around, their guns pointing at customers and clerks huddled against the walls.

"We're gonna shoot one person at a time until we find Dante," threatened Tongue.

"Lookin' for me, guys?" asked Mr. D, pointing an old Colt .45 revolver at the bikers. He had crawled out from the office and appeared behind the state lottery machine. Juanita, who was hiding by the luncheon counter, slowly stood up. She was crying over her friend, Wanda, the grill lady, who lay motionless at her feet.

Dante pulled the trigger, but the gun didn't fire. It only made a loud and embarrassing click. He looked at the revolver and realized it was empty.

"Aw, Mr. D," said Baker, relieved. "That's too bad." He and Tongue walked toward Dante who stood frozen.

"No!" screamed Juanita as she ran to Dante's side.

The bikers aimed their guns as Juanita tried to shove Dante towards the back offices. Just as Tongue and Baker leaned over the legal lottery counter to shoot Dante and Juanita, they were interrupted by voices behind them.

"Hold it right there, motherfuckers!" came the cry of several armed and dangerous patrons. Among them were Buffalo Man and Pink Lips, two small-time hustlers who dabbled in nefarious trades; old Ms. Washington from across the street; Al "Mad Man" West, a saxophone player at a local nightclub on the Avenue called The Sphinx Club; Fast-Talking Frank Bey, a Muslim preacher; Clayton Tyler, an unemployed longshoreman; and "Precious" Tracy, a street hooker from east Baltimore.

First Baker, then Tongue, whirled around ready to open fire. They were a split second late as eight customers pummeled them both with gunshots and knives they had hidden in their clothing. The bikers were cut down quickly as they were hit on all sides by a barrage of bullets and different-sized knives. Neither body fell to the ground, both impeded by the storm of gunfire.

Mr. D and Juanita slowly approached the counter as the sound of police sirens grew in the distance. Acknowledging Dante's muted thanks, the customers scurried to their feet and ran out of the store in different directions.

CHAPTER 80

Louis Dante sat cross-legged with his head leaning on his left hand, which patted his cheek. His mind was spinning. He was sitting on a dark blue sofa in his cousin, Estelle's, home on old Route 1, several miles south of the town of Bel Air in Harford County, about 45 minutes north of downtown Baltimore. It was almost five p.m. and Dante had been speaking with Margaret for the past two hours. She was adamant about not going home until he closed down his bookmaking empire. Currently, Margaret had gone to the kitchen for a soda and was discussing dinner with Estelle.

The past 24 hours had been hectic ones for Mr. D. While

effectively dodging newspaper and television reporters, he and his attorneys had met with representatives of no less than eight branches of government enforcement agencies including Baltimore City and Baltimore County Vice, the Maryland State Police, the DEA, the FBI, the City State's Attorney's Office, the State's Attorney General's Office, and the City Homicide Squad. Surprisingly absent was the U.S. Attorney's Office.

Dante's concern about continuity for his business had forced him to recruit Paul and his right-hand man, Gordon, to work the phones the previous night, along with Lanny who received a "battlefield" promotion for the beating he had taken. Arrangements were already in place for Mr. D to pick up the tab and other expenses for the funerals and hospitalizations of his customers and staff injured or killed in the mayhem of the previous day. Mr. D had also spoken with the late Big Nick Mattesick's brother, Wayne, to arrange for a healthy stipend for the rest of Donna's life.

Mr. D glanced at his Rolex watch.

"Have an appointment, Louis?" asked Margaret as she walked back into the living room.

"Naw, baby. I gotta go to work at six and it's a 45-minute drive," said Mr. D.

"Get the fuck outta here!" she yelled. "How can you think of business. Your business ruined my life . . . It killed people."

"I can't just close it up like that . . ."

Margaret began to cry and Dante rose to console her. She hugged him tightly and whispered, "Louis, let's leave the country. Tonight. Anywhere. The Caribbean, Bali, Mexico. You name it."

"I can't baby. Not yet."

"Yes, you can, Louis. You've got enough money. Please. It's the only way you and I can ever work out. Please?"

"Listen, Maggie. Lemme think about it. I gotta work tonight and . . ."

Margaret pulled away from Dante. She glared at him and wiped her eyes and nose with a Kleenex.

"It's over Louis. Your insensitivity has destroyed whatever feelings I still had for you. Go to work. That's your lover."

She turned and hurried away from Dante, heading toward an upstairs bedroom. Mr. D began to call out to her and stopped. He turned and walked out the front door to Big Nick's Porsche.

CHAPTER 81

The U.S. Air flight from Pittsburgh to Los Angeles and then to San Francisco was boarding. Michael Thompson, the chemist, had his head buried in the *New York Times* as he handed his ticket to the steward at Gate 41.

The night before, he was having dinner at McCabe's Place for Ribs in Laurel, Maryland, 20 minutes from his airport hotel, when he saw the television coverage of Tongue and Baker's massacre at Charlie's. After paying his check, he took an expensive taxi ride to Washington's National Airport and flew to Pittsburgh where he stayed overnight at a nearby Econo Lodge.

While the chemist entered the plane at five-thirty p.m., Mr. D discreetly parked the Porsche on Fullerdale Avenue near Stierhoff's Pub and got into a beat-up 1979 Plymouth Volare, which Lanny had acquired. He drove south on York Road for the next 15 minutes to the quiet community of Stoneleigh, parking the car a block away from his new betting apartment, a third-floor walk-up in a restored colonial at the end of Epps Street.

As Mr. D walked from the car towards the apartment, some dollar bills and betting slips fell from his coat pocket and started to blow away. He went after the papers and grabbed them, ignoring the few bucks that had blown down the street.

Book Three

CHAPTER 1
Winter, 1992
Magellan Prison Camp
Magellan, Virginia

"Did ya see the mayor gettin' blown?"

"What?"

"You heard me, Dante. Did you see the mayor . . . the former mayor having sex with a female visitor?" The deputy warden was losing his patience.

"No, sir," said Mr. D. "Can I be excused now? I wanna work out at the track before the sun goes in."

Deputy Warden Murphy sighed. He'd been questioning two dozen prisoners for over half the day and needed to file a lengthy report to the warden and the Bureau of Prisons before he could leave the complex by nightfall. For two days now, he had been investigating the allegations of several prisoners.

"Listen, Dante. You've followed the rules and stayed clean for months. Don't mess up now."

Mr. D did not want to fuck up. The government owned you in prison. The wardens, the guards, and the Bureau of Prison officials could fuck with you all they wanted, and there was nothing, absolutely nothing, you could do.

He was in the Visitors, or Recreation, Room that day when the former mayor, convicted, he thought, for smoking crack with his girlfriend and denying it, received a visit from a pretty woman from out of state. Mr. D was speaking with his old pal, Marvin, who had been driven down to see him by his male nurse, "Suitcase." Suitcase had pushed Marvin into the Visitors Room in his wheelchair and had gone outside to smoke. The room was filled with wives, relatives, and friends of about 20 convicts, along with several other prisoners who were using the vending machines or watching television.

Almost everyone saw or knew of the hanky-panky that was going on between the former mayor and his visitor. Incredulously, the on-duty guard was oblivious to it. Had it not been for several inmates who considered the former mayor an arrogant son-of-a-bitch, nothing would ever have been said.

"Mr. Murphy, I never saw anything going on," Dante lied. "My visitor was in a wheelchair, and I was bent over speaking to him the whole time."

The deputy warden shook his head. "Get the fuck outta here."

Dante stood up and left the room. He and Murphy knew that, regardless of the outcome of the investigation, the mayor was history at Magellan. Once the story hit the newspapers, it was only a matter of time—a short time—until the former mayor would be transferred far away; punished for embarrassing the warden and the Bureau of Prisons. He would pay dearly. No one could save him—not his attorneys, the ACLU, nobody. Nothing could interfere with violations inside of the walls. Justice was theirs.

CHAPTER 2
Baltimore, Maryland

"What kinda flowers are they?" asked Handsome John. He was staring at the flowers in the center of the old tire at the edge of the pavement. The tire was painted white and weighted with dirt. A makeshift flowerpot leaned against the inside rim of the tire.

"Begonias," said Runner Oppenheim. He handed money and paper slips with numbers to Handsome John.

They were on McHenry Street, or Numbers Runner Street, seated on the white marble steps of an occupied home in the middle of the block.

"Heard from Mr. D?" asked Runner.

"Yeah," lied John. "Three, sometimes four, times a week." Runner knew that John was lying. Word on the street, after Dante went to jail, was that Mel the Tailor and some guys had taken over. Temporarily or permanently, it didn't matter. The numbers runners and low-level bookies needed a lay-off operation. They just hoped that Mel, or whomever, maybe even Handsome John, would cover the big hits. If not, everyone would be out of business.

Chapter 3
Magellan Prison Camp
Magellan, Virginia

Louis Dante was into the fifth and final mile of a power-walk around the quarter-mile track of the federal correctional facility in Magellan, Virginia. Since the fall of 1991, he had been incarcerated at the Magellan Minimum Security Camp across the way from the Maximum Security Prison.

Fitter and trimmer from when he arrived at the camp, Mr. D had lost 22 pounds as a result of the poor quality of the food and a daily exercise regimen. He fast-walked like a tin soldier with his elbows tucked in, arms swinging, and legs stepping widely. Dante wore khaki-colored pants and shirt and Nike Air 180 running shoes. He averaged ten-and-a-half-minute miles, considerably quicker than the sixteen-minute miles of five months ago.

Mr. D had also found a way to divide his thoughts during the exercise regimen around the track. This mind-control program cordoned off his life in distance instead of time. The first mile consisted of personal issues: Margaret, Shirley June, and Juanita; and family and friends not associated with business. Following those four laps, which he forced himself to confront first, he addressed current legitimate business issues. The third mile dealt with his crumbling gambling empire and legal issues related to bank accounts, hidden funds, and investments. The next to the last mile was dedicated to miscellaneous problems, which sometimes ended before the final laps. The final mile or so always pumped him up. It dealt with his arrest and conviction, what led to it, and who was behind it. Over the term of his incarceration, he developed more conspiracy theories than there had been with the Kennedy assassination.

Why Louis Dante was even in jail was difficult to comprehend, especially to anyone who had followed the case in the newspapers. Months after a court-ordered wiretap had been thrown out, in desperation, the prosecutors had announced that they would proceed against Mr. D from an earlier wiretap on the telephones of Lanny Oswinkle. But that didn't work out either.

Baltimore (AP) Baltimore City prosecutors dropped their case against Louis Dante, the alleged ringleader of a multi-million-dollar-a-year gambling operation, yesterday after a district court judge threw out the last remaining bit of evidence against him on a legal technicality. In a case that has been marked by bizarre twists and turns, Judge Barry Glass ruled that prosecutors could not use information gleaned from a court-ordered wiretap because the order did not specify the exact hours during which police could eavesdrop on telephone conversations.

Although the application for the wiretap gave the times of 11 a.m. to 9 p.m., and the police only listened during those hours, Judge Glass found that this was not sufficient under Maryland law to protect an individual's right to privacy.

"The federal [appeals] court has said that a cavalier, carefree and careless attitude toward

any part of a wiretap should be severely condemned," the judge said.

In the face of the ruling, Will Hayden, a
deputy state's attorney, dropped the charges,
which cannot be reinstated. He said that because the trial had already begun, the action
was tantamount to an acquittal.

Richard Karson, one of Dante's lawyers,
said that in light of Judge Glass's ruling, Baltimore County prosecutors will also drop related gambling charges, which would allow Mr.
Dante to recover several hundred thousand
dollars in alleged gambling proceeds that had
been seized from his home.

But Mr. Karson acknowledged that Dante
(a.k.a. Mr. D) is under investigation by federal
prosecutors for allegedly trying to avoid federal cash reporting requirements and has a
multi-million-dollar federal tax lien against
him.

"This is a hell of a start," Mr. Karson insisted. "We've won a major victory in this court
by suppressing all three of the wiretaps."

So things looked good, except for the feds. And they wanted
Dante. They were prepared to go after him on gambling, tax, and
bank structuring charges; even though they acknowledged a less
than fifty-fifty chance at conviction. Mr. D and his attorneys liked
the odds against the government, but, as the meetings and nego-
tiations wore on, things changed. It was similar to the shifting
odds in a football game. The lawyers felt very confident that the
gambling and tax charges, based on the original wiretaps, could
be beaten in court or on appeal. However, the bank structuring
charge was stickier. A conviction meant five years, no parole,
regardless of whether an individual was a first-time offender or
chronic criminal.

In the end, Mr. D decided, with the concurrence of his coun-
sel, that in return for the government dropping gambling charges
and the multi-million-dollar tax lien, he would let them keep the
confiscated money and agree to serve six months in prison and
six months under house arrest. Had he been younger, he would
have fought it. But the "Intolerance of Ambiguity" was driving

him crazy, and the legal fees would have soared to way past a million dollars. It was his only move, and once decided, he never second-guessed it.

Dante's plea bargain was about the only thing he didn't second-guess as he moved quickly around the prison track, day in and day out.

CHAPTER 4
Baltimore County

"Maggie!" screamed Phyllis McTyre, a tall, thin black-haired woman of twenty-eight, as she hurried across the south campus of the Sheppard Pratt Hospital in Towson, Maryland. She was wearing loose-fitting green slacks and a baggy brown sweatshirt.

Nestled into its remaining 100 acres, the Sheppard Pratt Hospital was one of the finest psychiatric institutions in the world, treating over 4,500 outpatients per year. The 322-bed, private, not-for-profit facility was also a teaching and research center. Located inside of the Baltimore Beltway, it was surrounded by acreage it had sold off in the sixties to the Greater Baltimore Medical Center Hospital, Towson State University, and the St. Joseph's Hospital. Established shortly before the Civil War as the Sheppard Asylum from a trust by a Quaker named Moses Sheppard who was concerned with the plight of the country's mentally ill, enslaved, and imprisoned, the hospital trust was supplemented 40 years later by philanthropist, Enoch Pratt.

Margaret Dante looked demure in an oversized, blue print dress from Laura Ashley. Her blond hair was shoulder-length now, and she wore little, if any, makeup.

"It's so good to see you," said Margaret. "What's it been, three years?" They hugged each other tightly.

The women had met in 1987 when they were both inpatients in the dually-diagnosed wing of the hospital. They were being treated for mental health and addiction problems, and they bonded following several group therapy sessions.

"Actually, Phyllis, I'm sorry. Maybe it isn't good to see you here. Is everything all right?"

"Yeah," said Phyllis. "Great! I'm here for my semiannual aftercare checkup. I come back twice a year to see my mom and to check in with Dr. Harbin. How about you? You're not inpatient again, are you?"

"No," said Margaret, shaking her head.

"Partial hospitalization, detox, intensive outpatient? Talk to me, girl." Phyllis sounded like a clinician spouting treatment modalities. Margaret smiled.

"Right now, I'm only seeing Dr. Harbin once a week and on a crisis basis."

"Still not completely right, huh, baby?" asked Phyllis, stroking Margaret's arms.

Margaret nodded and tears welled in her eyes.

The last five years had been bad. The brutal attack, separation, and, later, divorce from Mr. D led to other problems. The only hope she held on to was Handsome John. She always felt that one day they would be together. But she was wrong. John immediately distanced himself from Margaret. Even when she visited him, unannounced, he refused to touch her. Finally, he fabricated a story that he was going back with his wife. She cried and begged him to make love to her one last time. He refused. Cruelly, he told her that he was afraid. Lying, he informed her that he had heard that the bikers both tested positive for the HIV infection following their autopsies. Margaret freaked out.

The rape and separation had caused enough anxiety and depression to require brief outpatient psychiatric help and medication. Occasionally, Margaret took too much medication and drank. Handsome John's allegations took Margaret to the brink. She demanded and took six AIDS tests, all negative. She didn't believe the results. Her mind was floating from too much vodka and Valium. She became suicidal and was admitted to Sheppard Pratt Hospital where she stayed for six months. It was during her first "tour" there that she had met Phyllis.

Although younger than her, Phyllis had had enough negative experiences with men that she was able to help Margaret as much as the therapists. But after Phyllis was discharged, Margaret became chronically depressed. Over the next four years, Margaret returned to the hospital as an inpatient for a total of nine more months. She also stayed in a mentor home, a residential site where she lived in the home of a trained mental health clinician for 90 days. In the last year, she had totally given up alcohol and drug abuse and was progressing positively.

The separation agreement from Louis Dante was beyond fair, and Margaret had no financial problems. After her doctor approved, she left her cousin, Estelle's, home and moved into the Penthouse condominiums in Towson. Her place cost $250,000 and was paid for by Mr. D, whom she rarely saw.

"Are you dating?" asked Phyllis. She and Margaret sat on the ledge of the new conference facility, the National Center for Human Development, which included a 195-seat auditorium. They overlooked the wooded road into the complex and the entrance off of Charles Street that still retained the original stone gatehouse of the Sheppard Asylum.

"No! I hate men!"

"I didn't mean men."

CHAPTER 5

The Baltimore City Police Department's multistory, glass-enclosed building on Fayette Street was literally under siege from the media and public-interest groups. Day after day, a barrage of new statistics concerning violent crime pummeled the first black mayor and third black police commissioner of the City of Baltimore.

Nationally and locally, new data was being released driving Baltimore's reputation as one of the best cities to live in to one of the better to die in; or at least be victimized in.

The latest profile of Baltimore in the newspapers had sent officials reeling, and included more than crime statistics:

● *In a city which boasted more single women with children than married with children, over two-thirds of all births were to unwed mothers; public school students were absent from class more than thirty days a year; and in 1990, there were 78,000 crimes reported.*

● *Single women with children in the poorest areas outnum-*

bered married-couple families by ten to one, the population was extremely young, most families there were on welfare, less than ten percent of women having babies were married, and violent crime was common.

• *In the wealthiest part of Baltimore, only 78 of nearly 1,000 school-age children even attended public schools, welfare was rare, not one teenager was reported to have given birth in 1988 or 1989, and crime tended to be against property, although armed robbery was not uncommon.*

• *Baltimore's most murderous streets in 1990 were those between Eutaw Place and Pennsylvania Avenue, south of North Avenue and north of Laurens Street, in the Madison Park and Druid Heights neighborhoods. Fifteen homicides, thirteen rapes, seventy-three armed-robberies and one hundred four aggravated assaults were reported in an area housing forty-four hundred people. (This area was also the location of Charlie's.)*

• *The city's most truant-filled streets were in two areas of southwest Baltimore and the area around the Maryland Penitentiary. The statistics showed that in one southwest Baltimore neighborhood— south of Baltimore Street between Carey and Gilmor Streets—not a single student graduated from high school in 1990-1991.*

It was lunchtime and Detectives Van Feldman and Hal Byron of the Records Division of Administration, formerly of Vice, left the side entrance of the police department building and walked down Baltimore Street to the Block, the city's adult entertainment section. They picked up three Polish hot dogs with the works from Polack Johnny's stand near the corner of Baltimore and Gay Streets and headed across to the south side of the Block. In the middle of the street, they entered the empty Midway Bar and walked towards the rear where they spied Detective Clarence Copley of Baltimore County Vice seated in front of a long-neck Corona beer. Without speaking, the city cops laid a Polish dog in front of Copley, and the bartender placed two Pepsis at the corner of the bar.

The three ate in silence. Finally, Ron Bell, the bartender and owner of the Midway, spoke.

"One of you guys wanna explain to me those articles in the *Washington Post*. First it said there were more murders, per capita, in Washington than anywhere else in the nation; probably the world. Later, it said there were more shootings in Baltimore than in Washington. Yet Baltimore wasn't even in the top five murder capitals in the U.S. I don't understand."

"Nobody does," said Feldman as he munched on his hot dog. "But from what I gather, it comes down to this. Either the gunmen in D.C. are better shots than the ones in Baltimore or our emergency medical system is the reason."

"What?" asked Bell, who was pouring ice over his cooler of assorted domestic beers.

"It's like this," said Detective Byron. "When someone gets shot in Baltimore, our ambulance system and Shock-Trauma Center are quicker and better than most cities. The first hour is crucial, and usually our emergency medical technicians have arrived and applied the lifesaving techniques. In Washington, a guy could lay bleeding on the streets for hours, maybe days, before help comes."

"I dunno," said Copley. "I still think they're better shots in D.C. But if what you say is true, where were the medics when Watowski got it?"

Feldman and Byron stared at Copley, and Bell took it as a signal to walk away to the front of the bar.

The heat was on the police department for arrests—arrests for unsolved murders—like Clem Watowski's. The mayor was the former state's attorney. He demanded action from the newly-elected state's attorney—his former deputy, Will Hayden. And Hayden wanted somebody for Watowski's murder or suicide, or whatever.

There was no dearth of suspects. Even with alibis, Shadow Creek, Jimmy Bop, Louis Dante, Paul Douglas, Gordon Baines, and another dozen people had motives and opportunities to kill Watowski. And there were other suspects.

"Internal Affairs is investigating me and Feldman," said Byron, "about Watowski."

"Jesus Christ," said Copley, wiping the mustard from his mouth. "With all that's fucking going on, who cares about the murder of a sleaze-ball bookie . . . Look, I need your help with the kid who's taking over for Mr. D and . . ."

"Hold it," interrupted Feldman. "We're not in Vice, anymore. We're in Records."

"You guys help me," said Copley forcefully, "and I'll help you. I'll check with a couple of my snitches about Watowski, and you guys give me some support with Handsome John Abrams.

CHAPTER 6

Handsome John drew back his custom pool cue and aimed low right at the cue ball, hoping to slice the nine-ball into the far left pocket to win the game. It was four-thirty p.m., and he was playing a series of nine-ball matches with Slick Stevie Miles, a pool hustler from Greenbelt, Maryland, outside of Washington, D.C. They were at table four in the center of Mel's Poolroom, and a small crowd had gathered to watch the $500-a-game match, which had been going on for over an hour. Miles was up $1,500.

"Hey, John, I need to see ya!" yelled Mel the Tailor as he came out of his office behind the cash register.

"Soon," answered John as he stood up and, once again, studied the shot.

"Now, man! It's important!" yelled Mel. He was holding his bifocals and some sheets of paper.

"Lighten up, Mel. I'm losin'."

Melvale Dennis, a.k.a. Mel the Tailor, walked back into his office and slammed the door. Handsome John laughed, lined up his shot again, and sunk the nine-ball to win the game.

"Gimme a coupla minutes, Slick," he said, and he walked away from the match into Mel's office carrying his pool cue.

"What's the rush, big man?" asked John sarcastically as he sat on a small sofa facing Mel's desk.

"You're creating problems. Things on the street are getting sloppy . . ."

"What are you talking about?" interrupted John as he unconsciously stroked the pool cue.

"You haven't picked up lay-off money from some of the bookies. You haven't paid off a bunch of number hits. Several checks at Charlie's didn't clear, and Juanita wants to be paid . . ."

"Fuck her black cunt!" said John. "She don't own Charlie's like everybody believes. Dante still runs it."

"That's not what I'm told," said Mel. "And besides, we need the place to cleanse our money. Shadow Creek said that he had three major number hits that he had to hold and pay off himself; and another hit for $14,000 that you still owe him . . ."

"Fuck that nigger, too!" said John, louder than before. "Let him take some risks."

"We're in business together, John. You and me. And we're gonna lose it if you don't do business right. These guys have guessed by now that we're not temporary replacements for Mr. D. Unless we're on the up-and-up, they'll lose faith in us and look to someone else to run things here. I want you and your boys to straighten up . . ."

John stood up and stuck his pool stick in Mel's neck. "Don't boss me around, you sloppy fuck. We're partners. You're not the boss."

Mel pushed the stick away and got up from his chair. "This is still my show, Abrams. I made you. I paid my dues. We've got Dante's empire here for the taking. I've got Paul and Gordon waiting to get indicted. There's millions out there for us and you're gonna fuck it up with your ego and sloppy business practices. I figured you for more brains than that!"

Handsome John stood pensively for a few seconds, regained his composure, and decided to cool things out. "You're right, Mel baby. Ever since Dante went to jail, I've gotten lazy. Ya know, the challenges are disappearing, and I need to be challenged . . . Hell, Dante'll be out of jail soon and then we'll really have some fun."

John turned and walked out of Mel's office. In his mind, he was already figuring how he was going to take Mel the Tailor down next. Mel, too, had reciprocal thoughts.

John took out a roll of bills to pay Slick Stevie Miles with.

"I gotta go to work, Slick. Here's the thou'. We'll play again next week, double the stakes."

"Where's my money, you thief?" shouted Old Man Lindy from the crowd of onlookers around the pool table. "You and Mel and that dead fuck robbed me!"

Lindy grabbed John's arm and tugged at it. Mel came out from his office and watched in amusement as John smacked Lindy repeatedly with the pool stick until he crumbled to the floor.

"Throw that old fuck outta here," ordered Mel to one of his workers as Handsome John strolled out of the pool hall.

CHAPTER 7

Ramone Blande ran down the front steps of the State of Maryland's Clarence Mitchell Jr. Courthouse onto St. Paul Street. The paper detective was working on a personal injury case for State Farm Insurance, which had just recessed for lunch at twelve-thirty p.m. He was wearing a full-length, oyster-colored Armani raincoat as he headed to Harbor Place, four blocks south.

At St. Paul and Fayette Streets, he recognized the two men in a Yellow Cab who waved him over. It was Paul and Gordon.

"Get in," Gordon commanded from the front seat as the back door opened and Ramone jumped in. The taxi pulled away and headed west.

"What's up, guys?" asked Ramone. "I've gotta be back in court by one-forty-five."

"That's okay," said Paul as he shifted in the seat and looked out of the rear window. In the front seat, Gordon made small talk with the Russian-immigrant cabdriver.

"Actually, Gordon and I have to appear before the federal grand jury in a half an hour; so you'll have plenty of time to get some lunch."

"Grand jury . . . Is it the one on loansharking?" asked Ramone. Paul nodded.

"What are ya gonna say?" asked Ramone.

"Say? We never say anything, Ramone. It's too incriminating. That's what the Fifth Amendment's for."

"Rumor has it that you guys have lots of trouble," said Ramone.

"We know," said Paul. "That's why we wanted to see you. It's getting very heaty for me and Gordon to be snooping around. We need your help, and we'll pay you handsomely. But it's imperative that you find out certain information as quickly as possible. Even if your findings aren't a hundred percent, that's okay."

The taxi had driven west as far as Green Street and turned left, past the University of Maryland Hospital and professional schools. At Pratt Street, the cab went left again and veered off to the right for the occupants to admire the handiwork of the development of the new baseball facility—Oriole Park at Camden Yards.

"What do you need?" asked Ramone.

"We need to know who is ratting us out to the feds. Who killed Watowski? Who is trying to take over Mr. D's business now? And who was behind Dante's problems in the beginning? I'm aware that Handsome John Abrams and Mel Dennis are trying to step in temporarily, but that doesn't make them guilty of everything, or anything. It may just be smart business. Oh, I also want to know if Shirley June McCutcheon had anything to do with Dante's trouble. His trouble, Ramone, is all of our trouble. Also, Louis wants you to visit him in Magellan."

The taxi pulled up in front of the Light Street Pavilion at Harbor Place, and Ramone stepped out. As he turned to walk away, Gordon called out, "Don't call us. We'll catch up next week."

Chapter 8
Magellan, Virginia

Every pair of inmate eyes in the Visitors Room caressed the body of the lithe black woman in the black wool suit with three-inch black pumps. She sat next to the convicted felon in the vinyl orange chair. The correctional officer, Facet, stared intently at the couple, certain that nothing embarrassing to the Bureau of Prisons would happen on his watch.

She had driven three hours south from Baltimore, taking Interstate 95 through Richmond and finally arriving at the Magellan Prison Camp. Parking off the rural road in the visitors' parking lot, she had followed the explicit instructions, walking up the opposite pavement to the guard tower, then crossing the street and announcing herself into the intercom at the base of the tower. After the guard verified her visitation, she again crossed the street and walked past the maximum security facility to the crosswalk leading to the camp. Crossing the street one more time, she proceeded to the Visitors Hall, presented herself to the correctional officer, Facet, and waited for Louis Dante to appear.

"Jesus, Louis, where the hell did the mayor do the dirty deed?" joked Juanita, looking around the room with the pool and Ping-Pong tables and vending machines. "I guess grabbing your cock is out of the question, huh?"

Mr. D fought back a smile. "Cool it, Juanita. The feds are sick over the incident. You shouldn't have dressed like that."

"Actually, Louis, I almost put on a nun's habit, but I figured that would turn you on more. I'm sorry. I just wanted you to keep me in your mind after I leave."

"Don't worry. If I forget, these horny 'mothers' in here'll remind me . . . Tell me what's goin' on."

"Well, you're definitely being missed on the street. Since Paul is under scrutiny, a coupla small-time bookies have tried to replace you, but they're not up to it. The biggest chunk of business is being handled by Handsome John Abrams and Mel the Tailor. Their business acumen, however, leaves a lot to be desired. They forget pickups, they don't treat big players like you did, and they don't pay off on time, or at all, sometimes."

"Great," said Mr. D, turning his head and glaring at Daryl Winkler, a convicted attorney in for tax fraud who had been staring at Juanita's legs. "For 20 years, I serviced those unappreciative pricks. Let 'em suffer over my demise."

"They think you'll be back. That's what Handsome John tells 'em," said Juanita.

"That's okay. It's smart business. But I'm never going back to bookin'. It's over. The stress killed me. I've got other ideas . . . How's your business?"

Dante was referring to Charlie's, which he had sold to Juanita legally for one dollar before he went to prison.

"You know, Louis, it's still yours as far as I'm concerned."

"No, sugar, it's yours. Forever! So, how's business?"

"Not as good as when you had it, but no complaints. Handsome John passed some insufficient-funds checks from four of his clients, but Mel said he'd see that they're covered."

Dante shook his head. "Those two'll never make it. But John's a good kid. He's always been in my corner, and he was once family, ya know."

CHAPTER 9
Baltimore City

Shirley June's eyes were squeezed shut. Her right hand was tightly grabbing her flowing red hair while her left one was digging into the brown striped sheet through to the mattress of the bed. Lying naked on her stomach, she appeared to be burrowing into the bed as she groaned in ecstasy. Hovering behind her, Handsome John's face was between her legs, his tongue moving from her vagina to her asshole.

She had experienced oral sex often, but never this variation. On the nightstand by the bed was a steaming cup of coffee which Handsome John would sip every thirty seconds or so before sticking his piping-hot tongue back into Shirley June.

It was lunchtime, and they were in a room on the fourth floor of the Hyatt Harbor Place Hotel, not far from her investment office. She had met Handsome John a couple of months earlier at a charity event. He told her his name was Jack Sprague, Jr., a shopping center developer from Montreal whose father was extremely wealthy. They were looking for investment opportunities in the States. Shirley June was immediately impressed with "Jack" and found his good looks and free-spending attitude appealing. After she corroborated that Jack Sprague, Sr. existed in Canada, something John knew she would do, she began seeing him whenever he "visited" Baltimore. She screwed him on their second date and envisioned a long affair and escape from the Dante fiasco; and maybe marriage and living in Canada down the road.

For John, it was another trophy-fuck, another conquest of a Mr. D lover; although he was really turned on to Shirley June's body and cunning mind. However, he knew it couldn't last, and yet . . .

John felt great. Vengeance was his. He'd put Dante out of business, ruined his marriage with Margaret, fucked Shirley June, and was close to being the top man in gambling. It was only a matter of time before he would dispose of Mel. He thought Mel was getting too much of their deal, and John detested being bossed around.

Handsome John, carrying an overnight bag, came down the

escalator from the garden restaurant. He kissed Shirley June goodbye and walked over to the checkout counter on the right. She passed through the revolving door of the front of the Hyatt. Both were totally unaware of the heavyset, rumpled-dressed man seated in the lobby with a *USA Today* hiding his face—Detective Copley of Baltimore County Vice.

My, my, Copley thought, cradling a manila file marked "Margaret Dante—CONFIDENTIAL." Late last night, he had "acquired" this file from the private office of Dr. Gary Harbin of Sheppard Pratt Hospital. That makes two surprises in less than 12 hours. What a wonderful day.

CHAPTER 10

At three p.m., Mel left his poolroom and drove north on Liberty Road across the Carroll County line and through the city of Westminster to the Westminster Pike heading east. Three miles later, he pulled into the State Vehicle Inspection Site to have his annual emissions test.

It was the end of the month and the absolute busiest time to get a vehicle inspected. There were at least 40 cars in line ahead of Mel. Quickly and quietly, the passenger from a metallic green 1991 Chevrolet Berretta behind him entered Mel's black Lincoln Town Car. He wore an off-the-rack blue pinstriped suit, starched oxford shirt, and rep tie.

"What's up?" asked the suit. It was Investigator Blume, formerly of the Maryland U.S. Attorney's Office. He was now operating out of the Attorney General of the United States' Office in Washington, coordinating a six-state loan-sharking investigation.

"Did ya sic the city's Internal Affairs boys on Feldman and Byron?" Mel barked.

"Yeah, a couple weeks ago. They're out of Vice. What's your beef with them? Was Watowski your close buddy?" asked Blume with a hint of sarcasm.

"Nah. I hated him. So did everybody else. But, believe me,

those ex-Vice cops are never 'ex.' I'm afraid they're also associated with Paul Douglas and Gordon Baines, and Dante," Mel lied.

"So what. You've got nothing to fear. We'll protect ya . . . I need some more names—friends of Paul, primarily, in Philadelphia and New Orleans."

The cars moved slowly, stopping and starting every few minutes. The drivers had their nine dollars and emissions applications in hand, hoping their vehicle would pass the standards.

"Smells like burning sulfur in here, Mel. Phew! You may not pass."

"It's not the car, it's me. Gas. Nerves."

"Jesus. You're brutal. I gotta lower the window."

Mel began citing a string of names and nicknames of gamblers and loan sharks in the two cities, along with some background material on each one. Occasionally, he threw in an innocent name of a fellow whom he disliked. He considered his "testimony" payback time. When he was finished, he decided on one more payback.

"Blume, there's a growing problem-child here in Baltimore that I'd like hassled." Mel's car was now third in line to be tested.

"Who's that, Mel?"

"John Abrams. Handsome John Abrams. Very dangerous. Also a Dante protégé."

"Okay. I'll see what I can do," said Blume as he prepared to leave the car. "By the way, Mel, it looks as if the AG's office'll need you to testify in court. Not against these new names or other ones, but against Paul Douglas and Gordon Baines."

"No fuckin' way!" screamed Mel. He pounded on his steering wheel and grabbed at Blume's suit coat. Blume removed Mel's hand and calmly told him, "Don't ever touch me again or I'll hurt you in places you didn't think possible . . . We didn't believe we'd need your testimony in court originally. However, our prosecutors tell me that in order to go to trial against Douglas, we need more than hearsay and affidavits from enforcement officials. We need a live body who's been victimized—you."

"But what about the other guys I told ya about who borrowed from him?" pleaded Mel.

"None have panned out. Not a one."

The black Lincoln Town Car was next, and the attendant tapped on Mel's window. As Mel's window retreated electronically, Blume got out of the car. "I'll be in touch," he called back.

"Fuck you," Mel muttered under his breath.

Chapter 11

Cousin Dickie slipped his key into the pale blue door of Margaret's condo and let himself into the marble foyer. At twenty-six years old, Dickie was slightly overweight for his five-foot-six frame. He weighed 170 pounds, with most centered in his belly and enormous thighs. He wore elastic-waist red sweatpants and a matching red hooded sweatshirt. Dickie's black hair was permed and tied in a ponytail, which hung about five inches below his neck. He had a baby-faced cherubic look and a pointed nose. He was carrying a large shopping bag full of groceries and meats that he had picked up for Margaret at Graul's Market out in the valley. His mother had insisted that after Maggie had moved from their house, she and Dickie would still help her out until she was fully recovered. Dickie didn't mind running chores for his cousin. He liked to hang out at her luxury condo and watch the large cable television, which he didn't have at his house. Cable meant sports, and sports meant gambling to Dickie in his own recovery from compulsive gambling.

Over the past few years since Dickie began seeking therapy, he had suffered several relapses. Anytime Mr. D found out, Dickie blamed it on his "disease;" and whenever his mom or Margaret discovered him gambling, he blamed it on Mr. D. When Dickie's insurance coverage was exhausted, it was Margaret, through Mr. D's alimony, who paid for Dickie's treatment.

Dickie had no problem finding treatment programs, even after he was put out of Gamblers Anonymous and, later, the state-funded treatment center in Mt. Wilson. Maryland was the first state in the nation to legislate and fund a public pathological gambling treatment program. Previously, only the Veterans Administration Hospitals in Brooklyn, Miami, and Brecksville, Ohio provided care. Since 1978, over six private facilities had operated in Maryland, and Gamblers Anonymous chapters grew from one to thirteen. And during the eighties, another dozen states passed similar legislation.

Dickie was so slick that he even conned money out of other gamblers in Gamblers Anonymous and ripped off the petty cash and checkbook at the state-run Mt. Wilson facility. In another scam, he went into the upholstery business and convinced his clinician and program director at the private psychiatric facility, Nyman Manor, that he could completely reupholster all of their antique furniture for below cost. Several thousands of dollars worth of sofas, chairs, and other items were removed from the hospital and carefully packed into Dickie's Ryder rental truck. After two years and numerous phone calls from the sparsely furnished Administrative and Conference Center, the executives at Nyman Manor quietly acknowledged that the upholstery job was a scam. Unable to admit that they were ripped off, they wrote the furniture off as a bad debt.

For the last two years, Dickie's behavior had improved. He no longer relapsed. "Slipping" was what he called it now, and that happened infrequently. And, on the occasions that he did place a bet, he always laid the money up front. This afternoon was one of his slipping days, and he was prepared to watch the Louisiana State-UCLA basketball game at Margaret's while she was in group therapy at Sheppard Pratt Hospital.

He placed the groceries in the spacious kitchen and was about to relieve himself in the guest bathroom when he heard soft voices coming from Margaret's bedroom. At first he thought it was the CD player, which she always left on, but when he rounded the corner of the hallway, he saw two figures. Silently, he crept around to the doorway and peeked in.

Margaret was at the left side of the king-size bed in front of the mahogany night table with the antique Chinese blue and white flowered lamp. The curtains were drawn, and the light of the lamp shone on Margaret's face, blond hair, and breasts. She was naked to the waist, her brown silk top hanging closely over her hips. On her knees on the bed was a woman with close-cropped brown hair wearing a lightweight gray sweater and stonewashed jeans. Dickie could not see her face, which was burrowed in Margaret's chest, kissing, licking, and gently biting her swollen nipples. Margaret's eyes were closed and her head rolled around her neck in ecstasy. He could not see the woman's hands, either, as they were both hidden under Margaret's skirt.

CHAPTER 12

"Had to bring in a handwriting expert to decipher Dr. Harbin's notes," said Detective Van Feldman.

"Yeah, yeah," groaned Copley.

"Then we had to get a shrink to explain the notes to us," added Byron.

"Yeah, yeah. You guys wanna take credit for my work," growled Vice cop Copley. "I took the risks. Remember that, boys . . . Anyhow, what's the story on Mrs. Dante?"

"Tell 'em, Hal," ordered Feldman. "And make it short and simple. We ain't got all day."

The three veteran cops were roaming through the inside stalls of the Lexington Market in downtown Baltimore. Stalls selling food, produce, drinks, candy, pastry, and other assorted goods dotted two square blocks between Howard and Green Streets. Hundreds of shoppers strolled and ate at lunchtime in the newly renovated market.

"Originally, Margaret Dante suffered from major depression, compounded by prescription drugs and alcohol. She was later diagnosed with posttraumatic stress disorder. During the therapy, it was revealed that she had past sexual abuse episodes as a child involving an aunt and uncle."

"Jesus," said Copley. The three ordered corned beef sandwiches from Lenny's Deli stall.

"Wait, it gets better," said Byron. "Later, Dr. Harbin finds that she has multiple personalities. Because of her drug problem, they put her in this special women's program. While she's there, her homosexual leanings are awakened and she begins an affair with another female patient."

"You fuckin' kiddin'?" interrupted Copley.

"No," said Byron. "She had a lot of setbacks, but his recent notes suggest that the psychotherapy, without medication, worked her through the trauma, and his prognosis is that she'll come out of this shit even healthier."

"But won't she still be gay?" asked Copley.

"Yeah," said Byron. "But here's the popper, my friend. In Dr. Harbin's earlier notes, Margaret spoke of an affair she was having behind Mr. D's back. And guess who it was with?"

"Who?" asked Copley on cue. He had stopped at Wallace's Bakery and ordered a slice of rainbow cake.

"Handsome John Abrams," said Byron.

"Sonofabitch," cursed Copley. "Now it makes sense. I had a Pen Register on Abrams a few years ago and kept seeing Mr. D's phone number pop up. I figured that Dante was never dumb enough to call another bookie from his home. Thought it was his nephew or cousin, Dickie . . . Never figured it'd be the fourth . . . or fifth Mrs. Dante."

CHAPTER 13

Ever since the early caveman borrowed his neighbor's ax and, upon returning it, found that he owed him two axes, or a piece of his "significant other," society has frowned upon the act of usury or loansharking. Taking excessive interest in exchange for a loan was against the law between the ancient Hindu and Chinese. The Greeks, although allowing small interest rates, scorned usurers. Aristotle felt that money could only be used as a means of exchange, and his philosophy greatly impacted the church in the Middle Ages, which condemned the charging of interest.

People who loan money at interest rates exceeding those approved by law, and who use threats and intimidation to obtain repayment, are known as loan sharks. Although the penalty for usury is forfeiture of interest and/or a fine, the punishment for loansharking is usually a prison sentence.

When Paul loaned Mel $90,000, he charged him 20 percent for 20 weeks as interest, or juice. This meant that Mel had to pay Paul $108,000 at $5,400 a week, $900 of which was interest. If Mel couldn't pay the entire $5,400 a week, he still had to come up with the $900 interest and would then have to pay the full monthly amount for an additional week. The common practice for loansharking money is usually over 10 or 20 weeks at 20 percent, although there are groups or individuals who charge 25 to 30 percent.

Mel's troubles at repaying the loan began in his third week, and he skipped payments, including interest, for three consecutive weeks. That's when Gordon paid him a visit and roughed him up, and scared Mel into running to the feds.

There's not a lot that gamblers can do with their profits. They need lots of liquid money to use for big hits, investment opportunities are scarce, and they surely can't deposit the money in banks. Thus, they put money out on the street to loan to risky people at exorbitant interest rates. When the loan repayments are delinquent, extortion and intimidation are their only recourse.

Guys like Paul and Mr. D seldom, if ever, resorted to intimidation and physical harm with deadbeat gamblers. They just cut them off and communicated the deadbeats to other bookies. To gamblers, this was worse than death. When it came to loaning money, it became necessary to instill fear in the borrowers. But aside from some minor beatings, no one was ever seriously hurt or killed.

However, the borrowers had no knowledge of this practice and feared for their lives.

CHAPTER 14

"You ain't small-time anymore, asshole!" screamed Mel through the pay phone outside of the 7-Eleven near his poolroom. He had been arguing for 10 minutes with Handsome John who was calling from a pay phone inside the lobby of the Pikesville Hilton at the Beltway and Reisterstown Road in northwest Baltimore County.

"Mel," said John, trying not to lose his temper. Inwardly, he wanted to kill him. "This is too much like hard work. I no longer have enough time to work out, hustle the babes, play around . . ."

"Exactly," said Mel. "How do you think Dante amassed his fortune? Why did you think all of the other BMs laid off to him? For 20 fuckin' years, he worked his balls off . . . same as Paul Douglas."

"Where do you figure Mr. D stashed his money?" asked John. He was speaking quietly now as two nuns in their thirties, dressed in modern-day habits, shared a phone call three stations down in the row of telephones.

"In his mattress," said Mel sarcastically. "Now don't keep breakin' appointments, John. Pay off the runners on time, and pick up the money that's owed us. We look like a couple guys off the pickle boat running this operation."

"Okay," said John. He was finished with Mel and had more lucrative thoughts in his mind. "I'll take care of business and see ya tomorrow."

"Tonight!" screamed Mel as John hung up.

Handsome John smiled at the two nuns. He thought for a moment about seducing them and then looked in his small black book for a telephone number. Finding it, he dropped a quarter in the coin slot and dialed.

"Dickie, my man," said Handsome John. "How's it goin'?"

"John," said Dickie cautiously. "I'm paid up, right?"

"Of course. 'Cept for some juice. But forget it . . . Listen, I've gotta proposition for ya, and I need to see ya real soon. How fast can you get to the Pikesville Hilton?"

Dickie stood by the phone in his kitchen and played with his earlobe, which he did only when he was nervous.

"'Bout 35 minutes," said Dickie.

"Great!" said John loudly. "I'll be waiting in the lobby with two nuns." He hung up as the nuns looked over at him in surprise. They had also completed their call.

Smiling, John approached the Sisters.

"Say, where you girls from? Krypton?"

※

"Where do you think your 'Uncle' hid his stash?" asked Handsome John. He and Dickie were sitting on a bench in the tennis barn attached to the Pikesville Hilton watching the pro give a tennis lesson to three overweight women dressed in designer warm-up suits and too much jewelry.

"I dunno, John. If I did, I wouldn't be sittin' here with you."

"Think his ex-wife knows?" asked John. He purposely didn't refer to Margaret by name. He was sure she had never mentioned their affair to anyone.

"I dunno," said Dickie.

"How'd you like to work for me, Dickie?"

"Doin' what?"

"Doin' what Mr. D never let you do. Being a real good bookie."

"Don't con me," said Dickie. "What are you looking for?"

John was silent for a while as the two stared at the tennis pro who was hitting balls to the three women. None had returned one shot inbounds.

"Here's the deal, Dickie. Dante must have salted away millions over the years, and some of it's gotta be hidden. You help me find it and we'll split it down the middle. If we don't find it, I'll still give you 25 percent of my action as long as you work the streets for me."

"What do I need you for to find the money?" asked Dickie.

"'Cause I've got ideas about how and where to look for it. If you could've found it, we wouldn't be talking now."

"I don't think Maggie . . . Dante's wife, will help us. And I doubt if she knows, anyhow," said Dickie.

"How 'bout you get me in to see her, alone. And I'll work my charms with her," said John as a tennis ball flew up and hit the netting in front of them.

"Maybe a while ago, John. But she ain't into men anymore. Keep this to yourself, but she's a lesbian now."

"No shit!" exclaimed John, surprised. He fell silent again. Then he spoke. "Can you get into her apartment?"

"Yeah," said Dickie. "I gotta key. But she's always home, except when she sees her shrink."

"Just get me the key and I'll figure out what to do," said Handsome John.

"I need a show of good faith," said Dickie.

The hour tennis lesson was breaking up and the pro seemed relieved. The women seemed elated.

"I'll show you more than good faith, Dickie. Here's a thousand dollars now," said John as he peeled off ten hundred-dollar bills. "As soon as you get me the key, you get another thou' and a list of collections to begin your job as my new 25-percent partner in the numbers business."

Dickie smiled as he took the money. Cockily, he responded

to the offer. "I want 25 percent of the sports gambling, too, or it's no deal."

"Fine," said Handsome John, knowing that he wasn't going to deliver on any of his promises, anyhow. "I want the ex-Mrs. Dante's schedule and a key to her place within 48 hours."

Chapter 15
Magellan, Virginia

Mr. D not only improved his appearance and speed around the track, he regained his considerable skills as a pool player. Within a few months, he had become the best pool player at the Magellan Camp. There were even some who were convinced that Louis Dante could beat Reggie Constanza, the reputed Mob boss of Cleveland. Constanza was the top pool player in the maximum prison across the street. No such game would come about, though, since the Bureau of Prisons frowned upon such fraternization.

"Goddamn, Dante, how many balls did you just run?" asked Chooch Tranor, a black former social worker serving three years for embezzling welfare funds in Wilmington, Delaware.

"I wasn't counting," answered Dante.

"I was," said Joseph Morstein, a former developer from Rockville doing 18 months for diverting Housing and Urban Development (HUD) funds. "He sunk 78 straight balls before he missed."

"What's the world's record?" asked Tranor as he watched Mr. D rack the balls and begin to play again.

"I think Willie Mosconi ran over 500 balls once," said Morstein. "How many do ya think you can run, Dante?"

Mr. D moved gracefully around the pool table, never looking up at Tranor or Morstein. He sunk six balls, two of which were excellent bank shots. Then he stood erect, chalked his cue stick, and spoke to his fan club.

"Records don't mean shit! I saw Mosconi, Lassiter, and Minnesota Fats all play. I also saw guys in filthy pool halls in one-horse towns run more balls than anybody when money was on the line. A guy is at his best or worst when the pressure is on. Playing for fun, for championships, and for records is for chumps. When your own money is on the table, that's when you can talk records."

Dante thought to himself and smiled. He turned to his audience of two fans.

"Greatest pressure playing I ever saw with pool was a few years ago in Atlantic City at the world championships. Not the competitions, but the side betting earlier in the day. Mickey Seidel, from Baltimore, challenged everybody at 'jacked-up-one-handed' pool for $1,000 a game."

"What's that?" asked Tranor.

"There're three ways to shoot pool: the traditional way with two hands; one-handed, using the rail to rest the pool cue on; and jacked-up, or up in the air, one-handed where you can't use the rails. You have to have very steady nerves, timing, and great concentration 'cause you're holding the back end of the pool cue and shooting with it.

"Anyhow, Seidel couldn't get any of the champions to play him straight-up, even money. So he gave them two ball spots in nine-ball games, increased the odds, and walked outta Atlantic City with $150,000. That, boys, was pressure!"

"Wow! That's a great score," said Morstein. "A hundred and fifty thousand dollars!"

"Not exactly $150,000 net for Seidel," corrected Dante. "He didn't have all of the up-front money. I was backing half the action."

Mr. D went back to shooting pool, and Morstein and Tranor continued talking about records. Ten minutes later, Deputy Warden Murphy walked over to Dante.

"You got a visitor."

"I don't think so," said Mr. D, eying up a shot. "Nobody scheduled to see me 'til the end of the week."

Dante hit the cue ball toward the six ball, shooting high right English, hoping to just nudge the ball into the side pocket and continue on to drop the ten ball in the corner. But the six never dropped. Murphy grabbed it. He then walked over to Mr. D and stared in his face as the cue ball continued on, knocking in the ten.

"This guy don't need an appointment . . . Outside, now. Assistant Warden Martin's office."

Mr. D smiled at Murphy, contained his anger, and tossed his pool cue to Morstein. He hurried through the Recreation Room and down the hallway to his "appointment." Inside of the assistant warden's office stood a lean, tall man of 38 wearing an off-the-rack black wool suit from Sears. He wore prescription sunglasses with green tint and black rims. Grinning, he introduced himself to Mr. D.

"Detective Brandon Carr, Internal Affairs, Baltimore City."

Dante sighed. "You've made a long trip for nothing, Carr. I've got nothing to say to the police, . . . and what's Internal Affairs got to do with me? I'm not a cop."

Continuing to grin, Detective Carr motioned Dante into a chair by the door and lifted himself up on top of the assistant warden's desk.

"Oh, you've got me wrong, Dante. I didn't come down here to ask you anything. I'm here to tell you something."

CHAPTER 16

Once in the late seventies, the feds paid a surprise visit to Mr. D with a search warrant and several very large FBI agents intent on laying waste to the Dante homestead. Mr. D watched in silence for five hours as the U.S. government tore apart his home looking for his stash. At one point, two agents were inches away from a safe in the concrete wall in the den, which hid four million dollars in cash. Nothing was ever found and the charges against Mr. D for interstate gambling were dropped a few months later. The government didn't offer, and Dante didn't ask, for someone to pay for the cleanup after the FBI had ransacked his home.

Bookies need money to pay off big numbers and sports betting hits within days. Unlike the state-run lotteries, which, for a one-million-dollar jackpot, will pay $50,000 a year for 20 years, remove taxes beforehand, and print the winners' names in the newspapers, bookmakers pay higher odds, deliver the entire amount at once (e.g. one million dollars in cash), take no taxes, and maintain confidentiality. Bookies also need immediate funds to loan out.

The problem for the bookmaker is where to hide his stash. It needs to be close by and under cover. Safe deposit boxes don't work anymore. The government's been on top of them for years. Surveillance by the authorities also makes visiting a "stash" too often very dangerous. Thus, the bookmaker must operate more than one stash and, hopefully, have a trusted friend or family member to either keep a stash or know of its whereabouts in case of an emergency.

Paul always had his brother, Benson, his uncle, Little Billie, a network of trusted transporters between Virginia and Maryland, and later, Mr. D.

Louis Dante had Paul, and his trusted wheelchair-bound friend, Marvin.

CHAPTER 17

It was three a.m. and Mel was half-asleep on the long, worn black sofa in his poolroom office. The door was locked and Mel was slouched halfway off of the sofa dressed in huge white boxer shorts. The VCR was playing *Taboo II* on the television, a porno film from the early eighties.

Mel was oblivious to the flames and smoke bellowing from the back left outside corner of the poolroom. The fire had begun fifteen minutes earlier, and only the two-day downpour of rain, which had stopped the day before, kept the soaked building from burning quickly. An elderly woman, whose semidetached house was situated 200 feet behind the poolroom, had noticed the fire when she woke up to let her dog outside. She immediately called 911.

The wail of the sirens and roar of the fire trucks were not enough to jostle Mel's attention initially. However, the sound of axes busting into his precious poolroom sent Mel scurrying for his pants. Within seconds, Mel had dressed, gathered his money strongbox, and fled outside to the street.

An hour later, as Mel watched two fire officials sifting around the smoldering remains of two-thirds of his poolroom, a man in civilian clothes who flashed his ID approached him.

"Mr. Melvale Dennis? I'm Brian Nepper, Baltimore County Fire Department, Arson Division."

"Are you here to see if somebody set this fire?" asked Mel. He was breathing heavily and shivering.

"Actually, this fire didn't take much investigating," said Nepper. "It was certainly deliberately set. Whoever did it didn't even try to hide it. Coupla' our firefighters found the gasoline container and rags lying out back."

"Motherfucker," said Mel, enraged.

"Do you sleep here often?" asked Nepper.

Mel nodded. He was still clutching the money strongbox under his left arm.

"Got any enemies?" asked the arson investigator. "Could be someone was trying to kill ya. I'm gonna turn this one over to the police. They'll be in touch with you."

"Thank you," said Mel, dismissing Nepper. He walked halfway down the block to his car and locked the strongbox in his trunk. Taking one last look at the charred ruins of over half of his pool hall, Mel got into his car and drove off. There was nothing more he could do. He had notified his insurance agent from a pay phone earlier. Anything of value or danger to Mel was safely in his trunk. And the Dante gambling business, which he had usurped, needed to be run every day, regardless of the circumstances.

In his mind, Mel was conducting his own investigation of the arson, sifting through the possible suspects who wanted him scared or dead. It boiled down to Paul and Gordon or Handsome John.

Four cars behind Mel's Lincoln Town Car, slouched down beneath the steering wheel of a 24-year-old white Chevy Nova, was Old Man Lindy. He was perfectly still; except for a grin that grew wider and wider as he watched Mel the Tailor drive away.

CHAPTER 18

Shirley June McCutcheon was feeling adventurous and had, for the first time in years, cut her hair and permed it. Elated with the results, she uncharacteristically hugged her hair stylist, Jon, and skipped out of Salconi's Salon to her new black Lexus.

Suddenly she stopped, feeling her throat closing. Leaning against her new car was Detective Copley.

"Jesus, you asshole! What are you doing here?" cried Shirley June, looking up and down Montgomery Street.

She was dressed in a gray wool suit with a black Burberry raincoat draped over her shoulders.

"You said we'd never meet again if I helped you. Leave me alone." She was shaking.

Copley had his arms folded across the front of his worn, old herringbone, tweed sport coat. He looked the beautiful redhead up and down admiringly.

"Miss McCutcheon, even at my age I still appreciate beauty; and you're a fine lookin' woman. But I liked your hair better the way it was."

"Why are you here?" she whispered. "Please, get in my car. I don't want to be seen talking to you."

Copley walked around to the passenger side of the slick mahogany auto and waited for the electric door lock to pop up. He had trouble sliding into the front seat since it was pulled up close to the dashboard.

"Miss McCutcheon, I'm an honorable man, and I meant what I said about never bothering you again about Louis Dante."

"Then why are you here?" she asked, her hands tight on the steering wheel.

"I'm here to ascertain if you're involved in illicit gambling, or just a bookie groupie . . . How's this seat go back?"

Shirley June started the car and pressed an automatic seat adjustment button.

"I don't know what you're talking about," she said.

"How about Handsome John Abrams?" asked Copley.

"Never heard of him," said Shirley June, relieved to hear an unfamiliar name. "What's he got to do with me?"

"He's a bookie who's takin' over for Dante. And I saw you with him a coupla days ago coming out of the Hyatt Hotel after a little tryst."

"That wasn't a bookie, you bastard. How dare you follow me. That's my boyfriend from Canada. His name is Jack Sprague, Jr., and you're gonna get in trouble if you mess with his family." Shirley June was livid.

"Calm down, Miss McCutcheon. You've been suckered. I wasn't following you. I was following the bookie, Abrams. He's takin' ya for a ride, my dear. I'm just trying to figure out why."

Two hours later, Shirley June reached Ramone on his car phone. Hysterical, she threatened and, later, pleaded with him to get the word to Mr. D to leave her alone. Without mentioning Copley or sex, she told Ramone that she had recently discovered how Handsome John Abrams had fooled her and that she believed Louis Dante had put him up to it for revenge. Ramone never divulged that he was on his way to visit Mr. D, or that she had called him outside of Washington D.C.

CHAPTER 19
Magellan, Virginia

"Say, Dante. There're some guys who'd pay a lot of money if you sent your visitor over to 'maximum' for a few days," said Officer Facet, referring to Ramone Blande.

Instead of a business suit, Ramone had worn a casual outfit. Casual for him, but embarrassing to Mr. D. Already taking "ribs" from fellow inmates over Juanita, the appearance of the homosexual Ramone bedecked in a tan ultrasuede suit and royal blue silk shirt had Dante blushing.

"Christ, Ramone. Couldn't you have toned it down a bit?" whispered Dante as he chose a chair rather than the two-seater sofa which Ramone had plopped down on. "If I was across the street in the prison instead of the camp, after your visit, I'd be gang-raped."

"Oh, what a terrible thought," giggled Ramone. "Why don't you sit next to me, Louis? I've got some very interesting information to relay to you."

"Cut the jokes," said Dante. "I've got some problems. Internal Affairs for Baltimore City paid me a visit and . . ."

"Wait," interrupted Ramone. "Lemme' tell you about a call I received on the way down here."

Ramone proceeded to tell Dante about Shirley June's frantic conversation on his car phone blaming Mr. D for putting Handsome John up to humiliating her. Then Dante topped Ramone's exposé by telling him what the Internal Affairs cop, Brandon Carr, revealed to him about Handsome John, Maggie, and Shirley June.

"Why would he do this to you?" asked a shocked Ramone. "Or haven't you figured it out yet?"

"Ramone," said Mr. D softly, "in here, there's plenty of time to figure things out. As far as I can break this down, it's far too sophisticated to be solely a Handsome John show. I'm speaking only of the takeover of my business. Mel the Tailor seems to be the major player here, and Abrams always worshiped him. As to Maggie and Shirley June, my guess is jealously, vengeance for his sister, both . . ."

"What was the motive of the Internal Affairs guy to tell you this?" asked Ramone. He stood up, walked over to a vending machine, and bought a can of apple juice. Mr. D walked with him.

"They want somebody for Watowski's murder," said Dante. "Plus, Copley's probably involved. Maybe they're looking to dismantle my network before I get out. I had a feeling the cop thought Handsome John was working for me."

"All right, Mr. D, what do you want me to do?"

"Ramone, I want you to go to Santo Domingo in the Dominican Republic."

"What?" asked Ramone, flabbergasted.

CHAPTER 20
Baltimore County

"Get out of here or I'm calling security," said Maggie, lifting the telephone in her kitchen.

"Put the phone down, Margaret. Please," said Handsome John softly. He stood up from the sofa in her living room and walked towards her.

An hour earlier, Dickie had casually walked Handsome John through the lobby, past the security check, up the elevator, and into Margaret's condo. Together they had searched the place for over a half-hour. Finding nothing that would help in locating Mr. D's stash, John dismissed Dickie and waited. When Maggie entered her condo and saw John sitting in the living room, she was surprisingly calm, ordering him out without so much as a hello or a question about how he got into her home.

"Just give me five minutes. I'll tell you the whole truth, no matter how badly it'll hurt." He took the phone from her hand gently and stood inside of the entrance to the kitchen.

"Hurt who? You or me?" asked Maggie. She was wearing blue jeans and a yellow Towson State University sweatshirt.

"Maybe both of us," said Handsome John.

"Okay," she said. "But as soon as you're finished, you're out of here."

"Fine," he said. "If that's what you really want. Louis Dante was responsible for the death of my sister, another one of his ex-wives. I wanted revenge. So I purposely devised a plan to seduce you, which you went along with willingly. I lied to you about my having a wife and where I worked. I lead you on hoping you'd leave Mr. D. I also wanted to see him lose his business. When it all came true, my revenge was complete."

That much was true. But now John began to segué into his con.

"But then things got confusing," sighed Handsome John. "I had fallen in love with you and was trying to fight it off. I avoided you. I hurt you with that bullshit AIDS story with the bikers. I even tried to escape mentally by trying to take over Dante's gambling empire."

He swallowed hard for effect.

"Nothing worked. When I heard how sick you had become, my guilt turned to anguish. Finally, I couldn't take it anymore, and I decided that I had to confront you and admit what I had done. And to ask your forgiveness . . . God, Maggie, I'm so, so sorry."

John began to cry. Maggie was moved. Hesitantly she came to him. They hugged. Tears streamed from her face. Handsome John slowly began to press against Maggie, sliding his hand down her back to rest at the top of her buttocks.

"No . . . stop," she whimpered. "It's not you, it's just that . . ." She grappled for the right words, unaware of her present feelings.

"After those animals attacked me, and the trauma that followed . . . well, I just don't . . . can't . . . handle anything physical with men. Hell, John, I'm only attracted to women now."

Handsome John released his hold on Maggie.

"Don't feel uptight about it, hon. I understand. The same thing happened to my sister," he lied. "Look, I'll leave now. I've said my piece, and I upset you. I hope you'll forgive me someday."

Maggie was touched. She believed everything John told her and understood his need for revenge. She felt sorry for him. She even felt a slight sexual pang for John that she didn't quite comprehend.

"Stay a few minutes, John. I'll make some coffee. We'll talk. But no touching," she added with a smile.

CHAPTER 21
Baltimore City

"Look guys, the feds keep pushing the idea on the state's attorney and the mayor that cops killed Watowski," said Internal Affairs Detective Brandon Carr to former Vice cops Feldman and Byron. "I'm under intense pressure to provide evidence to indict somebody, particularly you two."

The three members of the Baltimore City police force were huddled in Carr's cramped office on the third floor of the police department building on Fayette Street near the southern end of the Jones Falls Expressway.

"Why are the feds so hot after us?" asked Byron. He was more pissed off than upset.

"They've got an informant who swears you guys did it. No solid evidence, yet. But if we don't get someone for Watowski quick . . ."

"Do you have any idea who their snitch is?" asked Detective Van Feldman.

"It's probably one of the bookies they've given immunity to. Take your pick. Most of 'em have gone before the loansharking grand jury."

Hal Byron sipped on his sixth cup of coffee for the day. He occasionally yawned, the caffeine having no effect on him whatsoever. It was like Ritalin on a hyperactive child.

"Was Dante surprised at what you told him? Did he tell you anything about Watowski?" he asked.

"You guys should know," said Carr. "Dante'll never help. He's no snitch. However, as cool as he tried to appear, I think he was wigged out over Handsome John fucking his women."

"The black bookies musta done it," insisted Feldman. "No one else makes sense. I've gone over and over the suspects." He pounded on Carr's desk.

"They have better alibis than Dante, Paul Douglas, and Gordon Baines," said Carr. "I've grilled them and their henchmen for hours. Look, Hayden's gonna impanel a grand jury in three days, and even though you guys go way back with him, it's politics. Does Copley have anything new?"

CHAPTER 22

The Hippopotamus Club on the corner of Charles and Eager Streets opened its doors during the disco era in the late seventies.

Until 1983, half of the customers were heterosexual. Now, in its thirteenth year of operation, the "Hippo" was ninety percent gay and still generating large crowds. Baltimore, unbeknownst to many residents, has one of the largest homosexual populations in the United States.

Like fish out of water, Paul and Gordon stood at the large circular bar by the rear of the Hippo watching the all-lesbian band, *Mild Spring Men*, entertain the dance crowd with the *Rolling Stones'* classic "Sympathy for the Devil." Paul and Gordon looked nervously around, trying to spot Ramone Blande, who had insisted on meeting with them as soon as possible at the Hippo. Both men kept their dark topcoats on despite the warmth of the room.

"I always hated strobe lights," said Gordon. "I dunno how these dancing people keep from fallin' down."

"Maybe that's why they hold onto each other so tight," joked Paul. "Jesus, there's Ramone."

Ramone walked through the crowd on the dance floor wearing a skintight black jumpsuit with red cowboy boots. The huge bulge around his crotch caught intense and approving stares from the homosexual assembly, plus Paul and Gordon, who tried not to look for too long.

Purposely, Ramone hugged Paul and Gordon to enhance their embarrassment.

"If the cops are following you two, this'll give your dossiers some needed juicing up."

"This had better be important, Ramone," said Gordon, "or I'll probably have to kill ya!"

"Oh, that's so kinky, Gordon," giggled Ramone, leading them to a small lounge by the back entrance that was set-aside for older gays who desired a quieter atmosphere.

Ramone's persona dramatically changed as they sat at a small booth across from the bar. He became dead serious and proceeded to relay to them the discussions with Louis Dante at the Magellan Prison Camp. After telling them about Handsome John and Mr. D's women, he brought them up to date on Mel the Tailor.

"Mel's not positive, but he told the feds that you guys probably started the fire at his poolroom. It looks like Mel and Handsome John are behind most of your troubles. I figure the feds'll look to arrest you two within days."

"Thanks, Ramone," said Paul. "Gordon and I will disappear in about 36 hours. Where are you going to be?"

"The Dominican Republic," said Ramone.

CHAPTER 23

Handsome John had convinced Maggie that if they could locate Mr. D's stash that the money would be turned over anonymously to AIDS research. Maggie truly believed him. There had been no physical relationship between the two, and she now considered them platonic friends. It was not difficult for John to persuade her to assist him in finding Mr. D's hidden treasure since she could trace all of her mental, physical, and emotional problems to her relationship with Louis Dante. And, at the same time, she could understand what had driven Handsome John to seek revenge on Mr. D. Unfortunately, Maggie had no idea where Mr. D had hidden his stash, but she felt that it was still somewhere in her former home. She called Juanita, whom she knew still had a key and oversaw everything that took place in the Dante household while he was in prison. She arranged to meet Juanita on the pretext that there were three pieces of artwork that she had a sentimental attraction to and which she really would liked to have taken, but had forgotten to ask for in the divorce settlement. She assured Juanita that there was no need to call Mr. D concerning the pieces since they were not expensive or of interest to Louis. Juanita promised to meet her on Wednesday morning, explaining to Maggie that she was not authorized to give her a key and that Maggie could not be in the home alone. Maggie readily agreed to this stipulation.

✳

That same morning, Mr. D walked briskly around the quarter-mile track at the Magellan Camp. He had two weeks left to go before his release, and contemplated what he would face. He knew that Ramone was presently in Santo Domingo in the Dominican Republic on a business deal that could return him millions of dollars in profits. He knew that Paul would have to leave town for good and go undercover, and that Gordon would have to assume a new identity and act covertly as a go-between for Mr. D and Paul. The bookmaker also thought about Handsome John and what devious tricks he was presently up to; and Mel the Tailor whom he was 90 percent convinced was orchestrating events.

✳

Mel the Tailor was at his mother's home. Anticipating his mother's quick return with breakfast and the morning newspaper, he opened the front door only to face an angry Gordon Baines.

Mel's mom lived in the Fells Point section of Baltimore. Part of the eastern Baltimore harbor, it had undergone a massive ten-year revitalization. The old homes were bringing in lucrative prices, and new condos and town houses were rivaling the high-priced homes in suburban and rural Baltimore County. Some compared Fells Point to old-time Georgetown in Washington, except at prices more affordable to middle- and upper-middle-class people.

Mel's mother, Bernice Dennis, lived in a brand-new town house on Ann Street, down the street from Henderson's Wharf, a new hotel and marina. The cobblestone streets were reminiscent of a bygone era, and Mel enjoyed staying at his mom's on occasion. This was one of those occasions. He knew that someone was trying to scare or kill him because of the fire at the poolroom, and wanted the confinement of the town house and the narrow cobblestone street to make it difficult for someone to sneak up on him. However, Mel failed to look through the mail slot before opening the front door, and, thus, was shocked to find Gordon, pushing his way inside.

"Long time, old pal," said Gordon as he shoved Mel into a newly upholstered pink sofa in his mother's living room.

"What's the matter?" cried Mel, looking around for an escape route. He knew he was in trouble. "My mom will be back in a few minutes, Gordon. You better make it quick. And don't get any funny fuckin' ideas."

"I don't need that much time, Mel. I'm just gonna kill ya. So it'll take only seconds . . . unless, of course, you have somethin' to tell me that can keep you alive."

"Like what?" asked Mel. He had a lump in his throat the size of a cantaloupe. He was about to piss himself as he saw Gordon pull out a gun and screw a silencer onto the top of the barrel.

"Well, first of all, Mel, what's goin' on with this loansharking grand jury?"

"Gordon, please," begged Mel. "I don't know what you're talkin' about. I just . . ."

Gordon smacked the gun barrel over the top of Mel's head and then put his hand around Mel's throat.

"Don't fuck with me, Mel. Don't lie. I don't have any time. Talk to me or you're fuckin' dead."

Mel's mind raced. His head hurt. Gordon's pressure on his windpipe tightened. He tried to find a way out. He knew that Gordon's visit was strictly business, and if he could come up with a proposition, something, anything, it would save his life. He decided to spill his guts, to tell Gordon everything and hope something would work.

"All right, Gordon, I'll level with ya. I went to the feds. I was desperate. I couldn't pay you and Paul, and I figured you guys would kill me. It was my only shot, strictly a business decision. I had to give you guys up. I didn't want to. And then Handsome John Abrams came to me with an interesting deal. He said we could take over Dante's empire, along with Paul's, if we got rid of everybody involved. Now, Handsome John has always had it in for Dante because he blamed him for the death of his sister. He's been workin' on this revenge thing for a long time."

"You're a fuckin' liar," said Gordon, about to smack Mel again with the barrel of the gun. Mel winced and put his hands in front of his face.

"That's not all of it, Gordon," cried Mel. "Handsome John is out to kill me, too. He's not happy with me telling him how to run Dante's gambling business. I don't know who set the fire to my place. I thought it was you and Paul, but it could have been Handsome John. I don't need this aggravation. I'm gettin' too old for this. Gordon, you and Paul need me. Without me, you guys are history. I can get you guys out of a lot of shit. I swear, I'll make it up to you. Maybe there's somethin' we can work out. Maybe . . ."

CHAPTER 24

Handsome John had parked along the wooded street, four homes down from Dante's. On foot, he hurried up the road and private driveway and got into Maggie's car, which idled roughly by the house. She was keeping the heater on in the cold of the morning, waiting for Juanita to arrive.

"I still don't understand, John, how we're going to get Juanita to tell us where Louis hid his stash. She's totally loyal and dedicated to him. She'd die first."

"Let's just play it by ear," said Handsome John. "You get out of the car when she pulls up and then the two of you walk in, leaving the door open. Make sure it's unlocked. That'll get me in there. In the meantime, you start talking to Juanita, keeping her occupied. Then, take her to your old bedroom and stay in there for a while. Maybe let her believe you've become depressed, being back in the house. Start crying, whatever. Give me time to search the house and see if I can find the stash. After that, we'll just have to take some chances. I'm gonna slouch down in the seat where she can't see me."

CHAPTER 25

"See here, Dickie," said Runner. He was showing him a crumpled piece of paper with dozens of three-digit numbers. "I make a copy of every number I give to you guys, and here's 999 from Friday and 101 from Monday. The Friday hit was for over $12,000, and you're telling me it wasn't among the numbers I gave you?"

"That's right," said Dickie, emphatically. "It wasn't on the sheet. And neither was the 101 from Monday. You must be slippin', Runner."

Dickie stood at the base of the marble steps on one of the vacant houses on McHenry Street. Runner Oppenheim sat on the top step. He was dressed lightly for the cold weather and was shivering, his arms wrapped tightly around his body.

Runner stood up slowly and motioned to Dickie. "We gotta straighten this shit out. C'mon inside here where it's warmer. I can't talk out here much longer."

Without waiting for a response, Runner turned and entered the house through the door, which was already open. Dickie followed him into the hallway, which was partially lit from the sunlight. The wood was rotted and the paint had chipped away from the walls and staircase. A urine stench pervaded the area where the two men stood.

"Ya know, Dickie, it's one thing that you, Handsome John, and that fat fuck, Mel, are slow and late and inaccurate when it comes to running the numbers business. And maybe that could be forgiven 'cause Mr. D spoiled us for 20 years . . . but Mr. D was always honest. He paid off no matter what the hit. My numbers were always on his sheet . . . ."

"Listen up, Runner. Dante's history. He's never comin' back to run things. Me and my partners, John and Mel, call the shots now. Those two numbers weren't on the sheet. I think you're just trying to beat us for $15,000."

Dickie knew that Runner was correct. He had spoken to Handsome John about the two hits and was told not to pay. Although Dickie didn't initially approve of stiffing Runner's customers, after John advised him that the hit would cost Dickie $4,000 personally, he easily acquiesced. Being much heavier than Runner, and a former bully, Dickie not only didn't fear him, he almost relished a confrontation.

"You forget somethin', Runner. Ain't nobody but me and my partners around who you can lay-off to."

"Dickie, are you telling me that my customers are being 'armed'?"

"No, Runner. You just made a mistake. Neither of those phantom digits of yours were on the sheet."

"That's too bad," said Runner. "Me and my guys can no longer do business with you and your partners. We're officially ending our business association."

"Yeah," laughed Dickie as he leaned on the staircase. "That'll put your crew outta business. Nobody'll take your action."

Ignoring his remarks, Runner added, "Now, the 15 thou' you owe us, that was due yesterday."

"Kiss my ass," said Dickie as he turned to leave the house.

"Wait a second, ya schmuck!" shouted Runner. "I want you to meet my new lay-off bookies. I've also hired them as a collection agency for you and your deadbeat partners."

"That's it," said Dickie. He turned, balled his hand into a fist, and lunged for Runner. But Runner was gone. In his place stood two very large black men. Dickie froze. His back was to the rotting wall, and the route to the door was blocked by the larger of the two men.

"Do you have the money? The 15K?" asked the menacing form opposite the doorway.

"Lemme' explain," pleaded Dickie. His plea was unacceptable. The two figures proceeded to punch and kick Dickie repeatedly. His screams receded quickly to whimpers, and soon, only the constant thuds of the beating could be heard.

Five minutes later, the assailants walked out of the house. They nodded to Runner who stood by the curb. It was Shadow Creek and Jimmy Bop.

CHAPTER 26

Juanita had her arms on Maggie's shoulders as she consoled her in front of a large vanity in the bedroom. Dressed in matching blue jeans and jean jacket over a white turtleneck sweater, Maggie sat in a high-back, French-style chair with her head bent over the table, weeping. She had convinced Juanita that she was reliving the assault five years earlier.

After an unsuccessful cursory search of the home for Mr. D's stash, Handsome John found his way to the bedroom. Softly he came up behind Juanita, pulled a Beretta handgun from the right pocket of his light blue, silk Windbreaker, and stuck it in her neck.

"What the . . . " said Juanita as she whirled around. "John, take that gun away from me."

"Sit down in this chair," ordered John. "Maggie, get up and find something to tie her hands with."

"Maggie," said Juanita. "What's this about?"

Margaret got up slowly. She didn't understand Handsome John's need for the gun, or why he wanted Juanita tied to the chair, but she followed his commands.

"Get two ties from the closet, and tie each hand around the arms of the chair."

John pushed Juanita into the chair, keeping the gun leveled at her chest. She wore a black suit with a black and white polka-dot blouse and short black high heels. Margaret took a couple of Louis Dante's Nicole Miller ties and tied Juanita's wrists securely.

"Maggie and I want Mr. D's stash. All of it. We're going to donate it to AIDS research. Tell us where it is or you'll be sorry."

Juanita smiled and turned to Margaret.

"Girl, have you lost your mind? Handsome John is a sleaze-ball crook. He's using you. He'd never give a dime to a charity or anything. Just to himself."

Then she turned back to John.

"I'm not about to tell you anything. You're a lowlife thief who's taking advantage of this sick little girl. You oughtta be ashamed . . ."

John smacked Juanita across the face with his left hand. It was a stinging blow. Both of his hands wore tight white racquet-ball gloves. "Shut the fuck up, you black whore!"

"John, no," cried Maggie. "Please don't hurt her."

"Okay," said John. He moved the gun from Juanita, pointed it at Margaret, and shot her in the right shoulder.

Both women screamed briefly. Margaret grabbed at her bleed-ing shoulder and fell back onto the bed. She began to cry and then passed out from shock.

Juanita regained her composure. "Why'd you shoot her?"

"'Cause I don't think you can stomach that. You're a tough cookie and too loyal to Dante. But you'll tell me where his money's hidden, or I'm gonna keep putting bullets in Maggie every time she comes to . . . Maybe I'll blow her knee cap off next . . ." He aimed the gun carefully.

"No, don't," Juanita pleaded. "Outside. Underneath the dog-house. Use the shovel by the kitchen entrance."

"Very good," said John, who bent over and kissed Juanita's neck.

He walked out back, grabbed the small shovel, and ap-proached the doghouse of the deceased pet German shepherd, Lilly. The brown-stained doghouse had been vacant for over five years since Lilly had been poisoned. Handsome John kicked it over and dug into the hard ground. About two feet under the interior of Lilly's doghouse was a silver metal briefcase. John lifted it up and brought it into the kitchen, placing it on the side of the sink. He opened and closed a number of cabinets and drawers, eventually finding a hammer and screwdriver, which he used to jimmy open the metal briefcase.

Inside were packets of money tied with red rubber bands. Various denominations of bills— hundreds, fifties, twenties, and tens—were piled neatly in rows. John began to count the stash when he heard noise coming from the bedroom. He grabbed the briefcase and hurried back to Maggie and Juanita.

Maggie had regained consciousness and was writhing in pain on the bed, pressing the sheets onto her wound, trying to stop the bleeding. Ignoring Margaret, John plopped the money down in front of Juanita.

"This can't be more than 60 or 70 grand. Where's the rest of it?"

"That's all of it, John. Now, help Maggie, please."

"Sure," said John. He took his gun out and shot Maggie in the left kneecap. Blood and bone splattered off of the bed onto Juanita's lap. Margaret vomited and passed out again. Juanita also threw up.

"The rest of it, cunt," ordered John, holding the gun up, pointing again towards Margaret.

Juanita began to cry. "Jesus Christ. You're a madman . . . The guest bathroom. False floor. Bottom of the linen closet."

Jackpot, thought John. End of the rainbow. He rushed out of the bedroom, through the dining room, and into the foyer where he found the guest bathroom. He opened the linen closet, threw towels, light bulbs, soap, and other toiletries to the bathroom floor, and began feeling for a lever or handle. Frustrated, he ran into the kitchen and retrieved the hammer, returning in seconds. Haphazardly, he swung the hammer into the hardwood floor. Shards and splinters of wood flew up. Suddenly, he caught a glimpse of a similar silver metal briefcase. He tried to pull it through the hole that he had made, but it was too small. Grabbing the hammer again, he pounded it into the false floor, this time freeing up the briefcase. He carried it into the kitchen and, with the assistance of the hammer and screwdriver, opened it as quickly as the first.

This jackpot seemed to have less than the one found under the doghouse. John went back to the bedroom. He bent over Juanita and whispered in her ear.

"I know Mr. D saved more than $100,000 in his life. Where's the rest of it?"

"That's it. That's all I know of. I swear it," sobbed Juanita.

"Fine," said John. "We'll continue to play the game. Your way."

He untied her right wrist and placed his gun in her hand, forcing her finger onto the trigger. Aiming at a still unconscious Maggie, he pressed Juanita's finger with his own, shooting Maggie once more. This time the bullet took off the top of her left ear.

Juanita began screaming hysterically, forcing Handsome John to slap her in the face several times before she stopped.

"Please, John. I swear there's no more money in here. None."

"Where's the rest?" He went and stood over Margaret, moving the gun above the sprawled and bleeding body.

"Marvin! His crippled friend, Marvin! But I don't know where . . . Oh, my God!" Juanita cried uncontrollably.

"Thanks, Juanita. You've really been quite helpful. Just one more thing."

John again forced the Beretta automatic into Juanita's hand. She tried to ball her fingers into a fist, but he was too strong, and Juanita was once more positioned into the role of an accomplice. This time the gun was aimed and fired through Maggie's chest, killing her.

Juanita lurched back, trying not to black out, and, by reflex, relaxed her grip on the gun. As she fought off a wave of nausea, John twisted her wrist up and away from the bed and held the gun pointed at her temple. Startled too late and not strong enough to fight off Handsome John, Juanita was helpless. John squeezed her trigger finger with all his might, firing the gun. She died instantly.

✳

There was no rush, John thought as he drove slowly towards his apartment. Soon he would visit Dante's old friend, Marvin, and confiscate the millions Mr. D had stashed there. For the time being, he would count his newfound money slowly and hide it in a safe place. He liked the false floor hideaway idea of Dante's and figured to duplicate it at home. Although he was upset with the blood and bone fragments splayed over his silk Windbreaker, Handsome John knew he could well afford a new one. The old coat would have to be destroyed. It was the only evidence that linked him to the slaughter at Dante's house.

When he arrived at his apartment, John was surprised to see no messages on his answering machine, or any attempted calls on his caller ID box. Surely, Mel or Dickie would have called by now, although he knew that Mel was probably in a panic, laying low because of the fire at his poolroom. He wouldn't worry about it, though. Dumping the money from the two briefcases onto his bed, John lost himself in the merriment of counting his new windfall.

CHAPTER 27

Lindy sat in the Little Tavern hamburger joint on the corner of Guilford and Holiday, two streets over from The Block. He had been up for 48 hours after being evicted from a flophouse a few blocks away on East Lombard Street. Slowly, he chomped away on a plateful of Little Tavern hamburgers.

In its heyday, the Little Tavern had two dozen locations around Baltimore. Open 24 hours a day, they sold small hamburgers with the works by the bag to thousands of Baltimoreans daily for over five decades. Now only three restaurants were left, and two were in danger of closing.

Poor Lindy, he still couldn't fathom how his financial position had crumbled so quickly after saving and scrimping for most of his life. True, the scam perpetrated upon him by the late Jeff Hall, Mel the Tailor, and Handsome John had accounted for the largest chunk, but he still owned, at the time, his poolroom and home. Then his wife took ill with cancer. Although his health insurance covered the traditional expenses, Lindy desperately tried every would-be cure with his beloved Kate who was given six months to a year to live. He mortgaged everything to obtain the funds to take her to the Bahamas for a series of nontraditional modalities of cancer treatment. Transfusions, injections, radical diets, and housing for the two of them left Lindy in serious debt. When Kate died, Lindy was totally dependent on public assistance and charity. He felt humiliated, and was forced to seek out old poolroom customers for handouts.

Over the years, he became obsessed with plotting revenge upon Mel the Tailor, whom he considered the architect of his demise. When confrontations failed to provoke a positive response from Mel, Lindy tried to burn Mel's poolroom. It was a small but hollow victory for Lindy, who now sat brooding and desperate in the Little Tavern.

He had $28 in cash, his old car, and a half a tank of gas left.

CHAPTER 28

"Guess we got indicted," said a dejected Detective Feldman to Detective Byron. "Why else would we get called up immediately to IA?"

The two former Vice cops climbed the stairs from their office in Administration to Internal Affairs.

"We need to call a good lawyer, man," said Byron. "It's gonna probably cost us everything we own, plus our pensions, to afford the kind of attorney we'll need to get us outta this shit."

Standing outside of Detective Carr's IA office, they knocked once, nervously glancing at the other cops peering from their cubicles.

"Everyone must know," whispered Feldman as they entered the room.

"Hey, guys, why the long faces?" asked Carr. "I've got good news for ya. Sit down. I may need your help with something."

Feldman and Byron looked at each other quizzically. They were both in dark pants with white shirts and ties, wearing their revolvers on their hips.

"Must be open season on Mr. D's family," said Carr. He looked out of his window onto Fayette Street. "Earlier yesterday, his cousin, Dickie, was found in a vacant house on McHenry Street. Somebody beat the livin' shit outta him. Beat him so bad, he'll be a babbling idiot if he ever gets out of intensive care.

"Then, later in the day, Baltimore County Police found a bizarre scene at Louis Dante's home. His ex-wife, Margaret, was found dead from multiple gunshot wounds, killed by his loyal employee from Charlie's—Juanita. And Juanita is dead after shooting herself in the head. Your bosom buddy, Copley, called me. Said the place was a mess. They're trying to piece it all together, but can't make head nor tails of anything, yet. Nothing fits."

"What's this got to do with us?" asked Byron, nervously.

"Oh, yeah. I almost forgot. Preliminary findings on the gun used at the crime scene indicate it might be the same one that killed Watowski. We'll wait for Ballistics to confirm."

Relief and glee began to bubble from the throats of the former Vice cops.

✳

Two hours later, Deputy Warden Murphy of the Magellan Prison Camp interrupted Louis Dante's exercise regimen at the track, escorting him off of the cinder track to a bench on the grass field. The warden informed him of the telephone call he had received from Dante's attorney, Richard Karson—Maggie and Juanita were dead and Dickie was in intensive care.

Dante thanked Murphy for coming over and consoling him, before resuming his fast-walk on the track. Murphy walked back to the Recreation and Visitors Building. A lump formed in Mr. D's throat, tears welled in his eyes, and his heart began to thump heavier in his chest. He stopped moving and dropped to the track on his knees, his hands resting in the cinders. He began to gag, the gagging giving way to the dry heaves. The bookmaker rolled over onto his side and started sobbing. Murphy had turned back before heading into the building and saw Dante lying on the track. He called out to two other prisoners having a smoke by the basketball court, and together they ran toward Dante.

CHAPTER 29
Dominican Republic

Ramone dug his heels into the soft dirt of the tropical mountainside of Duarte Peake, trying to maintain his balance on the downward cycle of the hiking trail. He was drenched with perspiration as he tugged at his olive drab shorts and matching tank top which were sticking to his body. In front of him were his two hiking companions, now residents of the Dominican Republic, but formerly citizens of the U.S. The three men were taking the abbreviated version of a typical two-day hike up the highest mountain in the Caribbean, Duarte, located near the border between Haiti and the Dominican Republic.

The location and activity were necessary to prevent visual and auditory surveillance of the conversations that were precautionary following Ramone's earlier meetings with two casino representatives in the capital city of Santo Domingo on the previous day.

The two companions were Mickey Seidel and Ira Charles. They wore surplus camouflage army fatigues. Seidel, the current world "jacked-up-one-handed" pool champion also wore a brown beret to cover the bald spot atop his head. He had a deep tropical tan and was in excellent shape, weighing 175 pounds on a 5'10" frame with very little fat. Seidel represented the U.S. interests in the newly built casino and hotel, La Casa Verde, The Green House.

Ira Charles represented certain Dominican nationals who fronted for the Americans in the casino, but were also connected to gambling networks in the eastern and midwestern United States. Charles was in his late forties, short and wiry, with a very thin mustache. He was an African American immigrant from Houston, Texas who had visited the Dominican Republic in the early seventies as a civil-rights militant doing graduate work in History. He was writing a master's thesis on the town of Samana, 170 miles northeast of Santo Domingo. English-speaking American slaves founded Samana in the early 1800s. Enamored with its history, Ira Charles decided to move to Samana permanently. A distant relative from Virginia, Uncle Little Billy, paid for his education.

Seidel's arrival, although more recent, paralleled Charles' to an extent. He married a woman whose parents were among the founders of the Dominican town of Sosu'a on the northern coast facing the Atlantic Ocean. After World War II, a number of German Jews settled there and, over the years, it became a drawing card for North Americans because of its beautiful beach and scenery.

The two immigrants of the Dominican Republic were aggressively courting the designee of Louis Dante, a.k.a. Mr. D, for one of two reasons, or both. The first was that connected "high rollers" like Dante could prove invaluable for handling Las Vegas-type junkets and for increasing the sports betting programs in the embryonic-stage casinos on the island. Second, they wanted Dante to set up toll-free "800" phone numbers at clandestine sites on the island to receive sports bets from mainland U.S.A. These would prove profitable from an investment standpoint, or for allowing the casinos a place to lay-off their bets without having to worry about moving the wagering lines.

Since the mid-eighties, a few large bookmakers, tired of being arrested and harassed, had been conducting offshore betting through "800" numbers in the Bahamas and elsewhere in the Caribbean. Networks were set up for delivering winnings to bettors and/or collecting losses that were still made and conducted in the United States. There were very few problems with moving money in and out of the country.

The gambling elements of the Dominican Republic wanted to get into this action in a big way and were actively seeking bookies the caliber of Mr. D to set up operations on their island. There were, however, some problems. One was that it was against the law to accept bets from out of the country, and two, with the Dominican Republic being a democracy like the U.S., it was very concerned with alienating the U.S. Justice Department. Unlike the sixties, when anti-American sentiment was high, the two countries now got along famously.

On the plus side of the gambling interests was that the economy of the island depended on tourism. Since the Dominican Republic was not in a league with the more progressive Caribbean destinations where modern facilities and utilities made them more attractive, they needed a hook. And gambling was the key to enticing high rollers, jetsetters, and tourism.

Ramone had decided that he would recommend an "800" number business for Mr. D to be run out of the Dominican Republic. He liked Seidel and Charles, and also recognized that Louis Dante needed to leave the States following his release, home

detention, and parole time. As he traversed the lush green tropical forest footpath down the side of Duarte Peake, he prayed he
would survive the hike to make his recommendation.

CHAPTER 30
Baltimore City

Carr, of Internal Affairs, caught up with Feldman and Byron
as they strolled down Baltimore Street towards their lunchtime
routine on The Block.

It was cold and blustery, and steam exited their mouths as
they spoke.

"Wait up, guys. We need to talk," said Carr. He had forgotten
his topcoat and was shivering.

Feldman and Byron threw up their defensive antennae recognizing that Carr's tone of voice was once again that of the
inquisitor.

"I've got good news and bad news," he said. "What do you
want to hear first?"

"The bad news," said Feldman as they huddled in the doorway of Polack Johnny's hot dog stand.

"Why don't ya ask me for the good news first?" asked Carr.

"Fuck you, man," said Byron. "I'm gettin' sick of this shit . . .
All right, what's the good news?"

"The gun used to kill Watowski was the same weapon used
at Dante's house on the two women."

"Great!" shouted Feldman. "How bad can the bad news be?"

Carr shoved his hands deep into his pants pockets and looked
around the street.

"Where were you guys Wednesday morning?" he asked.

"That's it!" said Byron. "I'm gonna kill you!" He lunged at
Carr as Feldman interceded, standing between the two.

"Cool it out, man," ordered Feldman. "Carr, what's this about?
. . . And, by the way, we were working and only have about a
dozen eyewitnesses to verify it."

"Okay. That's great then," said Carr, relieved. "I'm just doing my job. The autopsy on Juanita Colter, the black female alleged suicide, revealed that she had two broken bones in her fingers. Somebody forced her to shoot herself in the head. Watowski's murder is, therefore, still unsolved."

Feldman grabbed their order of Polish hot dogs and French-fried potatoes sprinkled with Old Bay crab seasoning, motioned to Byron to pay the cashier, and took Carr with them across the street to the Midway Bar.

As they entered the poorly lit establishment, Byron apologized to Carr.

"Forget it," said Carr. "I'd have reacted the same way."

"What happened at Dante's?" asked Van Feldman.

"They still can't figure it. Someone overturned an old, out-of-use doghouse. There's an empty hole there, too. And one of the bathrooms had a false floor that was busted up."

"Shit, man," said Hal Byron. "Somebody's looking for, or already found, Dante's stash. That's what it was all about. Do us a favor, Carr. Talk to the deputy commissioner and get us back in Vice temporarily, or assigned to you. Then let us visit Dante. Me and Van want whoever these motherfuckers are real bad."

"I'll see what I can do," said Carr as he took a long bite out of Feldman's hot dog. After he swallowed it down with some ginger ale, he smiled.

"You guys won't need to travel to Virginia. The feds are letting Dante come up for the funerals."

CHAPTER 31

Handsome John was mad at himself. After reading the headlines in the newspaper and watching the television coverage of the murders, he realized that he didn't have as much time as he thought to snatch Dante's major stash at his friend, Marvin's. He was pleased that the police had kept news of the robbery from the media. Surely, he felt, the holes in the closet and under the doghouse was evidence enough of a burglary attempt.

John thought through his predicament and the need to rip off Marvin as quickly as possible. He needed a plan, a strategy. That would take time; time he didn't have, especially at the moment. Handsome John was in the middle of an intense racquetball match at the Towson Racquet Club for the championship of the Men's Open "A" Ladder.

By concentrating on Dante's stash, he had fallen behind two games to one and was losing the current game in a best-of-five series. The games had been rough, with lots of bumping, shoving, and staring. John's opponent, Rich Safron, 10 years his senior, was a gifted player with a very aggressive streak.

Twice they had almost come to blows over balls which John had hit Safron with; balls traveling at 130 miles an hour which drew blood on the back of his muscular legs.

Safron was a husky, good-looking salesman for Nikon with thinning blond hair and powerful arms. He played with wide-barred goggles that gave him a menacing appearance.

John never liked Safron's cocky attitude to begin with, and he had also been frustrated in the previous games with Safron's tricky, slow, high serve and devastating backhand shots. Now, as they volleyed over a crucial point, Handsome John hit a "Z" shot upward around the court ceiling. Something hurt in John's shoulder, and it caused his follow-through to catch Safron on the left cheek with the side of his racquet, opening up a bloody gash.

Safron turned and grabbed John, thrusting him up against the glass at the rear of the court, and slamming him repeatedly against the partition.

Immediately, the referee and two fans came onto the court and broke up the altercation. John stomped off the court, defaulting the match, picked up his gym bag, and hurried to the locker room.

Safron's day will come, he thought. But, right now, it was time to drive over to Marvin's, conduct some surveillance, and proceed with a plan to find the Dante stash. After that, he would go to the Cayman Islands and "kick back" for a couple of years.

Baltimore was becoming too heaty. He had already heard about Dickie's beating and Mel's poolroom fire, and he figured his gambling business acumen would never survive the next month.

On the way out of the racquet club, John got into his car and drove west on the Beltway to the Greenspring exit, north towards Marvin's home. It was time for some surveillance.

CHAPTER 32
1968-1969

The years 1968 and 1969 were up and down for Marvin and Louis Dante. As true Baltimore sports fans, they mistakenly bet with their emotions on the pro-football Colts, the pro-basketball Bullets, and the pro-baseball Orioles in their championship series against New York's Jets, Knicks, and Mets, losing badly.

However, as emerging small-time bookies, they won a lot of money that year and began to comprehend the foolish role of "betting with your heart."

Marvin was engaged at the time to a beautiful, leggy model named Loretta who was also an instructor at the Barbizon Modeling Agency in Baltimore. Returning from a four-day trip to Jamaica, they were hit head-on by a pickup truck that had crossed the centerline of Greenspring Valley Road. The driver of the pickup had fallen asleep at the wheel and was killed along with Loretta. Marvin was paralyzed from the waist down.

Rehabilitation was slow and painful, and Louis Dante was instrumental in giving Marvin back the desire to live. He made Marvin a silent partner and arranged for tutors to teach Marvin financial management, real estate development, and investment planning. With the help of a two-million-dollar insurance settlement, Marvin developed intricate investment schemes to launder and invest Louis Dante's gambling dollars. He also became keeper of Mr. D's major stash, which fluctuated between six and ten million dollars.

Marvin lived in prestigious Greenspring Valley on a beautifully landscaped estate, two miles from where his fateful accident had occurred years before.

He employed a male nurse nicknamed Suitcase and a driver named Stanley. Stanley also performed household chores and ran errands for Marvin. Both men had been with Marvin for over a dozen years, were well paid, and totally loyal. However, neither was privy to Louis Dante's business dealings or the location of the stash.

CHAPTER 33
1992

Mel was worried about Handsome John's whereabouts. Since the fire, he had not heard from him, even with the violent events of the week that John would have normally relished discussing.

The gambling ring that Mel and John had hastily put into action to replace the Dante empire was in tatters due to John's lack of commitment. He felt for Handsome John who had helped him with some great hustles, like the Lindy scam, and who had always been there for him during Mel's down times. Their scheme to break Dante was remarkable.

But Mel was also afraid of John, whom he considered an absolute sociopath capable of doing anything: the poolroom fire, the murders of Dante's women, and the beating of Dickie. However, Mel wasn't sure of his motives, and, of course, maybe Handsome John didn't need motives. But, then again, maybe he hadn't done anything, anyway.

In the long run, Mel needed someone to take the fall, to get him out of all of his predicaments with the loan-sharking grand jury, Gordon and Paul, and the hits his organization had taken that John had refused to pay off.

Thus, he had arranged for a meeting with Federal Agent Blume at his burned-out pool hall. They were to get together in Mel's old office, which had been temporarily boarded up and cordoned off from most of the charred remains of the pool hall. Mel was not concerned with meeting a cop at his place since it was 10:30 p.m. on a cold, drizzly night, and there was poor lighting and little pedestrian and car traffic on the street.

The Tailor had no set strategy since he knew that the enforcement people would find a way to tie up the loose ends, keep his identity safe, and allow him to operate his own gambling shop, albeit very quietly. It was that loose kinship between cop and criminal. It was the only way the enforcement community could put the "big fish" away and win points with the media and the public.

Mel did know that he would have to give up Handsome John for Watowski's murder, but the police would keep him out of it. He would also back off of testifying against Paul and Gordon, but they would still have to drop out of sight. Then, without Handsome John, Paul, Gordon, and Dante, Mel could take whatever piece of the gambling pie he desired, and leave the rest to the blacks.

Mel parked his big Lincoln across the street from his pool hall, looked around the street, and locked the car door. He was wearing a green and orange Miami Dolphins football cap and a floor-length blue trench coat with a heavy wool plaid lining. Turning his collar up and pulling the wide brim of his hat down over his forehead to avoid the rain, Mel hunched over and proceeded to cross the street. When he was two-thirds from the opposite side, a small white blur of an automobile came hurdling towards Mel, hitting him with such impact that his body was flung backwards into the side of his own car.

The white blur was an old Chevy Nova that skidded to the curb, uprooted an old green bench reserved for bus riders, and came to rest on the sidewalk.

Mel the Tailor would have only sustained a broken hip and left leg had the impact not knocked him into the Lincoln, where the side of his head hit the steel frame of the door with such force that he was killed instantly.

Several minutes later, as a small gathering of drivers stopped to offer assistance, and the distant sound of an ambulance grew closer, Federal Agent Blume arrived at the scene. He walked over and observed Mel lying in the street, his back propped up against the car. It was obvious that he was dead.

A young couple was consoling an old man who was driving the Nova. He was explaining to no one in particular, over and over again, that he never saw the victim until he darted out into the street in front of his car.

" . . . Then I lost control," he said. "It was wet and there was nothing I could do. I'm so sorry. I've been driving for 60 years and this is my first accident."

An officer with a notepad in hand approached the old man, ushering him to the sidewalk.

"Sir, I need to ask you a few questions. First, what is your name?" inquired the officer gently.

"My name is Lindy."

CHAPTER 34

Louis Dante sat impassively in the front row of mourners at Ruck's Funeral Home on North Harford Road in east Baltimore County near the Harford County line. He wore dark sunglasses.

The minister had completed his somber eulogy and was giving friends and family of the deceased directions to the cemetery where Maggie was to be laid to rest.

Earlier in the day, Mr. D had attended the funeral of Juanita in downtown Baltimore at the Evans Funeral Parlor. It was a much more spirited eulogy, and the mourners were more demonstrative.

Two federal marshals had escorted Dante, along with his attorney, Richard Karson, and his paper detective, Ramone Blande.

"We'd like a few minutes alone with our client," said Karson, more as a statement than a request.

The two marshals shrugged at each other. One, the senior member of the federal custody team, a tall, lean man in his early fifties, looked up and down the hallway for an empty viewing parlor or office.

"Use the front office. You've got ten minutes. Then we take him back to Magellan."

Karson, Dante, and Blande walked into the empty funeral director's office and closed the door. Karson walked over to the window. He did not wish to hear any discussion between Ramone and Mr. D.

"Your assessment," said Dante, removing his glasses. His eyes were swollen and red, but this was business.

"There's a lot of competition already in the islands, besides the Dominican Republic. However, with the right network, the "800" betting line has a high probability of success depending on several variables. The feds are already hip to what's going on in the Bahamas and the DR. There's an ongoing investigation with some guys from the West Coast, but it involves alleged fixes of games and races, bigmouths, and poor organization at the top of the pyramid.

"My recommendation would be a small local staff run by Charles and Seidel with the capacity to move the operation around to other islands as things grow heaty. People like myself and other trusted guys could collect and distribute in the U.S., and keep you as far from jeopardy as possible."

"What makes you think I trust you, Ramone?" asked Dante. Ramone wasn't sure if he was joking or not and didn't respond to the comment. Karson continued to stare out of the window, occasionally glancing at his watch.

The knock on the door announced, "Two minutes!"

"What are our immediate needs?" asked Dante.

"Lots of seed money. Four million dollars in cash to the Dominican ASAP."

"Richard," said Dante to Karson. "Go out and tell them I'll be ready in a couple more minutes. Thanks."

Relieved, the attorney opened the door and huddled outside with the two federal marshals.

"Since I can't give this business up, I've gotta trust you," said Mr. D, who stood and put his hands on Ramone's shoulders. "But trust has not always been good for me. Sometimes even the most loyal guys . . . for whatever reasons . . . turn on ya. Remember that . . . Anyhow, my friend, Marvin, the one in the wheelchair who left the funeral service with his male nurse, is the one to see."

Mr. D jotted something on a piece of paper he tore from a Ruck Funeral Home notepad and handed it to Ramone.

"Give this to him. After he looks at it, say, 'Betcha can't eat ten kosher dogs in one sitting.' Got it?"

"Yeah," answered Ramone.

"He'll get the money for ya and even tell ya how to move it safely. Good luck!"

Dante hugged Ramone and turned to leave.

"Thanks for the hug, Louis," joked Ramone.

CHAPTER 35

Marvin lived on a circle that was accessible by a single-lane road, off of Hillside Avenue in beautiful Greenspring Valley. At the top of the circle, past an old farmhouse, was a fifty-yard private driveway leading to two two-acre homes on Keller Road. The house to the right with old western-style fencing around the perimeter was Marvin's.

A blacktop driveway led to the three-car garage and seventy-five-hundred-square-foot home. The long brown-stained rancher blended nicely into the wooded lot. Behind the home was a seven-foot-high fenced-in area surrounding a large swimming pool and a long, circular deck. Black-stained railroad ties supported shrubbery gardens opposite the house, and neatly trimmed hedges, trees, and bushes encompassed the pool area.

Strangely enough, the pool had been covered for most of the years since Marvin bought the home in the early seventies; and the staff would never think of taking a swim. The pool cover was forest green in color and attached to permanent hooks in the rough-grained surface around the pool. Leaves from the fall and winter months lay atop the pool cover hiding the broken pump used to clear off the rainwater and melted snow.

Although the pool cover was stretched fairly taut, the weight of the leaves and seasonal precipitation had caused it to sink in the center at least three feet below the surface of the water.

A gate at the far side of the pool and deck area led to the sliding glass doorway of the master bedroom, which had a ramp for Marvin's wheelchair.

Handsome John took in everything he could from his exterior surveillance of Marvin's house on three occasions over a 24-hour period. He had been careful not to be too obvious to any nosy neighbors or the elderly farmer tilling the thawing soil near the circle of Keller Road.

John had concluded that even an exhaustive search of the interior and exterior of Marvin's estate could take weeks, and then still prove fruitless. He realized that he would have to duplicate his strategy with Maggie and Juanita. Surely, the camaraderie developed over the years between Marvin, his male nurse, and his driver would force Marvin to confess the hideaway of Louis Dante's stash. John actually convinced himself it would be a study in behavior between men and women. Would Marvin break before Juanita? he thought as he rubbed his right shoulder which had grown increasingly sore. Hitting the racquetball or being shoved by his opponent into the wall had somehow damaged his shoulder, and he could barely lift his arm without severe pain.

CHAPTER 36

Mr. D's attorney, Richard Karson, quickly left Ruck's Funeral Home shortly after Dante and Ramone emerged from the office. Karson always prided himself on his ethics, never allowing himself to be privy to a conversation involving potentially illicit activities. Ramone followed seconds later, leaving Dante to wait with one of the federal marshals as the other went to the john.

The parking lot was almost deserted by the time Dante and his escorts walked outside to the light purple Chevrolet Caprice waiting to transport him back to Magellan.

As Mr. D opened the back door and slid into the seat, the opposite door opened and Baltimore City Detective Van Feldman jumped in.

"I'll just be a minute, Louis," he said. The city Vice cop had been on a first-name basis with Dante for all of the years he had pursued him.

"First, my heartfelt condolences. I'm so, so sorry. Second, I need your help."

Dante sat perfectly still, staring at Feldman.

"Your assistance will help to avenge you, and nobody'll be the wiser."

"I don't talk to cops," said Mr. D. "Never have. Can't. Nothing personal. Just business."

"I understand, but hear me out," said Feldman. "The gun that killed Juanita and Margaret killed Watowski, too. We have no leads on Dickie's assailants. The feds main snitch, Mel the Tailor, was supposedly about to give them someone major, but he got run over, coincidentally, right before he was about to talk. Driver of the car was Lindy, who used to own . . ."

"I know, I know," interrupted Dante unexpectedly. He rarely responded to anything the police said, but the news was very interesting since it could help Paul, Gordon, and himself later. However, he sensed that the cops were looking to pin everything on Lindy, or at least make him a co-conspirator.

"Feldman, I want you outta this car as soon as I shut up. Lindy had nothing to do with anything except that Mel Dennis destroyed his life. Let him be. But, the process of elimination should point you guys to one conclusion. I'd have never, ever suspected that he could have masterminded it or have been so cold-blooded. You know who it is—your Internal Affairs buddy told me all about him in Magellan. Goodbye!"

CHAPTER 37

"I'm with Cal-Tech Cablevision Services. We're investigating customers who may be pirating Pay-Per-View channels," said Handsome John as he was confronted by the old farmer, Willis Perry, while walking up the driveway towards Marvin's home.

Perry looked weathered and slow in his overalls as he took off the heavy-duty gloves he wore while operating the tiller.

"You people shouldn't be showing that pornography on TV. Caught my grandson, Percy, watching it on one of them free weekends."

"Sorry about that," said John. He kept a Baltimore Orioles baseball cap pulled low over his forehead, not wanting the farmer to recognize him later.

John carried a toolbox in his left hand. His sore right shoulder had made lifting anything with his right hand too painful. Inside of the toolbox was a German Glock nine-millimeter semiautomatic pistol with an extra loaded clip and a silencer already screwed on the barrel.

"I've just gotta check a coupla more signals comin' from the telephone wires and then I'm outta here," explained John, dismissing the farmer. As John spoke, a car passed behind him carrying Ramone Blande to Marvin's house. Someone extra to deal with, thought John.

The telephone poles supporting the cable TV lines were located in the back of Marvin's property, a few yards behind his fenced-in pool area.

Handsome John made his way through the thick underbrush, "fake-checking-out" the metal box hooked to a telephone pole five feet from the ground. He could not see over the fence from where he was, so John inched closer to the site where the pool motor was located just outside of the northwest corner of the enclosed area.

He saw the wheelchair-bound Marvin, Ramone, and Suitcase, the male nurse, as they came out of the kitchen door onto the deck. After some brief conversation, the three made their way down the ramp leading from the deck to the swimming area. Handsome John knew that no one else was around. During his last surveillance check, he had seen the driver, Stanley, leave after calling out that he would see Suitcase the next morning.

Opening the toolbox, John picked up the pistol with his left hand, disturbed that he was unable to function with his right hand, and stalked around to the gate near the garage.

He entered the pool area swiftly, surprising the three men. He waved the gun at Ramone and Suitcase, who were still dressed in dark suits from the funeral.

"Sit down on the ground with your hands behind your heads," he ordered. Turning to Marvin, who was also still wearing his funeral suit, John spoke rapidly and softly.

"I don't have a lot of time. I know you have Dante's stash. Juanita told me. They were the last words she spoke. Show me where it is or I'll kill your two boyfriends right now."

"Okay," said Marvin, matter-of-factly. "Eighty percent of Louis's money is invested in various stocks, bonds, commodities, short- and long-term notes. It'll take some time to turn that into cash . . . but you said you didn't have much time, right?"

John slapped Marvin's face weakly with his right hand, forgetting that his shoulder was hurting.

"Where's the other 20 percent, asshole?" He pointed the gun at Suitcase.

"Easy, John," said Marvin. "It's right here." He pointed toward the pool where everyone was standing near the edge.

"How much?" asked Handsome John. His right shoulder was throbbing now.

"Two million, five," said Marvin.

Ramone was wide-eyed. He couldn't believe Marvin was giving up the information so easily.

"Why would you hide that much money out here?" asked John menacingly.

"The pool cover is on all year. Been like that for 15 years. Lots of leaves and debris in the pool and overtop of two very waterproof and secured strongboxes. It's safer than anywhere else."

"All right. Get it up now then," ordered Handsome John, satisfied with Marvin's answer.

Marvin smiled at him and remained still. Handsome John had a quizzical look on his face as he felt something stick into his sore right shoulder.

"Drop that gun slowly, cableman," said the old farmer. He held a 30/30 lever-action Winchester rifle on Handsome John, who started to turn. Earlier, the farmer had phoned Marvin and warned him that someone was snooping around.

With great swiftness, Marvin grabbed the German pistol from Handsome John by squeezing his left wrist at a pressure point tightly and pulling the gun out of his hand. Although paralyzed from the waist down, Marvin's upper body was in great condition, having worked out with Suitcase using free weights four times a week for years.

Recognizing the pain in John's right shoulder earlier, Marvin tossed the gun to Suitcase, and then reached over and wrapped his hands around John's wrist and arm. He tugged hard, shocking Handsome John, and then shoved him onto the slick pool cover where his body automatically slid towards the middle.

Finding himself suddenly submerged in water and leaves on the slimy pool cover, Handsome John fought with his feet and left arm to keep from drowning. But he couldn't remain above water. His weight stretched the cover even further down in the center, and the surface was so slick he couldn't get any traction at all. It was worse than being in quicksand.

Marvin, the old farmer, Willis Perry, Suitcase, and Ramone watched as John struggled to get his head above water. But as hard as he tried, he found himself running in place, unable to even stand or tread water. No one moved to help him. He died a gruesome death in minutes.

Ramone looked at Marvin, feeling somewhat guilty.

"I had a black Lab years ago that I loved with all my heart," said Marvin. "One night, he was chasing a squirrel around here, and somehow slipped onto the pool cover. Horrified and unable to help, I watched him drown. He couldn't get himself out of that center area. No one was here to save him, and I don't know how they could have, anyway. Ever since that day, I've kept a rope and long stick with a hook up by the kitchen in case another animal falls in . . . but no one wants to save the kinda animal who's in there now.

"Gentlemen," he concluded, "no one saw this animal come in here or leave. Correct?"

Everyone nodded in agreement. "Suitcase, that long stick with the hook is also available for bringing up two lightweight, water-proof boxes that Mr. Blande has come for. Replace the boxes with the dead animal, please."

CHAPTER 38

"I think we need to issue a warrant for Handsome John Abrams' arrest," insisted Detective Feldman. Standing next to him, Copley nodded in agreement.

"Abrams is a state problem," said Federal Agent Blume. "But I don't think you've got enough on him for a warrant. By all means, bring him in for questioning. Maybe you can scare him. You don't really have enough evidence to make him the killer of Watowski or the women. Nor do you have enough evidence to accuse him of arranging Mel the Tailor's death and Dante's cousin's beating."

"We gotta make an arrest and charge somebody," said Byron. "And what are the feds gonna do, Blume, now that Mel's dead?"

The enforcement personnel from the city, county, and federal governments were waiting for State's Attorney Hayden outside on the steps of the Clarence Mitchell Courthouse on the Calvert Street side.

"The grand jury will go ahead and indict Paul Douglas and Gordon Baines," said Blume. "Maybe we can get a plea outta them, although without Mel Dennis, we could get thrown out of court. However, it's a multi-state loan-sharking investigation, so we'll lose some and win some."

Hayden came out of the marble courthouse and walked over to the men. He listened to their arguments and shook his head.

"So, we could go after Abrams and get laughed out of court, or just leave Juanita as the shooter and tidy it up nice and neat. Is that basically it?" asked Hayden. He was frustrated.

Blume looked down at the steps. He knew Hayden wouldn't like it, but he had to ask.

"You could indict Dante as the one who ordered Juanita to kill Watowski and his ex-wife. Then she got remorseful and shot herself."

"Jesus, Blume. You sound like the former U.S. Attorney. Win at all costs. You guys will never be satisfied 'til ya put Dante away forever. How do I know that Mel the Tailor wasn't the real killer, and that you guys were protecting him?"

"Why you motherfucker!" yelled Blume as he went for Hayden, who pulled away as Feldman stepped between them.

Hayden strolled away down the street towards his office and called back to Blume.

"Maybe I'll drop that 'dime' to the press."

Epilogue

In September of 1992, the *San Francisco Examiner* head-lined the story of a federal investigation into a bookmaking, sports-fixing, money-laundering organization operated by two former Bay area bookies. The article detailed how two Santo Domingo homes had been converted into a bookmaking parlor with over 40 toll-free lines and a mainframe computer for taking bets from thousands of gamblers in the continental United States. The Dominican police assisted in the case.

This incident caused the Dante operation to relocate onto the three small islands of Andros, Bimini, and San Salvador, situated among the seven hundred islands and twenty-five hundred keys in the Bahamas. Ira Charles, Mickey Seidel, and Gordon Baines ran the offshore operation.

✳

Paul Douglas became a fugitive and went to live out his remaining years with his Uncle Little Billie in Virginia. They continued to fund black causes and the greatly expanded Baltimore gambling operation of Shadow Creek and Jimmy Bop.

Paul and Gordon were indicted by the federal grand jury investigating loansharking, but never appeared for arraignment. They became absconders.

✳

The police never located Handsome John for questioning in the murders of Watowski, Margaret, and Juanita, and the beating of Dickie.However, Ramone Blande, disguised as Ray Abrams, a cousin of Handsome John from New York, showed up one day and met with a dozen bookies throughout the Baltimore metro area. He told them he represented Handsome John Abrams and paid them off for all outstanding and questionable sports bets and numbers hits. Advising the bookies that John was in hiding due to police harassment, he informed them all that their lay-off action would be handled, payoffs would be prompt, and the now-retired Mr. D would stand behind Handsome John.

This pleased the bookies, and they agreed to lay-off to John's designee, Ramone, a.k.a. Ray Abrams.

✳

The police never solved the murders publicly. The state's attorney embarrassed the feds, as he had threatened to do, implicating them with Mel the Tailor.

Lindy lost his driver's license and was placed in the Pikesville Nursing Home.

✳

Mr. D was visiting his old friend, Runner Oppenheim, on McHenry Street.

"How's business? I understand you went into sports betting as well as numbers," asked Louis Dante as he sat on the curb in front of the same vacant house where Dickie was beaten. Miraculously, Dickie recovered and moved with his mother to Deerfield Beach in southeast Florida.

Runner shifted, leaning from one leg to the other, fidgeting with his hands.

"Ya know, the action has dropped dramatically since '90," he said.

"Dramatically's a big word for you, Runner," laughed Mr. D. But Runner wasn't laughing.

"Guys who used to bet a thousand now bet 500. And guys who used to bet 200 now bet 100. There's a 50 percent decline due to the recession. Plus, the bettors are sharper. No longer are they all stiffs."

"So," said Dante, slowly rising from the curb, "you want out?"

"Are you crazy?" yelled Runner. "How could anyone ever leave all this!"

ABOUT THE AUTHORS

Bob Litwin has worked for the federal government for almost forty years. He holds B.A., L.L.B., and J.D. degrees from the University of Maryland, and has taught writing courses at the College of Notre Dame of Maryland and Towson University. He collaborated with Chip Silverman on *The Block*, an historical mystery novel set in Baltimore's red-light district.

Chip Silverman, Ph.D., M.P.H., M.S., C.A.S. is Vice President of Government Relations and Addictions Programs for Magellan Health Services. Prior to that, he was Special Advisor to the Governor of Maryland for Substance Abuse Policy and Director of the Drug and Alcohol Administration. He worked for the state for twenty-six years. His first book was *Diner Guys* in 1989. *Aloha Magnum,* co-authored with Larry Manetti, who co-starred in the TV series, *Magnum P.I.,* was published in 1999.

Chip and **Bob** have written for the *Baltimore News American* newspaper, served as contributing editors at *Baltimore Magazine*, and produced and hosted segments of the *Evening/PM Magazine* television program.